APPOINTED BY FATE

Skye McNeil

For information, contact the publisher, Hot Tree Publishing.

WWW.HOTTREEPUBLISHING.COM

EDITING: HOT TREE EDITING

COVER DESIGNER: CLAIRE SMITH

FORMATTER: RMGRAPHX

ISBN-10: 1-925655-10-5

ISBN-13: 978-1-925655-10-0

10 9 8 7 6 5 4 3 2 1

For my bosses, Mike and Ryan. You supply me with endless coffee, superlative cases, constant support, and friendships I'll never forget.

CHAPTER ONE

Fog drifted over the beaten path at Gray's Lake as the patrol car slowed to a stop. Officer Levi Quinn rested his palms on the steering wheel and studied the end of the makeshift road. Halloween night wasn't his favorite to be a patrolling police officer.

Per routine, he radioed his status and position to dispatch before opening the car door. A harsh gust of wind slapped his smooth-shaven face. Clicking on his flashlight, Quinn cursed his damn luck when he heard a cat hiss from the nearby bushes. The calico beauty darted in front of him, making his breath hitch. The seven-year veteran could survive getting shot, but felines set his skin crawling.

Radio static filled the air, but Quinn ignored the report of a theft. His call was more important. Gang activity occurred often in Des Moines, Iowa, but particularly thrived under a new moon and mist to hide wayward acts. The drug deals and drownings were so prolific that the city installed security cameras and posts along the running trails with emergency call buttons. Heinous crimes were more common at Gray's Lake after midnight, and tonight fit the bill perfectly.

Tall grass whipped at his black combat boots the farther he walked into the copse of ancient trees. A sizzle in the crisp air warned him that this night wouldn't solely be kids playing tricks in the park. "Damn you, Ollie. Of all nights to be sick," he cursed his partner, reaching an opening between the trees.

The lonely picnic tables took on eerie forms, opposite of their usual occupants in the daylight. Under the cloudy sky, he shone the light across the graffitied benches and spotted an unusual form. The hair on his arms stood at attention. Shining the light around, Quinn squinted.

"Des Moines Police," he called, weaving through the table maze.

A rustle from behind him caught his attention for a moment. After checking behind the thick brush, he spotted nothing out of the normal for the wooded area, despite the looming form ahead of him. Chalking it up to another stray animal, Quinn approached the body at the end of the light's beam. Cautiously, he nudged the man lying facedown on the table. Getting no response, he checked for a pulse. Nothing met his fingers, so he grabbed his radio.

He swiftly called in to dispatch and was relieved when backup and an ambulance responded with their estimated time of arrival. Finding the man's wallet, Quinn compared the driver's license to the face. "Yep, Mr. Jimmy Nichols." He squinted, then reviewed the man again. "Holy shit, that's Nitty Nichols, the drug dealer." The man was long regarded as being the father of gangs in the Des Moines metro area.

A branch snapped and Quinn whipped around. "DMPD. Come out slowly with your hands in front of you," he commanded, though his voice wavered. When no one appeared after a full minute, he guessed it was a passing critter. The wooded reserve huddled between Des Moines's office buildings was crammed full of wildlife.

Quinn rifled over the deceased man's body for more information, but only found ten dollars, a lighter, and three bags of what smelled like marijuana. Placing the items in plain view, he let out a breath as he waited for the ambulance and additional police officers to make it to the scene. The wail of sirens was closer now, but the urge to take a look around before they arrived overwhelmed his better sense.

Quinn set off in the dewy grass. The moon was mirrored in the calm lake. He always hoped to never find a dead body on Halloween night. There was something especially creepy about this particular holiday for Quinn that he could never shake. Ghosts from his past crept into his mind, but he pushed them down to focus on the scene ahead of him. From his viewpoint, he couldn't determine if foul play was involved. The lake was a popular spot for junkies to ride out their fix, then pass out. It seemed the one tonight had a little too much, though the truth would be revealed during the autopsy.

The sirens were closing in as he walked deeper through the picnic area. Red and blue lights flashed amid the trees, so he quickly scanned the surroundings with his flashlight. On the last sweep, his light found another body in the grass.

Rushing over, he felt the man's pulse. "Still alive," he stated, grateful the night hadn't taken another soul.

Patting down the man, Quinn felt the harsh texture of metal. He moved it out of reach and continued his search. By the time he was done with one pocket, he'd discovered ten small bags of white powder and twelve small bags of a leafy substance. If his training and experience had taught him anything, this slumbering man was a drug dealer. One who carried a knife and happened to be within shouting distance of a cooling corpse. Quinn didn't believe in coincidences. Not tonight.

Before Quinn could check the next pocket, the suspect groaned, then took a startling breath.

"DMPD. Get up real slow now," Quinn directed, his hand on the gun holstered at his hip.

The man sat up and winced at the bright light in his face. Black eyeliner rimmed his eyes, and his hair was disheveled. "Whoa, calm down. It was a little cocaine, that's all." He rubbed his head. "No need for bashing my head, Officer. I didn't resist."

"Sir, do you have any identification on you?"

"Yeah. Hey, calm down. This isn't a strip club, buddy."

Quinn opened the wallet held together with silver tape and examined the Ohio driver's license. "Cameron Shearer, is that right?"

"Last I checked," he quipped, wiping his nose as he stood.

Not fond of the response, Quinn prodded, "Do you know what happened tonight?"

Cameron stuffed his hands into his blue hooded sweatshirt and took a step, but his left foot faltered. Leaning down, he dug a hand in the oversized boots and his face turned ashen. "What the hell is this?" he griped, his voice shaky as he pulled out a 9mm gun from the boot.

"Drop it! Now!" Quinn commanded, snapping his gun toward the man.

"Look, that's not mine. I've never seen it before. I swear," Cameron protested as he tossed the gun to the ground.

Voices carried along the lake, and Quinn breathed a sigh of relief that backup had arrived at last. He kicked the gun away from the suspect, his gut uneasy. "Put your hands behind your back."

When the frazzled suspect failed to obey, Quinn's heartrate skyrocketed. "Mr. Shearer, lie down on the ground, facedown."

"I didn't do anything," argued the tattooed man, pacing.

Quinn didn't give him the opportunity to speak another syllable before he flipped Cameron to the ground in one swift movement. That act resulted in a scuffle, the man stronger than he appeared.

"Get off me! I'm innocent."

"Cameron, I need you to stop resisting," Quinn instructed, struggling to cuff him. For a man who'd looked dead to the world minutes ago, he had a lot of fight in him.

"This is police brutality," complained the man now beneath him.

Ignoring the jab, Quinn all but smiled when he saw a familiar body clad in blue approach. He clicked the handcuffs in place but didn't move. He had a feeling his latest arrest would be a dumbass. "I thought you were sick," he shot, gripping Cameron's right shoulder.

Rookie Officer Ollie Richards offered him a pained grin. "Yeah, I was until my girl started throwing up too. I can't handle that shit."

Quinn hauled Cameron to his feet. "Well, you're the reason she's heaving, Ollie. You knocked her up."

Ollie grabbed the suspect's left arm and shrugged. "I'm kind of regretting that these days." He nodded toward the druggie. "Is that a bad Halloween costume or is he a suspect?"

Quinn chuckled as the man struggled to free himself. "A little of both. Let's get him back to the station. The county attorney will probably want to press charges of some sort." He nodded toward the grass. "Mark the weapons I found on him, will you?"

Ollie placed numbered cones by the discarded knife and gun, then called for a forensic intern to photograph the weapons. Falling into step, he walked alongside Quinn on the march to the group of police cars. The woods were bright with red and blue, a welcome sight.

They reached the picnic table soaked in light as the medical examiner pulled off her gloves. Quinn frowned at the blood that seeped through the table and onto the grass below.

"What's the verdict, Lucy?" Ollie asked.

The aged examiner flicked her eyes up. "This man was murdered. There's a gunshot wound to his groin and a stab wound in his heart. I can't be certain of the final cause of death, but I'm labeling it as a homicide."

Quinn's hand tightened around the suspect's arm. "It seems you were quite busy tonight, Mr. Shearer."

"No, you've got the wrong guy," Cameron insisted. "You're arresting me without a warrant or probable cause. I want an attorney."

Ollie rolled his eyes. "Oh goody, you know the system. I'll make this fast, then." He started peppering off the Miranda rights as Quinn intently watched.

The man didn't look guilty, but they typically didn't.

"I'm just trying to get home," Cameron spewed like a broken record. "Home."

Halfway to the patrol car, the alleged murderer wrenched out of Ollie's grip. The man made it five feet before Quinn tased him. Halloween night continued to suck, this year especially.

— — —

A kettle whistled from the open-concept kitchen, five feet from Joci Dorous's office door. She flicked an annoyed glance at the door and willed it to shut on its own. Only one person in the entire building drank tea. She was also the most obnoxious.

Dropping the case brief to her solid oak desk, Joci drummed her fingers as a form walked by her translucent glass wall. The shuffling feet soon transferred from the carpet to the tiled kitchen. Joci's right eye twitched at the knowledge that the dragon woman was on the hunt again.

Whenever her boss's fling of the year made a pot of tea, it meant she would soon irritate both floors of employees.

Though Joci had gotten used to the English-born terror, she wasn't a fan. Her saving grace had come when she learned that the woman screwing the firm's patriarch was a family law attorney. Since Joci wouldn't touch family law cases with a ten-foot pole, the illustrious Netty wasn't her problem—until the woman decided to ransack the second-floor kitchen instead of the one on her own floor. It made sense though, since the partners were on this level. Even her boss didn't want the woman within shouting distance. Joci smirked at that ironic truth.

Shoving the thought of her boss's love life from her mind, Joci focused on the post-conviction appeal brief. Reading the opening, she grabbed a blue pen and notebook. The plea wasn't hers but a coworker's. In their office, it was common to pass documents along for other attorneys to review. Unfortunately for Joci, she was a perfectionist, so most everything passed through her hands before it was filed with the court.

A knock at her doorway caused Joci to look up. "Oh, hey, Rayna." She smiled at the one attorney in the firm she thought of as a friend.

Rayna Alley smiled back and held up a red file. "You have a new one," she informed her. "Brett Petosa assigned it directly to you."

Intrigued, Joci stood and padded to Rayna's position in the doorway. "Oh really? I wonder why." She hadn't received a file from the boss in months, so her curiosity was piqued.

She opened the file and stared at the mug shot that met her gaze. The thirty-year-old looked as though he'd gone through the wringer before booking. His wavy brown hair held remnants of grass and twigs, while his deep brown eyes were cold. The black eyeliner only emphasized the nose and eyebrow piercings. "Huh. Looks like a punk," she pointed out. "My favorite."

She flipped through the pages and her eyes widened. "Wait a minute. Cameron Shearer?" Joci glanced to Rayna, then back to the booking photo. "This can't be the same guy."

"You know him?"

She focused on the dark eyes and realization hit her. "Yep. That idiot. What did he allegedly do?" She skimmed the notes. "Murder? Cameron? No freaking way."

"How do you know him? He's from Ohio." Rayna pushed back her auburn bangs.

Memories of playing in the creek behind his aunt's house drifted through Joci's mind. "He lived across the street. We used to play together after school. I can't believe he went off the deep end."

"Yeah, people are crazy. So, since this is your first murder case," she took a step closer, "please, please, please tell me I can help."

Joci tipped her head to the side and nodded. "Of course you can. I'll need all the help I can get." She perused the minimal information in the file. Her heart skipped just thinking about reconnecting with the man who used to be a happy-go-lucky kid in Ohio. *I doubt he'd even remember me.*

"Do you know who hired us?"

"Somebody rich, that's all I know. Brett did a video consult with him, I think. The file didn't get to me until two days later." Rayna snapped her fingers. "But I remember Brett saying the guy was adamant you were Mr. Shearer's attorney. No clue why."

"I can only guess because I know him." She shook her head. "*Knew* him. He's much different these days."

Rayna added in a small voice, "Oh, and the court attendant wanted to know your second chair choice."

"What?" Joci questioned, slamming the file shut. "Dammit, I forgot about the second attorney requirement on murder cases." Most of the time, they needed to be from the same firm for efficiency. The person also needed experience. Plenty of attorneys in the firm qualified, but only a select few could take on such a large case.

"Cooper and Hayes are already in a robbery trial, so I couldn't suggest them." Rayna laced her fingers together and cast her eyes at the floor. "The only other attorney qualified for a homicide is Adrian," she squeaked.

Setting the folder on her desk, Joci retreated to the giant bay window that overlooked downtown Des Moines. She straightened her shoulders. "Yeah, I was afraid of that."

"You can call the court attendant back," the newbie lawyer urged. "I'm sure you can change it. Maybe the firm down the street will agree to help out."

Joci weighed her pros and cons quickly. "No. Adrian is who I need on a murder case. I won't let my personal feelings get in the way of justice. Our client deserves the best, and that's us." She crossed her arms over her white blouse. "Please let him know. I want to see our client as soon as possible."

In the window's reflection, Joci watched Rayna slowly back out of the office. Once upon a time, she would've jumped at the chance to be Adrian Petosa's boss, but not any longer.

Blinding light streamed through the window as the sun rose. In the cooler months, a day didn't go by when Joci wasn't in her office to witness the sun's ascent. Pulling at the blinds, she lowered them, then returned to her desk.

A new e-mail from Rayna awaited her. The woman was efficient and her only female friend. Maintaining relationships outside of the courthouse and office was difficult, if not impossible, but the intern through law school had wormed her way into Joci's heart three years prior.

She smirked at the memory. From that day forward, she'd made it her business to help Ms. Alley any way she could. She was once in the position of having no friends in a law firm. The politics were enough to drive a sane person batty. Joci couldn't watch a sweet girl like Rayna self-destruct in the name of law. Now, thanks to her help, the younger woman had passed the bar exam just last week. Quite a long way from scuttlebutt to attorney under tutelage.

Clicking on the e-mail, she read the text. Adrian was in trial today, so he wouldn't be available to visit their new client in jail. Tapping her pen on her yellow legal pad, Joci refused to wait until Adrian was ready before meeting their client. She had been working the toughest cases for five years just so she qualified for a murder case, and she was not about to wait for the cocky son of the firm's founder to get a jump on the defense.

Dialing Rayna's extension, she waited for the recent graduate to answer. Though Rayna was officially ready to practice on her own, the firm's policy was for newbies to shadow another attorney for six months before beginning solo cases. Sadly, that meant Rayna continued her work as a glorified assistant for the time being. Soon enough, she would be the boss of her own legal team.

"Rayna, please cancel my appointment this morning and have someone cover my hearing at eleven. I'm going to jail."

"What about Adrian?"

Some days, Joci wished the woman wasn't so bright. She gritted her teeth at the bad luck. Only she would be forced to endure the intimacy of a brutal case with her ex.

"Adrian can catch up later. I'm not waiting for him anymore." With that, she hung up and slipped on her black heels.

"He better have one hell of an alibi," she grumbled, grabbing her red clutch, ironically a gift from the very man she wanted to ignore until the case was over, but had no choice in the matter since he was the other attorney now.

— — —

"I owe you one," Joci called over her shoulder to the front guard of Polk County Jail.

"One of these days, I may collect on that," Bill replied with a wink.

Placing her notebook under her arm, Joci clipped her badge onto her shirt and waited for the familiar click of the doors. Once she made it into the waiting room, another round of clicks echoed in the white space until the second door opened. A short woman sitting on the bench outside the door set her book down and greeted Joci with a smile. The prisoner liaison led her through the winding hallways, chatting about the weather.

Joci made polite conversation but kept her mind focused. Her favorite jailor would eventually call in that favor, though most likely for his grandson who continuously got in trouble with the local police department.

Connections made the legal world go round. When she'd initially started practicing, Joci doubted she would find anyone to aid her cases. That quickly changed when the Petosa Law Firm scooped her up from the Drake Legal Clinic.

"And here you go," the inmate stated with abnormal merriment. It seemed the woman was thankful for an alternative way to work off her mandated stay. Joci couldn't blame her; she would also rather escort attorneys instead of passing the time mopping floors.

"Who are you here for today, Miss Joci?" the jail guard asked, looking up from his computer screen. He was surrounded by monitors on all sides of the circular deputy desk. It sat a step above the ground, so when he met her gaze, they were nearly at eye level.

From her location, Joci could see flashes of live video streams from the north and south wings of the jail, as well as the visiting rooms. "Hey, Larry. I'm here for Shearer, Cameron," she advised, handing him the slip of paper with the offender's information.

"I'll let him know you're here," Larry said, standing. "We'll head to the second room."

Joci followed her second-favorite jailer to the room. It wasn't hard to find friends among the jail staff. One simply had to not be a bitch. She grinned as she remembered one of her professors making that statement. It was true. In fact, when she needed a favor, she didn't have to look far. Thanks to her kind smiles and the free advice she'd dished out over the years, the jailers trusted her.

Settling into a room that reeked of body odor, Joci reread the police report. The arresting officer was more than familiar to her. She made a mental note to chat with Officer Quinn at his earliest convenience. The more information she could glean from those at the scene of the crime, the better prepared her client would be in court.

Studying her surroundings, she frowned at the small bookshelf lined with law books. A tiny table with a book under one leg sat in the opposite corner, with an ancient computer on top of it. It made sense now why prisoners filed pro se pleas with out-of-date materials. Their connection to updates were limited, if any, within these walls.

She debated telling Cameron straight away about how they knew each other, but part of her wanted to see if he'd recognize her. It'd been quite some time since they last spoke, but surely he wouldn't forget their friendship.

Before she could open her yellow notepad, the door

swung open. Joci watched the man at least three inches taller than her six-foot frame waddle into the room. The jailor removed the leg shackles, then locked the door behind them. Her client slunk into the seat across the table from her, and Joci couldn't help but study him. His black eyeliner was smudged beyond rescue, and the shady bags beneath his eyes told of sleepless nights. Tattoos peeked out from the neck of his green jumpsuit and covered his forearms below the pushed-up sleeves.

"Cameron Shearer?" she asked.

His eyes slowly lifted from the table until he met her gaze. The intensity of the brown hue instantly made Joci crave a dark roast coffee.

"I don't need a shrink. Thanks, sweetheart," he bit out, his pierced eyebrow elevated.

"Actually, no—"

"Oh, I didn't know Iowa jails had conjugal visits." His eyes grazed her with approval. "I think I can handle you, though."

"No, you fuckbag, I am Joci Dorous, your attorney." She cleared her throat. "My colleague and I were assigned to your case. Due to its delicate nature, you get two lawyers."

Cameron leisurely slid his eyes down her face to her body. Though this was common, never had Joci felt her cheeks burn under an inmate's scrutiny. She wished she could vanish from the room. Her high-necked white top suddenly felt like a camisole. Though he didn't peek beneath the table, she was positive he would ogle her red pencil skirt on the way out.

"I don't need an attorney, much less two," he stated, toying with the tiny hoop in his right nostril. "Who hired you, anyway? I'm not complaining, per se. You have a filthy mouth. I find it extremely attractive on a woman."

The tone from his silver tongue sent a jolt straight to her stomach. His eyes all but stripped her down to the mismatched lingerie underneath. Even though she knew him, she needed to set him straight. It wouldn't do to have indecent thoughts about a client, friend or no.

She glanced to the file. "Unfortunately, I don't have that information."

"It's all right. I can figure it out. I'll have to thank him for the eye candy. You're a lot better looking than the last lawyer I had."

Joci wanted to pluck the piercings from his face. He resembled a rocker punk, and he was anything but a rowdy seventeen-year-old.

"You aren't allowed to have jewelry," she advised matter-of-factly.

He smirked. "You're right, but I don't follow many rules." He pointed to his outfit. "Obviously."

"You may not want a defense team, but you have one anyway. Deal with it." Staying on topic was the only way she was getting through the initial interview. There'd be more time to argue how the hell he convinced a guard to let him keep his stupid earrings. It happened more often than not in the jail. Things tended to slip through the cracks when it came to the inmate codebook.

She pulled out a sheet of paper Rayna had drafted.

"This is a waiver of speedy trial. I need you to sign it in order for us to get a proper defense in place." She placed a pen on top of the sheet. "Otherwise, your trial will be in roughly one-hundred and twenty days, since the county attorneys, Mr. Bell and his second chair, Ms. Lord, are on top of trial information filings for the first time in five years," she muttered with annoyance.

"That's a quick turnaround."

"The court likes to get through cases as quickly as possible. Iowa law goes like this: there are ten days from initial arrest to your preliminary hearing. You waived that hearing yesterday, but they set your arraignment forty-five days out, and now we have ninety days from your arraignment date to trial. Usually a pretrial conference date is set thirty days from your arraignment hearing, and then a trial date is secured within thirty days after that date. Continuances are common, but not always granted. All cases must be tried within one year of the arraignment date unless the defendant files a waiver." She nudged it closer. "The clock is ticking."

Cameron slouched forward and skimmed the document. "Nah, I'm not signing."

Joci adjusted her ponytail, then straightened her black-rimmed glasses. "It would be in your best interest if you gave us the chance to prepare so we can have these charges dropped or get you acquitted. Four months isn't an ideal amount of time to get everything done for such a serious crime."

"If I'm going to prison, I want to go sooner rather than later." He held up his cuffed wrists. "If that's all, I have a riveting game of solitaire to return to."

Startled by his words, Joci propped her chin in her fist as she flipped through his file. It came as no shock that he had a history of criminal acts, though predominately in Ohio, not Iowa. With his attitude and candor, she half expected he'd served in prison at one time or another. Somehow, he never spent more than thirty days in the clink. It was curious by anyone's standards.

"Look, Cameron, I don't like to lose cases. Ever. I am devoted to a client until I bleed their defense. You have an explicit criminal background. A Polk County jury will chew you up and spit your guilty ass out within an hour. I don't want that on my conscience or on my record." Joci tilted her head and shoved the waiver back to him. "Sign it."

She watched with bated breath as her client slowly grabbed the blue ink pen and twirled it between his fingers. His movements were so methodical, so easy, so mesmerizing that Joci forgot he was a supposed murderer. He looked so very different from the kid who smeared mud on her face the first day of summer break after second grade.

Finally, he scratched his bushy eyebrow and broke the silence with his baritone voice. "Ms. Dorous, put that damn thing in front of me one more time and I'll show you precisely where you can shove it."

Joci's mouth popped open at his crude yet calm sentence. She held in a smirk. The Cameron she knew would say something like that. *Always a smartass.*

He moved to the door and signaled the jailer. After the door opened, Cameron glanced behind him. "Wear blue next time. It'll bring out your eyes," he insisted, jingling out of the room.

Silence simmered around Joci once the door closed yet again. The cocky bastard had managed to intrigue and piss her off in the same conversation. That wasn't her usual experience with clients. She'd failed to invoke her dominant personality, and Cameron Shearer had stomped the fight right out of her. She felt a tingle of attraction for him, but chalked it up to the childhood crush she'd had on him. She couldn't deny he was decent-looking.

Stacking her file and notebook, she looked around the room. "He stole my pen," she realized. "With his mouth, he's bound to need a little protection."

Joci tugged the door open and sailed through the hallways, not bothering to listen to the chatter between inmates mopping the floors. Her mind was consumed with getting her latest and greatest jackass of a client out of jail before he got himself killed.

— — —

"Shearer, try to stay out of trouble, all right?" the jail attendant advised, pulling the cell door closed. "If you keep this up, Ms. Dorous will have my hide."

Cameron raised his chin and licked his bottom lip. The metallic taste of blood met his tongue and he touched the swelling mass with care. He couldn't help himself; fighting was in his blood—and his profession. "You know my lawyer?"

Bill huffed and jangled his keys. "Oh yes. Joci is the daughter I never had. She takes care of her own."

"She sounds like a peach. Does she do this for all of her clients?" Cameron asked, wiping blood from his hands. Having an attorney actually give a shit about him wasn't normal. Then again, his boss didn't purchase legal services the other times he'd landed in county jails. The Italian would pay for his early release, but he'd let Cameron sit around until the case was dismissed. The disruption had occurred not thirty minutes after leaving his attorney's side. The other guy looked better than him, but Cameron wasn't beefy. Sure, he had muscle, but his assailant had had two others supporting his actions. He couldn't help but wonder if the attack had been orchestrated from outside of the jail walls. It was more than a possibility. His line of protection was never necessary in Ohio, but this was new turf.

Bill thought the question over, then shook his head. "You're a Petosa client now. The firm tends to take extra care of their clients.

"And if I get into another fight?" Cameron prompted. It was curious that the woman he'd met an hour earlier hadn't abandoned him. *There's still time for that.*

"All I know is if you keep it up, they'll put you in the Shoe. Believe me, you don't want that." Bill handed him a pad of paper. "That's where they put the loons."

Cameron took the extended paper but couldn't fathom the man's diligence. It shouldn't matter where his actions placed him. Moreover, the aging jailer shouldn't offer favors to any attorney. Of course, in his opinion, Joci wasn't a typical woman. He could tell that from the meager time spent in the visiting room. He liked her despite the whole lawyer profession. In his experience, people of the law were uptight. So far, Joci fit the mold.

"Am I supposed to write a letter to Santa with my blood?"

Chuckling, Bill bobbed his head and took two steps back. "Aw, boy, you already swiped a pen. You're set."

Reaching through the cell bars, Cameron watched the man retreat to the safety of the hallway. It was abundantly clear that Bill didn't work behind the locked lobby doors. He was much too chipper for grunt work with inmates.

Sighing, Cameron moved to the flimsy mattress and stared at the blank sheets of paper. Any normal man would demand a bond review, but he knew better than to waste time when no one awaited him beyond those walls. He was a flight risk. Still, it'd be worth it to see Joci again.

He had no one to call or write to. Tapping his toes, he considered his ex-girlfriend in Ohio, but she'd left him two years ago. The few friends he managed to keep were no better than he and wouldn't drop a penny to help him. He was in too deep with his benefactor if the swanky attorney firm was any indicator. Adding another tenure to his term wouldn't suffice. Not when he was so close to escape. Why the Del Rossi mob footed the bill for not one but two attorneys was curious. He and Bernard went way back, but the boss always had a hook for the help he gave.

Instead of reflecting on the past, he lay on his back and toyed with the pen he'd stolen from Joci. Now she'd been a welcome sight to bloodshot eyes. The perfect way her slender body filled out that outfit made him grin. He was stunned at her height. Surely she came from a tall family, but had she chosen to be a model, he'd buy whatever she sold. Long and toned legs to go with her equally attractive arms. His eyes couldn't help but slide up and down her torso either. It was perfect, but he'd rather see it without the baggy shirt to come to a final judgment. *Oh yeah, she's got a rockin' body.* She looked familiar somehow, but he couldn't place her. Partying and getting hit in the head too many times could do that to a guy. With her fiery attitude, he could get accustomed to seeing her fierce face ideally framed with eyeglasses on a regular basis. Lucky for him, he would have that exact opportunity.

A smirk danced along his lips at the memory of his attorney's slight nose scrunch when he first walked into the shoe box they called a room. She did it so fast, he almost missed it. But it was adorable, even if it was a reaction to him.

Cameron rested his elbow behind his head, baffled that his appearance hadn't swayed her against him. It was common for women who crossed his path. He was never more than a passing whim. His job didn't attract stable love interests, and his hobby as a drummer didn't assist his cause either.

Rubbing his eyes, he noticed the black kohl from his eyelids on his fingers. He hardly ever wore the stuff unless he was with the band. As the Rejected Misfits were touring the Midwest, it was the only explanation for the night he was arrested. His memory was fuzzy, but he recalled playing a gig at a local bar, then bits and pieces. "Where are those bastards, anyways?" he wondered aloud. An inmate down the hall yelled for him to "shut it," but Cameron ignored the guy. It was perplexing how Jared, Tommy, and Eddie didn't get mixed up in his fiasco.

Without a doubt, the drugs and booze in his system had caused his blackout, but he'd never hurt anyone before. He shrugged. Well, he had been in a fight or twenty, but he always knew when to stop, and never used weapons. That was for pansies. If a man couldn't protect himself with his fists, he had no right to cheat with a gun or a knife.

Sitting up, he picked up the notepad. He really ought to scrawl a letter to his ex-girlfriend, but the woman he craved an audience with was his very own lawyer. Joci appeared to have her head screwed on right. He would trust her, but only in part.

"Maybe someone will finally get it right," he heckled as he set pen to paper. If she didn't respond to his notes, he knew one surefire way to get her attention.

CHAPTER TWO

Joci tapped on the counter in the lobby while she waited for Bill to return with her purse and cell phone. Normally, she didn't bring them into the jail, but she'd had more than one client to see today. After visiting with her newest inmate, she'd managed to speak with three others before her stomach rumbled.

Glancing out to the bustling area, she noticed every computer was occupied by family members video chatting with inmates. A baby's shrill cry echoed in the high-ceilinged expanse, while the high-pitched buzz of the metal detector chimed. The niche in the far side of the lobby was filled with people viewing the court proceedings. If she strained her ears, she could hear the judge's gravelly voice and the hum of bystanders. Turning her head, she saw a line forming in front of the inmate account deposit machines. The jailers at the front were busy with visitors asking questions through the bulletproof shield. Without a doubt, it was another successful day at Polk County Jail.

"Here ya go, Ms. Dorous," Bill announced, handing her the belongings.

Grabbing them hurriedly, she offered him a smile. "Thanks. I appreciate the help."

"No trouble. I can't say the same about your murder guy though," he said quietly.

Scrunching her nose, Joci huffed, "Did he get into a fight?"

"How did you know?"

"I have a knack for these things." It came as no surprise that Cameron Shearer had set his fists to blaze once she left. She caught him once fighting on the school playground, but he always sported a bloody nose back then. *Seems like he's comfortable with his fists still.* Somewhere between elementary and high school, Cameron got to know the courts and wasn't a fan. She was half tempted to recall the help plea she'd made to the jailer, then thought better of it. Just because he hadn't recognized her didn't mean he wasn't worth her aid.

"Thanks, Bill. If he gets out of hand, let me know. He'll learn eventually," she commented, checking the messages on her phone. Two missed calls from Adrian. "Looks like he finally answered Rayna's call," she mumbled, then stuffed the iPhone into her clutch.

"Counselor, what are you in for this time?"

Spinning on her toes, Joci grinned when she spotted the familiar face of Officer Levi Quinn. She waved at Bill, then took a step away from the desk. "Oh, you know, the usual."

Quinn placed his hands on his hips. "Got caught stealing

a man's heart again, didn't you?" he teased with a serious face.

Scribbling her name on the sign-out sheet, she smirked. "Hush now. They haven't traced that one back to me yet."

Quinn let out a hearty chuckle as he closed the distance between them. He held up his cuffs. "If you would stop being irresistible, I wouldn't have to handcuff you, ma'am, but I see no other way around this."

Meeting his humor-filled green eyes, Joci took in the addictive vision of Quinn. Only once had she called him by his first name. It didn't work. Not for their type of relationship. She scanned his getup. He wore a black tee under a matching bulletproof vest with 'Police' on the front. His gold badge easily rested on his hip alongside his gun holster. By anyone's standards, Quinn was handsome. Joci knew that better than the rest. A five o'clock shadow around his mouth told her that he'd done back-to-back patrols. His long legs and even longer torso gave her height of six feet a run for its money at a good two inches above her.

"You know I like it a bit rough," she flirted, her voice low.

He ran his fingers through his relatively short brown hair, a knowing smile playing on his lips. "Yeah, I'm quite familiar with your wiles."

Joci nodded. "Walk with me. I'm on my way out." He immediately fell in step, and she adored how smoothly their paces matched. Her heels clicked through the front lobby until they reached the double doors to the world outside of jail.

November greeted them with a surprising heat wave of eighty degrees, unusual for the Icelandic state for that time of year. "This weather is ridiculous," Joci commented as they walked away from the massive building lined with barbed wire fences.

"Oh, I don't know. It gives you more time to sunbathe," Quinn pointed out.

Joci rolled her eyes, and he pulled his sunglasses out of his pocket.

"What are you doing later?" he inquired when they reached her Mercedes.

Unlocking the door, Joci leaned against the black C300. "Why? What did you have in mind, Officer?"

Quinn positioned his body directly in front of her and rested his hand on the car roof. Without rush, he trailed her body with his eyes. "Well, I do have the night off, so I thought we could get dinner."

Joci pondered that notion with faux intensity. At last, she brushed a speck of dirt from Quinn's shoulder and looped her fingers through the vest straps that did little to hide his toned chest. "Sorry. I think I have a hearing to prep for."

Not put off, Quinn leaned closer until his lips were centimeters from hers. "Are you sure? I think you might like dessert."

Doing her best to resist him, Joci met his gaze and immediately regretted it. Saying no to Quinn was more difficult than finding parking in front of the courthouse at eight in the morning. "In that case, I can move things around to accommodate you."

Maintaining his proximity, Quinn graced her with a contagious grin, then lowered his gaze to her lips. "Good. I'll see you at seven." He drew back and slipped on his shades. "Try to stay out of custody until then." He turned around, allowing his best assets to entice her before he added, "Later, counselor."

Joci couldn't pry her eyes away from Quinn's vanishing form. He looked as good walking away as he did approaching.

Opening the car door, she forced her body to obey. She needed to focus her attention on the newest case to cross her desk. Though after meeting the offender, Joci decided that she'd earned a bit of mischief with her favorite police officer. Normally, cops and lawyers didn't mix. The draw of opposing sides sparked her interest to the handsome man in the first place. Battling it out in a courtroom led to spicy rendezvous after hours at her firm or in a storage closet in the courthouse. It wasn't anything but sex, something she had no problem with since her divorce.

Pushing that thought from her mind, Joci put the car into gear and set off toward her office. No doubt, she'd have to deal with the other half of Cameron's defense team upon arrival.

— — —

Joci hit the button for the ninth floor and waited for the elevator doors to close. Two men in business suits stopped it, and her left foot tapped the shiny floor. After leaving the jail, she'd run to the cafe down the street from the firm for lunch. Now that her belly was full of broccoli cheese soup, she was ready to dive into the rest of her workday.

Her phone rang from the confines of her purse, but judging from the ringtone, it was Adrian. Nothing quite like Justin Timberlake's serene voice to remind her of her ex. The elevator jolted to life as a new voice mail vibrated. She didn't have time to explain herself, especially since Adrian would eventually hunt her down. It was a specialty of his.

The elevator stopped at her floor and she squeezed through the group. The moment both heels met the carpet, Rayna came into view. "You're back. Thank God. The jail has been calling for you."

Cocking an eyebrow, she asked, "For what? Did I forget something?"

"Uh, no. It's your new guy, Shearer. He keeps asking the jailers to call you." Rayna clicked her heels together. "I guess he wants you to visit him."

Joci took in a cleansing breath. "I was there an hour ago," she ground out. "Will you call him back and let him know Adrian and I will visit later this week. He's going to be one of those clingy clients, I can sense it already."

"Speaking of people who are relentless, Adrian is driving me nuts," Rayna informed her, keeping up with her boss.

"You wouldn't like dating him, then," joked Joci as they walked through the front lobby. The firm was changing the flooring from carpet to marble, so the women had to dodge bare spots as they ventured through the maze of cubicles.

"How long has he been terrorizing you?" she asked when they made it to her office without being jumped by an intern. It was usual for Joci, and she detested the loss of carpeting in that moment. The bloodsuckers would hear her coming from a mile away when the floors were complete.

Rayna closed the office door. "His trial went a whole two hours, so since he got out of the courtroom."

Reviewing the mail stacked to perfection on her desk, Joci didn't bother answering. She'd predicted that behavior. It was a constant for Adrian, as was his behemoth defense in any case he touched. He didn't lose unless it was necessary. She admired that about him, even if it had been her downfall.

"Did you visit the murder guy?" Rayna questioned when Joci sat down.

"Actually, yes. It was weird to see Cameron like that."

"Did he know who you were?"

"No, but that's fine. I'm a lot different than the girl with braids, crooked teeth, and no glasses."

"Hmm, then why'd it take you so long?" Rayna asked innocently.

Joci saw right through the bullshit. "I also saw a few other clients."

Peering at the file, Rayna studied the mug shot. "You know, he's awful cute. What did he look like in person?"

Joci typed her password into the computer. "He's fine."

"Fine? That's how you describe a morning latte, Joci. I mean, I don't go for the bad boys, but damn." Her eyebrows wiggled under her bangs. "Remove the half-assed makeup, put him in a black suit, and he's a dream come true. He has tattoos, doesn't he? God, I love those."

Joci threw her assistant turned coworker a disgusted glance. Cameron was drool-worthy, she wouldn't deny it, but she wouldn't encourage her friend's antics. The woman couldn't handle that piece of work. Plus, a tiny tingle of jealousy surged through her at Rayna's giddy nature. Watching Cameron with her would be more than awkward. "If you put it like that, then every jailbird is sexy," she settled on at last.

Rayna plopped down in the seat across from her. "Ooh, I get it. You like him for yourself. Aren't you a selfish one?" she teased.

Lifting her eyes, Joci studied the gray-eyed beauty. Her auburn bangs needed a trim, but otherwise she was on point. In more than one way, to her chagrin. "I admit, Mr. Shearer is attractive in the boy-band type of way, but he pales in comparison to Quinn, who I also saw at the jail."

The other woman squealed and clapped her hands over her mouth. "I thought you were only friends with benefits."

"We are."

"You can't hog all the hotties, Joce."

Surveying the onslaught of e-mails, Joci spilled, "Fine, have at it with Cameron. Good luck with him."

"Oh, I'm sensing a little jealousy. Did your blast from the past stir up feelings for the drummer boy?"

In truth, Rayna was right. Some part of her lurched to the past and then back again when she was face-to-face with her childhood crush. He'd never known and she'd never told anyone. It was better that way since she moved shortly after their time together. Still, she needed to get Rayna off her case. If she let emotions play into this job, she might end up being a sole practitioner in Butt Crack, Indiana.

"Come on, Joci! Your reason for liking Cameron isn't his rugged body alone, is it?"

The second Joci parted her lips to comment, another voice filled the void. "Now that would be ridiculous, Rayna. I'm also massively wealthy."

Both women's gazes shot to Adrian Petosa, who stood in the doorway wearing a fabulous grin. "No need to gossip about me behind semiclosed doors," he pestered good-naturedly. Clearly, he only heard the last bit of their conversation.

Rayna scurried out of the office, shutting the door.

Ignoring the six-foot shadow in a tailored blue suit, Joci opened an e-mail. Adrian craved female attention the same way he was addicted to winning at scratch off tickets. Both were a boost to his ego. Keeping their interactions all business was safer.

Her silence didn't rile him. "You're looking beautiful today, Joci. I always did like you in skirts. They're much simpler to shimmy out of the way."

A less seasoned attorney would've taken the bait, but Joci refused to give in. She logged in to her electronic filing system and scanned the notifications. "It's glorious outside today, Adrian. You should get a touch of sun before winter."

She took a sip of her lemon water and almost choked on it when she raised her eyes. Her ex was scrutinizing his pale skin in her window. It wasn't his fault that his bright red hair came with pasty pigmentation, but she liked to badger in the office as much as in court.

Adrian crossed to her desk and leaned his knuckles on

the edge. "I tried to call you. Several times."

"Huh, I guess I missed them. Must be this damn phone. Time for an upgrade," she replied, holding in a smile at his fiery blue eyes.

He shuffled an organized stack of papers to the floor, an act that used to have a different effect on her. Now the fluttering papers only pissed her off.

"This is *our* case. You should've waited for me," he said deliberately.

Joci swiveled her chair to face him. "No, I don't need to, Adrian. It's not like I got much information from him. You can come next time. I'm sure he'll be thrilled to meet you."

"Who wouldn't be?"

Joci bit her tongue to remain professional. "Okay, well, I'm going to get back to work now."

Adrian straightened his striped tie. "Or we could pop down to the pub and grab a drink."

"It's a little early for drinks, so thanks, but no." When he didn't scamper from the room, she stared at the pleadings in front of her until she was certain she was going cross-eyed.

"I can come back later if you'd rather."

Joci rubbed both hands over her face, bumping her glasses up. "Adrian, please go."

"We used to do it all the time, Joci. Don't be a downer." He took a step closer. "Remember what would happen after a couple drinks? You'd sing a little karaoke, then—"

"Then I'd smack you for getting handsy." She chuckled at the memory and shook her head. "But that was the past. We've both moved on, which reminds me, I need to draft this petition to plead guilty."

Leaning over, Adrian snagged her hands in his. The thick gold band of his Harvard Law School graduate ring clashed with the single silver band on her middle finger. A day hadn't gone by when he didn't wear the ring proudly. Even when they were married, he'd remember to put that one on and forget the wedding band. "Does it have to be like this?"

Straddling the line of staying professional and having a fight with her coworker, Joci ripped her hands away. "Yes, now go the hell away." Her temper simmered when he sighed. From the sound of it, he was going to walk out of her office. She could handle a case with him, but not when he brought up their failed marriage.

"I've been waiting for us, Joci. I want to try again."

Any control she possessed flew out the door at his soft admission. Screw being civil in the workplace. He was throwing low-blows now. He deserved her wrath. She'd never given it to him after the event. He'd simply moved back to the apartment the firm owned and filed for divorce. No crazy makeup sex or yelling matches. No begging to get back together. Nothing. Well, she was done with his cocky attitude. If she didn't get this off her chest, it'd just bubble as tension through the entire case.

"Then maybe you should've waited until I left the office to screw an intern," she barked back.

Adrian snapped his eyes shut. "That happened one time, Joci, and it was an accident."

"Uh-huh, right, because I slip and fall out of my clothes and onto a hot guy on a daily basis," she ground out.

He held up his hands. "Wrong choice of words." He cleared his throat. "A mistake. Sleeping with her was a mistake."

Joci harrumphed. "Only because you got caught."

Slapping his hand on the desk, Adrian huffed, "You knew what I was going through at that time."

Accustomed to his Irish temper, Joci took in his red face. "Oh yes. I'm well aware of what *we* were going through, Adrian, but I didn't screw the first guy who smiled at me to cope."

Cramming his hands into his pockets, he paced the floor. They didn't speak about their personal life. Not in the last two years. They ignored one another and existed when their paths intersected.

She watched his fluid movements and her heart lurched. Reliving the past only hurt. It sent shock waves through him as well, though neither of them had attempted to patch up their relationship.

Snatching Cameron's file, she tossed it toward him. "Rayna is unearthing all of his criminal past, but here is what we have so far."

Adrian halted and pressed his fist to his lips. His eyes drifted to the red folder teetering on the end of the desk, then back to her. "I never stopped loving you, Joci. You have to understand that."

Uncertain how to react, she continued, "He's a bit of a troublemaker. Already, Bill had to move him because he was involved in a fight. They'll resort to the Shoe if he keeps it up, which I'm sure he will. He's a pain in the ass.

Been calling all morning."

Her words didn't distract him. "If I could change what happened, I would. I should've been at home with you, helping you through it. I went back to work too soon, but you know the reason why."

"Cameron has been in and out of the system in Ohio, so I'm curious to find out why he was in Iowa. His eyeliner was horrible when I saw him. I'll send Rayna to buy court clothes since he won't sign the stupid waiver. He's set on seeing through to a speedy trial," she continued as tears pricked her eyes. She didn't want to cry, not in front of him.

"We would be together if I wasn't selfish back then," Adrian put in, stuck on his one-sided discussion.

Joci crossed her arms, her heart quickening. "Quinn was the arresting officer. I can get some information out of him tonight when I see him."

Adrian froze, forcing her to ramble on with a shaky voice. "Rayna thinks our client is attractive, but only in the obvious ways. He's the poster boy for what happens when your music dries up along with your dreams. We can spin that in court."

"I would give up gambling for good if I could have you back," Adrian promised, kneeling in front of her now.

Joci's stomach dropped at his pleading tone. He was dead serious. Once upon a time, all she'd desired was him. That changed in an instant. "We may be successful if we tag-team him about the waiver—"

"Dammit, Joci, will you look at me?" he rudely interrupted.

Slowly, she moved her eyes until they clashed with Adrian's dark blues. Too much history lay between them for her to ignore. It would do her no good to fight it during this case. Their lives were linked once more, whether she liked it or not. "He would've been two this Christmas," she uttered bitterly.

Adrian pulled her hands free and encompassed them with his own. "I know. Not a day goes by that I don't think about him and what happened."

Tears flowing down her cheeks now, her mind whirred back to the worst day of her life. A happy family on their way home from the hospital—until their car was trapped between two semitrucks and battered by another. Their son had died on impact, but Joci and Adrian were forced to see the mastermind behind their demise. One of the firm's criminal clients had sent a posse to destroy them when they'd failed to get a deal that didn't involve prison time.

Luckily or unluckily, Joci hadn't decided, they'd somehow survived. Their assailants did as well, but only for another month. Their fate caught up to them in the county jail. Attacking two prominent criminal attorneys put the firm on edge, and Joci was glad they had the support when they needed it. If it weren't for the firm's less than kosher clientele connections, justice would've never found them. Either way, from that day forward, neither Adrian nor Joci had been the same. His father had insisted that the firm's employees never discuss the matter. The media had done more than enough in the weeks following the tragedy.

"I want to be with you," proclaimed Adrian, wiping the

tears from her face.

"And it took you two years to come to that conclusion?" she fired off, her eyes flashing.

"We both needed time apart. I'm willing to give us another chance."

Joci sniffled and furrowed her brow. "I don't know if I can, Adrian. There's too much water under the bridge for us to start over."

Handing her a tissue, Adrian kissed the top of her head. "Tell you what. We do this case together, and if after we kick ass you still feel the same, I'll leave the conversation alone until you bring it up again."

His suggestion sounded reasonable enough, even if Joci was wary of the outcome. If she let herself fall in love with Adrian all over again, she'd never forgive herself. Studying his resilient eyes, she saw the truth. He wouldn't give up until she relented, so the path of least resistance was the way to go. It would give her the experience of the good side of Adrian for a few short months and give their client a superb defense. Though her stomach flipped at the idea of them as a couple, it wouldn't move beyond the case. She would make certain of that no matter how much she still found Adrian attractive. "All right, it's a deal, but don't expect me to be all lovey-dovey and crap."

"And what about Quinn? I know the two of you are more than friendly."

"Yes, we are, but it's just sex with us. Sure, he's my friend too, but he knows I'm not looking for anything serious."

Adrian let out a relieved sigh, though she was certain part was from the underlying tension. He never had to deal with any sort of competition before. Women fell at his feet, her included. Well, she was determined to keep her word with Adrian, but also make certain she didn't get attached.

"Good. If you're available, let's go see our schlemiel on Friday. That will give me enough time to catch up on a couple of cases."

Wiping her eyes, Joci adjusted her glasses. "Yeah, sure. Friday is fine." Standing, she forced a smile. Revisiting her living nightmare wasn't the best start to her afternoon, but it felt good to get her side out there. It should've been done years ago.

Adrian swiftly pulled her into his hold. With her heels, they were the same height, but Joci didn't care. Being in his arms once more brought a plethora of emotions and memories to mind. His touch instantly calmed her as his Ralph Lauren Red cologne washed through her nostrils. He smelled as good as the day she met him.

"Hey, Joci, I have Javier's depositions scheduled for—" Rayna's voice cut off abruptly, and Joci broke the lingering hug.

"Great. Send out the subpoenas, please," Joci instructed, rubbing her lips together.

Rayna eyed both lawyers, then backed out of the office, her face flushed.

"She tends to have issues with closed doors, doesn't she?" Adrian asked the moment Rayna's shadow disintegrated.

Joci slipped off her heels. The damn things were killing

her today. "Yes, but she's my best friend and I don't hug people in my office every day so it normally doesn't matter."

Adrian nodded. "I'd hope not."

Reaching over, he pressed his lips to her cheek. "I need to get going. I have a hearing in half an hour."

Hustling to her desk, Joci groaned when she spotted a hearing on her docket for the same time. She had been so preoccupied with the murder case that she'd neglected the rest of her clients. "Shit! I have one too. Can I hitch a ride?"

Smoothing his suit jacket, Adrian smiled. "You bet. I'll meet you by the elevator in fifteen minutes." He paused in the doorway and added, "Thanks, Joci."

Leaning back in her comfy office chair, she replied, "Don't thank me yet. You don't know what I'll decide."

Adrian patted the doorframe. "No, but I hope I do."

With that, he left Joci to mull over the events the day had brought thus far. If she wasn't careful, all of that male attention may overwhelm her circuits.

CHAPTER THREE

The obnoxious foghorn forced Cameron awake, and he jerked up to a sitting position. Sweat raced down his face and he attempted to steady his breathing. His dreams haunted him almost as much as the case looming over his head.

Five days had passed since meeting half of his dynamic duo defense team. He swung his feet off the bed. Since then, he'd kept his nose clean. He smirked. "As clean as I can."

A second fight had come to his cell yesterday, and he felt the remnants now. This time, the tatted thugs made it evident that Cameron's enemies knew where he was hiding. It didn't take long for the inmates to know a member of the Del Rossi mob was among the ranks. After all, the Del Rossi family owned all but the very ground the Windy City sat on. His boss, Bernard, was one of three brothers who orchestrated the mob from their corners of the States. The choice to cross over into Iowa wasn't his two weeks ago, and it certainly wasn't his now.

Tenderly, he felt his ribs. By his guess, they weren't

broken. Not yet, at least. Though if his late-night fight clubs continued, he would sport more than a few shattered bones. His silent adversaries were out for his blood, and thus far, they'd collected a substantial amount.

He should tell his attorneys this information, yet he had no desire to do so. He couldn't be certain that an Iowa prison was safer than the county jail, but for now, he would keep his mouth sealed. The last thing he needed was a death sentence before he was thrown before a judge.

Since the misunderstanding, he'd been secluded for his protection. *Yeah, like that's going to do anything*, he scoffed. Hearing from his boss needed to happen soon. He was fairly certain hiring the law firm meant that Bernard Del Rossi was willing to forgive the slight misgivings when it came to his sister, Bambi, also Cameron's ex. They'd been on the outs ever since he'd broken it off with the blonde bombshell, not that he blamed Bernard. Back then, he called him Jerry, but that name was reserved for family, not men crawling out of disgrace. Hell, Cameron was shocked when he didn't lose a finger, much less his life, after shunning Bambi. A broken arm was all he'd been given. Not a bad deal for breaking the heart of a mobster's sister.

His foot touched a crumpled sheet of paper on the floor. Reaching down, Cameron snatched the balled-up attempt of a letter to his benefactor. "He wouldn't appreciate the paper trail," he amended, reading the note. It wasn't the first time Bernard had bailed him out, though this time, the charge was a bit steep. He knew why, though. The big man himself asked Cameron to look into the Mikkelsen mob's movements. They were slowly taking over smaller gangs the Del Rossis usually kept control of. It was bad for business, hence the reason why he was sent. Cameron wasn't sure what to expect when he started trailing a string of deaths due to overdosing on a new drug sold by the Danish crew. His on-again off-again band was the best cover he could find, and he paid for the majority of the gigs, so the other men agreed without much debate. The information led him to whispers about an attorney who was helping the mob in Iowa of all places. He'd yet to find out who the attorney was, and he was scheduled to meet with Jimmy "Nitty" Nichols to discuss who had sold him the bad batch of drugs when he'd blacked out.

He'd originally agreed to the wild-goose chase, but with the contingency that his time with the organization be cut short. Now Cameron wasn't sure if it was worth all this hassle. He wanted out of the Italy-born mafia. He'd done his time, and he was ready to start fresh in a place where people didn't know what the intricate tattoo with vines of black ivy surrounding D and R meant on his left arm. Instead, he was locked in a jail cell with less-than-friendly gangs letting him know they had issues with the Del Rossis. *No shock there.*

For the next hour, he doodled on the notepad, left ankle propped up on his right knee. The blinking yellow light above his head drove him to break a pencil, but thankfully he'd grabbed a few.

"Shearer, you have visitors," a jailer called, advancing on his cell door.

"Who is it?" Cameron stood and rubbed his face briskly.

Never one to let his facial hair run wild, the rough bristles set his mood to dire. Little by little, his life was falling apart, and he couldn't glue the pieces back together.

The guard unlocked the door. "The tooth fairy," he stated sarcastically. "Who else would it be but your lawyers?"

Cameron's pulse quickened at the thought of being in the same room as Joci Dorous. There was something about her that rocked his subconscious. She was familiar, but he couldn't nail down why. He may act as though he loathed her, but the pretty brunette had grown on him faster than he anticipated.

"Well, I suppose they're better than no one." He scratched his back. Since his arrival, his shower privileges had been reduced to every other day thanks to the facility's fear that he'd be stabbed after the recent brawls, and he was in desperate need. "Can I shower first?"

The man grunted his disapproval, so Cameron tried again. "How about breakfast? A man facing murder charges needs his energy," he asked, pushing his luck.

The man passed him a pastry that had once resembled a cinnamon roll. "Here. Your friends had first crack at it. Eat at your own risk."

Opting to go with a more sparse diet, Cameron refused the offer. "Forget it. I'll starve first." He spun around while the man patted him down before clicking the cuffs into place.

"You look like hell," the oaf pointed out with a snicker.

"Thanks, princess. I try." His snarky reply led to him tripping over the guard's baton.

The man nudged him forward, and Cameron had never thought he would be glad to see bureaucrats in suits as much as he was in that instant. The room's lone table and three chairs welcomed him as he walked inside, his eyes pinned on his female attorney. She stood near her chair, which was occupied by a briefcase. To his disappointment, his other attorney wasn't a woman but a redheaded man.

Without ceremony, he slouched in the lone open chair. It was as uncomfortable as it looked, but he couldn't complain. It was better than being shark bait in his cellblock.

Ignoring the man, Cameron openly gaped at Joci. Her exquisite navy-blue dress hugged every delightful inch of her long body. The sleeves hung three-fourths of the way down her alabaster arms and flared at the ends. A bow on her left hip accented her small waist.

When she stuffed her hands in the dress's pockets, Cameron didn't stop the smile on his lips. The beige pumps weren't his favorite, but he was no fashion expert. The best part of her outfit was her cherry-red lips. Those were enough to quench whatever hunger he felt.

Swinging his gaze to the other man in the room, he was mildly put off when the ginger glared at him. It seemed his new attorney wasn't a fan of Cameron's intimate perusal.

"So, what's up, darling? Did you get my case dismissed yet?" he offered with a wave of his hand.

Joci took the lead, a particularly attractive trait. "That's doubtful right now, Cameron. We have an immense way to go before we can discuss that possibility."

Cameron rolled his shoulders back and nodded. "Who's the suit?"

"Adrian Petosa," the man informed him, his voice as crisp as a potato chip. "Your second attorney."

Surveying the final link of his defensive chain, Cameron couldn't fault the guy. He'd detected a high-end cologne at first entrance to the room, but it was Adrian's Kiton K-50 suit that set him down the path of jealousy. The details he knew about high fashion included being able to spot an imposter designer, but what his attorney wore was flawless. He didn't want to imagine the price tag on the suit that was one of two-hundred and fifty made per year. Cameron was in hands void of calluses now.

"Well then, it looks like I was given the wealthiest asshole alongside you, Ms. Dorous."

Joci pressed her lips together, then ripped the briefcase from her chair. "Mr. Shearer, please keep it up so I have a legitimate reason to request a withdrawal of our services. I'm pretty sure 'he's a jackass' doesn't fly with our judges, but I'm willing to take a crack at it," she warned, her bright eyes flicking to her coworker.

Loving her gumption more and more, Cameron scratched his wrist. He was still amused by their first encounter, and he didn't want the visits to end quite yet. "That won't be necessary." He eyed Adrian. "Yet."

The spitfire took her seat, then glanced to her partner. The look that passed between them made him speculate if they were together. With their incredible attractiveness, his attorneys would make a stunning couple.

"Let's go over the night of the arrest. Walk us through it," Adrian began.

"I already danced this with the cops. Read the report," Cameron directed.

"Mr. Shearer, you asked for a lawyer even before they read you the Miranda rights. If you knew to do that, you also didn't tell the police everything," Joci stated.

Cameron rested his elbows on the sticky table. He didn't care to know how it had become that way. "Fine. My band, the Rejected Misfits, played a bar downtown that night. We did a lot of drugs, drank gallons of booze, then hit on women. I woke up in a wet field with a cop shining his flashlight in my face, and suddenly I had a knife and gun. I don't carry weapons ever. It's not my style. There ya go." He glanced between the two. "The end."

"Okay, that's a start. What kind of drugs? Who were the other band members?" Adrian questioned, whipping out a notepad.

"Jared Malone, Tommy Lu, and Eddie Cianciaruso are the guys who play in the band with me. They're probably in Vegas by now, though. That's where they talked about going next." Joci held out her hand for more and he rubbed his chapped lips together. Accepting that these two wouldn't stop until he spilled his story, Cameron did what they wanted, save numerous details about his less-than-savory way of life. Part of what got him in this mess was because of his big mouth. He didn't need them to know anything about the Del Rossi mob unless the boss told him to spill it.

When he was finished with his tale, Adrian tapped his

index finger to his upper lip. "Is it possible that you killed the victim when you were high?"

"Nope. I'm not violent." He saw Joci roll her eyes. The bruises on his face and fists didn't help his cause, so he added, "All right, not very violent. When I get high, it calms me down. Usually. I'll admit, I've had my fair share of fist fights. On that night, I did a line of cocaine before our gig, but it only makes me play the drums better. I'm not capable of murder. I would know if I did it."

"Not necessarily." Joci pulled out a stack of research papers. "If the drugs you took were laced with something you're unaccustomed to, it could've increased your adrenaline and resulted in homicidal acts."

He decided not to mention the tidbit that he hadn't taken enough drugs to induce a blackout. He'd promised himself to never become his dad, but his boy band cover usually included recreational use of drugs. Cocaine wasn't his drug of choice, but he'd done a small line that night before he met with Nichols. In the past, he'd done too much and felt the repercussions the next day. He knew for a fact someone shoved a needle in his arm with more illegal substances. Glancing to his right arm, Cameron frowned. He wasn't a leftie and he'd never shoot up, which meant someone got the drop on him. He was determined to pin the person to the wall if only to make them suffer for the slight way his body came down from the unexpected high. He didn't crave another hit, hell no, but his stomach let him know it was a horrible decision to do any in the first place. He'd stick with marijuana. It didn't hurt.

Cameron shoved the documents away, not ready to divulge any information to the duo. "Learn all of that in your fancy office chair, did you?"

"No. I looked it up at the research library, but thanks for putting a golden spoon up my ass." Joci shoved the file into her briefcase. "A real confidence boost."

He'd meant to rile her, but from the looks of it, she was done with his brashness. Typical day in his life. Cameron liked to see the fire skewer her eyes at his words. He shouldn't try to upset her, but it was too addictive to stop.

"We'll get a private investigator to look into your story, as well as the bandmates," Adrian stated, scribbling on his notepad. "It may take a little while if they're hopping from state to state."

Not caring what the well-dressed man did, Cameron focused on the prettier form of law in the room. Joci took off her glasses and wiped under her eyes. It was then that his mind whirled to a time when mobsters were just the bad guys on television and not real-life nightmares. "Joci. Joci Dorous."

She glanced to him. "Yes?"

Realization smacked him in the jaw. "You didn't used to wear glasses."

She slowly shook her head, but he couldn't tell if she knew who he was or not. She didn't say anything the first time they met, so maybe she didn't recognize him. That stung a little too if it were true.

"Um, what does that have to do with anything?" Adrian asked, clearly annoyed by the derailing train.

Cameron attempted to remain collective as memories popped up surrounding a lanky girl named Joci who lived across the street from his aunt. Without a doubt, the woman in front of him was the same girl all grown up.

"Shit," he mumbled under his breath.

He understood why Bernard picked the Petosa firm now. He met Joci's eyes but found them guarded. *Does she know or has she forgotten me?* He wasn't sure which option he'd prefer. Either way, he needed to keep the sexy siren at a safe distance. If she felt even a fraction of what he did when they were kids, she'd regret ever seeing him again. When women got too close, he tended to burn them.

"Cameron, we want to help you, but you have to trust us." Adrian stood and pushed in his chair. "And that includes everything. Whatever you're not telling us will find its way out one way or another. We'd rather it not be in front of a judge and jury."

Watching in silence, he envied Adrian. No doubt the man would spend all his free time with the tall beauty beside him, while Cameron wasted away in a rank jail cell. He considered breaking the news to Joci about their past, but opted against it when he recognized Adrian's body language toward the gorgeous woman.

"I'll think it over," he offered. He locked eyes with Joci. Hers reminded him of an afternoon in the forest. It was a one-of-a-kind hazel tint. Just like he remembered. *Damn, how did I not identify her before now?*

Joci stood and clutched her briefcase. "We'll be in touch," she told him, then swept around the table, as cool as a Canadian breeze.

Cameron decided not to turn around. He could already guess Adrian's firm hand was on the small of Joci's back as he led her to safety. His insides ached. It was something he hadn't done in too long, and it was doubtful he would get the chance in the next twenty years.

— — —

"Do you want another drink?" Adrian asked, two hours after they finished up at the office.

Tipping the glass to her lips, Joci sipped the remaining scotch and set the tumbler down with a thud. "I'm good. Thanks."

Adrian snatched his glass and headed toward the bar while she stayed behind. To her amusement, he'd doted on her every whim since they chatted the other day. It was quite the difference to his previous cold shoulder. She'd missed this side of Adrian. It was the same side she'd fallen in love with.

Staring at the empty glass, Joci regretted not ordering another one. She needed it if she was going to give Adrian a glimmer of hope. In all honesty, she didn't think she should entertain a change to their circumstances, but she couldn't help herself. Other than his one bout of infidelity, Adrian had treated her better than anyone else.

"I thought you could use it," Adrian's warm voice stated as he placed a full glass on a napkin.

"You always sensed when I needed something." She grabbed the scotch and took a greedy gulp. "Most of the time."

Adrian cleared his throat and took a drink of his matching single malt. She didn't know why she'd added that last bit. They'd called a truce, and yet she couldn't let the past go.

"So, I was thinking we get Shearer evaluated. Maybe by Dr. Kinnard. If he has a serious drug and alcohol problem, we can get him into treatment and out of jail. That would look pleasant to a jury." Adrian rolled his neck. "What do you think?"

Joci took another drink and reminded herself that they were coworkers at the moment, and not lovers. She couldn't count the number of times the simple tilt of his neck resulted in a massage gone awry. That was a thought she'd never imagined would pop into her brain ever again.

Shaking her head, she focused on the present. "Um, yeah. I think it's a great idea. May also help sort his life out. I get the feeling that he has deeper issues at play."

Adrian chuckled. "Don't we all?"

Joci swirled the ice around in her drink. "Hey, just to keep you informed, I know our client."

"What?" he choked out amid the scotch. "You know him personally?" He squinted. "Did you screw him?"

"No, you dick. He was my neighbor when we were in elementary."

"Oh, all right." His brows knit together. "Will it be a problem?"

She recalled the way Cameron ogled her, then shook her head. "No, I'll be fine."

"Room for one more?" a deep voice asked from behind them.

Jumping at the sound, Joci spilled her drink. After dabbing the table with a napkin, she set the glass down. Lifting her gaze, she swallowed hard as she met Adrian's icy eyes. She knew that look well, and it sent shivers down her spine.

Dabbing her mouth with another napkin, she groaned at the timing. "Hey, Quinn," she greeted with cheery resolve.

Quinn placed one hand on the empty chair beside her and the other on Joci's. "You ready to go, or do you need a few more minutes?" He glanced to Adrian, then back to her. "I can wait if you're working on a case."

His understanding settled Joci's gut, but the drastic change in Adrian's demeanor irked it once more. Getting to her feet, she chugged the rest of the burning liquid. "I think I'm good."

"You're going with him?" Adrian inquired.

After giving Quinn a quick grin, she cracked her neck and stood. "Yep. I had to cancel on him the other night, so I'm making it up to him this weekend."

Adrian glanced at Quinn, then settled his gaze on her. In one swig, he drained his glass, and pushed a smile on his face. "All right, if that's who you have to do."

"Adrian!" Joci seethed, her eyes wide. Envy wasn't one of his best traits, but it also showed her how much he cared. "We're not together and you know it."

"It's cool, Joci. I get it," Quinn filled in. "I'd be the same way." He looped his arm around her waist. "Except I wouldn't lose you in the first place by being a dick."

Adrian's jaw tightened and he stood to his full height,

despite being several inches shorter than the off-duty police officer. The two men glared at each other while Joci's head pulsed in pain.

Thoroughly aggravated with the testosterone levels in the bar, she unlatched from Quinn's arm and stalked to the front door. She overheard the men exchange words but couldn't decipher them as she rushed outside.

The chilly November air whipped at her coat lapels as she moved toward the parking lot. She'd ridden with Adrian to the bar, but her apartment was within walking distance. Her ankle turned on a crack in the sidewalk, and she cursed when she tripped. Her nerves were officially shot. She could handle an intense cross-examination, but seeing two people important to her life at odds did her in.

Now that she thought of it, telling Quinn to meet her at the bar hadn't been the best idea. It sounded good at the time, but she hadn't expected Adrian to get possessive. He hadn't given a shit for the last two years, so she hadn't given it a second thought.

"Joci, hold up!" Quinn called, his voice closer than she'd expected.

She didn't slow her pace. Five more blocks and she would be home. She would walk with pride until she got there too. Her heels, on the other hand, may be on their way to the trash bin before that. "Go home, Quinn," she shot back.

"Let me give you a ride," he insisted, now at her side. "You shouldn't walk in those things this late at night. Someone may think you're a hooker," he pestered, but she wasn't in the mood.

"No," she rejected.

Quinn grabbed her arm and twirled her around to face him. "Stop! I know you're pissed, and I'm sorry. I thought the two of you were done." His green eyes turned a shade darker. "Is that not true anymore?"

Joci didn't resist his hold. It was one that had helped her through when no one else could. "I don't know," she admitted. "He wants to give it another shot, but I'm not sure what to do."

Wrapping his arms around her, Quinn simply held her. "Well, I'd be lying if I told you that I would be okay with you and him, but I understand. I'm here, Joci, and I'll support you no matter what. That's what friends do, whether they're screwing or not."

Joci clung to Quinn's Carhartt coat. He was much too good for her. That was probably why she couldn't let him go. Tilting her head up, she cradled his smooth jaw in her hands. "Thanks, Quinn. You're my knight in Kevlar."

Quinn smirked. "I do what I can."

But he did more than that. Without hesitation, Joci pressed her lips against his. He reacted like every time before, his lips parting as he consumed the breath in her lungs with his exuberance. The way he moved her entire soul with such a simple act destroyed her.

Reluctantly, she pulled away when raindrops splattered them. Giggling, she tugged his hand. "Come on! Let's get inside before it opens up."

Instead of racing back for his pickup, Quinn scooped

her into his arms and sprinted down the sidewalk. Without a doubt, Joci had her work cut out for her when it came to the men in her life. She hoped life didn't become more complicated.

— — —

Rustling the early December newspaper to the next page, Joci studied the stock market trends. It was more of the same, and she seldom followed it. The sole reason she was reading the boring part was to ignore the slumbering man beside her. Quinn's bare chest had beckoned to her from the instant she woke on Sunday morning. Knowing he had to work that evening, she let him snooze. It was the least she could do for the man who calmed the demons that lurked in her dreams.

She and Quinn never discussed a future together. She wouldn't allow it. Friends, sure, but a relationship, no. He knew where they stood, which was why occasionally shacking up with him wasn't a big deal. His job all but guaranteed danger at every clock-in, and she couldn't lose another person to a criminal warlord.

Joci ran her fingers through her hair and pushed her glasses up her nose. Attachments were a means to a cruel end in her mind. The death of her son exemplified that. She'd had no one to comfort her. Adrian had drifted too far away to grasp, so she buried herself in work. Whether that was the right call or not, she wasn't certain. Had she made another, her kinship with Levi Quinn would've never blossomed.

Skipping the comics, Joci turned to the classified section as her mind revisited the day she'd met the officer. She had just lost a domestic abuse case in the courthouse and was marching down the steps outside. There he was, sporting aviator sunglasses, in full police uniform. Every woman drooled for the man with a smile as bright as the July sun. When Joci caught his glance, her brain spun in place. Slamming into one of the limestone columns that held up the building was the least of her bruised ego that day.

Joci bit back a smile at the memory. As expected, Quinn had rushed to her side and helped her up. He even collected the papers the wind tousled. Her life had altered for the better at their meeting.

Accepting him as her fate wasn't a pill she was willing to swallow. Quinn was her best friend. One she told every dark secret to, and yes, tangoed with in the sheets when the opportunity presented itself. She wouldn't change their arrangement for the world, but she often wondered if that was all her love life would amount to. The thought of succumbing to a full-fledged relationship sent her mind into convulsions and her body to full panic mode.

From the bedside table, her phone buzzed with an incoming call. She dropped the paper and plucked the iPhone up. Rayna's name was illuminated alongside a photo of the two of them. "Morning, Rayna, what's up?" she greeted, slipping on a pair of Drake University sweatpants.

"Just checking in. How're things going with the kinky cop?" Moving to the living room, Joci tried to imagine her friend. No doubt she wore a giddy smile along with flannel pajamas.

"It's good," she conceded.

"All righty then, on to other news. What the hell did I walk in on with you and Adrian? You haven't explained that. Are you two shaking desk drawers or what?"

Flipping the switch for the coffeemaker, Joci glanced out her fourth-story apartment window. The sun sat on top of one of Des Moines's tallest buildings and cast ideal lighting on the city below.

"Joci, are you listening?" Rayna's chipper voice broke into her admiration.

"Sorry, no. What did you say?" She prayed the question about Adrian wouldn't resurface.

"I asked if you and Adrian are more than coworkers."

Hmm, now that's a loaded question.

Seeking out a mug, Joci poured a cup of freshly brewed arabica. "It's a bit complicated, I'm afraid," she divulged as the last drop of coffee hit the top.

"What do you mean? You know I won't tell anyone."

Joci knew that was true. The majority of the office rats didn't speak to Rayna. Their jealousy of how easily she climbed the intern ladder made her the main subject of the watercooler gossip. With her office so close to the kitchen, Joci heard a few too many secrets.

"Yeah, I know you won't." She padded to the sofa and sank into the plushness. "I'll tell you about it sometime," she promised, catching sight of Quinn's form.

"What? Why can't you tell me now?" Rayna complained.

"I'll be in at seven in the morning tomorrow. Can you get court clothes for Shearer? His arraignment is coming up. I gotta go." She ended the call before the woman could respond.

"Working on weekends again, huh?" Quinn asked, crossing his arms. The sole tattoo on his chest jerked at his movement.

"My job is demanding, what can I say?" She placed her phone on the cushion beside her. If she had her way, she would stay in this spot and devour Quinn's body until she passed out from exhaustion. He bore the typical fit body of a cop. Since he wasn't one for donuts, his lean muscles captured every woman's lust and every man's envy.

"That's too bad," he commented.

Deciding now was as good a time as any, she asked, "What can you tell me about the Shearer case?"

Quinn let out a breath and rubbed his forehead. "So it's to be one of those Sundays." She shrugged, and he mirrored her. "Okay, I'll play ball." He moved to the seat across from her. "Off the record?"

"I wouldn't have it any other way," she retorted, wrapping her fingers around the cup of joe. This was how she preferred her investigations: half-naked and swimming in caffeine.

"One of the emergency buttons at Gray's Lake dispatched me there. I spotted the deceased, then called for backup. Your client was about fifty feet away with a knife in his possession. He also had baggies of cocaine and marijuana. The gun came into play when he found it in his boot. Ollie and I tag-teamed him."

"I forgot he was there."

"Yeah, he showed up late. Typical Ollie."

She made a mental note to catch up with the rookie

another time. "How did Cameron act?"

Quinn knitted his brows. "He was nervous. A little cocky about the drugs, but acted like he'd never used a handgun before," he recalled. He leaned over and stole her coffee. After taking a satisfying sip, he added, "Between the knife matching the wounds on the victim, the drugs matching those in the victim's body, and Shearer's admittance of taking drugs, it all points to him."

"What about the other footsteps in the grass?" She waved for the coffee.

He offered her a humoring expression. "Joci, it's Gray's. Dumbass kids trample through the woods every night. That particular night was Halloween. The ground was covered in shoe prints, but we don't have the resources to track down each misfit who was there. It won't help at all."

Joci crossed her legs and handed him the mug. "But maybe the real killer was among those prints. You know how it goes. Shearer could've been a decoy found to pin the murder on. Drug deals go on too often at the lake."

"If that was the case, they wouldn't have left the drugs," he reminded her. "But your guy passed out and would've stolen the goods once he woke. It was Jimmy Nichols, Joci. That man is bad news. If Shearer contacted Nichols for a drug exchange, then decided he wanted money too, it wouldn't be unheard of. Open and closed case."

He drained the cup and went to the kitchen to refill it. "I don't see any other scenario."

Fully aware of the odds, Joci chewed at her thumbnail. Quinn hated Halloween for reasons she sort of knew, but if he was telling the truth, her client was a cold-blooded murderer. She wasn't fond of that thought. Had Cameron truly changed so much since she last knew him? It seemed so if she believed the cop's version of events. She wasn't about to relinquish into defeat. Whether for Cameron or any other client, she dug into files and reports until she could piece together the crime. It didn't add up. Not with mismatched information.

"I don't know, Quinn. There's something missing. The motive is fuzzy."

Returning to the couch this time, Quinn patted her thigh. "All I know is the county attorney determined our case was enough to convict on. I'm not sure what motive he'll present." He wrapped his arm around her shoulders. "That's not my particular forte."

Joci leaned into his body. "True, but you do excel in other facets."

"Oh yeah? Like what?" he asked when she lolled her head on his shoulder.

Swiping the steaming cup of coffee, she placed it on the table. Joci ran her fingers along his jawline, then plunged them through his hair. "The Sunday crossword."

Quinn lifted his eyebrows. "No, I suck at those."

Smiling coyly, Joci kissed his cheek. "Oh, I didn't mean the paper." Her hands fluttered over his chest. "I mean the puzzle two people form."

Comprehension flickered in his eyes. He dropped his gaze to her lips. "Oh. Yeah, I'm excellent at puzzles when they involve you."

"And cocky too," she chastised with a smirk.

Leaning in, Quinn shook his head. "Not yet, but I'm willing to bet you can fix him within seconds."

A giggle erupted from Joci's lips just in time for Quinn to swallow it whole. She may still be floundering for a viable defense, but she was positive she'd discovered the instigator in the passionate crime she was about to commit.

CHAPTER FOUR

"Here's the latest." Rayna produced three white envelopes stamped with the Polk County Jail logo on the front.

Studying the penmanship, Joci didn't have to check the return address to know who had sent another round of fan mail. "Ah, I see he's into calligraphy now," she uttered, grabbing a silver letter opener. With one zip, she had it open, sighing at the note. It was humorous in a way, the number of times Cameron wrote her in the last month, and her alone, requesting a visit. Thanksgiving had come and gone with nothing new to tell him. She was determined to keep their old friendship on the up and up so she didn't get any personal feelings jumbled in there. The county attorneys were gathering discovery materials, but they had managed to file the trial information on time.

"Has he signed the written arraignment yet?" Rayna asked from across the desk.

Joci looked up and noticed her friend wearing a fetching lavender suit today. The color suited her, but what else was new? She set the group of envelopes onto the stack of the "Shearer memoirs," as she liked to refer to them. She still hadn't confronted him about their connection, but that was because Adrian always tagged along to their meetings. Their conversation was meant for just the two of them. Adrian wouldn't understand.

"Nope. Adrian went out to see him, but Shearer refused to come out of his cell. I'm just glad Adrian covered the bond review hearing a few weeks ago." She pushed up her glasses and pinched the bridge of her nose. "But since neither of us has seen him since then, it's time to attempt another appointment."

Flipping her straight hair over her shoulder, Rayna assumed, "And you're the lucky pick?"

"So it seems," Joci replied, glancing to the letters. She read each one, because billing had to be accumulated for such a case, but also because she was curious. Cameron didn't act like a criminal, but not many of them did in her experience. Something about him was different. He was too clever for a crime such as homicide. But then again, it'd been a while since he was the kid doing backflips on the trampoline in her backyard.

Joci couldn't believe Cameron was guilty. Not of murder. Perhaps he was guilty of another offense, but there was too much coincidence for her mind to accept.

"I think I'm going to try out my signature move," she advised, snatching the expanding folder for the miscreant.

Rayna eyed her. "I thought he was your friend. Your tactics sort of swing over that line."

"Oh please. We were kids when I knew him. He hasn't said he's recognized me and probably won't if he's a druggie." She slid mint balm over her lips. "Plus, it'll be kind of fun to mess with him."

"Hmm, what happened to that being a last resort?"

Tossing her an annoyed glance, she nodded. "If this doesn't rattle him, I don't know what will. I never go too far. Don't worry, Ray."

"Well, have fun with him." Rayna pushed off the chair and made her way to the door. "By the way, how's it going with the sexy police officer?"

"Shit! I forgot about Quinn." In one fluid movement, Joci stood and checked her phone. Sure enough, Quinn had sent her two text messages. "He's going to be pissed." She sailed to the exit, then turned on her heels and snagged her coat from the hanger behind the door.

"I thought you said the two of you weren't in a relationship," Rayna prodded as she followed her boss.

Joci rummaged through the pockets of her coat and rubbed her lips together. "We're not, but I was supposed to meet him for breakfast." She glanced to the clock. "What day is it?"

"Tuesday."

"Aw, crap. I thought our meeting was for tomorrow," she wailed. She didn't wait for Rayna to offer a witty response. It would be iconic for sure, since Joci wasn't known for letting anything slip through the cracks when it came to her cases. Managing time for handsome guys wasn't high on her list. The only excuse she had was due to her late-night work on a theft case. She'd spent the early hours drafting the appeal brief and didn't bother to crawl into bed once she was done. By then, her alarm chirped its early time and she bustled to the gym for a quick run.

"I'm going to the jail after I meet with Quinn," she called, all but running to the elevator. "Let Adrian know, will ya?"

"You have his number, remember?" Rayna hollered as the elevator dinged its arrival.

Joci acted as though she didn't hear as the doors closed. Settling into the back of the small metal box, Joci pulled out her phone and sent a quick text to Quinn.

Joci: Hey, sorry about bailing on you. Can I make it up to you?

She tapped her left foot on the floor as she awaited his response. For the most part, he replied within minutes, but seeing how she'd flopped on him, she didn't expect a hasty reply.

The ride down the building passed in what felt like slow motion. They stopped at just about every floor, yet no text from Quinn.

Reaching the first level at last, Joci trekked through the busy lobby. With her phone attached to her hand and her head down, she smacked into a solid body. "Oof!" she muttered.

Steady hands swooped around her middle, keeping her from teetering backward on her heels. "Well, that's one way to get you in my arms again," a smooth voice laced with humor joked.

"Adrian." Joci righted herself and pushed out of his grip. "Sorry. I was preoccupied."

The tall attorney straightened her lapel. "I'd say that's putting it lightly." He nodded to her phone. "Got a big date you're rushing off to or something?" His question, though innocent, harbored a hint of resentment.

"As it turns out, no. I was on my way to see Shearer." She waved the red folder. "Maybe he'll see reason and sign the written arraignment so we don't have to go to court later this week."

"Hmm, well in that case, do you want me to go with you?" His hand rested on her forearm. "He can be quite difficult."

"I think I'll be okay." She took a step away. "I've got one last Hail Mary up my sleeve."

Before she could reach the outer doors, Adrian snaked his arm around her waist. If she wasn't set on running to Quinn and then subsequently Cameron, Joci would've enjoyed his touch.

"You're going to pull a Dorous?" he questioned, his blue eyes quizzical.

Her lips curved in a smile. "You mean there's a name for it?"

He inched her closer to him and lowered his voice. "For what you do to the poor souls to get your way, yes, there is a name for it. One I've heard spoken in hushed tones at the jail." His eyes slid over her face. "It's not safe, you know. One of these times, the guy will want your attentions."

Joci leaned over and pecked a kiss to his cheek. "Aw,

don't worry. It hasn't failed yet." She wiggled out of his grip and pasted on a bright smile. "Plus, it's not like the guards aren't watching everything that happens in those rooms. I never do anything too risqué that would get me in trouble."

A wary expression crossed his pale face, but he nodded nonetheless. "Be careful, Joci."

"Always."

Adrian's brows bunched together, but he added, "Let's meet later today to discuss what happened, okay?" He closed the minimal distance. "And not about the case alone. You promised to try. So far, you've ignored me more than the time I spilled pho on you."

Chuckling in remembrance, Joci waved her hand. "I smelled like soup for my client's trial on assaulting his wife with a cheeseburger. The stains didn't help his defense either."

"I won't do it again," he swore, holding up his fingers like a Boy Scout. "Meet me at the Royal Mile. I'll buy the first round."

Joci rolled her eyes and adjusted her glasses. "You'll buy all the rounds." She turned around and bit back a giddy grin. Flirting with Adrian was easy. Allowing herself to open up to him was a much more troubling situation.

"Anything for you," he called as she crossed the threshold to the outside world.

Jingling her keys, Joci didn't bother to stop the excitement that filled her gut. One way or another, she would enjoy her day, whether it was with Adrian or Quinn. A gust of wind blew her hair in her face. *Or with Cameron,* a little part of her mind reminded despite fighting the urge. After seeing him last month, she'd dug out the old photo albums until she found the ones with him in them. Back then, they were as thick as thieves. Seeing how they used to swipe cookies from his aunt's kitchen, they weren't exactly hardened criminals. They had good times together, which made her heart seize when she thought about him potentially facing life in prison. She wanted a different future for the boy who'd climbed trees with her and sang Disney tunes.

As she made it to the curb, her phone buzzed from her pocket. Digging it out, she saw Quinn's name. "Hey, Quinn."

"Hey yourself, stranger," his deep voice greeted.

She could imagine him now, sitting in the patrol car with his window down and the heat cranked to full blast. "So, I wanted to apologize," she began.

"It's cool. I get it. You're a busy lady, and your ex probably wants to monopolize your time."

Joci passed a group of tourists and entered the parking garage. One perk about working downtown was that her firm had ground level parking attached to the building. "Well, I have been busy, but not with Adrian."

In the background, she heard the police radio mumble a code. His silence told her more than she wanted to know. "It's this case. You know, the park murder one."

"Oh yeah. That guy. He hasn't pled out yet?"

"Please," she scoffed. "The county attorney won't offer him a deal." Joci ducked into her car and started the engine. It was slow to warm up, so she sat with her seat belt unbuckled. "Don't hate me."

Quinn's laugh sounded strained but comforting at the same time. "I could never hate you, Joci. It's a complicated situation, you and me. We both knew it from the start." He sighed. "I always thought you would change your mind, though. About us."

Opening her mouth to refute his words, Joci was interrupted by the wail of a siren.

"Hey, I've gotta take this call, but if you're free later, I'd love to get together," he said amid static.

She heard the engine rev on the other end and smirked. Quinn loved his job like any other man would when it came to speeding for a cause. "All right. I'm going to stop by Akebono for lunch if I ever get out of the parking garage." She buckled, pulled up to the street access, and tapped her finger on the steering wheel.

Squealing tires met her ears and she smirked. "Try not to flip that thing, will you?"

Another chuckle from Quinn made her lips itch to meet his. "Tell ya what. I bet I can get done with this call and meet you there before you."

Cocking her eyebrow, she took the bait. "You're on."

"Perfect. Loser buys, and I never lose," Quinn stated with confidence.

His siren blared across the line. "Loser loses their shirt," she heckled.

More tires screamed around a corner, and he laughed. "You strike a hard bargain. You know what, I think you're about to get stopped by a friend of mine."

Joci heard him muffle a phrase over the police radio, and she shrieked, "So not fair, Officer."

"Good. You can arrest me later."

A blush met her gaze when she looked in her rearview mirror. As predicted, red and blue lights flashed behind her. "You're an ass."

"One who doesn't lose," he said. "All right, I gotta run. Be nice to Ollie, now."

If she weren't so impressed with him, she would be furious at Quinn's antics. He didn't like to fail, and this was no exception.

Following the rules, Joci pulled over to the side of the road and rolled down her window. From her viewpoint, Officer Richards was trolling on his laptop. It took five minutes before he even set foot on pavement.

"Is there a problem, Officer?" she asked with enough sugar to make him diabetic.

Ollie popped his head into her window, invading whatever space she had left. "As it turns out, ma'am, you were speeding."

"I didn't realize. I'm sorry." She handed him her license and registration, though he didn't bother to look at them. "What can I do to make this right?"

A boyish grin covered the cop's handsome face. He checked his watch, then pointed to the street. "I'm supposed to say something super-inappropriate, but I think it would be better if Quinn said it instead of me."

Joci retrieved her documents and stuffed them in their place. "Have you stalled me long enough?"

Grabbing his radio from his chest, Ollie said, "Unit 2754, are you prepared for departure?"

They both waited with bated breath for the response. After a minute, Quinn's voice came across the line. "You can release the suspect, partner."

"Ten-four. Over and out" came Ollie's reply before he eyed Joci. "You're free to go, but I'm going to have to ask you to be generous with my buddy. He could use a bit of legal advice, and I hear you give the best."

Clicking the car into gear, Joci shot, "I'm going to ignore that insinuation, Officer." She smiled. "But I'll take it under advisement."

Ollie saluted, then waltzed back to his patrol car. Despite knowing the situation was a farce, Joci couldn't stop the nerves from bubbling inside. With ease, she slid onto the street and set off in the direction of Akebono. A fierce debate in court was nothing compared to the adrenaline that Quinn set off within her brain. It was addicting, almost as much as he was.

— — —

Cameron eyeballed the creamy slop on his tray. If the smell didn't curdle your appetite, the sight of the food would do the trick. He shoved the plastic away and leaned his elbows on the table. Thanks to his protective attorney, the majority of his time was spent in his cell. Chow times were a different story. Three times a day, he had the opportunity to stretch his legs, which resulted in fistfights nine out of ten times.

Today, his ribs yelled at him to quell his masculine urges, and for once he listened. He sat alone to avoid confrontation, but his solitude didn't last long. A group of inmates sat around the beige picnic table, not bothering to acknowledge his existence.

Ignoring them, Cameron surveyed the open area surrounded by guards. It was a large enough space, with vending machines on either end, not that he could afford the jacked-up prices. If he could, the mystery meat wouldn't be on his tray in the first place. At least a dozen tables were bolted to the cement floor, each with six inmates.

He lifted his eyes to the upper decks, which held more deputies and various prisoners as they watched the others below. Jail cells lined the catwalks, but all the doors were open this time of day. Out of all the jails he'd frequented, Iowa's wasn't too bad. It was clean, and the employees weren't complete assholes.

"What're you in for?" a gruff voice asked from beside him.

Returning his focus to the present, Cameron turned his head. "Nothing much. A bit of a misunderstanding." He nodded at the man covered in black tattoos. "What about you?"

"Burglary," he mumbled, then stuffed a potato chip into his mouth. "Who's your attorney?"

"Joci Dorous," he stated. Letting these men know he had more than one attorney would seal his indictment among the inmates. They were all innocent until proven guilty in a courtroom, but the inner walls of a jail were another situation.

"Nice." He whistled low and lifted his eyebrows. "She's mine too." He moved closer and offered a chip. "She's known for her success rate, you know?"

Cameron took the proffered chip hesitantly. "I've heard such a rumor."

"I'll tell you what"—he waved the bag—"never has one of my other attorneys flirted with me like Miss Joci."

Now engrossed in the subject, Cameron folded his arms. "Oh really?"

"Yep." The man crunched away, then wiped his mouth with the back of his hand. "She grabbed my leg one time she visited me."

Cameron held in a snort. "There. Feel special now?" he said, grabbing the man's knee.

The older inmate chuckled and tossed his trash to his buddy across the table. "No, I mean she wanted some of ol' Russell." He moved Cameron's hand up his thigh.

Uncomfortable with his placement, Cameron removed his hand. "I see. And when did she do this?"

The criminal scratched at his overgrown beard. "The day before my arraignment. Wanted me to sign some stupid paper."

A wicked grin crossed Cameron's face as Russell kept going. He was liking Joci even more thanks to the man's story.

"Well, I wouldn't sign it, so she came over and sat real close." The man demonstrated on his fellow inmate to his left. "And she talked real sweet to me. A bunch of legal mumbo jumbo, if you ask me, but when she started moving her hand up my leg, damn, I couldn't resist."

"And you signed the paper?" Cameron filled in, tapping his finger to his lips.

Russell nodded with enthusiasm. "You've seen her. She's a beauty. I signed the damn thing." He laughed. "My signature was a bit shaky, but it made her happy."

The inmate continued on with his gaudy story about the attorney, but Cameron stopped listening. It was clear that she liked to use ploys on her clients, but he'd never heard of that one before. Most women didn't want to come within spitting distance of inmates, but it seemed his lawyer was a new breed. One who got her way whenever possible.

"Shearer, your attorney's here," one of the deputies stated.

He nodded slowly, then stood. Patting his new friend on the back, Cameron asked, "Has she done that again?"

Russell unwrapped his candy bar. "Nope. Haven't seen her since." He took a bite and frowned. "Damn woman."

The look on his face must've tipped the other man off, because he added, "Oh don't worry, I'm sure she'll give you the proper treatment too. Her other clients in here have told similar stories."

Cameron rubbed his side and chuckled. "Let's hope so, because she's in for a surprise when she tries her subtle move on me."

The other man waved him off and returned to his sweet treat. If Joci was anything like the girl who used to scare the living shit out of him at Halloween, he could almost predict her ploy.

Glancing around the room, Cameron wondered how many other men Joci Dorous had tried her seduction on. If Russell was any indicator, it happened often when she couldn't get a man to do what she wanted. *Well, she's in for a real treat*, he thought as the guard buzzed him through the door.

— — —

"You're here at last," Joci greeted when her client strolled into the tiny room. She shuffled the files in front of her to steady her hands, eyes glancing up to the video camera recording, though not audibly. From her experience, there were few blind spots in the room, but she wasn't worried. Cameron wouldn't hurt her. She clicked her pen. *I think.*

The moment he entered, the room shrank another six feet. He wasn't too stocky, but his build was impressive nevertheless.

"Sorry, had to finish lunch." He plunked into the plastic chair. "It was a surprise today. A disgusting, yellow surprise." Cameron's brown eyes met hers. "Ever tried the food here?"

Joci rolled her shoulders back. "Can't say that I have."

"Little Miss Goody-Two-shoes, huh?" he prodded, spreading his legs out beneath the table.

Moving her feet out of his way, she scrunched her nose. "Not always, but more than you." She wasn't fond of the way he was eyeing her. It was as if he knew something but wanted to keep her in suspense.

"How'd you like my letters?" Cameron asked, bobbing

his head to his file. "I get bored in here. Hope you liked the drawings."

Clearing her throat, Joci skirted that specific subject. His artwork, while impressive, wasn't appropriate in any sense. "You should probably stop sending doodles of guns and marijuana plants. It doesn't help your case," she warned.

Cameron kept his gaze locked with hers. "I never said they were my guns and weed."

She forced a smile to her face. "I already warned you once, Mr. Shearer. It's no skin off my back if your cell abruptly gains one more resident."

Rubbing his thumbs together, he leaned forward. "What brings you here today, Ms. Dorous?" He glanced to the empty seat. "And without the redheaded wonder."

"You're awful chipper for a man charged with homicide," she shot back. He was still the mouthy ass she remembered.

"You bring out the best in me, what can I say?"

Flipping open the file, she pulled out a plea. With precision, she placed the paper and a pen in front of him. "You need to sign this. An arraignment hearing is a formality. One you don't need to deal with."

He ran a hand over his face. "That's what your dumber half said about the bond hearing. I found it quite interesting."

"You're baiting me," she called him out.

Leaning forward until he was inches from her face, he smiled. "Is it working?"

Determined to not give in, she pressed past his game. "You need to sign this written arraignment," Joci said for the second time. She watched her client trace his finger around the pen. Somehow, he managed to maintain eye contact and annoy the hell out of her with his act. He was a cocky dude, and he hadn't changed in that respect.

"Hmm, tempting, but no," he shot back with a tilt of his head. "I like the red, by the way. It really makes your eyes take on a dreamy look."

Taking a calming breath, Joci studied him. He bore new scrapes and bruises, but damn if they didn't make him look like a stud. She chided herself for her apparent attraction. He was a cutie at nine years old, but now, hell, even a nun would give him a second glance.

"You wouldn't have to leave your cozy cell. Larry says you like it there." Her eyes drifted over the jumpsuit stained with blood.

"Nope." He sat back and rolled the pen to her. "But thanks for the option."

Unnerved by his complacent attitude, she grabbed his wrist. The moment she made contact, she regretted it. His skin sent a warm shock through her hand. *This is why you poke a finger at the guys instead of grasping them.* "What the hell is wrong with you?" she seethed. "You're facing murder charges, Cameron. Murder. You know, like go away for life charges, and you're sitting here like it doesn't matter."

His eyes dipped to her hand. "It doesn't matter. If I'm meant to get out of here, I will." His lips spread in a smile. "I do like this, though. You touching me." He met her gaze. "I could get used to it."

Joci withdrew her hand and glared at him. "I don't get you." She shook her head in frustration. "The psychologist's report came back," she advised.

"Ooh, goody. Am I crazy?" he asked.

She flipped through her folder until she reached the filing. "No. You're sane." She met his eyes. "Somehow."

"I find your lack of faith disturbing," he quoted, folding his arms over his chest.

Joci's eyes latched on to that chest. She shouldn't be curious about the tattoos that lay beneath the horrid shade of green, but she was. He'd more than filled out since their childhood sleepovers. "Star Wars jokes, huh? Well, I didn't think you were mental, but now I do."

Cameron chuckled, the low sound charismatic. "Aw, come on. I'm just bored, and you offer a perfect distraction. A pretty one too."

Amused, she sat back in her chair, disregarding his case for the present. "Is that what you want? A distraction from this hellhole?"

He lifted his eyebrows. "Something like that."

Sensing a tremor of hesitation, Joci decided to push him off-kilter. Normally, she would flirt with the client, maybe graze her hand over theirs, making sure the line wasn't crossed. But she and Cameron had a history, even if he didn't know it yet. When they were younger, she used to play dirty tricks on him, but nothing as forward as what her mind conjured up. She moved her seat around the circular table until she was right next to him. His breathing increased at her brazen move.

"What're you doing?" he asked, his eyes wary.

"Giving you what you want," she said with a sultry tone. Joci almost smiled at the expression that crossed his face.

It was a mixture of excitement and worry. She would've laughed out loud if he jumped up and ran. It was like the reaction she got in Ohio, except they were playing hide-and-seek and she decided a hairy monster mask was a good addition to their late-night game. Her maneuvers here were entirely different, but touching him felt more right than wrong.

Her hand ducked beneath the table and rested comfortably on his upper thigh. The hard muscles beneath told her he was a frequent flyer at a gym. "Is this the distraction you want, Cameron?"

He cleared his throat and attempted to move in the other direction. "Umm."

Not giving up, Joci trailed her hand farther to his inner thigh. "How about now?" She could see the beads of sweat form on his forehead at her act. Thus far, her signature move was working, albeit much more forward than her usual form of convincing a client. She didn't know what possessed her to straddle the line of ethics, but her fingers had a mind of their own now. She couldn't stop if she wanted. Pressing her luck, Joci moved farther in. Never had she resorted to this proximity; the guys usually bailed at her initial brush of her hand.

At last, Cameron reacted, but not in the way she predicted. His large hand captured hers, and she froze when he guided it farther up his leg. He leaned his head close to hers, and the sultry words washed over her as if he'd rehearsed them. "Darling, if you want to screw me, just say so. I'm more than willing to rattle your brains loose."

Joci tried to wrench her wrist free, but he wouldn't budge. Meeting his eyes, she saw they weren't filled with hostility or maliciousness. The brown depths swam in humor laced with a tinge of lust. He didn't cave to her. This was the first and sole time an inmate didn't let her get her way. "You knew," she spat.

He cocked his left eyebrow. "Knew what? Knew you were trying to play on my loneliness? Knew that your reputation precedes you when it comes to this sexy move on your clients?" He paused, then added, "Knew you would enjoy touching me as much as I do?" His bruised lip cracked in a smile. "Yeah, Joce, I knew." She struggled for release, but he wouldn't budge. "Try it again, Ms. Dorous, and I'll do more than let you trace my thigh." He dropped his hold on her as he finished.

Staggering back, Joci stood up and glared at him. "You're a sick bastard."

Cameron leaned forward and smirked. "And you secretly love it. So, are the pot or the kettle in this scenario? I prefer the pot, obviously."

Joci huffed in exasperation. It seemed her latest and greatest asshole of a client could read her intentions better than the majority. Gathering her items, she tossed him a maleficent glower. He offered a dazzling smile in response.

She tore the door open and glanced over her shoulder.

Cameron waved his fingers at her in a cute way. His words stilled her swift exit. "Oh, and next time, try not to be predictable. You always had a tell when we were kids. You rub your lips together. It's adorable."

Her mouth dropped open at his revelation. "You asshole, you knew who I was this whole time?"

He chuckled. "Not the whole time." He pointed to her glasses. "When you took those off, I recognized you, but wasn't sure if you knew me or not."

Joci plopped back on the chair. "How could I not? You were always a troublemaker. It shouldn't surprise me that you drifted a little far out of the lines."

"Kind of like you with your little act." His eyes, a mixture of concern and wonder, pinned her to the chair. "From what I hear, you do it pretty often. I never expected you to flaunt your body like that."

Immediately ashamed for her lack of control, she cleared her throat. "I don't do"—she motioned her hand between them—"that with my clients. I don't know what possessed me."

"So I'm extra special?" He leaned forward, fingers grazing the tops of her hands.

Feeling her cheeks burn, she eyed the camera. "Something like that." He had an eerie ability to enrage her so much that she didn't want him to stop, but then he'd do something sweet and make her forget why she was mad at him. It happened all the time back in the day. She wasn't sure why it was a shock that he still did.

"Well, I guess we can discuss the reasoning behind your sexy dance later," he teased. "Maybe next time, lose articles of clothing."

"It wasn't a dance, and that would've been a striptease. I don't do whatever that was with my clients."

He shrugged. "Whatever you say, counselor."

They sat studying each other for a good thirty seconds before Joci looked away. Maintaining eye contact made her remember the juvenile attraction she once felt for him. Those sensations needed to disappear if she expected to stay on the right side of the table.

"Did you have a nice Thanksgiving? They served turkey here, but it wasn't very good. Reminded me of when my aunt tried to cook us pot roast. Remember that?"

She smiled. "Yeah, it was pretty bad." Despite wanting to remain professional, she couldn't help but recall the time Cameron's aunt attempted to make them dinner. If she passed it off as beef jerky, it would've worked. From that day on, most of the dinners at his aunt's house were Chinese delivery or pizza.

Checking her watch, she gathered her folders. "I need to get going, but I'll come visit again, okay?"

"No worries. I'm not going anywhere."

"Smartass." She paused at the door and cast one last look to the man who was definitely no longer the freckled boy. As she clopped down the hallway, Joci couldn't get a grip on him. He wasn't like every other criminal. He was her first crush. *First kiss too. And I reacted to his touch.* She bit her lip. *Bad, very bad, Joci.* Crossing the boundary with a client, even if he was a long-lost friend, was territory that could result in a disbarment. Somehow, her body craved the dirty activity Cameron incited. She saw it on his face and felt it in his grip. He didn't see her as a freckle-faced kid anymore and it scared the hell out of her. Once upon a time, they made a pact, but he'd probably forgotten all about it after all the years. Now she understood why bringing along another person would be safer when it came to jail visits. She didn't trust herself alone with a man who sent her body into a tizzy.

— — —

Cameron sat in the room for a moment, digesting what had transpired a moment ago. He liked her. She was gutsy and not afraid to put him in his place. She was the best version of the girl who broke her leg when they went sledding together. It was his idea, and not the greatest as it turned out.

Pushing off the table, he stood and walked to the door. Since his booking, the guards were becoming accustomed to him little by little. They didn't cuff him anymore when he moved between the rooms of the jail. For that, he was thankful. The rigid shackles seemed like a bit much.

Knocking on the door, he smiled when it opened right away. "I'll see myself back to my bed," he advised, not caring to hear the response.

At a leisurely pace, Cameron sauntered down the hallway. He spotted a fellow inmate mopping the floor but kept his gaze set to up ahead. It was a slow day for the facility, not that he minded. The constant comings and goings annoyed him more than amused him.

When he reached his cell, all thoughts of Joci flew out the window. "What're you doing here?" he asked, curious at the invasion.

Russell patted the cot. "I've come to deliver a message."

Aw, shit. He'd been waiting for such a delivery, but hoped he was flying under the radar. From the grim expression on the other man's face, his luck had run out. "Well, go for it, then."

"J.J. knows where you are," Russell regurgitated. "And if you don't continue to keep your mouth shut, he'll come for you."

"I always did love a good riddle," Cameron replied. "Anything else, old chum?"

Russell nodded quickly and stood. "Yep. Sorry, buddy. You seem nice, but the money is good."

Before Cameron could react, the wider inmate plunged his beefy fist into his stomach. Doubling over at the pain, he failed to see the next swing. This one struck his jaw. It wasn't until Russell punched his kidney that Cameron fell to the floor.

"There's more where that came from if you don't go away for murder," Russell finished.

Shaking his head against the pain, Cameron didn't dare watch the inmate leave. The man's friendliness made sense since he probably got paid a decent penny for his recent act. No doubt, the brute could deliver on his promise.

Cameron edged up to the cot and lay flat on his back. Calling for a medic wouldn't do any good. Not when more bruises would accompany the ones forming at present. He was on his own yet again. Joci's face swam in front of his blurred vision. Wincing, he reran the events from earlier. A crooked smile played his battered face. Thinking of Joci was the best medicine he could ask for.

Adjusting his body with care, Cameron let out a frazzled grunt as he punched the pillow to make it more comfortable. If all he had was her face, scrunched up in exasperation, running in his mind, it would work wonders on his soul. The injuries wouldn't heal on her smile alone, but a hope that somewhere inside her tough outer shell, she cared about him, even if just a small amount, made him relax. Why else would she allow him to keep an intimate distance earlier? She could've escaped his grip with ease. He'd barely held her hand in place. They were friends so long ago, but he didn't see her as a kid anymore. That happened when she not so subtly groped him. Smirking, he was surprised how much he enjoyed seeing her frazzled. The soft gasp that'd slipped through her lips earlier wouldn't easily be forgotten. He could go for a multitude more of those.

He tucked his hands behind his head. She'd wanted to be there with him. Some part of her desired to feel his touch. It wasn't a miracle, but it was close enough for Cameron. She was the type who would be easy to talk to once they both opened up. He could handle exposure if she was the recipient. They'd shared a kinship in grade school, but the stakes were much higher these days.

Sighing, he closed his eyes and imagined a life where he could be fortunate enough to have a woman like Joci. Not just as a booty call or one-night stand, but as the person he woke up beside each morning.

CHAPTER FIVE

Pressing the gas pedal, Joci couldn't escape Polk County Jail fast enough. Small snowflakes dotted her windshield, but she didn't see them. All she saw was Cameron. Turning onto the side road, she turned up the radio. She didn't want to think about the client who pushed any button she exposed.

A new tune from Maroon 5 filled the speakers, and she focused on the lyrics instead of the last hour. After singing the chorus, Joci found her mind wandering back to the jail. She should've known better than to trust him, but it was her one shot. She made a note to go back and see him again to discuss the time he'd been out of her life. She was curious as to how he'd gotten involved with drugs—not that his parents were the best role models.

She checked the time and was shocked to see her appointment with Cameron had taken longer than expected. She was set to meet with Adrian in about five minutes. Picking up speed, she grumbled under her breath when a semi pulled out in front of her. The road to the jail was littered with industrial businesses and junkyards. Chugging along with glee was never possible, no matter the day.

Adrian's distinct ringtone met her ears. Making a mental note to change it to a different Justin Timberlake song, Joci answered. "Hey, I'm running late, if you couldn't tell. I'll be there in ten minutes."

"No worries. I ordered a drink, so if I'm soused before you get here, it's your fault." He was smiling, she was sure.

"Oh please. You hold your liquor better than anyone I know."

"Yeah, not sure if that's supposed to be a compliment or not, but I'll take it."

Joci veered onto the interstate and checked her speed. She'd already been pulled over once today. The second time wouldn't be by the rookie. "Okay, see you in a few."

"All right, drive safe," he signed off.

When a ding from the phone met her ears, she grabbed it and noticed a new message from Quinn. Her face broke out in a smile when he sent a photo of his handcuffs with the caption *Later, babe. You owe me.*

Shaking her head, she bit her bottom lip. Of course she'd lost the race to Quinn. He made it up to her by promising to never use police resources against her again. "Yeah, because I believe that," she mumbled.

The Des Moines skyline met her view and she switched lanes. The quick lunch at Akebono was anything but quick. She was certain they would've stayed until close if Quinn hadn't been called away and she didn't have appearances at the jail to make. It was easy to talk to him. He was the best person in her life, and spending time with him was as simple as breathing.

Still, she didn't have the ability to maintain the level of relationship he wanted. Quinn kept his motives to himself most the time, but every now and then he would sneak them into conversation. Today was no different.

"He wants more than just random hookups," she said aloud, as if testing the words on her lips. She shuddered at the thought. All she wanted was a friend with benefits, and Quinn had plenty of benefits to choose from. He knew the request was too much, but she couldn't blame him for trying.

She hadn't reacted. In fact, she'd disregarded the words in their entirety and steered the conversation to a case. It worked, but she knew the subject was far from dead in Quinn's eyes. "One of these days, I need to cut him loose," she told herself. If Quinn wanted a boyfriend and girlfriend relationship, she wasn't the right woman for the job. She'd said as much earlier at lunch, but he ignored her. *He still thinks he can change my mind.*

Her exit loomed ahead, and a small part of her wanted to keep going and take the ramp to her apartment instead. It wouldn't help in the long run. Adrian lived in one of the firm's posh apartments rent free. It was close enough to jog to her place, and an ideal location downtown. Ironic that they'd lived so close to each other before meeting yet never crossed paths. It came as no shock that his father, Brett, never rented the place out while she and Adrian were married. It became the 'cool off' apartment, as Adrian liked to call it. He used to frequent it after heated fights where he walked away the loser.

Second Avenue bustled with life as the sun crept closer to the horizon. She managed to avoid incoming traffic and whiz by the Events Center. A stiff drink was the best diversion she could ask for. Between Cameron's flirtation and Quinn's badgering, Joci needed something strong to muddle her thoughts. She recalled whom she was meeting and groaned. Adrian wouldn't help much, but free drinks would.

The painted brick of the bar beckoned to any who approached, so she pulled into an open parking place. Thus far, the streets were full of people sneaking out of the office before closing time. This was the ideal time for bars in the downtown area, and one she knew well.

Yanking on the brass door handle, Joci stepped into the dim expanse. A Celtic rock band echoed over the speakers as she pinpointed Adrian's position. He was in his favorite spot; the dark corner booth may as well be reserved for him alone. Walking in his direction, she couldn't count how many times they had frequented the pub after work and sat in those exact seats.

"Looks like the jail decided to let you out," he teased when she arrived at the booth.

Shedding her coat, Joci slid into the seat across from him. "Well, it was touch and go there for a while. Larry thought the inmates could use some entertainment. It was down to me and a newbie attorney from the King firm. I won."

Adrian handed her a tumbler of scotch. "Damn, I owe Larry now."

Joci rolled her sleeves to her elbows and picked up the glass. "Cheers to that, then."

He took a sip of his drink. "Did Shearer give you hell?"

Sloshing the scotch over the cubes of ice, she thought over her time at the jail. If she gave Adrian a play-by-play, he would be furious and no doubt ask for her to withdraw. It was endearing in an odd sort of way, his protectiveness of her.

"Nothing more than usual," she settled on.

The vein in Adrian's forehead relaxed at her response. "Good. He's a pill if you ask me." He drained his glass and lifted his fingers to the bartender. "If we weren't getting a nice paycheck from this, I don't think I ever would've taken his case."

The bartender was swift on the draw and delivered two fresh drinks in record time. Joci watched the thirtysomething man return behind the counter. Adrian had handled his case about seven years ago, and now his booze was on the owner for life. Joci took another sip and studied the man across from her. Any other lawyer may have abused the ever-flowing drinks, but Adrian was different. Sure, he frequented the establishment time and again, but he tipped the owner more than the cost of any beverage he ordered. It was one of the quirks she admired about him. Despite coming from money, he wasn't quick to mishandle it. *Unless it's to gamble.*

"He's something all right," she put in, switching to the new scotch.

Adrian leaned over the table. "Okay, so in all honesty, I don't want to talk about work."

Joci smirked when he pulled his pinstriped purple tie loose from around his neck. That act alone made him look more down-to-earth. "Fine, what *do* you want to discuss?"

He let out a slow breath. "Us."

"That's pretty obvious," she teased. "You mentioned it earlier."

Adrian pushed his right hand through his bright hair. "Oh, yeah." His eyebrow twitched and he batted at it. He was nervous. It was cute too. This wasn't normal for the high-rolling attorney. He maintained control almost as much as she did.

Deciding to let him drive this train wreck, Joci sat back and nursed the scotch in her hands. Watching Adrian fumble for words was almost as attractive as when he spoke with eloquence. He threw back the second glass and drummed his fingers on the wooden table. She had to fight the smirk wanting to break over her face.

In the office, he was a beast. *And the bedroom.* But when it was the two of them, they either spoke about work or, well, you know. His discomfort was liberating. Adrian Petosa, speechless. It was a miracle above all else.

A waiter brought a plate of cheesy nachos to their table. Both stared at the mouthwatering concoction topped with jalapeños. Her phone rang from within her purse, but she disregarded it. She was much more absorbed in this face-off. Plus, it was probably Quinn, and she should focus on one man at a time.

"Do you know how bad I want to kiss you?" His quiet query surprised her.

She shook her head, not daring to speak. This was his time to grovel. He had lots of compliments to shower on her to even begin to dent his transgressions.

His blue eyes pierced her. "Because I do." He scratched his forearm. "And not just since we've had this case together."

Intrigued, Joci took a bigger sip to calm her nerves.

"You may think I forgot about you, but I never did. I saw when you walked by my office, looking like a dream come true." He glanced at his hands and grinned. "You did it on purpose, didn't you?"

Joci lifted her gaze to him. That knowing expression covered his face. "It may have happened a time or two."

She couldn't deny her actions. Some sliver of her wanted to show off to Adrian. Since their split, she'd lost weight and worked out until all of her clothes were a size eight. Coming from size fourteen, it was quite a bit of a change for the woman teetering over six feet.

Adrian's hand shook as he lifted the tumbler to his lips. "And each instance made my heart break all over again."

Downing her drink, she nodded once. "Good. It was supposed to." She tucked her hair behind her ears. "You can't expect me to roll over and act like nothing happened, Adrian."

In one quick movement, he was beside her. "I don't." He inched closer on the bench. "I'll be sorry about what I did until the day I die. You never deserved my selfishness."

Swallowing hard, Joci attempted to stabilize her breathing. With him so near, every inch of her body willed her to collide with him. She craved more than a sideways glance of lust when she strutted by his office. Each fiber of her being desired to feel him again, if only once more.

"Joci, I'm sorry." His eyes dipped to her lips, then returned to her eyes. "I know you may not care, but I've done a lot of work on myself over the last two years. I've been to therapy and stopped my more rakish ventures."

She wasn't sure if he was serious about the gambling bit, but she wouldn't doubt him. He'd been an avid lottery player, among other activities, when they met. The pull of money and chance was common among lawyers, but Adrian had it the worst. If he was truthful in his statement, she had to commend him. It wasn't easy to let go of your addictions.

"Okay," she replied at last. If she offered more, she was afraid her mind would shut off and her body would act on its own. It was already too close to a hostile takeover for her to handle.

Adrian brought his hand up to her hair but stopped short of touching her. "Let me try, Joci." His palm cupped her cheek. "Please. I won't let you down."

Staring into blue depths, Joci was certain she would drown in the adoration and longing there. Not four hours ago, she'd been sitting similarly to this with Quinn. It was wrong on more levels than she cared to admit, yet felt right too. Adrian was the guy you married. Quinn was the one you fucked to forget all others. The problem was she *had* married Adrian and it ended in disaster.

Placing the scotch on the table, she took a deep breath. "I can't yet, Adrian. You might be ready for a relationship, but I'm not. If you said you wanted to hang out, which could lead to some Netflix and chilling, then I'd be all for it."

Joci's lips were covered by Adrian's. It wasn't a long kiss, since the bartender interrupted them within seconds.

"What about now?"

"You're a dick," she breathed, though didn't reject the kiss. It still sizzled on her lips despite her words.

"Hey, guys, I didn't know you were back together. That's great!"

Adrian groaned and pulled away. "Thanks for the cock block, man."

Giggling at the embarrassed face of the man in front of them, Joci replaced Adrian's lips with her scotch. The slow burn eased her mind and she sent a silent thanks for the interruption. She wasn't sure if she was ready to divulge in the ecstasy of her ex. For now, she would sit back and watch the two men while the ice melted in her cup.

CHAPTER SIX

Eyeing the suit and tie steamed to perfection, Cameron felt out of place. The outfit provided by his lawyers cost more than a year's worth of rent. He rubbed his wrists when the jailer removed the handcuffs, glancing at his surroundings. The staging room was where inmates could change into more court-appropriate clothes if they were blessed enough to have someone to provide them.

Now as he stared at the pretty redhead from his attorney's firm, Cameron wondered if that hair color was part of the job description.

"I'm Rayna Alley," she started with a dazzling smile. "The one who's been intercepting the million visit requests from you." She offered him a pointed glance. "I believe these should fit." She held up the hanger. "Adrian and Joci want you to look sharp."

Cameron hid the smile his lips wanted to grace her with. He didn't feel bad in the least for all the phone calls he asked the jailers to make on his behalf to his lawyer.

He was bored, and bugging Joci was better than staring at blank walls. They used to play phone tag all the time as kids. *Apparently she doesn't like that game anymore.*

"Here, try these," demanded the woman who could pass as a beauty queen.

He took the outstretched hangers. This was a new experience for him. In Ohio, his public defenders didn't give a shit if he smelled, much less what he wore. He'd never been to court without the jumpsuit attire. "Thanks. I think."

Rayna nodded, her bangs sweeping into her gray eyes. "I'll let you change. They'll be in once you're done." She all but ran out of the room filled with convicts, leaving him alone with his worries.

"Don't look now, boys," he heckled, undressing. The soft fabric was a welcome relief as he buttoned the white dress shirt. He'd been graced with a ten-minute shower that morning. Even though the water was freezing, he relished the cleansing.

Glancing to the mirror that was no doubt a two-way, he frowned at the fresh cut marks on his bottom lip. Yet another gift from the person responsible for his arrest. All his years on and off the streets didn't give him the treatment bestowed upon him in the Iowa jail. It was his own fault for not being careful. He'd overturned one too many rocks, and the Mikkelsens wanted it stopped.

"Well thank God, you look like a human instead of a washed-up drummer," a sultry voice commented.

Joci's reflection came into view as he flipped the tie

around his neck. She fit the typical lawyer part today in a gray skirt suit. The black camisole beneath the pleated suit jacket accentuated her bosom. Fashionable high heels graced her feet, and their black hue matched to perfection. He found himself wondering if she dressed herself or if someone else organized her closet.

"Glad I could resurrect for you," he replied, attempting to fasten the silk tie around his neck. No matter how he tried, the blue noose failed to obey.

"Here, let me," Joci offered, approaching.

Reluctantly, he spun around. Her berry perfume attacked his senses. The scent wasn't overwhelming, but it made him crave fresh raspberries. "Who taught you?" he asked as she straightened the knot.

Her eyeliner held a bold shade of blue today, but the gorgeous hazel orbs were focused on perfecting his outfit instead of on him. The desire to force her to look at him absorbed his thoughts.

"My dad. When I was ten, he told me that if I was going to play with the big dogs in business, I better learn how to do everything they can do." She slid the tie to the right. "Only better."

Cameron liked that story, but he liked her hands on him more. It was oddly comforting to be eye-to-eye with a woman for a change. He wasn't used to it, but could be if she was the one beside him. "I take it when you moved to Iowa, you didn't bathe in rubies like your partner."

Joci met his gaze. "Hardly. You knew my parents." She took a step back and studied him, adjusting his coat before nodding her approval. "I worked my way through college and law school. Everything I have, I earned."

"I admire that," he complimented, shuffling to the door.

"Hold it. What the hell is going on with your hair?" She stalked over to him and ran her fingers through his unruly waves. That act alone was the gentlest caress he could wish for.

"It gets crazy when I don't have my special conditioner," he joked, shooting his hand to the mass. It collided with hers and he hid a smile at the softness of her skin. It felt like satin to his coarse fingertips. Instantly, he wondered if the rest of her body would feel the same under his touch.

Joci withdrew her hands and huffed. "I suppose we'll get you a haircut too. Can't have a shaggy head for trial." She eyed her dainty wristwatch. "It's time. Let's go hurry up and wait, shall we?"

"What?" he questioned, closely following her, but his question fell on deaf ears as they entered the condensed version of a courtroom.

He would've been lost in the crowd of inmates and police officers if Joci didn't grip his hand. The silver ring on her middle finger dug into his flesh, but he didn't complain as they reached Adrian.

"We're here. How far did he get?" she questioned, nodding to the judge. The old man was speaking but incomprehensible. Cameron chuckled.

"He's to the M's," Adrian informed them, reviewing his client. "Much better, but I think green would look better on him."

Joci scrutinized Cameron, then agreed. "Yeah, you're right. I'll send Rayna out later."

From his spot beside them, Cameron watched silently as the two fluidly conversed. They didn't allow a millisecond of dead air, which told him that they had some form of history.

"Cameron, when the judge addresses you, be sure to answer clearly and use 'Your Honor' like a badge," Adrian instructed. "O'Dell is a stickler for that shit. He's one of the old-school judges."

"How can I understand him when he has marbles in his mouth?" Cameron jabbed.

"Yeah, and maybe no snarky comments," Joci warned. "He's not a fan."

Accepting their advice, he observed Joci scan the room. Her eyes locked on a tall police officer in the closest corner of the room.

"I'll be right back," she assured them, weaving through the horde before either man could answer.

Boredom ensued when Cameron listened to the drone of the court hearings. It would've made the worst reality show. Sneaking a glance at Adrian's phone screen, he noticed the man was texting furiously. Despite a glare from the lights overhead, he managed to decipher the words 'Mike' and 'Rose.' He frowned at the similarities between those names and the code names the Del Rossi used in correspondence among the mob.

Surely he was mistaken. His lawyer couldn't be involved with the Mikkelsens.

"Do you mind?" his lawyer asked, moving the phone out of view.

"Sorry, just haven't had my phone in weeks. My fingers are itching for a fix. It's worse than drugs."

Adrian rolled his eyes at the obvious sarcasm, then glanced toward his coworker when she reached the man who could've passed as a body builder. Chuckling, Cameron recognized the officer as the one who arrested him. "She sure knows how to pick them," he said, nodding to Joci. She directed a brilliant smile toward the man, who was equally enraptured by her. Their closeness unnerved him, but not as much as it seemed to bother his male attorney.

Adrian straightened his tie. "They're not together."

Swinging his gaze back to the slender attorney, Cameron clucked his tongue. "You sure about that, compadre? They look pretty cozy."

Scowling over at him, Adrian snapped, "You don't know Joci, so shut it." He buttoned his suit jacket. "She's experimenting with a few things. It'll flush out of her system."

Confused at the apparent triangle, Cameron probed, "Then you guys are together, but on a break?"

Adrian positioned himself directly in front of Cameron. "Joci and I have history. That tool is a bandage. One she'll outgrow."

Taking it as the best he would get from that half of the duo, Cameron laced his fingers together. "Whatever you say, boss man."

His attorney cast him a frown but quickly recovered

when his female counterpart reappeared. "What is Quinn here for?"

Joci pulled her ponytail tighter, while Cameron wanted to obliterate the hair tie that held it in place. She hadn't worn it down yet, much to his dismay. "Preliminary hearings. He has a few this morning," she said with a cavalier smirk.

It was astonishing to Cameron, the amount of tension between his legal team. The redhead had only told him part of the truth. If a woman like Joci didn't reciprocate those vibes in full, she had a solid reason. Curiosity filled him, but he didn't have a chance to work it out before his name was called.

Adrian and Joci ushered him to the shabby defense table. He snuck a glance to the balding county attorney, who was sweating through his brown suit. The woman beside him was pretty, but not enough for him to drool over. He preferred legs over bust any day.

The elderly judge peered down at Cameron through his tiny glasses, then began to read aloud the trial information and minutes of testimony. In reality, Cameron couldn't decipher but twenty words the entire time. If Joci hadn't sent him the document ahead of time, he would swear the man was speaking Klingon.

After what felt like an hour, the judge looked up. Cameron shifted his eyes to his defense counsel, then remembered his role in the day's events. "Not guilty, Your Honor," he stated confidently.

The jailhouse courtroom exploded into chaotic shouts from the inmates awaiting their own hearings. All at once, the goons who had battered him at the jail appeared from the crowd and lunged for him. No one stood in their way as the group of five men threw punches and kicks after dragging him to the ground. He aggressively fought back, but the odds weren't in his favor. It seemed his mob enemy shelled out more money to make him understand the severity of sticking his nose in Mikkelsen business.

Sirens blasted and red lights flashed through the bodies hovering over him. Guards blew whistles loudly enough to bust eardrums, but that didn't stop the entourage from jabbing his ribs until he couldn't breathe.

The attack went on forever in his mind, but by the time the jailers yanked the men from his bloody body, not two minutes had passed. Fellow inmates continued to holler for more, clanging their chained wrists together.

"Everybody facedown!" the judge screamed, slamming his gavel.

Two guards helped Cameron up, his legs shaky. Joci's face swam into his plane of vision, her expression outraged. Adrian stood close beside, a protective arm around her.

The entire courtroom buzzed with fury. This was a new scenario, if Cameron read it right. His attempt to smile at the buffoons who'd jumped him as they lay beneath ten deputies only reopened his busted lip.

"Your Honor, my client has been continuously attacked in this facility." Joci stomped toward the bench. "Petosa Law will post his bond so he can be removed to our firm's secure care with an ankle monitor and house arrest pending trial." Her demand silenced the room, and all eyes were glued to her form.

The judge scowled down his nose at her, then curtly nodded. "Ms. Dorous, I'm going to grant your request on the contingency that Mr. Shearer attend appropriate treatment with a licensed psychologist. Once this situation is sorted out here, a hearing will determine if that placement is in the public's best interest." He pointed to the bailiff. "Now get him out of here before another riot starts."

Cameron stood in awe. No one ever stuck up for him like that. Blinking furiously, he held in the urge to tackle Joci with a bear hug. And he never hugged unless forced. *What the hell is wrong with me?* Blood dripped off his eyebrow and onto his cheek. The pain disintegrated when his focus was on her.

The subject of his thoughts thanked the judge, then stepped over to him. "You ready?"

He gulped, tasting the metallic tang of blood. "Um, yeah."

"Good," she stated, hustling by him. "Our first stop is the hospital."

Cameron couldn't stop staring at the sassy way she sashayed from the room. Every male eye was fixed on her, but he was the only soul to follow her out of the courtroom. Even his other attorney stood dumbfounded at her reaction to the attack. It became obvious that she was not only putting herself on the line, but her firm as well. Yeah, he was growing rather fond of his attorney.

— — —

"Joci, are you on meth? The guy is a lunatic murderer!" Adrian reprimanded on the ride in the elevator. He hadn't spoken two words since her display at the jail, but now he was ripping into her like she was a present on Christmas morning.

"The doctor said he's not crazy." She figured now was as good a time as any to include "Plus, when I lived in Ohio, he was your typical neighborhood kid. He's innocent," she argued.

"Should I be worried about you bending the rules because you played tic-tac-toe with him when you were children?" He let out a disgruntled huff.

"You're being ridiculous. He's not guilty. I can feel it."

"You think all the clients are innocent." Adrian loosened his tie as they neared the building's top floor.

"No, I'm quite observant when I catch someone in the act," she poked, then stepped off the elevator. Joci immediately regretted her words. Every relationship had ebbs and flows, but all theirs did was pivot since they started being on speaking terms again.

Adrian was hot on her heels, not ready to let her get away with that. "How am I supposed to get through to you when you keep pushing me away?"

Stopping short of the state-of-the-art apartment for the firm's wealthy yet abominable clients, she turned to face him. "I'm sorry. It's a coping mechanism for me. This is how I've gotten through the parade of girls that's gone through your revolving office door."

He opened his mouth but Joci beat him to it. "I haven't had

an actual relationship since us, for obvious reasons. I don't plan to change it anytime soon either." She glanced to the door, the person inside pulling her to it. "You moved on more times than I care to count. Stop acting like I'm yours or we'll never function outside of this case."

She swiped her key card and the handle flashed green, so she pushed through. A cinnamon smell greeted her, instantly calming her. Adrian sailed past her, but Joci stood in the entryway as she took in the splendor.

Never had one of her clients inhabited the million-dollar glorified jail cell. Hers usually didn't come along with money to spare. Adrian, on the other hand, was accustomed to the place. With two thousand square feet, the apartment was anything but shabby. An interior designer had flown in from New York City to create the masterpiece. It was fit for kings and, often enough, the firm's clients resembled members of a monarchy.

Gray marble lined the floors while a mural of the Paris skyline welcomed new visitors to the penthouse. Never in her lifetime could she afford a fraction of the lavish pad, but she did enjoy the amenities.

Closing the door behind her, Joci delicately traced the antique justice scale that sat on the entry table. Every inch of the top floor was decorated in memorable fashion. No penny was spared for their clients with unending pockets. The space even included bulletproof windows for those clients who preferred extreme protection.

Male voices carried, and she made out Adrian's as well as who she assumed was a member of the sheriff's department.

The armored county van had transported Cameron here following his short stint at the hospital.

Reaching the living room where Cameron sat on the red sofa, his leg propped against the glass coffee table, Joci smiled slightly. Her client looked horrid despite the hospital's attempts to patch him up. The stitches stood out, but not as much as the dried blood and dark bruises.

"If you so much as sneeze outside the front door, the county sheriff will be up your ass," the middle-aged deputy warned, clicking the anklet in place.

Cameron eyed the flashing monitor. "I think you'd like that a bit too much," he harassed with a goading grin.

The deputy stood to his full height, then grunted to her. "Just because O'Dell likes you guys doesn't mean we do."

Joci settled her purple Prada purse on the wet bar. "Duly noted," she answered, not giving him the satisfaction of meeting his gaze.

The man blazed from the apartment, slamming the door. Awkward silence filled the area as Joci reviewed the fully stocked bar with a keycode panel. Punching in the five-digit password, she plucked out an aged scotch and poured a shot. Adrian's eyes bored into her back, but she refused to turn around.

"All right, Shearer, you just won the lottery today," Adrian announced. "If you screw this up, neither of us will come to your rescue. Understand?"

Swallowing the single malt, Joci watched the exchange in the mirror above the sink. Adrian was uptight. Most likely because of her bold move at court that morning. It was in his nature to be the savior, not her. *Times have changed, indeed.*

"Okay, I get it. Calm the hell down," Cameron growled, sprawling on the couch.

She hid her smile behind the glass when Adrian looked her way.

"I need some air," Adrian muttered, moving to the exit.

Swiveling in her spot, she extended an olive branch. "I'll meet you for lunch." She connected with his blue eyes, and his quick nod appeased her before he stormed out.

The room echoed his departure as she poured another drink.

"Why did you do it?" Cameron's quiet question enveloped her like a fog.

Throwing back the shot, she met his gaze. The liquefied pool of chocolate in his eyes drew her to take the seat beside him. "You're my client. I'd rather not have you six feet under."

"And?" he led.

Joci pushed up her glasses. "And you're my first murder trial where I've been lead attorney. I won't let you get shivved before I can free you."

Cameron shifted to sit up. "Do you think I'm innocent?"

"I've seen the damning evidence. Right now it's swaying me to believe the police reports," she retorted logically. It was the truth.

"Great. What now?"

"The private investigator is digging into the night of the event. He should have something by next week. I think since the victim was Nitty Nichols, spinning a self-defense argument for your case could work with a jury."

"He didn't have any weapons."

She picked up a yellow folder and opened it. "But he did. This just arrived from the P.I. Take a look."

Cameron scanned the pages. "The gun in my boot was his."

"Yep, so if you guys rolled around for control and the gun went off or your knife stabbed him, we'll use the defense that you were protecting yourself."

He handed the information back to her. "That's great and all, but I doubt anyone would buy it."

Joci shifted her weight and regretted wearing the cute—though extremely uncomfortable if worn more than an hour—heels. She wasn't sure why she chose them earlier. They weren't a pair she wore unless it was to a date. Her eyes drifted over him. This was most assuredly not a date.

"Unless you have more information for me, it's the best we have."

He scratched his scalp and tilted his head toward her. "All right, thanks."

She fingered her left earring. "All part of the job."

"Oh, sure." His smile faltered, and he leaned into the cushion.

Joci's eyes surveyed the damage inflicted on him. Despite the wounds, he wasn't hard on the eyes. His suit was long gone, since the ruffians tore it to shreds. *Probably to teach him a lesson.* The casual jeans and blue T-shirt he wore now suited him better anyhow. The police still stowed away his street clothes he'd worn during the alleged murder as evidence for the case, so Rayna had to find clothes fast for the tall man before he returned from the hospital. As usual, the woman worked miracles in a short time.

"Are you all right?" she asked, then laughed. "That's a dumb question."

He shifted his eyes to her, and her attention caught on his eyebrow piercing. It was intact, but the nose ring had been torn out thanks to the morning's activities. She didn't miss it but was somewhat attracted to the one that remained. He was an enigma to her. One she almost didn't want to figure out.

"I'll live, thanks to you." His eyes slipped down her figure. "I don't understand the real reason why. I'm a nobody."

Joci didn't know why either. Sure, she told him the lawyer defense, but she didn't get emotionally involved for her other clients as she had for him that day. When she saw the first punch thrown, her stomach dropped. She was zealous for all her clients, but they weren't the childhood friend she thought she'd never see again. She didn't want that happening for real.

"I think it's because you remind me of someone," she offered. It was half true. Months of helping juvenile delinquents made her pity their futures. Well, she was staring at it now, and she wanted to help him in any way she could.

Her eyes fluttered to his hands. The right one bore two tattoos. She realized his fists were swollen and scabbed. "You need to ice those."

She grabbed two ice packs from the freezer, then with a careful touch, wrapped his hands around them. "There. That should do the trick."

"Thanks, Joci," he murmured.

When she lifted her head, his face was inches from her. Panic etched in her mind, but her body wouldn't move. She was stuck gazing into his charming dark brown eyes. Abruptly, she lowered her gaze, but found that to be a mistake when it landed on his tattooed arms. They were marvelous too. She could spend all afternoon sorting out each ornately connected masterpiece. The intricate ivy crawling up his forearm instantly brought questions to mind, but she ignored them for the time being. Now wasn't the time. A moth on his left bicep snatched her attention. The pattern looked too familiar, yet she couldn't recall the reason.

The longer she looked, the more figures stood out to her. Two bicycles leaning against a tree with red buds and tiny initials carved in its trunk forced her to pull away. They reminded her of the time she and Cameron had raced bikes down the street. Surely these weren't the same ones. "I'm sorry. I shouldn't stare."

Cameron pressed the ice to his hands. "They're on me for review. Don't feel bad."

"What do they all mean?" she wondered, then slapped a hand over her mouth. "That's too personal and none of my business." She stood, knocking a pillow off the couch. "I should go."

Cameron stood as well, his stature astonishing her. When

he wasn't locked up, he towered over her. "Please don't. It'll take a whole ten minutes alone before I get bored." He nodded to the television. "Even with that." Lacking shame, he gripped her hand. "Stay a while, and I'll spill the stories behind a few of my tats. You know you're curious."

His soft request startled her, and she shook free of his hands. "I can't. I'm meeting Adrian for lunch."

Walking to the panoramic window, he inquired, "What's the deal with you two anyway?"

"What do you mean?" She hoped she wasn't so obvious.

He twisted toward her. "Adrian all but claims you as his, but you flirt with police officers while he looks on. Are you together and in a tiff?"

"It's complicated," she huffed. Why did she care what this man thought about her relationships? She wasn't sure, but she needed to clear the air. "We have a past."

"Adrian told me as much." Cameron closed the distance between them and ran his eyes along her face. "What does that even mean? You two were friends and he did something to hurt you?"

Joci gasped at his insight. His demeanor was a far cry from that of the oaf in a jail cell. Perhaps she'd misjudged him. "How did you know that? What the hell did he tell you?" Her temper flared at the possibility that Adrian was yammering to people.

Cameron held up his hands. "Nothing, simmer down. He didn't say anything." His gaze softened. "But it's in your eyes."

"What?" She self-consciously fingered her square frames.

"They're beautiful, by the way," he offered with a shy smile.

Joci wasn't sure if she should run for her life or hear him out. When he continued, her pulse quickened.

"A shade of green with a smidge of brown to make them hazel. I like them, but they harbor loathing whenever Adrian's around. I want to know why."

On edge from the obscure hold he had over her, Joci clutched her purse. "Just because we went to summer camp together when we were kids doesn't mean I know you now," she reminded him. "All you need to know is he and I aren't together. We can work together without our personal lives interfering, if that's what you're worried about."

Cameron shook his head, his curly hair flipping to the side. "I wasn't worried about that. I have every confidence in you to try your best. Just like when you tried to show off at recess in first grade."

"I won't simply try," she scoffed. "I'm going to kick county attorney ass, with or without Adrian's help." The nerve of him to think she couldn't do anything by herself! "And the monkey bars would've been a success if you hadn't distracted me."

"Me? Really? You were climbing the playground equipment in a pair of flip-flops and wearing a sundress. You wouldn't listen to reason, and what did that haughty attitude get you?"

Her cheeks flushed red as she stomped toward the door. "A broken arm at recess, but I still did the bars better than you." She put her feet in motion again. The memory of his arrogant dare that he was better at climbing than her resurfaced. His tortured face when she'd fallen, and his worried expression when he rushed to her side drifted to her mind. She couldn't hate him then, just like now.

"Joci, wait!" he called, easily catching the door before she could tug at it. "I'll bet you wouldn't fall off the playground equipment anymore. Well, unless you wear those stupid high heels."

"Move," she directed, but he didn't obey.

"No. Not until you listen to me," he replied, forcing his body against the door.

With him now blocking her escape, she crossed her arms. "Get on with it, then."

"Oh, okay. I thought you were going to slug me or something," he joked with a smirk. It was an addictive sight to Joci's unstable mind.

Pressing her lips together, she glared at him. As though reading her thoughts, Cameron placed his hands on her arms. She wasn't certain why she allowed his bold move, but she couldn't shun it. *Because we know each other.*

"You haven't changed much. You're still bullheaded and ready to prove me wrong. I always liked that. Plus, you're a great attorney. I can tell from the few times I've seen you in action," he praised. "But if you don't want to be with Adrian, you should tell him before he invests too much time. Believe me, guys need to hear that shit or we never stop."

The insight frightened her. "You're not the person to offer relationship advice, Cameron," she hurled.

His eyes lowered to her lips, and Joci's stomach pitched. Why she didn't stomp on his foot was lost to her. This wasn't how she acted with clients. She didn't engage with them unless it was case related. Their interaction was unprofessional, yet felt more right than arguing in front of the Supreme Court.

"And what do you know about my life?" His low voice drew her closer as if by magic. Somehow, she was chest to chest with him, their breath mingling.

"My investigator found your juvenile record," she noted.

His hand snaked up her back, pressing her nearer. "Pretty sure that was sealed."

"It still is. I just got a quick peek at it." Though it wasn't illegal to probe into the Ohio court system, Joci felt bad about opening the documents. She needed to know any skeletons in his closet before moving forward.

Cameron brushed her ponytail from her shoulder. "Somebody's been doing her homework."

"I told you, it's my job. You're my job." Her gaze flipped between his alluring lips and captivating eyes. "You were caught trying to steal from Bernard Del Rossi. He's a huge mobster, Cam. What the hell were you thinking? I'm shocked he didn't kill you himself."

A sad smile covered Cameron's face as he pulled her hair free of its confines. Chills instantly covered Joci's skin at the bold contact and made her shiver at what he could do to her next. "My mom was sick and couldn't afford the medicine to help her, and my dad owed a lot of money to Del Rossi. I took it upon myself to right both of those. Too bad I didn't know the liquor store I nabbed the money from was owned by the boss himself. A bit ironic, isn't it?"

"Yeah, I'll say. So what happened? The court file was redacted for a lot of the transcripts."

Tangling his hands through her long locks, Cameron bent closer. "Because Del Rossi likes his privacy. But I can't hate him. He helped my mom get a doctor who'd actually help her and arranged a repayment plan that didn't include sleeping with fishes for my dad. He's done a lot for my family over the years."

His sentiment shifted Joci's impression of him. Behind his sarcastic jabs, he was a good person when it came down to it. "So you're in good graces with a mobster?"

"Let's just say Bernard and I go way, way back," he stated, lowering his eyes. "You don't know me as an adult yet, Joce, but I hope you'll give me a chance. You'd be surprised what I would do for the people I care for."

Confused by his candor, Joci's mind whirled at the possibility that he truly was guilty of a crime. If he was friendly with the Italian mob boss, it wasn't a far stretch that he was more involved with the Del Rossis than he cared to admit. "I need to go," she whispered.

Reluctantly, Cameron stepped aside. "Wear your hair down. It's too pretty to keep back all the time."

Joci didn't bother to retrieve her hair tie as she turned the doorknob. Her heart pounding, she rushed down the hallway and into the elevator, where she leaned on the rail. Cameron was right. She didn't know him, and she needed to steer clear of being alone with him. There was no telling what she may do if confined within the same walls as the mysterious tattooed drummer.

CHAPTER SEVEN

Clicking through the three hundred channels slowly drained Cameron of all motivation. The Christmas season was upon them, but he was left in dismal isolation in the extravagant apartment cell. "At least in jail, there're dumbasses to laugh at," he complained when he found a show that seemed interesting. For the most part he didn't go for Western flicks, but he was out of options.

The pre-trial conference last week was boring as hell, but he'd seen Joci at least. She didn't stick around since she had another hearing in the courtroom next door, so Adrian filled in the blanks for his questions. Reluctantly, he'd agreed to moving the trial so they could complete depositions. He wasn't fond of stretching his time out, but it also meant he had more chances to interact with Joci. She stirred something long lost to the mobster way of life.

To his disappointment, the ritzy apartment didn't come with a drum set. Feeling the beat of a song throughout his body was exactly what he needed to clear his head. He was getting attached to Joci already. How could he not when she smelled like summer and looked like a daydream? It happened in Ohio, but she left him high and dry. If history repeated itself, he would be the one to leave this time around.

After tossing the remote to the couch, he sauntered to the window. The view from the tenth floor was astonishing. It was no Chicago, but Des Moines held its own Midwestern charisma. People flooded the snowy streets below, and he urgently wished he were among them. The sweet December air swept through the top of the window in the kitchen and ruffled his hair. How he wished that was an intimate touch instead of a flippant breeze!

A rap on the door signified the deputy's arrival. There was a slew of security guards in an office down the hall, but a member of the Polk County Sheriff's Department stopped by every now and then to verify his confinement. Apparently they thought he was a mastermind escape artist.

"Hey," he greeted when the buzz-cut hair came into view.

The deputy harrumphed, then went on his round of the apartment. It was the same each time. The sheriff would make sure he wasn't harboring drugs or an alternate route from the glamorous cell, then pat him down before leaving.

The prepaid cell phone rang from the coffee table, pulling Cameron away from the impromptu raid. He grabbed the phone and grinned when he read the caller ID. "Hey, Joci," he answered, feeling giddy. *Stop it*, he chided. She was the best part of his day. Hell, if she patted him down as thoroughly as the cops, he'd never let her leave his side.

She called daily to ensure his food arrived three times and on time. He didn't know why she didn't ride the damn elevator up a flight to see for herself, but he appreciated the consideration nonetheless.

"Hey yourself, jailbird. Everything kosher up there?" Her voice sounded strained, and Cameron wished there was some way he could assist her. She was doing a lot for him, yet if he told the real story, it would invalidate her hard work.

"For the most part. Sergeant whatever is here now," he commented when the man came into view and roughly frisked him. "He gets a bit handsy."

The deputy rolled his eyes, then left him to his conversation. Any other day, Cameron didn't mind the company. Watching television and using the treadmill entertained him for only a small amount of time. He was fond of the exercise equipment, though.

"You shouldn't aggravate the police. I may need to use them as witnesses." She sighed. "Try to behave."

"It'd be a ton easier if I had someone to talk to," he badgered. "When I'm alone, my imagination gets the better of me."

"In that case, I can send Rayna up in an hour," she offered, seeing right through him.

Cameron thought it over, but couldn't handle the bouncy auburn today. She was sweet and all, but she got on his nerves too fast. "She's nice, but I would rather you came up here. I'll show you my secret tattoos." He held his breath, and wasn't disappointed when the sound of falling files and fluttering papers echoed across the line.

"Uh, uh, I don't think that's the best idea," she whispered into the phone.

He chuckled. "Afraid you might like spending time with a man on his way to prison?"

Joci giggled, but it was shaky at best. "Look, we need to keep things professional, okay? No flirting or whatever."

Taking a seat at the kitchen table, Cameron rubbed the back of his neck. "Darlin', you'll know when I'm flirting with you. It'll knock your pretty Prada shoes right off you."

She huffed, and he was certain an eye roll accompanied that delectable sound.

"Depositions are coming up after the holidays. I'm sorry you have to be cooped up for Christmas."

"You've done more than enough." He waved his hands at the apartment. "This is a much better view than a jail cell, so thank you for that."

"One of us will talk to you before we leave for the weekend. The court's closed on Friday and Monday, so nothing new on your case should come for a week at least," she concluded.

"What're you doing for Christmas?" he asked, though he almost didn't want to know. If she told him she was spending it with that snake Adrian or the cocky cop, he'd break into the liquor cabinet and drink all the remnants.

"I'm not sure yet. My parents invited me out to Colorado, but I doubt I'll head out there."

"Why not?"

He heard the ding of the elevator. "You know my

parents, Cam. They're a bit much sometimes. I already have enough stress in my life. I don't need my mom antagonizing me about being an old maid."

"Believe me, you'll never ever be an old maid. It'd be a sin."

Joci chuckled but didn't agree. "All right, drummer boy, I need to sign off. I'll touch base later," she promised, then hung up.

"Okay, then nap time it is," he muttered and moved to the couch. The cashmere blanket beckoned to him, so he snuggled beneath it and fell fast asleep.

Two hours later, someone nudged his foot. Thinking it was Joci, he groaned, "Five more minutes, berrylicious."

"Berrylicious?" Adrian's voice yanked Cameron from his warm slumber.

"Oh shit." Cameron opened his eyes to see his attorney giving him the best death glare on planet Earth.

He forced out a chuckle. "My bad. I thought you were Joci. You know, she smells like berries," he offered. Adrian tossed the cashmere to the floor. "It's a joke. Lighten up."

"Well, I'd appreciate it if you stopped. You're making her uncomfortable," Adrian advised.

Not buying that, Cameron stood. "If that's how she feels, she'll have to tell me herself. I don't take hand-me-down rejections to my charm."

Adrian squinted his blue eyes. "Maintain your distance. That's all I'm saying."

"We were friends back in the day. I see no problem with building on our history."

He jerked his head to the box at his feet, ignoring the last part of his client's plea. "Now, I brought over some case work. This is all the discovery the state has provided so far. The medical reports, photos, police reports, etc. are in there. We need to go over as much as possible. Joci and Rayna are going over their copies, and we'll regroup later with notes." He crossed to the kitchen. "I'll start the coffee. It's going to be a long night. I hope you like bloody photos. The autopsy reports always make me queasy."

Seething, Cameron cursed. If he was forced to review a murder he didn't commit, he would have more fun if the attorney was a brunette with sparkling fervor, not the one who made him wish he was back in jail. Adrian rubbed him the wrong way, but it wasn't because he was a douche. *Okay, that's part of it.*

He flipped through the photos, recognizing the park in daylight. From the little he knew about Adrian, he liked to win and would do almost anything to guarantee it. The whole reason he was in Des Moines was because of the whispers from a neighboring mob about a well-known attorney being in the Mikkelsens' pocket. Del Rossi sent him to investigate since it affected the mob's dealings in the Midwest.

Cameron studied the redhead after he returned from the kitchen, head bent over the police reports and sleeves rolled up to his elbows. He didn't resemble a mafia man, but that didn't mean he wasn't one. If being with the Del Rossis taught him anything, people were not always as they appeared.

He was just getting into a report when the cell phone next

to Adrian buzzed. "I need to take this," he stated, standing.

Watching him retreat to the bedroom off the kitchen, Cameron could've sworn he heard Adrian say, "Hey, J.J., what's up?" but he wasn't sure. *Stop being paranoid. He's not the lawyer involved with the Mikkelsens.*

He tossed one folder to the side and grabbed a blue one, hoping it didn't contain gruesome evidence against him. The conversation with Joci nagged at him. He should've come clean about his true connection with Del Rossi. His time with the group didn't cease as she may suspect. Gritting his teeth, he rolled his shoulders back. His deadbeat dad didn't repay the mob boss. Not even close. Instead of being good, normal people, his parents bailed on the debt and him. He pinched the bridge of his nose as a headache grew. His options back then were either join the Del Rossi mafia or say adios to his life. Obviously, as a dumb sixteen-year-old, he chose the former. He enjoyed breathing. Especially now, because Joci took his breath away whenever she smiled at him.

— — —

It had been two weeks since she and Rayna went over the potential exhibits, and she was thankful when the P.I. called her. Despite the cold January winds, she trudged out of her warm pajamas to meet with him. Now, as they rode the elevator to the top floor, the recent festive holidays crept into her mind. Christmas came and went, but she didn't. She almost caught a last-minute plane to Denver, but a wicked ice storm hit Des Moines just in time for Christmas

Eve. Instead of chancing dismal outcomes, she stayed in her apartment. Alone on the day that used to be her favorite holiday. She felt bad she didn't visit Cameron, but she did manage to call him and wish him well. They'd spent a few holidays together, including Christmas morning, and she could still remember the smell of gingerbread cookies and the sleepy expression on his face when she ran across the street to tell him about the presents left beneath the tree.

Smiling reminiscently, Joci wondered how his day went this year. She'd set up a small tree in her apartment, but no presents were left beneath it. She felt a little bad she hadn't done anything to make Cameron's abode more festive. New Year's Eve went as to be expected—alone, yet again. This time she chose not to stray from her apartment. Going out and celebrating the cusp of a new start didn't feel right. She chalked it up to not having Quinn around anymore. He took some time off and went to southern Iowa for the holidays. Surprisingly, she didn't miss him all that much.

"So, when we arrive, I'd like to go over my preliminary findings," the private investigator noted.

Joci nodded. "Sounds good. I'm sure Cameron will be interested to see what you found.

They walked in silence to the armored door. She'd used Todd Combs a number of times for her cases, but his quiet demeanor unnerved her. Rarely did he visit unless the information was crucial to a case. Noticing the new streaks of gray in his hair, she wondered which case caused them. As an ex-cop, Mr. Combs was the best in the area, and his invoices showed it.

She swiped her card, then turned the doorknob. Cameron didn't know they were coming, so she hoped he was decent. The clock at the end of the hall struck ten at night, and she wondered if he was awake. *He will be now.*

"Let's set up in the kitchen." She pointed Combs in the right direction, then dropped her purse onto the entryway table. "Cameron, are you awake?" She checked the living room but saw no one sprawled out on the couch.

Moving through the kitchen and down the hall, Joci poked her head into the gym area and was disappointed when he wasn't there either. "Great, you had to be sleeping."

She moved to the largest bedroom and pushed the door open. To her surprise, a very awake Cameron sat on the bed with a book in his hands. The serenity in the scene made her heart palpitate. She could imagine him doing the same thing twenty years in the future, his hair gray and tiny-rimmed glasses on his nose while he read.

As if hearing her thoughts, Cameron raised his eyes. "Come for a nightcap, counselor?" he baited.

Clearing her throat, she stepped into the room. "No, sorry. Maybe another time." She jerked a thumb toward the kitchen. "The private investigator and I are here to discuss your case."

He stuck a bookmark between the pages and tossed the book to the other side of the bed. "Anything good?"

"No clue. He hasn't told me yet," she replied, lacing her fingers together. Joci took a step backward when Cameron swung his legs to the floor. His limited apparel of sweats alone didn't help the lurch of desire in her gut either.

"Should I put a shirt on?" he asked, catching her staring.

"No," she squeaked, a little too quickly. "Um, I mean, a shirt would probably be good."

Slinking over to the dresser, Cameron grabbed a T-shirt and slipped it over his shoulders. Joci scolded herself for being sad when his tight muscles and decorative tattoos disappeared. "There, all better." The hue of his eyes darkened. "I can take it back off later when the P.I. leaves, if you want."

Joci gawked at him and slammed her mouth shut. He was sassy and sultry, a very dangerous combination for someone prone to the same behavior. "Professional, Cameron. Keep this professional."

Cameron padded over to her and grazed his index finger over her arm. "That'd be easier if you didn't want the opposite from me." He moved beyond her, skimming her body with his. "You must be the guy digging into my life. How nice to see you, said no one ever," she heard him call from the hallway.

Returning to the kitchen, Joci watched as the two men sized each other up. It was humorous, the way men worked. Adrian did the same thing with Quinn, but this match was ridiculous. While in her opinion Cameron was more handsome than Jason Momoa, poor Mr. Combs's features weren't anything to boast over.

"Mr. Shearer, I'm Todd Combs. Nice to meet you," Combs replied, not bothering to address the blatant hostility. "Have a seat."

Joci reached the table in time for her client to plunk into

a chair. "Let's get started, shall we?" She pulled out two notepads and handed them to both men.

"Good idea." Combs rifled through his stack of paperwork and produced two folders. "This is what I've found so far."

Joci skimmed the contents. "You found the band members? That's great."

Combs shrugged. "Yes and no. They were in Salt Lake City and weren't helpful at all. After the concert, each man said Mr. Shearer took off on his own. They didn't see you again until your mugshot hit the Internet."

Cameron's hands laced together on top of the table. "Yeah, they're dicks sometimes."

"I thought they were your friends," Joci assumed.

"I wouldn't go that far. We were four guys who played songs, got high together, and fought over who had to pay for pizza." He scratched his left wrist, his eyes steady on the files. "Not the greatest definition of friends, honestly."

"This is what I truly wanted to discuss with you," Combs interrupted, pulling out a flash drive and laptop. "The state provided video footage of the area, but there was barely anything there, so I decided to dig into the possibility that someone tampered with it."

Joci's heartrate skyrocketed. She almost didn't want to see what was found. "And?"

"I wasn't able to get all the footage, but check this out." He plugged the drive into his laptop.

Grainy video flashed across the screen, October 31 noted on the bottom. They all watched in silence until a group of men moved from one camera angle to the next. The men wore black hats, dark clothing, and kept their faces covered by high lapels.

Combs pointed his middle finger to the man in the corner. "This one. He has something in his hands."

Squinting, Joci leaned in and her eyes widened. "It looks like a gun."

"It's probably a cell phone," Cameron concluded, sitting back. "There's too much fuzz in the footage. No freaking way anyone can scrub it enough to see what the guy has."

Frowning, she closely eyed her client. It was almost as though he didn't want her to find out who was in the park around the time the body was found.

"Unfortunately, he's right," the investigator added. "My techs cleaned it up for hours. This is the best they could do. It's unlikely the county attorney will use it."

"See?"

"Oh shut it." Joci glared at Cameron despite the grim grin on his lips. "I doubt it will help our case either, but you never know."

Combs took out photos and spread them out. "These are from the day after the incident. As you can see, footprints are everywhere. The scene was contaminated from the get-go. I took a few molds from indentations in the bushes, but I wouldn't hold out hope that they're helpful."

"Sure, makes sense. Let me know if the results stand out." Joci wrote a reminder to check back with Combs in a week on her pad.

"I did look into Mr. Shearer's criminal history in Ohio."

The moment the statement left the man's mouth, Cameron's right eyelid twitched. Pausing her pen, Joci watched him pick at a scab on his hand. His left leg bounced up and down while they waited for the P.I. to continue.

Combs glanced to his notes. "There was quite a bit of involvement with the Del Rossi mob."

Not sure whether what Cameron told her was all there or if there was more, she motioned for him to keep going.

"It appears your client is very familiar with Bernard Del Rossi himself." He pulled out black-and-white pictures. "These were taken about five years ago. I didn't find any recent ones of the two together."

"Five years, you say?" Joci did the math as Combs spoke, then shifted her torso to Cameron. "You said you were a kid when you became involved with Del Rossi."

"Sixteen, yeah," he produced, not looking her in the eye.

Fury filtered through her body and she slapped a hand on the table. "Look at me." He didn't comply, further pissing her off. "You and I are the same age, give or take a couple months." She stood and slid the picture in front of him, then stabbed it with her index finger. "If this was taken five years ago, you lied to me. You should've been done with Del Rossi within a year or two depending on the debt your dad had. Clearly your involvement went beyond that. Why the hell did you lie?" She was beyond livid now, and he still wouldn't meet her gaze.

"I'm not covered by attorney-client privilege should you answer, Mr. Shearer. Do you want me to leave?" Combs abruptly asked.

Cameron moved the evidence away from him. "Yeah, man, probably a good idea. I don't really want you knowing more than you already do."

"I'll walk you out," she offered, needing a moment away from the lying son of a bitch beside her.

Following the older man to the door, Joci managed a weary smile. "Thanks for your help. We'll be better prepared with what you've discovered."

The P.I. managed a smile, then curtly bobbed his head at Cameron before turning toward the elevator. "Not a problem. I'll check in with you later when I have more."

Joci nodded, then closed herself in the guarded apartment. She pressed her back against the solid door and her eyelids fluttered. Hearing and seeing potentially helpful and detrimental information was enough to make her want to drink an entire bottle of tequila, and she hated tequila. Homicide cases were an uphill battle, and her client wasn't helping. Now that the truth was out in the open, she needed to grind it out of Cameron.

"He's gone, then?" Cameron's question lingered in the air between them, willing her to open her eyes.

He stood with arms crossed over his chest, staring at her with an undiscernible countenance. "Because he was getting annoying. Reminds me of Adrian."

Maintaining her stance, Joci studied him. It seemed that any other male presence unnerved him. In that instant, she wondered if he acted like this all the time, or just when she was around. "You're not fond of other guys, are you?"

Cameron's cheek tightened. "Not when they like you."

A flush of heat rose in Joci's face. "You're being ridiculous. Mr. Combs is practically an employee and Adrian and I are…"

"Complicated. I know," he finished for her.

She moved to the living room. The couch beckoned to her almost as much as Cameron. He was tense, but she couldn't decide if it was from the inclination of him being jealous or his hidden secret she was trying to unearth. "Either way it's not your problem." She took a breath and steered the conversation back to topic. "Now, are you going to tell me about Del Rossi?"

His lips dipped in a frown. It shouldn't have been attractive, but it was nonetheless. "Is it mandatory?"

"Yes. You're being dodgy, and I need you to stop." She flung her hands around in aggravation. "You're my oldest friend and you've been keeping mob involvement from me. How can you do that? They're probably why you're in this shit storm."

"You're right. They are."

Startled by his admission, her mouth dropped open. "Seriously?"

He chuckled, the sound strained. "Yeah, I'm serious. I've done some bad shit in the past, Joce. I won't lie anymore. I was in Des Moines for a concert, but mostly on Del Rossi business. You know, sell drugs and fence some items."

"You're a thief as well as a member of a mob? Great. They were right about you."

Placing his hands on her arms, he nodded to the couch. "Why don't we get more comfortable."

The instant she slouched in the cushion, she wanted to fall asleep and forget what she recently uncovered. She didn't want Cameron to be this person, but he was. He was part of a mob, and not just any mob, but a dangerous one with plenty of unsolved murders pinned to them. She'd heard Quinn talk about them but never thought much on it. Now her mind whirred on the horrid things the mob could do to someone who got in their way.

Cameron sat beside her, though not too closely. "My parents left me and the debt to Del Rossi shortly after my juvenile court case came to be. I was given two choices, and I went with the one that kept me alive."

His words halted whatever anger she'd formed against him. Broadcasting dismal events wouldn't be the first thing she'd do either. The lies made sense. Joci subconsciously gripped his arm at the thought of him having to make a life-altering decision at a young age. Instantly, she wondered whether, if she hadn't moved, the same thing would've happened. Her family would've taken him in, she was positive of that. He was almost a member of the Dorous crew despite the short time she knew him.

"Since then, I paid off my dad's debt, but managed to collect a few of my own." His smile faltered. "I'm not proud of it, but I can't leave, Joci. If I could, I sure as hell would." He moved his arm to just above her shoulders on the couch.

Heart aching for his troubled past, Joci boldly reached over and gave him a hug. "I'm sorry, Cam. No one should ever be in such a position."

He smirked but didn't acknowledge her embrace.

"Thanks. Life's a bitch sometimes. That's what I've figured out."

"And you think Del Rossi may have pinned this murder on you?"

"Ha, no. I'm too valuable for that to happen. I think it was the Mikkelsen mob."

"Who? I don't recognize the name."

"You wouldn't. They're mostly in Denmark. Lately, they've moved to small areas in the States to see if they can make money." His eye twitched again. "I kind of pissed off one of their main guys by stealing a shipment of drugs from him last year. He never got over it, but that's small shit."

"Oh my God! That's why he set you up?"

Cameron shook his head. "Nah, my issue with J.J. goes a lot deeper than lifting drugs. I may have accidently gotten him thrown in prison a few years ago. There's more, but a sweet lady like yourself doesn't need to hear nitty-gritty details."

She wanted to question him more, but based on the scowl on his face, Joci opted against it. At the moment, she wasn't his attorney but his friend. Given the recent download she received, he didn't have many.

"It dealt with a girl. Let's leave it at that, okay?" His hand brushed her right shoulder.

"A ladies' man, huh?"

"Not exactly. I was duped and so was J.J. I just didn't know it until it was too late to help him." Cameron's leaned over and his voice dropped. "Don't worry, I'm not a man-whore."

She playfully shoved at him, but he kept hold of her hand. "I'll believe it when I see it. You were quite the talker when we were younger."

A peculiar flash of resentment crossed his face but was quickly replaced with mirth. "Maybe once upon a time, but not these days. My time with Del Rossi helped me understand what's truly important in life. Obviously, my family screwed me over, but I'm set on that never happening to someone I love."

Joci's breath caught in her throat. "You aren't going to stay with the mob the rest of your life?"

"Oh, I didn't say that." He laughed. "I'm sort of stuck with Del Rossi until he breaks me loose, but I always hope it'll happen sooner rather than later. I'm almost finished with my current repayment, so another five years and I expect him to give me the option of leaving."

"I didn't think that happened. You know, once in the mob always in the mob," she pointed out.

Cameron's eyes slid over her face before focusing on her lips. "When you're one of Jerry's favorites, you get special treatment."

"I thought you two were on the outs. You haven't seen each other in years, if you believe the photo Combs brought."

He stretched his legs and turned toward her. "Leaving may mean a less conspicuous job with the mafia. Don't you go worrying about me, counselor. I can handle myself."

Joci pointed to his anklet. "Obviously not."

Rich laughter filled the tall ceilings, instantly putting her at ease. It wasn't difficult when she was around Cameron. Initially, he was a pain, but outside of the jail's walls, he was more like the boy she adored.

Relaxing further into the couch, she rested her head on his shoulder.

"Life was so much better when we were kids."

"I'll second that."

They sat in comfortable silence, Cameron's warmth spreading over her and compelling her eyes to close. No doubt it was way beyond the normal time she fell into bed at night.

"Just so you know, neither the attorney douche nor the cop stripper will work for you," he whispered into her ear, forcing her eyelids to stay open.

Joci grunted. "You wouldn't know who works for me."

Cameron circled a bold arm around her waist, pulling her flush to him. His mild scent filled her senses, lulling her. "Maybe not yet, but I can tell neither guy could make you happy. Not in the long run."

Lifting her eyebrows, she let her eyes linger on his torso. He was magnificent up close, but even more so because she felt him beside her. She'd never thought the lanky kid with Metallica T-shirts would grow up to be more handsome than the majority of her exes. Why she allowed him to grip her like this, she'd never understand, but it was familiar.

"How would you know who would bring me happiness?" she questioned.

"I just do." With fluid movements, he reached back and tugged at her ponytail. "I hate these things, by the way."

He clutched the hair tie and slid it down until her hair fluttered into her face. "Much better."

"Why are you so much nicer when it's the two of us?"

He tilted his neck and trailed his hands up her sides. "I don't know. You've got this effect on me. I'm either an asshole because I want to see that angry crinkle on your brow." He smirked when she obliged. "Yeah, that. Or because I want to know how your lips taste on mine."

Joci's breath caught in her throat. No words could form in her mind. She couldn't admit to having reciprocal wayward thoughts. They were friends. *Even if he was my first crush.* Instinctively, her eyes lowered to his mouth. That was a mistake. His full lips curved in a smile.

"You too, huh?" Cameron's hands disappeared, making her whip her attention to where they were going.

With care, he eased her back to the couch and tucked her under his arm. She expected him to make a move—they both wanted it—but he didn't do anything. He simply kept her safe in his arms. With heavy eyes, Joci sensed her body drifting to sleep. The steady rhythm of Cameron's heartbeat in her ear calmed her. She shouldn't stay, but her tired body swayed her from the thought. Falling asleep in the sturdy arms of an ex-convict who also happened to be her oldest friend was her best definition of perfect. They used to build forts in the basement of his house and spend the night in sleeping bags, so what was the harm?

Startled to consciousness sometime later, Joci sat up and gasped. Somehow, the lights had been turned off, save the lone one above the kitchen sink. She glanced around the room and saw the clock on the wall. *Shit, it's three in the morning.*

Cameron shifted beside her, and her pulse quickened. He looked too damn handsome for a murderer, with his unruly curls and long eyelashes. The darkness hid his tattoos, but she ached to turn on a light to see them. They were always a deterrent before, but the ones he wore fit him and drew her in more each time she viewed them.

"Aren't you going to make me breakfast?" his sleepy voice mumbled when she managed to retreat from the cozy couch.

Cursing, Joci turned around to see him studying her. "It's not morning yet, so I'm off the hook," she teased.

He didn't try to stop her, just watched her instead. "Don't worry, I won't tell your boyfriend wannabe or your fuckboy about this."

Joci was startled when she realized that possibility didn't bother her. Thinking on it, she wasn't sure how either Adrian or Quinn would react to hearing she'd slept in Cameron's arms. She wasn't in a relationship with either one, so it didn't matter. Adrian would curse her out for putting herself in a compromising position with the ethics board, but they hadn't done anything, and they were friends long before her firm was retained for the case. Plus, it was sleeping, not screwing.

"It's fine," she reiterated, searching for her purse.

"Then you'd want to do it again?" Cameron appeared at her side.

"Shit, you move like a ninja."

He clicked his tongue. "Not an answer."

Swinging first her coat and then her purse over her shoulder, Joci shrugged. "It doesn't matter, Cameron. It can't happen again. I'm your attorney, whether we knew each other years ago or not."

His arms were around her in a flash, sending her off-balance. Cameron caught her against the wall, his dark eyes scouring her face. "Pretty soon you won't be." He pressed his body to hers, the act sending a ripple effect through Joci. "But it is kinda hot this way too."

She should move away from him, but the tender yet steady way he held her made Joci second-guess herself. By the time she talked her body into escape, his lips were there to silence her.

Erratic butterflies swarmed her gut when his mouth fastened to hers. Cameron plunged his hands in her tousled hair and tilted her head up to meet his. Any gasp she wanted to muster dissolved at his prodding tongue. The more he kissed her, the more Joci was positive this was a dream. She couldn't be kissing a client like a slut! It was a dream and nothing more, she was certain—until he came up for air.

"I want you to remember this in the morning, Ms. Dorous." His eyes dropped to her neckline and he let out a shaky breath. "Because you would be the type to think you're imagining this."

Not given the chance to answer, Joci's moan echoed in his mouth when his hands cupped her ass. His kiss bolted her feet to the floor, hurling her mind into fathomless wonder. Leisurely, his lips moved to her neck, then lower until he reached her shirt.

"Don't say I never gave you anything," he warned, dropping to his knees and lifting her shirt.

Joci's breath hitched. Having him in front of her in such an intimate way sent naughty visions through her imagination. She dug her nails into his shoulders when his lips clashed with the tender flesh of her breast. Her brain screamed at her for allowing his daring act, but the delightful pain he caused in her veins silenced her.

When he detached his mouth from her, Joci whimpered at the loss. Time was a foreign concept as he stood to tower above her. His breath washed over her face.

"Better scurry home, Joci. If you stay here much longer, I won't have any control of myself," he warned, his brown eyes filled with longing. His hand traced the breast he'd left moments prior. "Sweet dreams."

She bobbed her head in agreement. She needed to get out of there before he killed her with his lips. On a cloud of desire, Joci moved to the exit and felt his gaze on the back of her head. Checking over her shoulder, she spotted his tall figure, but couldn't decipher the emotions on his face.

Once outside the apartment, her hand fluttered to her chest. She reached the elevator and pressed the button for the ground level. What just happened couldn't be described. She didn't know why it happened or what it meant, but her body wanted more of it.

Curiosity got the better of her and she yanked up her shirt. "A hickey! That son of a bitch gave me a fucking hickey!"

She yelped at the sight of the red love mark. A smile overwhelmed her face before she could stop it. She had to hand it to Cameron; she wouldn't be forgetting what transpired anytime soon, thanks to his reminder on her body.

It was then that she was thankful she refused both Adrian's and Quinn's proposals for relationships. After feeling a portion of what Cameron could give her, she couldn't think about, much less accept another man's touch. The problem was she wanted more of what he offered. A craving that was both foolish and erotic.

CHAPTER EIGHT

An annoying sound met Cameron's ears five days later. It wasn't abnormal for this time of day, but not the voice he craved. He propped his legs on the coffee table and waited for the deputy to make an appearance. When the beige uniform came into view, he frowned and eyed the new officer with care.

"You're not the normal guy," he pointed out when the man came closer.

"No, I'm not" came a rough reply. "But I'm not here to make sure you haven't escaped."

A chilling revelation whipped at Cameron's stomach. "Why are you here, then?"

The man was upon him now and yanked at Cameron's arm. Once he was upright, the faux deputy said, "He's watching you."

Trying to pass off the situation as a joke, Cameron slapped at the man's hands. "Sure he is."

"I'm serious, Shearer. Bernard sent me," the man replied

in a hushed tone.

That got Cameron's attention. "What does he want? I'm doing what he told me to do. He should know that already."

His assailant narrowed his beady eyes. "He does, but this isn't good for business. He's dished out plenty of money for you to figure out who's giving the Mikkelsen mob insider information on the gangs here. If you can't handle it, you better tell him soon."

Cameron staggered away from the messenger and ran his hands over his shirt. "It'll be fine. I have a hunch who J.J.'s working with, but I don't know for certain. J.J. won't take over the Midwest, okay?"

"You better be sure" was the last warning Bernard's guy made before leaving the room.

Breathing again, Cameron surveyed the room. No doubt the guards had been on a paid coffee run during the impromptu visit. It was better that way. The less Joci learned about his dealings, the better. Yeah, he should've told her the whole truth, but he couldn't. Not when he suspected Adrian was helping the Mikkelsen mob plant roots in Iowa soil.

He paced the floor and glanced to the window. Joci was a floor beneath him. That realization made his heart pound. He cared for her more than he should. It wasn't planned, but he couldn't stop the sensations she spread through him. Touching her last week was a mistake. All he'd done since then was dream about her, about doing more against the hallway wall.

Picking up the cell phone, he let the ringtone calm his nerves. Knowing Joci had court, he dialed Rayna's number.

"This is Rayna" was the happy greeting.

"Rayna, it's me. Is Joci around? I need to talk to her." He gripped the phone and felt perspiration on his hand.

"Sorry, Cameron, she's in a hearing right now. Did you try to call her?"

"No, I thought maybe she'd be around."

"Sorry. Do you want me to take a message?"

Pressing his lips together, he shook his head. "No. No, it's fine. Just tell her to visit me, okay?"

"Sure, no problem," Rayna replied, then disconnected the call.

It was the same response each time he called. The excuses varied by the day, but Joci's unavailability remained constant. In part, he accepted his actions were the cause for her refusal to see him. He should never have kissed her like that. It was insane, yet he'd never felt anything so right until their lips meshed. She tasted as good as she smelled. *No, better.*

Moving to the couch, he plopped down and flicked on the television. A distraction was what he needed. His eyes caught on the cell phone. "No, what I need is her," he told the empty room. "But I scared her off." He couldn't resist the other day. She looked too damned beautiful when they were sleeping on the couch. He hadn't slept a wink. How could he when all he wanted to do was consume her body with his lips?

He buried his face in his hands and let out an aggravated sigh. He needed to pin down if Adrian was working for the Mikkelsens or not. It shouldn't be difficult if the man ever let go of his precious phone. A quick glance over text messages and calls would do the trick.

A knock at the door startled him out of his pity coma. "Who is it this time?" he groaned, standing.

To his dismay, Adrian came into view. *Fuck, just the asshat I wanted to see.*

"Why aren't you ready?" he asked, his brows knitting in confusion.

"What're you talking about?" Cameron barked back. "I'm not going anywhere."

"Depositions. The initial round of depositions is today. We're questioning about ten people."

"Shit, I forgot. Why can't we do it here or at your office?"

Giving his client an annoyed glance, Adrian replied, "Depos are held at either the courthouse or the county attorney's office. The conference room downstairs is currently being renovated, but we usually do smaller depositions in there anyways. If the proceedings were here, the witnesses may glean information about you." He pointed to the box of half-eaten pizza. "Such as how much of a slob you are. It wouldn't help you much."

"All right, fine. I need to shower."

He checked his watch. "We have less than an hour, so hurry up and get dressed."

"Will Joci be there?" Cameron queried, walking backward toward the bedroom.

Adrian's blue eyes dimmed. "Yes, why?"

Adrenaline shot through Cameron's body. "No reason. Be back in a few." He all but ran to shower.

Thirty minutes later, he sat in an uncomfortable chair in the courthouse with Joci nowhere in sight. "You said Joci would be here. Where is she?"

His second attorney squinted. "Late. She's running late." He shuffled the papers on the table. "Quit worrying about her. That's *my* job as her partner, not yours."

"You're doing an awful job," Cameron jabbed. He couldn't help it. The arrogant redhead got under his skin. Even more than the police officer who sat in the hallway, waiting for his turn on the stand. Both men rubbed him the wrong way.

The court reporter clicked her machine to test while the county attorney reclined in his seat. The woman beside was reviewing police reports and highlighting. No one seemed to be in any sort of rush but him. If the opportunity presented itself, he'd snag the phone in Adrian's hand. It was constantly lit up and hidden from his view. That couldn't be a coincidence. Adrian was hiding something. He simply needed proof.

After delivering a harsh yet silent judgment on everyone present, Cameron heard the door behind them open. Joci's light voice lifted his mood the instant she spoke.

"Sorry, guys, my hearing ran late." She moved through the room and settled into the seat beside him. "We're all set to go."

Cameron tried to keep his attention on the first witness, but his eyes veered to her. The brown suit wasn't his favorite, but the rich orange shirt beneath was becoming against her pale skin.

He listened to the psychologist who met with him drone on about how their weekly sessions were going and watched both Adrian and Joci scribble notes on their pads of paper. The shrink was boring, so he took his pen and started doodling. When he looked up from his sketch of the capital's skyline a time later, the witness was the forensic analyst, and Cameron's legs itched to move.

"Ms. Miller, can you verify that my client, Mr. Shearer, possessed the weapons on the scene during the murder?" Joci started.

The woman flipped her curly brown hair over one shoulder. "Mr. Shearer's fingerprints were on both weapons, but I cannot definitively say when they were in his possession."

"Then it's possible that someone planted both the gun and knife on him after he was asleep."

"I suppose."

Joci flipped through the woman's report. "It shows here that you can't determine whether the blood on my client's clothes was caused by stabbing or shooting the victim, Mr. Nichols."

"That's correct. Normally, during an altercation, blood spatter would transfer to the assailant."

Cameron swallowed hard when he realized where Joci was heading with her line of questioning. She was smart, but it was a jury's case, and they didn't always look at facts. The victim was a well-known gang member in Iowa. He'd have plenty of say up until his death. A jury may not like seeing their drug mule dead.

"So the blood could've been from Mr. Shearer giving CPR to Mr. Nichols?"

"Yes, but there was no evidence of broken ribs to indicate CPR was administered."

"Ms. Miller, I'm going to stop you there because I believe you're moving into territory better suited for the medical examiner."

Smirking, Cameron did his best not to preen at his attorney's quickness. *She said she was prepared, but damn, she's a little growly.* He knew of at least one way to help ease the frown lines on her face if she'd let him.

Joci walked a small circle, reading the documents in her hands. "Can you explain the drug test results, please?"

Ms. Miller nodded. "Mr. Nichols had opioids in his system, specifically heroin. Mr. Shearer had cocaine and marijuana in his report."

"Thank you. Would you consider the levels of heroin in Mr. Nichols's body to be lethal?"

"Mr. Nichols's heroin level was 50mg, so yes, it could be lethal."

Nodding, Joci produced a copy of the toxicology report. "Then it's possible Mr. Nichols overdosed or someone injected him with enough heroin to make it look like he was murdered by my client when, in fact, he wasn't."

A bead of sweat formed on the analyst's forehead. "It's circumstantial, but possible."

"That's all I need, thank you."

Once the lab tech completed her monologue, Joci spoke up. "I think we could use a recess." She nodded to the reporter. "Ten minutes should be sufficient."

A quiet hum filled the space as everyone left, until only the defense remained. Adrian pushed his chair back and got to his feet. "Do you want a drink, Joci?"

Joci pushed her glasses up and turned toward him. "Water would be great, thanks."

Cameron's needs ignored, he watched as his male attorney left them alone, cell phone left behind. When the door swung shut, he swiveled in his chair and carefully swiped the device. Turning away from Joci, he quickly slid the arrow on the touch screen. *Idiot doesn't even lock it.* He opened the messaging records and reviewed the recent ones. Several from Joci, but he was relieved when they were all professional. Ignoring the unusual jab to his gut of their constant chatter via text, he scrolled down until he found a slew of messages with the name Jay as the recipient. Tapping those, Cameron skimmed the conversation.

Jay: Did you destroy it?

Adrian: The P.I. managed to restore some of it.

Jay: Fix it.

Torn between wanting to yell 'I told you so' and slug the redhead, Cameron snuck a peek at Joci. If he brought this information to the prosecutor's attention, she would be affected and not positively. Sure, his case would be postponed, maybe even tossed, but she would be dragged through the mud because of Adrian's association with J.J. Allowing her to see any harm wasn't in him. He could beat a man to a bloody pulp, but any damage to Joci's body or life was unacceptable. He'd felt her come alive beneath his hands.

He wouldn't let her get tangled in the mess. *His* mess.

Swiveling the chair back toward Joci, he casually replaced the cell phone. "Why isn't the State asking many questions?"

Joci kept writing. "These are just for the defense's side of the case. The State has the opportunity to redirect, but mostly they're helpful to the county attorney to tighten up their case and witnesses."

"Ah, okay. I guess it makes sense." He laced his hands together. "So, I haven't seen you in a little while. How's your, uh, let's call it a mark? How's it doing?"

He anticipated a quick response and wasn't disappointed. Joci slammed her pen down onto the table and glared at him. The fire in her hazel eyes ignited one deep within his soul. Making her furious was almost more fun than kissing her. Almost.

"First of all, what we did will never happen again," she began, tightening her hair tie. "Second, do not mention it ever again." Joci rested her palms on her thighs, then took a breath. "And third, I'm attempting to save you from years and years in prison, so I would appreciate a little respect."

In that moment, he understood her problem. She thought their rendezvous was based on lust alone. Cameron studied her worried brow. It was true, in part. He desired her in every sense of the word, but not because of her looks. The woman sitting beside him drove him insane because of who she was on the inside. Sure, her body set him off too, but the brilliance of her mind enraptured him. She'd always been incredible, but seeing her all grown up reiterated his boyhood feelings. He craved more time with her that was clothing optional.

"Joci, I do respect you." He kept his voice low in case they were interrupted. She shot him a disbelieving glance. "Yeah, I shouldn't have kissed you like that." His eyes grazed her high-necked blouse, and he wished he could see his artwork. "But I won't apologize for it, and I definitely won't promise it will never happen again."

"You're my *client* first and foremost," Joci stressed, swinging her chair to face him. "I shouldn't have let you do that to me." Her voice strained despite its quiet tone.

Digesting her words, Cameron maintained eye contact. Her eyes resembled a grassy knoll today. A line of brown surrounded her irises, making him wish he could study her for eternity.

"Did you enjoy it?" he asked at long last.

A perplexed expression crossed her face. "Um."

Moving closer to her, he touched her hand ever so lightly. "Did you enjoy *me*?" he asked, this time emphasizing the words.

She opened her mouth as if to answer, then clamped it shut. When she rubbed her lips together, Cameron refrained from hauling her onto his lap and showing her exactly what she should be doing with them instead.

"I don't trust you," she admitted. "I want to, but I can't. There's still something about your story that doesn't compute. If we're going to win, I need more transparency."

Holding back a laugh, Cameron opted for a smile. "If you want transparent, then so do I. Maybe a nice negligee to start."

Her eyebrows shrugged together in question. "What are you—"

The door burst open, letting the flood of attorneys back into the small space. Cameron sank back into his seat and observed the frenzy. In another life, he could've handled being a lawyer. It looked decent enough. Yet the monotony of court didn't appeal to him. He needed a career that would keep him hopping. Too bad for him, that was what got him into this mess.

Adrian took over the next witness, the medical examiner. The cocky bastard was good too. He smiled and made the older woman feel like a queen. Hell, he even held her hand and helped her up the steps. The guy was good. *Too* good. His disapproval was true to form. The guy was part of the Mikkelsen group; he couldn't be trusted.

"Mrs. Butler, can you give us a rundown of what you found after the autopsy, please?"

"Certainly. Mr. Nichols died of asphyxiation."

Cameron's eyes swung to Joci, who didn't look surprised. Maybe he should've read those reports Rayna sent him.

"The gunshot to Mr. Nichols stomach and the stabs to his heart were done after he expired. I found tiny specks of dirt in his nose that indicates he was suffocated by someone with the same substance on their hand or glove."

Instantly, Cameron thought back to the P.I.'s video. Damn J.J. was pulling out all the stops for this one. Telling Joci about the bad blood between the Mikkelsen mob and Jimmy Nichols probably should come up in the next few conversations, but then he'd show his hand. Since Adrian worked with the Mikkelsens, it'd give them a head start.

"Interesting." Adrian smoothed his right eyebrow. "Do you believe the heroin in Mr. Nichols's blood had anything to do with his death?"

The examiner nodded. "Yes. His dosage was almost lethal, so it would take very little effort to smother him while he was in and out of consciousness."

"But the stab wounds and gunshot didn't kill him?"

"No, sir."

"Did you find any dirt under my client's fingernails or on his hands?"

She shifted on the hardback seat. "Yes, though the trace amounts found were too minimal for proper testing."

"So you couldn't match the soil in Mr. Nichols's nose to that on Mr. Shearer's hands?"

"No."

Adrian gave a pointed look to the county attorneys, Mr. Bell and Ms. Lord. "I think that's all I have. Thank you, Mrs. Butler."

Once Adrian helped the old lady down, he confidently sat down. "And that, children, is how you bring in reasonable doubt."

Joci simply rolled her eyes and prepared for the next witness, Officer Quinn. While the man in question switched places with the medical examiner, Cameron kept staring at Adrian. He didn't know how he ever got mixed up with J.J., but he figured some kind of debt was the reason. Being an asshole didn't fit the bill. He came from a wealthy family, one that would easily pay off any amount owed. *Unless he pissed off one of the bosses. Money can't buy you out of that.*

"Officer Quinn, thank you for taking time out of your busy schedule," she began with a smile.

"All part of helping the community."

Cameron hated to admit the cop looked decent up on the stand. His hair was slicked back, but not in a greasy fashion. It appeared his attorney wasn't lost on how delectable the uniform looked either since her eyes subtly dipped all over the guy. No one else would've caught it, but he did. He knew what it felt like to receive that look. Seeing her give it away to someone else made his stomach lurch.

"Officer Quinn, please describe the night of October 31 for us."

"One of the emergency buttons was activated and I was nearby, so I took the call. After searching the picnic area, I found Mr. Nichols and searched him."

"Find anything of note?"

"Drugs. Marijuana to be precise."

Joci crossed something off her list of questions, then continued, "And you're aware of who Mr. Nichols is?"

"I'm going to object there for relevance, Ms. Dorous," Mr. Bell interrupted.

"I'll rephrase. Are you aware of Mr. Nichols's criminal history?"

Quinn nodded. "Yes. He has been known to distribute illegal drugs. He also led a violent gang."

"And this gang, would it become worthless without Mr. Nichols?"

"Probably not the word I'd use, but they would be easier to take over with their boss gone."

Joci glanced to Cameron and he sent a silent warning. If she was going to ask what he thought, they were going to share many words later.

"Did you look into any rival gangs for this murder?"

"We did, yes, but couldn't find any significant evidence to suspect the other groups were responsible."

Don't do it, Cameron pleaded. If she mentioned the names, he was screwed, and not in a good way. Jerry would be pissed. The whole reason he came to Iowa was to stop the infiltration, not bring attention to the Del Rossis.

"Did you investigate any mafias, such as the Del Rossis or Mikkelsens?"

"Fuckity, fuck, fuck!" He continued to curse in Italian and English under his breath until Adrian poked him and frowned.

"Shut up," Adrian snarled.

Cameron pulled back from the attorney and focused on Joci. If she didn't look so damned cute with her glasses slipping down her nose, he might lose his temper.

Quinn cleared his throat. "Um, no. I believe neither of those mobs is in Iowa."

"But it's possible they are?" She stepped closer to where the officer sat. "They could be in Iowa and laying low."

"Yes, it's possible."

"Okay, let's go back to your search. After you found Mr. Nichols, where was my client?"

The court reporter clicked along with the words, the

sound aggravating Cameron's ears. He wanted this to be done.

"He was roughly fifty feet from the victim."

"Was he coherent?"

"Not until after I searched him."

"And that was when you found the gun?"

Quinn pressed his lips together tightly before responding. "No. I discovered the knife. He found the gun in his boot."

"His boot. That's an odd place for a gun, isn't it?" She showed him a photo of the 9mm.

"Not the most common place, no."

"Why didn't you search his boots?"

Quinn's eyes narrowed at her implication. "Mr. Shearer took a step, then reached down and grabbed it. During my initial frisk, the bulky boots didn't appear to have anything in them."

"And would you say they were an odd addition to his apparel since they were tall, rubber boots a farmer would wear?"

"Yes."

Cameron wanted to applaud but decided against it. Knowing a fraction of the history between the two up there, Joci was playing with fire. She could detonate her booty call status with Quinn for the case's sake, or she could play it safe.

"Then you admit you did not follow protocol."

And detonation is it. Cameron made a small explosion with his hands and saw Adrian smirk. It was funny even if Quinn didn't think so.

"Not entirely, no," the officer admitted after a long moment went by.

"With that in mind, do you believe protocol was used in the duration of this case?" She was standing farther from him, as if expecting an outburst.

"I can't speak for the rest of the department."

"That's okay, I got what I needed." Joci nodded to the county attorneys, who looked ready to barf. Yeah, his attorneys were badasses, even if one was a traitor.

— — —

With nothing but time on her hands, Joci reviewed the mountain of paperwork on her desk. To her gratitude, another attorney in the firm was helping pick up any slack that her murder case created. She wasn't fond of letting other people handle her messes, though. The bond she forged with clients wasn't one she wanted to toss.

The office was quiet in a calming way. She worked best alone, which was why arriving early was her mantra. Tonight, she didn't feel like going to an empty apartment where chow mein from last week was the only thing in her refrigerator.

After depositions yesterday, she was more than ready to go to trial. Between her and Adrian, they made great headway in the case. Cameron admitted as much, but was oddly quiet after the last witness. Quinn was pissed at her and rightly so. No, she wouldn't be experiencing any sexy interludes with him anytime soon. In truth, she didn't mind. She was content to put all her time and effort into Cameron's case. If he was set up for murder as she suspected, she wouldn't let him go away for it.

Kicking off her pink pumps, Joci skimmed a substance abuse evaluation for a client charged with operating a vehicle while under the influence. It was a common case and not one she lost often. Getting the best deal possible was her goal. Ninety percent of the time, she succeeded.

A vacuum cleaner droned from the office across the hall, signaling the cleaning crew had arrived late again. They were starting on the opposite end of the building, so the sound was quickly drowned out by the distance. Any other attorney would rat them out, but Joci personally knew the group that tidied the law firm.

Another sound met her ears, though it was faint. She waited to see if her imagination was rampant. When the low male chuckle came again, she stood. Every other employee left two hours prior and the cleaning group was three women, so this noise set her heart pumping faster.

As quietly as possible, she skirted her large desk and made it to the door. As common for her, the office light was turned off and a minimal glow was cast from the computer. The darkness helped her thinking skills, but now it made her question the act. Since her office was the last door tucked along the hallway, seeing any flicker of light was obscure unless the person was close.

She stepped out of her doorway and noticed the vacuum remained on full blast, though the door was closed now. Summoning her courage, she walked barefoot down the hallway. "Dammit, I should've grabbed my shoes," she mourned to the empty space.

Stopping shy of the cubicles, she listened for the sound. When she recognized it as a male voice she knew well, her stomach dropped. It was coming from the direction of Adrian's office. Flashbacks of two years prior filled her mind the closer she got to his corner spot.

Careful to stay in the shadows, Joci peeked to see why her ex was still in the office. She recognized Adrian's assistant. The beauty was sitting on his desk, her skirt pushed up to midthigh. It didn't take too long to put together why he was at the office late. He didn't do it often, so she was curious as to why that day. Sneaking closer, she watched him sign a stack of paperwork, flirting the whole time.

"Make sure he gets these as soon as possible. The boss will want to know the case's developments."

Her eyebrows rose until she swore they reached her hairline. *Who is he talking about?* She clenched her hands into fists. The mention of a boss had her concerned. Did he mean a supervisor—who was his dad, so doubtful—or did he mean a 'boss' as in a mob boss? *Dear Lord, did Cameron bring all the mobs to Des Moines?*

Moving out of sight, Joci shook her head and steadied her breathing. *What the hell is he involved in?* Settling her hand on her stomach, she went over the facts. She and Adrian weren't dating, so the whole slutty assistant shouldn't bother her. They were partners in a case. *He was supposed to be showing me how he changed*, she reminded herself. She didn't care to hear why he was at the office with the woman, though a pang to her chest told her different. What she did care about was why he was acting shady.

Doing an about-face, Joci set off to gather her cases to take home. Working at the office wouldn't transpire tonight.

By the time she reached her oversized cubicle, she'd decided what she'd seen didn't mean anything. They were colleagues and could have an actual reason for a late night. She didn't know his caseload, so his night owl tendencies could mean he was catching up on them. It'd make sense given the homicide case. Despite that, she gnawed on her bottom lip, unsure who he needed to send a message to. The hair on her arms stood up. Something wasn't right. She could feel it. Another airy giggle filled the air and she clenched her jaw. It shouldn't bother her, but somehow that sound was a splinter under her nail.

"Stop it, Joci. We aren't a couple." She snatched her heels, then pulled on her coat. Before locking the door, she remembered her purse and phone.

Shaking her head, Joci strutted to the elevator, set on making their status abundantly clear to Adrian in the morning. Even though he wanted to try again, she was wary now more than ever. *It would be better if we remained colleagues. Anything else would muck things up.*

Settling in the elevator, she watched the door close. Her eyes were glued to the floor number buttons. Every fiber of her being wanted to press the one for the penthouse. The more she fought the urge, the longer she stayed trapped in the silver box.

Stomping her foot, she closed her eyes and slapped the panel. Where she was heading, she didn't know. She kept her eyes shut until the door dinged. One eye at a time, she pried her lids open and studied the display before her. It was Cameron's floor. Her feet refused to move from their spot, infuriating her further.

"I should just get a cat," she complained, forcing her body into motion. Her brain may regret dropping in on her client, but her soul didn't.

Swiping her security card at the door, she held her breath as she pushed it open. Laughter immediately assaulted her. Thinking Cameron somehow managed to sneak a person by the guards, Joci whipped around the corner, then halted in her tracks.

"Joci, what are you doing here?" Rayna's kind voice asked from the sofa. She sat cross-legged with Cameron by her side. A stack of playing cards was the only thing between them.

At the mention of her name, Cameron flicked his eyes up to greet her. He tilted his head to the right and set down his handful of cards. "Yeah, Joci."

Unnerved by their apparent game night, Joci stalked farther into the room. "I was finishing up some tasks at work and thought I'd check in on you," she said to her client. "I didn't know you'd have company."

Rayna shifted and offered a sheepish grin. "I felt bad for him. He's locked in here with no one to talk to." She held up a fresh deck. "You're free to join us. Cameron was about to teach me poker."

"Strip poker, no doubt," Joci mumbled under her breath. When she glanced to Cameron, she saw he'd heard.

Fumbling with the buttons on her purse, she took a step backward. "Thanks, but I should go." Her eyes slid between the two on the couch. "Everything looks in order here."

Joci rushed toward the exit, her palms sweating. She never should've come up here. Of course, Rayna was the perfect distraction for a man looking at life in prison. It was obvious, she thought as she tripped over the rug in the hallway, Cameron was trying to pass his time as a free man any way he could. It seemed that included seducing any woman who set foot in his presence.

Yanking on the door, she was surprised when it wouldn't budge. Turning angry eyes toward the culprit, she saw Cameron pinning his arm against her escape. "Let go, please. I have work to do at home."

"You and I both know you'll get no work done if we don't talk. She's just being friendly," he stated, not budging.

She shoved him hard, which did absolutely nothing. "I don't care what you do with her or any other girl. It's none of my business."

Cameron slid his body directly in front of her. In one bold move, he captured her face between his hands. Joci, too stunned to react, stood compliantly. "But it is your business, Joci." His thumb ran across her bottom lip. "I'm glad you came to check on me. It means a lot. I also like you jealous. It's cute."

Joci tried to steady her racing heart, but it was no use. The one thing keeping her from closing the distance between their mouths was Rayna's presence. Steadying her mind, she said, "You're impossible."

"You love it." He moved out of the way that time, but managed to press a quick kiss to her cheek. Her face burned at his brave touch as she slipped through the door undeterred. Glancing back to the apartment, Joci swallowed the emotions in her throat. Thus far, her night had handed her too much information to handle alone. She didn't like the thought of Cameron schmoozing Rayna or anyone else, and she wasn't sure how to react to Adrian's late-night work ethic.

Punching the silver button for the first floor, Joci stuffed her hands into her coat pockets and rehearsed her speech for the upcoming press conference next week. It was Adrian's idea to get the public involved in Cameron's case in hopes to reach jury members before selection. It wasn't a horrible idea to plant seeds of doubt in the state's case and see if the jurors respond to the possibility that their client truly was innocent. If she rehashed the night's activities, she was bound to do something regrettable. She'd done enough of that in the last month to keep her mind humming for the next year.

Still, as she exited the elevator, she itched to call Quinn, if only to divert her for the time being. As if reading her mind, the phone in her purse sang the happy tune of the police officer's ringtone. She had some major ass kissing to do with him, and it was the perfect opportunity. No, she wouldn't be lonely tonight—or any other night if she could help it. It was why she preferred to be single. Plenty of freedom to mingle without emotions getting involved.

CHAPTER NINE

"Rayna, is it all set?" Joci asked from her office door.

The attentive gray-eyed beauty nodded from the kitchen. A cup of freshly brewed coffee rested in her hands, the colorful mug setting off the blue in her dress. "Yes. They're expecting you both at one o'clock." She glanced to the wall clock. "So, less than thirty minutes."

Straightening her gray pantsuit for the hundredth time that morning, Joci tried to steady her nerves.

In the months since they were assigned the homicide case, Adrian had been the ideal partner. *Well, except when he stays at the office alone with a hottie, but that doesn't make him a bad partner. Just a douche.* She hadn't discussed anything with him yet. A week had gone by since both seeing Cameron and Rayna cozy playing cards and Adrian punching the late time clock with his assistant. She would deal with him today, but only because she'd spent the last week between sweaty sheets with Quinn. He'd been mad about her deposition tactics, but she thoroughly made up for her sharp tongue with other uses of the muscle.

Joci turned her attention back to Cameron. She still felt he wasn't being truthful in his story. Shaking her head, she knew if she wanted to get more information out of their client, she would need to spend time with him. Alone, since he wasn't fond of Adrian.

As much as she wanted to stay at a safe distance, he drew her in like a beam on the top of a lighthouse.

"Super, thanks for the help," she commended.

"He's been calling for you again," Rayna said in a squeaky voice. She held up a stack of envelopes. "And sending more fan mail."

Eyeing the notes, Joci blinked several times at her client's failed attempts to communicate with her. The post dates were in succession, but she was sure there were more where these came from. Cameron was stubborn, but so was she. "He can keep calling and sending letters. I'm not going to see him unless I have to."

"I wonder why he's so obsessed with you. I mean, I spent a little time with him to pass the time, but he doesn't send me drawings of trees. They're not bad, actually. He could be an artist if he wasn't busy with illegal activities." Rayna tapped her chin. "You don't think he's dangerous, do you?"

"No," she answered. "He's fine. Annoying is all. He used to get like that when we were kids. It'll pass. He needs alone time."

"No, that's the problem. He's bored," the other woman added.

"Yeah, true." Joci smoothed her hair. "I'll catch you later."

Not allowing for a response, she ambled down the hallway. She needed to focus for the next hour, not go over the befuddled reasons that she shouldn't want to see Cameron.

Both she and Adrian would star in the interview, but she hadn't told their client about all the details yet. With Cameron's shady past, it would only rile him up. She saw how he almost came unglued during depositions when she mentioned the mob names. The drummer with a history of drug dependency didn't need to deal with that. He hadn't show signs of drug addiction, which made her wonder if he was a casual user instead of hardcore.

At the judge's direction, Cameron participated in rehabilitation from the tenth floor. A therapist came twice a week to steer him in the healing direction, yet Joci was certain he wasn't investing his full potential in the process. He wasn't opening up, but she couldn't blame him. He had a lot of history between his parents and the mob. Sharing that information could get him killed. It came as a complete shock that the latest resident hadn't disturbed the apartment's liquor cabinet. In hindsight, they probably should've cleared it out, but since it was locked with a code, she hadn't given it a second thought. It was there for wealthy clients, and Petosa didn't stray from giving in to whatever needs the person displayed. Most of the clients dealt with federal crimes and didn't need a babysitter.

"Knock, knock," she announced when she reached the corner office. It was the largest one on the floor, second only to his father's. Brightly colored saltwater fish swam with glee in their fifty-gallon tank to the right of the entrance.

Her gaze flickered to the expensive furniture, hitching on the mahogany desk. Her mouth dried. Many a time, her bare skin was on a first-name basis with the cool wood while under Adrian's vigilant care.

"Hey, beautiful." Adrian flashed her a magnificent smile when he looked up from his computer monitor. "You look fabulous. The press is going to eat you up," he complimented, taking in her business apparel.

Joci caught herself twirling a strand of her long hair between two fingers. She'd straightened it today, but she hadn't nailed down the reason why. Of course, Adrian preferred it straight, which was why she kept her hair hidden away in a curly ponytail or an artistic bun. *Yes, that is the reason why.* Surely there wasn't an outside force that urged her change.

"Thanks. You all set?" She closed the door and leaned her hands on the brass handle. "I think you should take the question-and-answer bit. I'll do the headlines, then let you wrap up. The women will prefer that."

"Sure." Adrian wheeled his chair from his desk and studied her. "Everything okay?"

Knowing her act of closing the door gave away her plan, Joci inhaled slowly. Even to her, she was acting odd, but she was determined to clear her mind. Quinn was part of her reasoning, but when it came down to it, her sudden moral dilemma could be pinpointed to one person alone: the cheeky bastard on the top floor.

Cameron swarmed her mind like a honeybee to a budding flower. His warning of her womanly wiles put her on edge.

Despite having Quinn to dispel the memory of Cameron, he didn't help. Sleeping with Quinn only made her more pissed at herself. He wasn't who she wanted between the sheets. It was rather unsettling, the way the mafia man slithered into her subconscious and forced her to stare at the problems she ignored. He told her to stop promising Adrian a chance. As time went on, she had to agree. She didn't want to lead Adrian on. There was nothing there any longer. She also couldn't pretend she felt no connection with Cameron.

"Actually, yes, I wanted to talk to you about something." She placed her hands on her stomach to settle the anxious bubbles.

"Oh my God, did Quinn knock you up?" Adrian blasted, shooting up to his feet. "That worthless bastard! I'm going to kill him myself!" His face turned a shade of red she had never seen before as he spewed explicit words.

"Adrian, stop. I'm not pregnant," she insisted, hustling to his side. Placing her hands in his, she felt his pulse slow. "I want to discuss us."

His blue eyes shrouded in confusion. "What's there to discuss? I have until the end of the case." Eyeing her with suspicion, he added, "Don't I?"

Joci swallowed the nervous energy. "I've enjoyed working with you these last few months. It's like it used to be," she started. "But I'm not convinced there is anything between us other than great teamwork." She left out the part where she'd seen him in his office with the pretty blonde and overheard him talking about a suspicious boss.

His brow wrinkled. "Like a spark?"

She bobbed her head. "More or less."

"Oh, okay. Well, I can help with that."

Joci parted her lips to answer but Adrian was suddenly there. He pulled her against his chest and tucked her hair behind her ears. Breathing shallowly, she met his electric blue gaze. His lips encompassed hers as her mind spun out of control. He tasted the same as the man she'd once loved. His Ralph Lauren cologne intoxicated her senses like every other time.

As she kissed him back, her gut churned. There was something wrong with their embrace. Too many memories were built into his lips that she couldn't erase. It was gone; the spark, the trust they'd once owned that shone brighter than the starry night, had dissolved somewhere between years one and two. His secretive behavior at the office didn't help convince her either. Trusting him never came easy.

Detaching from him, Joci cautiously opened her eyes. To her utter amazement, a smirk covered Adrian's lips. He brushed his hands up and down her back.

"I thought it would never go away," he confessed with a sad shake of his head.

"So did I."

"Don't get me wrong, I'm not happy about this, but the timing needs to be right. It isn't at the moment, and I can accept that." He kissed her cheek tenderly. "We may not have a spark, but I'll always love you." Adrian held her hand in his. "And that includes helping you commit felonies if the opportunity is warranted."

Joci giggled but was glad they were on the same page.

It made her indiscretions easier to accept. She didn't have to worry about Adrian being envious of the time she spent with Quinn or anyone else. "Then does this mean you want your key back and you'll walk me down the aisle when I find a firecracker?"

Backing up, Adrian rolled his eyes. "Yeah, I'll take the key, but I won't be walking you down any aisle. You already knew that, smartass."

"Just had to hear you say it," she teased, a weight lifted from her shoulders. Adrian wouldn't pursue her with his affections. He was there for her, but only in the way two people who shared the same heartache can be. If the time ever came to cross the line, she would be the moving force, not him.

"Now that the situation is all cleared up, shall we go kick some media booty?" he asked, pulling on his suit jacket.

"Let's."

They made it to the door before he added, "But if we're both single at forty, you're marrying me for real this time."

A laugh filled his office as Joci tried to stay sane. "What, the first one wasn't good enough for you?"

Adrian glanced to the ceiling then back to her. "Nope. Definitely not."

"All right, counselor, but I guarantee that you will be married by thirty-eight. Thirty-nine, tops," she predicted as they walked out of the room.

"As long as you're the flower girl, who cares?" he played along as they headed to the elevator.

Joci slapped his arm in jest. If anyone overheard their

conversation, they would be in trouble. Their relationship was complicated, but cleared for friendship. Nodding, she felt better about her path. *Then why do I sense that it's not enough?* she wondered as the elevator descended to the group of wolves with cameras and microphones.

— — —

"What the bloody fucking hell are they doing?" Cameron yelled when he flipped on the news. Rayna had told him to tune in, but he was sorely disturbed by the press conference his defense team was having without his knowledge.

Panic shot him through the roof at the mention of his name across the airwaves. "Bad. This is very bad." He fumbled with the cell phone and dialed Joci's number. For apparent reasons, she didn't answer, but he did hear the jingle on the news station. Adrian didn't answer either, but when Rayna failed to take his call, Cameron felt physically ill.

He sank onto the floor as Joci's ruby lips informed the media about the case and the potential of it being a wrong place-wrong time situation instead of coldblooded murder. He was as good as dead once Jerry got wind of the attention the suits were bringing. "He's going to assassinate me in my sleep." He was supposed to be quiet about the mob, but his attorneys were throwing Del Rossi and Mikkelsen across the airwaves like it didn't matter.

To his relief, Adrian accepted only five questions about why they believed Cameron's case was strong before the man wrapped it up with finesse. Cameron hated to admit it, but his lawyers were efficient and looked damn confident in front of journalists who were curious at the tactics they'd use at trial.

"Well, they are too freaking confident," he scoffed, redialing Joci's number when she was clear of the cameras.

"Cameron, what's wrong?" she asked, picking up the call at last. "You called a dozen times. Are you all right?"

"Both of you get up here," he directed. "Now!" He ended the call before she could talk her way out of his wrath. It wouldn't be difficult either. She spoke like a siren and drew him in like a vixen. But when their lips collided, she was kryptonite he never saw coming.

Pacing the floor, he racked his mind for any Ohio phone number. The cops had confiscated his cell phone as evidence. He wasn't sure why since his phone didn't kill the guy, but they still took it and hadn't returned it. Memorizing numbers wasn't something he'd thought to do since the first grade. He needed to get word back to his superiors before the Danish prick sent a stronger message—to wipe him out for good this time.

"Have you calmed down yet?" Joci inquired from the entry.

Storming to the door, Cameron paused when she met his eyes. God, but she was more majestic in person than on television. He shoved that thought aside and pointed his index finger. "You should have told me about that display downstairs *before* you did it."

"Why? So you could participate?" Adrian mocked. "You aren't getting anywhere near a television camera."

Cameron pulled on his hair in fury. He would pull it all out if he wasn't careful. "I don't want all of this attention."

"Why not? We're trying to subtly influence the potential jurors who see our conference. They need to view you as a man who was at the wrong place at the wrong time," Joci reminded him. "We normally don't hold that kind of conference, but we thought it'd help. If the jurors only saw what the news channels ran at the beginning of the case, they'll have a predisposed judgment of you."

Rapidly, he nodded. He knew the plan. Rayna had explained it to him last week in a doleful manner. It was a good one too. Except he was none of what they thought him to be. Sure, he wasn't guilty of that crime, but he was no innocent. Mob names weren't supposed to leak either. He'd blame Adrian for the oversight since it was probably his idea. He was in the pocket of the Mikkelsens, after all.

"If I die before my case makes it to a jury, what good was all your scheming?"

Adrian folded his arms. "What do you mean? What aren't you telling us, Mr. Shearer?"

Cameron let out a ragged breath. "Forget it. Just tell the guards to load their guns," he mumbled. "Nice knowing you. Please, no roses on my casket. They're clichéd."

His team exchanged a silent conversation, and then Adrian silently and swiftly slipped out the door. Alone with Joci, Cameron's mind decelerated and he sensed his blood pressure lower.

"Do you want a drink?" she offered, heading to the kitchen. "Oh wait, you probably shouldn't." She shrugged.

"But I could use one." She chuckled. "Or five. I'll let you have one, though. Drinking alone sucks. It'll be our little secret. Just like when we snuck bottles of pop into the movie theater."

Unenthusiastically, he followed. The stocked bar was one perk he hadn't indulged in since arriving. He didn't want to pay for it later. Plus, the need to drink only presented itself when Joci was around.

"Sure, I guess." He took a seat at one of the barstools and watched her concoct two drinks with an opened bottle of scotch.

"What's that called?" he questioned when she placed the tumbler in front of him. Guardedly, he took a sip. It was delicious. "Whoa, it's good."

Joci wiped up a spill. "Don't act so amazed." She grinned. "It's a Loch Ness Mystery. One of the popular ones I made when I bartended."

"You were a bartender?" He laughed when his voice went up a notch.

She took the seat next to him, her suit jacket long discarded. "Yep. I kept doing it even after I got this job, but only part-time. Once I started taking on cases, I worked a few shifts a month. It helped pass the time when my significant other was out gambling." Her eyes took on a faraway glint. "It was my favorite job outside of this one."

"Why's that? I'd bet pervs hit on you all the time," he guessed.

"I supposed that played into why I stopped, but I liked meeting people from different walks of life. The intrigue kept me there," Joci disclosed, tasting the drink.

He took a larger sip. "What was the reason, then?"

Her middle finger traced the rim of the glass. "For the most part because my job took over my life."

Always spotting her half-truths, he prodded further. "I'm not going anywhere, and we have a shit-ton of booze, so spill."

She turned her hazel eyes toward him and raised her glass. He watched as she drained the unique mixture. "Personal details."

"Could you be any more vague?" he wondered aloud.

"I could, yes, but I'll tell you." Joci leaned over and snatched his empty glass. "I got pregnant," she said, mingling something new with the booze. "And the guy I was with at the time didn't want me wasting my free time when I should be at home instead."

Wary of how to respond, he stayed mute and watched her flip liquor bottles around like it was second nature.

"Yeah, I don't fit the mom part, do I?" She laughed when she met his eyes, then grabbed a lime from the refrigerator.

"No, it's not that." He faltered. "You don't talk about a kid, so I assumed you didn't have any."

She splashed ginger ale with the liquor, then garnished the glasses with lime wedges. "There's a reason I don't talk about my son."

"And why is that?" he asked in a soft tone.

Joci pressed her lips to the cup. "He died," she stated, her voice heavy with sadness.

Sorrow scattered in his veins. He couldn't imagine what

her loss felt like. "Oh, Joci, I'm so sorry."

"Thanks. Me too."

Scrutinizing her intently, Cameron admired her ability to open up about such a private affair. It was clear she did it for a motive having to do with his case. Despite her efforts, he couldn't trust her. He wanted to do just that, but baring his soul wasn't a skill of his.

He polished off the second drink without hesitation. Comprehension hit him like a book across the face. "Wait. Adrian was the dad, wasn't he?"

"Bravo, Mr. Holmes," she joshed. "But yes, Adrian was my baby daddy."

"Do you mind if I ask what happened?" He wanted to know, but he also understood he would have to share some kind of secret too.

"It was a vendetta killing," she recalled. "An angry client took his misfortune out on us the same day we left the hospital. Our son wasn't even a week old when he died in a car crash."

Cameron's heart broke for her. He watched as she drained her glass, then met his gaze. "I don't know what to say," he divulged.

She lifted her glass in salute. "No one ever does. It's all good."

Joci propped her head up on her hand. Her glasses were lopsided. The urge to pull those damn frames from her eyes overtook him, but he refrained. She cleared her throat and rolled her neck. Clearly she was done with the exposé into her past.

"I'll bet you hate it here by now. All alone in a massive place. I'd be losing my sanity."

He surveyed her appearance. Her hair was pin straight today, no doubt for the television crews. "Nah, I can't say I mind anymore. Not with my present company. I rather like her."

"I doubt that very much," Joci argued, her lips secured to the bottle. "But thanks," she said into the glass neck.

A drip of brown liquid slipped down her mouth, and Cameron watched it in agony. It would be much too easy to lean over and lick it from her bottom lip. Still, he held his body at bay. Anytime he was alone with Joci, all he craved was to slam her against the wall and pull her hair until she begged for him to ravish her.

If he'd learned anything from her ignoring face-to-face contact, it was that she wasn't interested in him. Yet the way she caressed his tattoos with her eyes disproved his thoughts.

"One of these days, you have to tell me about your tats." She stood, then paused. "Do you want to talk about what happened at the press conference?"

"No."

"Oh please. You reacted the same way as during depositions. I saw how upset you got when I mentioned the mob names. My guess is I would've seen the same thing if I was up here during the conference. It's part of discovery, Cam. I need to find out if they were involved."

"You're playing with fire." He rubbed his lips together. *I really need to get lip balm.* "Look, when you say mob names, it scares the public and fucks up my plan."

"What plan is that?" She took a step in his direction.

"I'm trying to find a rat."

"And they don't have those in Chicago?"

He chuckled at her obviously manufactured blonde moment. "Wrong kind, sweetie. Part of the reason I came to Iowa was to find out who'd been helping the Mikkelsens get traction in the US. They were a blip on our radar until money transfers started coming through an Iowa bank."

"You think the person is here and he or she is watching your case."

"Not only that, I think they manufactured the case to keep me from uncovering the truth."

"Shit, Cameron, this is serious." Her brow furrowed in worry. It was adorable.

"My life is rarely carefree."

Joci locked up the liquor and twirled on her toes. "You should've told me about this. I would've been more discreet."

Letting his eyes trace her business outfit, he did his best to keep his hands from ripping off the damn thing. Her genuine care for his safety started a part of his heart he thought broken for all time.

"I'll try to be more upfront from now on, all right?"

Joci nodded and clutched her coat. "For now, I have a brief that's not going to write itself."

Feeling responsible for her need to leave, Cameron followed her to the front door. "Have fun with that."

"Oh you know it." She gripped the handle as if waiting

for something to happen.

Cameron took that as a step in the right direction, so he offered, "You know, you can work up here sometime if you ever need a little time away from the office. I'll be as quiet as a church mouse."

She studied him as if contemplating the option. "Stay out of trouble, okay? I don't want to lose you again."

He nodded but was somewhat aggravated when she ended their visit. He would've preferred a similar scene to their farewell that ended in falling asleep together, but mixing business with murder never resulted in happy tears. For the time being, he would wait to hear from the woman who piqued his interest more at every interaction.

CHAPTER TEN

Stirring vanilla creamer into her cup of coffee, Joci lost track of how long she had been sitting in her office. Time ticked by as her brew cooled. Interns buzzed by the door and construction workers drilled the new flooring in, but she remained frozen in her chair.

Other than the short amount of time she and Quinn hooked up for some post-deposition hate sex, she hadn't even thought about him. Sure, they were tense thanks to the case, but it was as if her body wouldn't allow her to entertain the thought of another man. She wanted to spend time with Cameron, not Quinn. *Fucking weird*, she noted, sipping the brew. Casual flings were fine. Until Cameron showed up. He made her want more and that realization frightened her.

Her calendar for the day stared back at her from the computer. Cameron's second round of depositions was that afternoon, and for the first time in her career, Joci was nervous about the outcome of the day's events. She lifted the paisley mug to her lips and winced at the cold liquid.

This feeling was creepy. Depositions were her forte on most cases. For an unknown reason, this case was different. The client was different. She and Adrian had prepared the night before for the remaining few witnesses. They just had the band members, who were being deposed via telephone since they were in California, the handful of police officers who secured the crime scene, and the emergency response team. Altogether, the depositions shouldn't take more than the morning hours.

Their client called twice a day for the last two weeks, but Joci answered once, if at all. Instead of going to see him, she took the coward's way out and sent Rayna, a task the woman was beginning to dread, since Cameron sent her packing within minutes. He didn't want Rayna or Adrian—he wanted her. Making a mental note to scold him for that behavior later, Joci pushed aside the coffee. Even if she wanted to see him too, she couldn't encourage their connection beyond attorney and client.

"Hey, do you want to grab a bite real quick?" Adrian proposed, strolling into her office. He flipped on the light as he entered. "I see you're going green again."

Peeking up, Joci momentarily regretted their joint decision to call it quits on their romantic endeavors. Adrian looked intriguing today with a fuchsia shirt tucked neatly beneath a midnight-black suit.

"I had a headache, but yes, food sounds good." She stood and grabbed her full cup. "It seems I was too distracted to drink my coffee, so I could use the energy."

Stealing the mug from her, Adrian smirked. "Now that

doesn't sound like the caffeine addict I know." He placed it back on the desk. "What's going on?"

"The case. I'm antsy." She swung her navy-blue jacket over her shoulders. "He's hiding some part of his tale. I'm afraid it's going to be the final nail in his coffin."

"Hmm. If that's all it takes, I'll grab the hammer."

Joci offered him a condemning glare. "Seriously?"

Adrian chuckled and patted her shoulder. "No? Well, okay. All we can do is our damnedest to guide him to the best outcome possible. You know the speech. We're doing all we can. It's the most we can offer our clients."

Tucking her shirt back into her pants, Joci shook her head. "I know. I just have this feeling." She waved her arm. "Forget it."

Linking his arm through hers, Adrian guided his coworker through the office. "If you think there's more, I believe you."

They passed a group of fresh intern blood, and Joci was shocked that he didn't eyeball the pretty faces. "Thanks."

"I don't want you to get hurt. Your sense of danger has always been on point. I trust you." He snagged the elevator button. "And if you feel this strongly that your coffee mantra is out of whack, then I'll do whatever it takes to make you buzzed again," he teased.

Joci followed him onto the elevator. "You know, maybe I was wrong about you," she said as the doors closed. "There could be hope for us after all."

Shrugging, Adrian released his grip on her arm and glanced at her. "I keep hoping, but I don't hold my breath.

Not when a lady like yourself has a cop on one arm and her mind full of a tattooed scoundrel."

She shoved him. "The first is a friend, and the second is a client and old chum. I have to be focused on him."

Smiling, Adrian poked her side. "Focused and obsessed are two entirely different beasts."

Joci frowned. "I'm obsessing over Cameron's case, not the man himself."

"Uh-huh, sure. Is that why you send Rayna to do your dirty work?" He leaned back against the steel wall. "Or are you too afraid of what might happen if you spend more time with him?"

Flipping her hair over her shoulders, she straightened her back. "You're insane. He's my client. *Our* client. All I'm afraid of is whether he strangles me or not." She offered him a haughty grin. "And I, for one, am fond of my neck." The door slid open and she concluded, "Last I checked, you were too."

Adrian shadowed her off the elevator and wound his arm around her waist. "Oh I am, believe me, but I think Cameron is a tad infatuated with it too. In the non-homicidal way."

Joci's lips parted but she clamped them shut. She knew as much, which was why she strayed from visiting. "Come on, you tease. I'm famished, and we need our strength to tackle these witnesses."

Holding the front door open for her, Adrian lowered his voice. "Now, now, counselor, I don't think it's acceptable to jump anyone while they're on the stand. Better wait until a recess."

Shooting him a devious grin, she shot back, "Aw, come on, Adrian, where's the fun in waiting?"

— — —

Bouncing his legs up and down in worry, Cameron sat at the table and awaited the first person for questioning. It was a different location than the first round of depositions. This room was intimate but less than inviting, with the stern county attorneys and carefree deputy chatting at the table opposite them. No judge occupied the top of the bench, but it put him on edge. Judges never looked on him in kindness. Of course, his sharp tongue was the reason the majority of the time.

Glancing to his left, he saw Adrian review the pages of questions. The male attorney was the epitome of business today. He much preferred the laid-back attire Adrian had sported yesterday when he dropped off the latest case pleadings. He wanted to strangle the man for putting Joci in a compromising position. It didn't help that he'd heard from Jerry. He shared the information about Adrian, but begged the boss not to act yet. Somehow, he'd figure out a way to get the Mikkelsens out of the Del Rossis' territory without Adrian or Joci paying. Even though he wasn't a Del Rossi hitman, he could see Jerry demanding blood penance for Adrian's crime. He wouldn't subject himself to such an act. He'd done some crazy shit, but he could never hurt Joci in any way.

Settled smack-dab between his defense team, Cameron didn't mind swiveling his head to the right. The unique-eyed brunette was ravishing as usual in her blue suit. Her demeanor was aloof since greeting him. He chalked it up to the handcuffs he'd had on up until five minutes ago. She hadn't looked pleased when she caught sight of them. He, on the other hand, could think of several uses for the cuffs that involved Joci.

"So, do we sit here all day and get bored or what?" he asked, tapping her hand.

Joci slanted her eyes toward him. "Be patient. We're waiting on the police officers who were at the crime scene to begin. It seems they got caught up on a call." She jotted on her notepad. "Their interview won't be long since they simply held down the perimeter while the technicians went over the scene."

Cameron heard Adrian move his chair back.

"I'll be back. Going to grab coffee," Adrian stated, not looking at either of them.

"I take mine with cream and sugar," Cameron called with a cheesy grin.

The redhead didn't acknowledge his order, so Cameron turned his body to face Joci. "I take it you and Mr. Expensive Suit are still on the path of rekindling your asthmatic love."

Joci dropped her pen and shoved a pad of paper his way. "Write down any questions or notes you have during the interviews. We may need them later on for cross-examination." She handed him a pen. "And no talking," she directed, her face strict.

Cameron eyed the yellow pad and blue pen. "I'm going to take that as a yes."

"Not that it's any of your business, but no, Adrian and I aren't trying to get back together," she mumbled beneath her breath.

Leaning forward in his chair, he locked his fingers behind his head. "Ooh, I get it. You need someone beefy like the cop who arrested me."

She let out a frustrated breath. "Quinn and I are friends," she stressed. "With occasional benefits," she added with enough speed to beat a cheetah.

Cameron's brow shot up. That wasn't what he'd expected to hear. A woman like Joci deserved more than a nonchalant booty call with any man. "How come? I'd bet my conviction that the cop would bend over backward for more than a casual fling."

"Quinn knows my intentions," Joci informed him briskly, then turned the questioning back on him. "God, you're being annoying today. Why do you care, anyway?"

As if on cue, a muscular police officer he didn't recognize sauntered through the door with another man at his side. "Are all the cops in Iowa hot or just the ones on my case?" muttered Cameron. He eyeballed Joci and was disappointed by the marvelous smile she shot both officers. He didn't like the hint that she was still hooking up with Quinn. She hadn't outright said it, but she didn't deny it either. He felt something when they kissed, but evidently it was one-sided.

Adrian appeared with three cups of joe. Rigidly, he nodded to the policemen, then returned to the table. "Sorry, they were all out of sugar," he noted, placing a coffee in front of him. "Not that I asked for any."

Cameron sipped the drink. "Mmm, bitter like your soul," he commented.

"Shut up," Adrian snapped.

Joci hushed them with her words. "Both of you need to sit still, look pretty, and watch how the master works." She pushed up off the table and nodded to the court reporter. "Let's begin, shall we?"

Cameron watched in reverent awe. Joci dominated the interviews with more class than he thought possible. If this were the trial, he'd bet the farm on her presentation. *No wonder Adrian wants her back. She's incredible.*

He sat there all morning, just taking in the experience. Joci was his favorite part of the day, but he had to give props to Adrian. These depositions paled when compared to how the ruthless attorney carved out reasonable doubt with the state's witnesses last month. For the first time since his arrest, Cameron felt confident in his defense. Jerry wouldn't let him rot without proper aid, but the Mikkelsens created a solid crime. Hell, if he didn't know from the get-go that he was framed, he'd be betting money on an acquittal.

His bandmates were no help for either side. Each one played dumb, an easy trait for the guys most likely smoking pot for the duration of the phone deposition. He knew they'd be worthless, but Jerry was paying good money for him to watch Joci at work. He might as well enjoy it.

After three hours, the team called it quits for the day. He was thrilled until the courtroom door swung open and Officer Quinn poked his head inside. He tried not to groan, but when Joci beamed at the man and ambled over to his side, the sound escaped. From his position, he couldn't hear what they were saying, but he wasn't alone in his dismal attitude. "Don't do it," he warned under his breath when Quinn leaned over to Joci.

"Oh, he's going to do it," Adrian pointed out. "He likes to make public displays."

The two men watched in anticipation, then grumbled in unison when the sturdy officer bent down and pulled Joci in for a hug. "Isn't that unprofessional? I mean, he's the person who arrested me. She deposed him last month."

Adrian placed the files into his brown briefcase. "Yes, but not completely. Separating work and pleasure doesn't come easy in the legal field." He gripped the handle tight. "I didn't think it would be this bad, but it's torture."

"You love her," Cameron assumed, his gaze locked on the officer and lawyer.

"How I feel about her isn't going to change her mind. She is the only one who can do that," Adrian advised, then nodded to the deputy. "I think your ride is here. I'll talk to you tomorrow. Rayna will bring over the transcripts when they come in, and then we'll need to go over them."

Leaving Joci to fawn over her beau, Cameron surrendered to the deputy at the door. "We can go now. I'm through."

The deputy clicked on the handcuffs and grunted. "This will all catch up, Shearer. Prison won't be fun for a guy like you."

Cameron took one last glance at the tall brunette before shrugging. "It's not like I have the royal treatment here either."

They made their way out of the courthouse and to the waiting van outside. Cameron couldn't wait to get out of the monkey suit, but he wasn't fond of the mandatory cuffs that accompanied him on the ride back to the firm.

When he was escorted into the penthouse jail cell, Cameron was stunned to see that Joci awaited his return in the living room.

"Come to gloat?" he greeted, ripping off his tie. It fluttered to the floor and landed in a heap. All he wanted to do was rinse off the day's events and fall into the fluffy feather comforter.

"Hello to you too," she shot back with a grin. "But no, my gloating can wait until after we win the case. Depos only give the prosecution time to hone their side."

Cameron kicked his shoes to the rug. "All right, then why are you here instead of smooching the cop?" He gave her a pointed scowl. "I saw the two of you canoodling in the courthouse. Pretty sure he was about to bang you like the gun in his holster if everyone cleared the room in time."

Standing, she wrinkled her nose. "Wow, okay. That was rude and random, but kinda funny too." She threaded her hands together. "I thought you could use a little company, maybe play a game or something, but seeing how you're in a mood, I'll leave you to your misery." In one quick move, Joci crossed the room in a path avoiding him.

Rubbing his face, he growled. "No, wait. Don't go. I'm sorry. I guess I'm tired."

"It's fine. I'll come by another time."

Cameron caught up to her within seconds and snagged

her hands. "Please don't." Her wrist felt so smooth that he couldn't help but rub his thumb along it.

"Ugh, you never change. You were an ass when we were kids and you didn't get your way and even more so now." Joci paused and spun around. "Why do you frustrate me so?" she wondered aloud.

"Because I don't know how to act around you," he disclosed. She offered him a confused glance, so he explained. "You're stunning, Joci. I've known that since we were ten. I could handle that fact if you were a bitch or if you were in love with some guy."

"How do you know I'm not?"

Her pulse thumped against his thumb. "Are you?"

She met his gaze and rubbed her lips together. If she was trying to torment him, it was working. "That's not your concern."

Cameron cupped her face and searched her stunning eyes. "You made it my concern when you told me about Adrian and the cop."

"Quinn," she input.

"Whatever. I don't care." He pulled her face closer to him, her fragrant body surrounding his senses. "All I want to do is kiss you until I can't breathe."

Joci's eyes flashed a warning and her sharp intake of breath told him exactly what he needed.

"But I can't do that."

Her brow lifted in confusion. "Why not?"

He traced his index finger along her jaw and rested on her lips. "Because I'm a horrible person." His eyes drifted to her neck. It beckoned to him, but not nearly as much as what lay beneath her shirt. "I would ruin you." He parted her lips with his finger. "Plus, I don't play well with others, and you have two very eloquent men clamoring for your affections."

"That's a pathetic slew of excuses," she confided, placing her hands on his chest. Her fingers drifted to the buttons and popped them open one by one.

Cameron's body reacted violently to the sultry tone of her actions. "Joci, I'm not a good guy. I've done things that would cause relentless nightmares."

Pausing her fingers on the last button, Joci met his gaze. "And you think you're alone?" She ripped open his shirt. "I paid off a dozen guards so I could have ten minutes alone with the crook who ended my family. Do you know what I did? I sent in lifetime prisoners to have a few uninterrupted minutes with him," she revealed.

Her eyes went from raging to regretful as he watched her. "But I got my revenge and so did Adrian. He had his own score to settle with the group that came after us." Joci traced his white shirt, her hands outlining the tattoos on his arms. "So you see, I'm a horrid person too. You don't scare me."

She pressed every switch in his body. Gorgeous and a vengeance streak? They were more alike than he initially thought. *Fuck, she's perfect.* His emotions raging, Cameron gave in to his body's demands and thrust her against the wall, his mouth devouring hers. She tasted as scrumptious as she smelled, but he needed more. His hands dove into her hair, crudely yanking her toward him. Her tongue dallied with his so intimately that he swore she was sent from heaven or hell or wherever goddesses hailed from.

"Damn, you have no idea how long I've wanted to do that," he confessed between kisses. She moaned in response, waking him from the situation. "Watching you today was torture. Every damn day apart from you is torture."

Abruptly, he tore away from her lips. He couldn't do this. He couldn't involve her any more than her job required. Jerry would have his head if he didn't figure out a way to get rid of the Mikkelsens. As badly as he wanted to explore every inch of her body, he couldn't. Not yet. She needed to stay as far away from him as possible. "But I killed him. I killed the man from the park."

Bit by bit, Joci's face shadowed at his statement. "What did you say?"

Cameron took in the slight swell of her rosy lips and cleared his throat. "I murdered Nitty Nichols, then passed out." He repeated the lie, willing her to believe him.

"No," she uttered. "No, you didn't."

"I did," he stated, backing away from her. "Still want to jump me?"

Disbelief flickered across her face, as well as overwhelming concern. She shook her head, but he could tell the words affected her. "I should go…." Her sentence dropped off, and she hurried out the door.

Pressing his fists against his forehead, Cameron closed his eyes tight and listened for the ding of the elevator. Once he was positive she was on a safe descent to the ground level, he flipped them open again. He willed her to accept his falsehood. "It's the only way she'll be safe," he told the empty apartment. If she didn't buy it, he would lose her too.

— — —

Knocking back a third shot of tequila, Joci ripped off her work shirt. It was smothering her just like her thoughts about Cameron. At last, all she wore was a white camisole. The entire car ride home, she'd cursed herself for stooping so low as to kiss Cameron again. It wasn't an act she completely regretted, though. He kissed with more fervor than any other man she'd locked lips with.

Somewhere during their embrace, he'd decided to push her away with his lie. She didn't believe his confession. It was too coincidental with their frisky moves. He had to be protecting her, but from whom, she wasn't sure. The Mikkelsen mob had no problems with her, so why would she need his protection? *What if he really did kill the guy and being close to me made him want to tell the truth?* She clenched her eyes together at the potential answer. *No.* His constant flirting didn't make sense if he was prepared to go to prison. She couldn't believe he killed someone. He admitted to being in Iowa on mob business, but there was more to the story. More he wouldn't tell. *What if he discovered the person helping the mob?* Either way, she shouldn't have allowed herself to be enraptured by Cameron once more. It was too easy when he was in the same room.

She studied her apartment in silence. Not an article of furniture was out of place. Any other day, that fact would reassure her, but today it made her feel hollow. She'd never dreamt of reaching thirty and having no family to push her insanity over the edge. Her parents were happy smoking pot in Colorado, and her one sibling was busy overseas.

"I have no one," she lamented, tears forming in her eyes. "It wasn't supposed to be like this." She held back the tears threatening to spill. Lying to herself was getting her nowhere. She told Quinn and Adrian she didn't want a serious relationship, but the more she went along with that notion, the less content she felt. Sure, having sexy hookups was fun, but they didn't cuddle her at night when a strange sound scared her awake. Shaking the mattress got her where she needed to go physically, but emotionally, she was empty. She missed the comradery of another person being around to enjoy a meal together.

She glanced to the kitchen. It was sparse of food since she rarely ate at home. The apartment was too lonely, she now grasped. It was why she threw herself into her job. She had no one to come home to and talk about their challenges with work. Each passing day reiterated her isolation despite trying to dissuade it. She couldn't anymore. Since seeing Cameron, she didn't want to kiss Quinn anymore; she didn't want to give a second chance to her ex-husband; she wasn't satisfied with casual relationships, but at the moment it was all she wanted. It didn't make sense since Cameron was almost a stranger. Somewhere deep in her soul told her the reason why. Accepting it was a whole different argument. Before spending time with Cameron, she was satisfied with flirting with Quinn and Adrian. Even if she slept with either of them, it didn't matter; she wasn't seeking anything but a good time, and Quinn accepted that.

"Dammit, Cam." Rubbing her lips together, she craved his touch on them. It wasn't like Quinn's or even Adrian's. It was all his own, possessive and familiar. It was what she dreamed about when she should've been focused on paying bills. She'd done her best to avoid the ex-con throughout the entire case, but he consistently pushed to the front of her mind when she was waiting for coffee or filing a petition. He was engrained in her memory, and now all the childish feelings she had for him when they were younger amplified when she took on his case. Their brief exchanges floated in her mind. She'd bet her savings account that he felt something real for her. It was why she kept distance between them. *So the only reason he's pushing me away is because of the case.* If they weren't nearing his trial, would it be different? Would she want to dip her toes into the proverbial dating pool with a relationship as the prize?

She shuffled to the spare bedroom that she'd transformed into a library. It was meant to be a nursery, but she never got the opportunity to design it. Instead, books piled up in orderly fashion on massive bookshelves.

Stepping into the room, she ran her fingers along the first edition books Adrian had bought. They were expensive, but looking at them made her head spin when she recalled each time he gave one to her. They would read the dusty things together, then create sweet havoc with their bodies. A sad smile crept over her lips. Those were the memories she adored, desperately coveting their renewal. Back then, she was happy. She was secure in her life, and it was all abruptly ripped away. She couldn't blame Adrian as much as she wanted to. They both let their relationship fade.

Joci's mind drifted to her recent encounter with Cameron. Somehow, he dove into her brain and found what she wanted him to do. It drove her mad. She didn't crave a fast fuck, not any longer. Quinn could offer that without a problem. She'd bet Adrian could too. But her body needed something different, something she hadn't had in a very long time. She wanted an emotional experience. With Cameron. He was the only man to make her realize how empty her life was. The irony wasn't lost to her either. "Fuck," she mumbled at the damning revelation.

"But he doesn't want me," she reminded herself. "Or he does and won't admit it."

Her body jonesing for an intimate touch, Joci retreated to the kitchen. After swallowing a mouthful of tequila, she gripped her cell phone. She had two options, though neither man was whom her body desired. If she drank enough tequila, she'd march right back to the apartment and exploit more than just the reasoning behind Cameron protecting her.

She couldn't have the man she wanted for obvious reasons, but she needed something. Someone. She needed someone to patch a bandage over her brittle heart caused by Cameron's rejection. Sending a message to the one man she'd written off, Joci didn't have to wait long for a response. He did live five minutes away, after all, so his journey wouldn't be difficult. She took a swig of the liquor, her mind swimming in apprehension. This was but a small part of what she wanted. These were the cards she was dealt, and if Cameron could shove her aside, then she would mirror his façade.

By the time she polished off half of the bottle, the doorbell rang. Staggering to the entrance, she swung the door open and offered her visitor a loopy smile.

"Joci, what's wrong? You said you needed me as soon as possible." Adrian's worry-lined forehead made her giggle.

"Oh I do need you," she advised, yanking him into the apartment. She slammed the door shut and pushed him against it. "I need you here," she said, turning the lock. "There." She nodded to the couch. "And everywhere in between."

Adrian's blue eyes clouded in longing, but he kept his hands at his sides. "Are you sure?" He leaned close. "You smell like you've had a few, and we just agreed to tap the brakes on us."

Joci shrugged her camisole from her shoulders, followed by her bra. "Oh, I'm very sure. I want you." She ran her tongue along his earlobe, resulting in a guttural groan. "Adrian, screw me like you mean it."

In one swift move, Adrian switched places with her and kissed her nape. With the cool metal door pressed against her, Joci was shocked at his zeal. This was nothing like the man she knew two years ago.

Hoisting her off the floor, Adrian's slipped his fingers into her pants. It was more than enough for her. Arching her back, Joci gasped when his teeth sank into her shoulder.

She ran her hands over his back, pulling up his shirt as they went. He tossed the useless item from his body before she could rip it to shreds.

Adrian shoved her pants off her hips and stared at her silky red underwear. "Damn, I've missed this."

Unwrapping her legs from his waist, Joci yanked his slacks down his legs. "Me too," she murmured when she took in his toned torso. Her head tilted to the side when her eyes took in his boxer briefs. "A lot."

After ridding them both of the last of their clothes, Adrian trapped her between the door and his body. His warmth spread through her more than the tequila in her blood.

"What made you change your mind?" he asked, his hand enveloping her bare breast.

Nipping at his neck, Joci caught his face with her hands. His blue eyes pinned her to the spot more than his body ever could. If she allowed them to cross the invisible line, she couldn't draw a new one.

"I missed you." She nibbled on his lip. "Us. I missed us together." Her eyes drifted down the front of his body. "Plus, you were so fucking sexy today. The two of us shredding the prosecution just like old times."

Not needing any other incentive, Adrian met her lips ravenously. Joci closed her eyes, taking in every trace of lust he scattered along her skin. She may be tipsy, but she needed this, even if she would probably regret it in the morning.

— — —

Cameron woke in a cold sweat in the middle of the night.

Sitting up, he gasped for breath. Patting the spot beside him, he frowned when he found it empty. "Joci," he mumbled, but saw no one had disrupted the bedding.

Inhaling the cold air, he sighed. "It was a dream. She's okay." He'd never been worried about his girlfriends' safety when he was in Ohio. Hell, the few he had didn't stay long, though they'd always been protected thanks to his mob. But now, Joci wasn't in his care. She was God knew where and alone. All alone. He ran a hand through his hair. He didn't want to revisit the rest of the dream where she'd been taken by J.J. The following scenes were far worse than a mere kidnapping. The prick had killed her because he wouldn't give up on the Del Rossi assignment. If Cameron knew what he did now, he wasn't sure if he'd accept the request from Jerry. The time spent with Joci made him shake his head. "No, I would. Even if just to see her again."

He threw off the covers and stood up. The hardwood floor felt like ice to his bare feet, but he ambled to the kitchen nonetheless.

He flipped on the light above the sink and sloshed scotch into a glass. He managed to figure out the code the other day. It wasn't too difficult since Joci didn't cover the panel when she entered the digits. Downing it with no problem, he rested his hands on the counter. Joci. The dream started innocently enough. They hadn't stopped earlier, and she was curled up beside him in bed. God, how he wished it were true!

But it wasn't the part that startled him out of sleep. He took another drink and let out a breath. When J.J. snatched her right out from under his nose, he was stunned out of REM. He thrashed beneath the sheets until his eyes popped open.

He drank straight from the bottle now. Never again did Cameron think he would spin his mind to losing her again. It had broken his heart to wave goodbye to her when they were kids, but losing her forever couldn't happen. He looked forward to whenever she'd stop by to have a slice of pizza in between hearings or when she played poker with him. He licked his lips. It was only regular poker. He couldn't convince her to play the more risqué version of the card game.

"Fuck, I love her. When did that happen?" He knew the truth. They shared more than sexual chemistry and a short history as adults. He'd wondered about her off and on when he did jobs for the mob. Staying sane wasn't easy when his boss was borderline crazy. The memory of having a friend with undying love for him kept him going. He never expected to see her again, but now he couldn't let her go. Now he didn't want any other man to be on the receiving end of the soft gasps he'd pulled from her lips. She was his.

Since the day she brightened the jail with her visit, he knew she was somebody special. How it'd taken him so long to figure it out, he didn't know. Forming attachments with anyone was difficult for him, particularly because of his past and his employer. Taking home the mobster boyfriend to meet the parents never went well in the past, which was why he opted for short relationships or none at all. He wasn't the best boyfriend either, but there was one woman to blame for that.

Pushing the past away, he focused on Joci. He wanted to be the person she relied on whether in court or at home. It was impossible until this J.J. fiasco was wrapped up. He needed to get in touch with Jerry and fast. "But first Joci."

Gripping his head in agony, Cameron wanted to call and tell her everything. He stopped short when he grabbed the phone. "No, I can't."

He'd rejected her and all but shoved her away earlier that day. She wouldn't buy into his madness. Not when she thought he was a killer. Still, he doubted she believed him. Her eyes said as much before she left him alone to sulk. He scratched his head in frustration.

He was a killer. He'd killed whatever mojo they had going. "So now she's gone too."

— — —

Tender fingers laced through Joci's disheveled locks the next morning, slowly waking her. She hummed in contentment, relishing the caress. "That feels good," she professed, opening her eyes.

Adrian's lopsided grin stunned her into reality. He looked rather content, resting a hand on his red hair. "You always were a sucker for a head massage."

Rolling over, she nuzzled into his chest and inhaled. "You know me best."

Silence enveloped the bedroom as Joci snaked her fingers along his naked chest. His skin pebbled under her delicate touch.

"Thank you for texting me," he stated. She opened her

mouth to answer, but he wasn't finished. "Instead of Quinn."

"Adrian," she began, but he turned toward her and silenced her with his lips.

Fire spread over Joci's bones as he held her lips captive.

"I don't know why, but I'm glad you did," he divulged, mere inches from her mouth. "And I get it if you don't want to do it again. We come with baggage, and that's not easy to overlook. I'm happy with the memory of an awesome night of sex, if it's what you want."

Supporting her head with her hand, Joci revisited the night before. Not once had Adrian questioned her intentions during their escapade, nor had she thought of anyone else while beneath the sheets. They were just two people exploring sexual energy together. No strings or memories attached.

Now as a hangover drummed her brain and the morning light cascaded through the window, Joci addressed the ramifications of their act.

"I don't regret it," she stated in all honesty, then smiled. "I guess all of our spark isn't gone after all."

Adrian tugged on her hair and grazed his eyes over the rumpled sheets. "That's fairly obvious."

She blushed at the memory of all the delicious ways they molded together. It had been one of their best qualities when they were a couple. "I don't know what to do the moment we leave this bed," she admitted.

Pulling her against him, Adrian inhaled the scent of her tousled hair. "Neither do I, so let's lie here for another few minutes before entering reality."

Thinking that was the best scenario for the time being, Joci cuddled into his arms and closed her eyes. "I think you're on to something."

They lay intertwined, the bustle of Des Moines blaring in the background. Their serenity was short-lived when Joci's alarm clock went off. "So much for that," she laughed. "Do you need to shower?"

Adrian rolled up to sit. "I should. I'm meeting a new client this afternoon. Smelling decent would be a good idea."

"Okay, I think I have some clothes that may fit you," she pointed out, sitting up as well. Her eyes rested on the lower drawer of her dresser.

"Do I want to know whose clothes these are?"

She smirked. "Probably not."

"All right. I'll swing by my place to get a suit."

Summoning her strength, she padded to the attached bathroom. "We may as well conserve water," she suggested, lingering in the doorway.

Adrian's gaze settled on her lack of clothes before he inched off the bed. "Yeah, I'm 100 percent sure we won't be doing any of that."

"Then I guess we better hurry," she teased, Adrian hot on her tail.

An hour and a half later, Joci snuck by Rayna's cubicle. Her silver heels gave her away when she reached the kitchen for her morning coffee. She didn't have a chance to make any at home, with Adrian consuming her time. A satisfied grin played on her lips at the memory of their time spent together.

"Joci, you're looking, well, sexy today," Rayna noticed, coming into view.

Pressing the brew button, Joci watched the water heat up. "Thanks. I think." She silently urged the woman to retreat, but luck didn't sway her direction.

"I couldn't help but notice both you and Adrian came in late today. Suspiciously late." She swiped her bangs from her eyes. "And together, no less."

"Yeah, we ran into each other in the lobby," she attempted, willing the coffeemaker to hasten in its task.

"Mmhmm, I'm not buying it, sister." Rayna propped her hands on her hips. "Spill."

After the machine sputtered the last drops of coffee, Joci decorated the brew with her creamer. "All right, we carpooled. My car is in the shop."

Rayna tapped her size ten shoes in disappointment and made an angry buzzer sound. "Try again."

"Damn, are you sure you're not a cop? You've got the investigator thing down pat." She waved her hand for Rayna to follow.

Once they were securely in her office, Joci relinquished her story. "Adrian and I slept together. Happy now?"

Squealing, Rayna shook her friend's arm. It was the one and only time Joci was glad she didn't have coffee in her hand. "How is this possible? Tell me all about it! Was he super incredible? I mean, he must be if you hooked up after all this time. Oh my God, this is so exciting! I need as many details as possible."

Positioning herself until she was comfortable in her

office chair, Joci prepared to tell her friend her sad, yet satisfying tale. It was inevitable, so getting it over with was in her best interest. Joci hoped she knew what the hell she was doing with her life.

CHAPTER ELEVEN

Sitting in the warm undercover patrol car, Joci waited for Quinn to finish his call. It was an odd feeling being in any part of a police vehicle, but she rather liked the sense of danger. They would often troll the streets of Des Moines together. Finding shady places to park was among the other activities they did in and on the unmarked car. She smirked at the fond memories made in the back seat.

The decision to speak with Quinn was her own. Not even Adrian knew about it. She felt a teensy bit bad telling him she wasn't free when she was going to chat with her boy toy instead. Despite the guilt, she needed to do this on her own and without Adrian's input.

A week had passed since she and Adrian slept together. It was just the one night and morning, but Adrian wanted more and told her as much. She couldn't, though. It was fun, very fun, but her heart wasn't in it. When she reflected on it later, she had to admit the truth that he was a stand-in for the man she wanted. Obviously, she hadn't been thinking it while licking whipped cream off Adrian's abs, but the hangover the next day reminded her of the fact.

"Sorry about that," Quinn apologized, turning toward her. "Work never ends, but you're accustomed to that." He turned up the heat. "Now, what's up? It's been a while since I've seen you outside the courthouse. Been hiding from me?"

Joci offered him a weak smile and saw his green eyes waver from his usual chipper attitude. "We've been friends for the last year and a half, and I've never shared myself with anyone else like I have with you."

Quinn flipped his radio down. "And I appreciate that. I think it helped us both with the cruelty we've been through."

Nodding in remembrance of his sorrowful story, Joci continued, "But Adrian and I slept together." She waited for a response, but not even a muscle jerked in his handsome face. "Clearly that's old news."

"No, nothing like that," he reassured. "I always assumed the two of you would give it another go sooner or later. I mean, I'm not a fan of the guy, for my own selfish reasons, but if you want to step into that pool again, I'll be on the sideline with a floatie."

"You are quite the detective," she teased. "But thank you."

"Not yet, but someday." Quinn started the engine and pulled away from the curb.

"It was just the once." She noticed his eyebrows lift. "Okay, well, one night and part of the morning, but I told him I couldn't continue with more."

"Hmm, that's interesting. I think I know why." He didn't

look at her even after the subtle hint. "I'm kind of surprised your client hasn't made a move, to be honest."

Joci's heart sped up. "Which client? What do you mean?"

Quinn eyed her strangely. "Cameron Shearer, the murder guy I arrested. Man, the way he looked at you during depos." He did a quick chef kiss with his fingers like . "It was intense."

Buckling her seat belt, Joci shrugged. "Huh. I didn't notice."

The officer snorted. "Yeah, okay. You'd have to be blind to miss it. Adrian saw it, which is probably one of the reasons he doesn't like the guy."

Her thoughts turned to that day not long in the past. She was well aware of how Cameron looked at her. He couldn't have been more obvious unless he held up a sign that said 'I want to screw you.' But he didn't move toward his desire. The day after her one-night stand with Adrian, she noticed he acted slightly different toward her, as if he knew what transpired between the attorneys.

Flicking the switch for the lights, Joci beamed at a driver. The car's brake lights flashed in response. "I love doing this a little too much."

"Yeah, there were a lot of things you loved to do with me." His smile dipped to a flat line. "So, I won't lie. I'm a little pissed you're not choosing me."

She tucked her hands in her lap. "I'm sorry, Quinn. I just can't."

"I get it. Still sucks though." Turning onto a street thriving with nightlife, Quinn slowed the car. "So does this mean we're not friends anymore?" His voice softened. "Not the benefit kind, but the regular kind of friend."

Playfully slugging his arm, Joci shook her head. "No, silly. I still need an inside man on the force," she reminded him with a splendid smile.

Quinn rolled his eyes and pointed to the dashboard. "All right, then I suppose I'll let you freak people out by switching on the siren while I drive around town. It'll be like old times. Well, except for what usually happened in the back seat." His eyebrows wiggled in jest.

With glee, she clapped her hands, her fingers trigger-happy within seconds. It may not be the most mature way to spend an evening, but it was entertaining, and she needed more of that in her demanding days.

— — —

Cameron shoved his food around on the plate. He should be grateful for the daily deliveries, but today he wasn't. A burner cell phone had been hidden alongside his scrambled eggs and pancakes. He couldn't eat. Not with the ever-looming possibility that it would ring, disturbing his life once more.

Without hearing the voice on the other end, Cameron knew who it would be. He nudged the untouched plate out of his way and sat back. He'd thought things were going his way in Iowa. His defense team was organized, and he'd finally grasped his underlying feelings for Joci.

Since waking up in the middle of the night last week, he'd gone over how to tell her about his affection. When he called the office line an hour ago, Rayna told him Joci was in court all day. Whether true or not, Cameron was thankful for the extra time. He reviewed all scenarios their conversation could lead to, including but not limited to: Joci removing herself from the case; her hating him; and his personal favorite, her kissing him until he was numb.

All of his plans shifted when his breakfast arrived with the special delivery. His main concern was not if, but when he would be murdered. J.J. held grudges, and he was more than due for a payment.

The phone loudly rang from the table. The bad phone, not the Joci one. With shaky hands, he drew in a breath and flipped it open. "Hello?"

"Cameron, you're alive. That's unfortunate," the bone-chilling voice taunted. "If it was up to me, I'd have slit your throat myself."

"J.J., hey, man. I haven't heard from you since you left me stranded in an Iowa park. Thanks for that, by the way."

The head honcho of the Mikkelsen U.S. group chuckled. "If you would've stayed out of my business, you wouldn't be in this mess."

Cameron gripped the phone until he thought it would shatter. "You threatened the Del Rossi organization with your move to Ohio and then Iowa, so it's only fair I stuck my nose in yours. We can't ignore the slew of bodies you left in your wake."

"Oh you're going to regret it, if you don't already," the other man mocked. "The Mikkelsens want you away for good. You're even more of a pain in the ass than when I liked you. Just think of it: Del Rossi's favorite soldier away for a murder he didn't commit. Classic. I thought for sure somebody in jail would've put you in a coma, but your boss was looking after you, wasn't he? Got you two lawyers and a private facility. Nice."

Standing, Cameron paced the marble floor. "Yeah, I lucked out. I guess that's what happens when you don't piss everyone off like you did. Believe me, once this case is taken care of, I'm coming after you," he cautioned with conviction.

"You think the tall brunette and her ginger lover boy will get this swept under the rug?" guessed J.J. "I looked into them. They're great and all, especially together, but I wouldn't hold my breath. Ask them how Tuesday night went. I'll bet the redhead will be happy to rub it in your face."

Lost for words, Cameron couldn't do anything but listen.

"According to my informants, Adrian gave it to her good. The next morning too." J.J. laughed. "You always had the worst taste in women."

"I don't know what you're talking about. Joci is my attorney. She means nothing to me other than a get out of jail free card," he roughly fibbed.

"Keep telling yourself that, Shearer, but I know the truth."

"And I know it's Adrian Petosa who's been feeding you intel and helping the Mikkelsens," he ground out.

"Well, bravo, Mr. Shearer. You aren't as dumb as I thought."

Cameron's victory was short-lived. Gloating would have

to wait until later when J.J. continued.

"Either plead guilty to the murder or I'll send my guys after your precious Joci this time."

Cameron's heart dropped when the kingpin added, "And she isn't protected by bulletproof glass, so it will be as easy as slapping a mosquito."

Envisioning the scenario, Cameron felt his stomach pitch. "Don't you dare," he growled.

"Guilty plea, Shearer. The Mikkelsens just need a fall man for killing Nichols. He was in the way of their expansion. Do it and I'll consider letting her live. You, on the other hand, I haven't decided yet. It'd be a shame to waste our history of fun banter. It keeps me amused. My bosses don't have to know if you live after the conviction." The Danish wonder dropped the call as the phone slipped from Cameron's hand.

He wasn't sure how much, if any, of the threat he should believe. J.J. Jepsen was cruel, but first-degree murder wasn't in his nature. Not for an innocent Iowan attorney. They went round and round ever since J.J. left the Del Rossi mob to join the Mikkelsens. Long ago, they were partners, friends even, but not since Bambi and that whole fiasco.

At the moment, he couldn't review the past. He needed to focus on Joci and any future in store for them.

He sank into the loveseat, J.J.'s words replaying in his mind. The possibility that the goon was right about Joci and Adrian aggravated him beyond fathoming. "If I hadn't tossed her aside, she wouldn't have slept with him," he muttered, then cursed a string of profanities.

Even though he and Joci were just two people who'd kissed a handful of times, his soul caught fire when she was near. He was the better part of himself, the childhood Cameron, in her presence. If she wanted back with Adrian, he was left to the truth. He was alone once more. The thought formed a lump in his throat.

His legs shaking, he stood and retrieved the cell phone from the law firm and dialed Adrian's number. He would hear it from the serpent's mouth before he took his next step. If he was about to risk his life for a woman he barely knew, Cameron needed to discuss the possibility that she didn't care for him as he'd thought.

— — —

"Where you at?" Adrian called from the entryway. "I have court in an hour, so make this fast."

Stepping off the treadmill, Cameron jogged to the hallway. "Sorry, I had my earbuds in." He popped them out of his ears and tried to catch his breath. Two miles typically weren't a big deal, but he was working off stress as well as calories. Keeping the secretive phone call between him and J.J. under the radar ate at him almost as much as the possibility of his attorneys knocking boots.

Adrian took in his shirtless attire and sweaty torso before nodding. "Getting a nice workout, I take it."

"Eh, it's okay." Cameron wiped his face with a hand towel. "Thanks for coming. I wanted to talk to you in person."

"Sure. What's this about?"

Taking in the man's casual blue T-shirt and dark jeans, Cameron had to admit that he was a catch. The young attorney exuded wealth and he was only in sneakers. Without argument, Adrian was the best possible person for Joci if he wasn't part of the Mikkelsen crew. The girl he'd known in Ohio had big dreams to help people, and the man standing before him could make them come true. Despite the truth, a nagging ache littered his heart. He couldn't get rid of his assignment without hurting her. The potential paths for the outcome became even more muddled.

Getting down to business, he realized he was standing in the hall staring at his lawyer. "Oh, um… I think we're in danger."

Offering him a hesitant glance, Adrian walked into the living room and took a seat in the leather recliner. "Okay, and you're basing this off what? A gut feeling? Pure speculation?"

Cameron trailed him into the room and tossed the burner cell to him. "No guessing needed. That came with my breakfast a little while ago, along with a threat to me and my legal team." He remained upright, as all his body wanted to do was run until exhaustion set in. "Particularly Joci."

That information snapped Adrian to attention. His back straightened and his eyes darkened. "Who was it? When did it happen? You kept this from us?"

Not wanting to divulge all of his secrets, Cameron shifted on his feet. "J.J. Jepsen. He's a bad dude from Ohio that I crossed."

"Dammit, Cameron!" Adrian yelled, pushing up to his feet.

"This is Joci's life, my life, your life we're talking about." His eyes blazed blue rage. "Start explaining."

"I should tell you both at the same time," Cameron attempted, but he was swiftly cut down.

"Hell no! You'll tell me now," his attorney snarled. "I'm about ready to make Joci withdraw from the case on this menace alone. Don't push me to completely toss your case."

Cameron didn't love that idea, but he also didn't want her harmed in any fashion. "She'll be fine if she stays here."

Adrian's face when from red to white in seconds. He shook his head and a small smirk appeared on his face. "Ah, I get it. You think she'll fall under some sappy spell for you."

The thought had crossed his mind, but he argued, "No. I want to keep her safe, that's it."

"And how are you going to do that? You have no weapons and you're wearing an ankle monitor. You're no help at all." The redhead studied the cell phone that J.J. sent. "I'm not leaving my ex-wife with you or any other schmuck. She stays with me. End of story."

Adrian's words punched Cameron in the gut. "Wait, she's your ex-*wife*?"

The man opposite him took apart the phone, searching for clues. "Yes. I thought she told you about our history."

Taking a seat now, Cameron let the development drench him in a new coat of sweat. "She said you were her ex. I thought ex-boyfriend or ex-fiancé. I didn't realize you two were married at one point."

"Well, we were, but not for very long." Adrian clicked

the phone's buttons. "A homicidal psychopath puts a damper on newlywedded bliss."

"You were just married when the accident happened," Cameron comprehended.

Adrian's brow rose and he discarded the phone to the coffee table between them before sitting once more. "I see Joci told you bits and pieces of the story." He leaned forward and pasted on a thin grin. "It would be my pleasure to fill in the blanks."

His body now aching for liquor to offset the startling information, Cameron tossed the towel over his shoulder. Sweat clung to his skin like a glove, causing the need to scratch until he peeled it all off.

"I stole Joci away from her nonprofit job one day after a mutual court hearing. She was zealously defending a delinquent kid, and I knew right then that our firm needed her." Adrian's eyes took on a faraway gleam. "I fell in love with her six months into her time at my father's law office." A sad smile crossed his face. "But she was dating a cop from Johnston at the time."

Unsure if he wanted to hear the story, Cameron slouched deeper into the couch. Disappearing into the void sounded better than listening to a love story for the girl he was in love with.

"I'm a persistent bugger though, and I managed to snag her away from him," Adrian boasted with a tip of his head.

"Then it must have really hurt when she went back to the cop type after you broke up," Cameron jabbed, with intent to wound.

After tossing his client a disgruntled frown, the man nodded. "Yeah. I supposed that's why it sucked even more, but you're not my therapist, so I'll stop there."

Cameron did find the tale intriguing, though he was more interested in the Joci parts.

"I'll skip the nitty-gritty details up to when she was nine months pregnant. One day after we finished our hearings, she dragged me into a courtroom and a judge married us."

"Let me guess, Judge O'Dell."

"Winner, winner," Adrian confirmed. "There was no fancy frippery like my family wanted, but we were happy." His face clouded. "We got divorced not long after our son died. Unfortunately, I played a big part in the divorce by not being there for her, and by staying late at the office with an intern."

His eyebrows furrowed, Cameron sat up pin straight. "So you married her, she had your baby, and then you cheated on her after you both lost your son to a lunatic."

Adrian scratched his chin. "To sum up, yes, but I never stopped loving her. I know she feels the same way, so you can see my problem with you holding out on vital information about a risk to the woman I love."

Cameron's left eye twitched at Adrian's plea. He would do the same if the roles were reversed, but he would involve his fists instead of eloquent words. Some part of him didn't want to accept that Joci was as engrossed in Adrian as he clearly was in her.

He hardly knew her, but when they kissed, the connection wasn't fake. He would've taken her several times in the hallway before she had time to utter a sigh if it would've changed anything. *And yet she hooked up with him the same night instead,* he bitterly recalled.

No, he was convinced that she used Adrian to prove to him that she could shove him aside like he did to her. The problem was Cameron's act had been for her protection, while Joci meant it as a painful knife to his soul.

Despite his mind waging war, his heart went out to his male attorney sitting across from him. It was time to pull out all the stops. He needed Joci safe, which meant showing his cards. "Here's what I can tell you," he began. "J.J. threatened Joci, but he won't hurt her if you're around."

"What're you talking about?"

"Cut the act, I know you're working for the Mikkelsens." He watched the blood drain from Adrian's face until the man resembled a ghost.

"What did you say?" he whispered.

Cameron rolled his shoulders back and cracked his neck. "You heard me. We're on opposite sides here, Adrian. You're a pawn of the Mikkelsens, and I'm one for the Del Rossis. I came to Iowa to find the person helping them move into our territory—you, as it turns out—and I'm not going to let a bitter rivalry with my old pal hurt Joci. So, that being said, you sure as hell better convince Joci to stay around you."

Adrian squinted but didn't argue. There was nothing to argue about. "I don't like this, but if what you're saying is true, I can't put our lives in jeopardy. Joci and I will take the other bedrooms until further notice. You're sure J.J. won't hurt her?" He seemed more worried about her than his own safety. Cameron didn't want to see it as a good thing, but he needed all the help he could get. If Joci was better off with Adrian, then so be it. But it wouldn't be permanent. He wouldn't let it.

"Not if his informant is attached to her. He wouldn't risk the Mikkelsen operation. Not yet, at least."

Nodding curtly, his lawyer stood. "I need to speak with Joci about this. We'll be over once it's done."

"Sure."

Adrian swiveled around and met his gaze. "And I assume my involvement with the mob will be kept quiet, correct?"

"Yeah, man. I won't tell her, but you should."

Adrian snorted and shook his head, not giving any other response before moving away.

Cameron waited until Adrian left the apartment before he let out a guttural groan. "I should've just screwed her," he complained, then chuckled at the logic. It wasn't like him to stop mid-embrace with a gorgeous girl in hopes that it wouldn't turn into a mere fling. "Oddly, Iowa matured me. Who knew?"

CHAPTER TWELVE

Ambling down the busy Court Avenue, Joci ignored the phone call from Adrian and sipped on her fall-flavored coffee as she paused for the pedestrian light to switch to white. The March day was mild for Iowa, but a hint of snow lingered in the breeze. Her phone buzzed again with Adrian's ringtone, still Justin Timberlake, but she didn't answer it. He'd called five times since she got out of the shower, but it wasn't uncommon for him. He didn't like to be ignored, and she most definitely wanted to ignore him. He was taking their hookup more seriously than she was. It wasn't that she regretted it, but she did. *I should've called Quinn.* She scolded herself. *No, you should've gone to Cameron.*

The cinnamon spice concoction warmed her hands as she waited for the lights to change. Her morning was unlike the rest in the fact that she'd actually made breakfast instead of the frozen waffles she guessed were two years old when she found them in the freezer. *Definitely letting go of those Eggos.*

Traffic slowed beside her and the light flipped in her favor. It was odd to accept that she didn't want a fling anymore. She felt quite grown up, despite the backslide with Adrian. Now all she had to do was act on her feelings. *Right.* Seeing how Cameron shied away whenever she showed her face, it wouldn't be easy. She needed to tell him about how she felt, how he made her feel, but the murder case kind of got in the way.

Snowflakes swirled around her, sending a hint of a pedestrian's cologne to her nose. It reminded her of Cameron's earthy tones. *Damn, the man is everywhere.*

Pulling her gray trench coat closer, she caught sight of the crowd shuffling behind her reflected in the window of the deli. Worry trickled into her mind when she recognized the same two adults from the corner at her apartment. Both wore black from head to toe, but their auras were anything but approachable gothic.

She picked up her pace, but found the act difficult with four-inch heels. The motivation behind the sparkly red shoes amazed even her, but with a bond review hearing at nine in the morning, they were necessary. The particular county attorney she was going up against wasn't keen on tall women, so Joci liked to use that to her advantage whenever possible, if just to send the man scrambling for words.

Joci turned down an alley in order to shave a couple of minutes off her time. "And to see if I'm being paranoid," she breathed, loud enough for her ears alone.

The sickening crunch of twigs behind her offered the regrettable answer. She snuck a peep over her shoulder.

The two stalkers didn't hide their obvious target as they closed in. Yanking her phone from her pocket, Joci dialed as fast as her fingers could move. No doubt they were related to the Mikkelsen mob in some way. Who else would follow her?

At the end of the corridor, she noticed the side street wasn't busy. That particular location didn't have cute coffee shops or offices either. *Damn.* She stopped and twirled around. "I called 911. The police will be here any minute," she warned, holding up the mobile device.

The shadows exchanged a glance. "Tell Shearer that J.J. is waiting for him to make good on his word. If he doesn't, we'll keep coming back to escort you to work."

Before she could react, they darted in the opposite direction. *Shit!* She liked being right, but not when it involved threats. Adrenaline still coursing through her body, Joci tossed the coffee to the ground. She didn't need to wake up any longer. The latte splattered along the broken concrete, innately mirroring her nerves.

"Joci? Joci, are you there?" a tinny voice called urgently.

Remembering her cell phone, she pulled it to her ear. "Quinn, thank God. These two people were following me."

"What? Are you sure?"

Joci's voice shook. "Yeah, very sure."

"I'm on my way to you. Where are you?" he inquired, the siren blasting in the background.

"The alleyway across from the office." Her stomach was queasy. She closed her eyes, fighting the urge to run into the office building and hide in law books.

"Perfect. Don't hang up. I'm almost there," he informed.

The wail of the siren was closer now, and Joci leaned against the brick wall beside her. "Breathe," she told herself over and over.

On a typical day, walking to the office didn't include this much drama. The most adventure in five years included a purse snatcher who was tripped by a granny with her cane. This was a turn of events she wasn't in favor of.

Never had Joci been more grateful to hear the screech of tires on pavement. Opening her eyes, she let out a muffled cry when she spotted Quinn rushing toward her.

He wrapped his arms around her, and tears flooded from her eyes. "Shh, you're okay," he reassured. "What did they want?"

"To give a message to Cameron."

"Whoa, really? Were they with the Mikkelsen mob?"

"Yeah." She wiped her nose. "I guess he's been in contact with them and isn't living up to his end of whatever deal they have."

Quinn gently rubbed her arms. "I'm sorry, Joci. You don't deserve any of this."

She shrugged. "All part of the job, right?"

"I'm not sure about that, but okay." Quinn glanced at her pumps. "Heading back to Kansas so soon, Dorothy?" he gently teased.

Smacking his chest, Joci chided, "Maybe I will if people keep stalking me." Her heart fluttered as her mind replayed her morning. "They stalked me from my apartment. I guess they really want Cameron to know he needs to stop being an ass."

Quinn reviewed their setting with watchful eyes. "Yeah, like that'll happen." He steadied her with his arm around her waist.

Nodding, Joci leaned her weight on him as they made the final trek across the street and into her building. Her legs wobbly, she was grateful that he didn't abandon her immediately. She and Quinn may only be friends, but he was the type of guy who would be there for her no matter what the risk. What she couldn't grasp was why the mob thought scaring her would motivate Cameron. They weren't a couple, and she was just an attorney from the outside looking in. How would the Mikkelsens know how to control Cameron unless her feelings were reciprocated? That train of thought made her even more breathless than the friendly stalkers.

The law firm hustled with activity when they stepped off the elevator. Quietly, the two drifted to her office, stopping when Rayna spotted them.

"Joci?" She glanced between them. "Quinn? What's going on? Why are you here? Why is she white?" She glared at Quinn. "What did you do?"

"Rayna, please get Joci a drink of water," Quinn directed without explanation. "She'll fill you in when she catches her breath."

Attempting a smile, Joci nodded, and the other woman hurried to the kitchen. She was glad for a reprieve. Rayna had a way with pestering until questions were answered. It made her an excellent attorney, but an annoying colleague.

Carefully, they stepped into Joci's office. "Wow, I love what you've done with the place," he ribbed, settling her into a chair. It wasn't *her* chair, but at least he was in the vicinity.

"The decorator comes next week," she played along. "She had to decorate Oprah's closet first."

Chuckling, Quinn took the seat beside her. "I'm glad you're safe," he said in all seriousness.

"Thanks. Me too." She unbuttoned her coat and noticed that it sported spots of coffee from her hasty movements.

"Next time, please call 911 okay? I would hate for something to happen to you." He went to brush her hair from her face as Rayna reappeared with a bottle of water, Adrian by her side.

"Are you all right, Joci?" Adrian queried, glaring at the uniformed officer.

Jerking his hand back as though burned by the penetrating cobalt gaze, Quinn stood. "She's fine. Two strangers followed her this morning. They had a message for your client. A warning, actually."

Adrian hustled to Joci's side, visually checking her for injuries. "I was talking to *her*, Officer Quinn. Why don't you go eat a donut?"

"For the love of God, Adrian, stop!" Joci commanded, jerking her head away to avoid his smothering touch. "He told you what happened. I'm fine. Just shaken up."

"I just got off the elevator to grab my file before I was heading to your apartment," her fiery-haired partner fumed. "Dammit, he was right."

Joci rolled her eyes in despair. "You were with Cameron this morning?"

Adrian set his shoes along the office floor, his hands in his once perfectly gelled hair. "Yes. He told me about a threat J.J. gave him about you." His eyes settled on her. "I tried calling you. Repeatedly. Why didn't you answer?"

All eyes shifted to Adrian now. "What threat?" Quinn boomed, resting his hand on his belt.

"And what does Cameron have to do with any of this?" Rayna piped in.

Joci took a swig of water and exhaled. "This has to do with what he wouldn't tell us, doesn't it?"

Morosely, Adrian nodded. "Yes."

"Tell me what he said," Joci requested, then jutted her chin to the door. "Rayna needs to hear it too, but not the whole firm." She smiled at Quinn. "And neither do you. Sorry, Quinn."

Quinn nodded his understanding. "I get it. Let me know if I can help with anything."

As the door closed, she prepared her mind for the worst, but knew there was more. There was always more than what it seemed when it came to Cameron Shearer.

— — —

"Cameron Anthony Shearer, where the hell are you?" Joci's voice shrilled.

Startled out of his nap, Cameron sat up in the bed and listened for her to repeat the words. Instead, the criminal counselor whizzed into the bedroom at lightning speed. He listened for additional footsteps from her worse half but didn't hear Adrian. *Good, because I'd love nothing more than to slug him.* The desire to tell Joci all about Adrian's dirty side job nearly overwhelmed him, but it wasn't how he wanted to win her over. He wanted her to want him because of him, not because Adrian was a douche. He didn't have to wait long for Joci to barrel into the room, and God, she looked delicious.

"I didn't realize you knew my middle name," he commented, not caring to pull a shirt on. *She'd* walked in on *him*, after all.

Joci's eyes fired greenish-brown arrows. "I'm your attorney, dumbass. I looked it up."

"For dramatic effect," he added when she paused to take a breath. "You were always a bit of a drama queen."

Crossing her arms over her chest, she narrowed her gaze. "Maybe, but that's not the point."

Inching off the bed, Cameron sauntered over to where she stood. "I'll bite. What's the point?"

Her eyes flittered over his partially clothed body, which made his blood warm. He craved for her to do more than look. Each second she refrained ate away at his resolve.

"You've been holding out on me. J.J.'s guys threatened me today. Told me to give you a message about keeping your word and some shit like that." Joci fixed her glasses, enticing him to toss them to the floor—along with her luscious body. "Not cool."

"What? They threatened you? Are you hurt? I'm going to kill that motherfucker." The instant his hands gripped her arms, he didn't regret calling Adrian out earlier that morning. The man could've kept it from happening if he'd just left when he told him to.

"I'm fine. They just scared me."

She didn't brush him away, and his heart swelled in hopes that J.J. was wrong about her affection for Adrian.

"Good. I'm glad."

Not in any hurry, he took in her appearance. Her outfit was one thousand times more expensive than his off-brand sweatpants. "I like the shoes, but I think you're missing Toto."

Joci exhaled a disgruntled sigh and threw her hands in the air. "J.J. Jepsen. We're talking about J.J. Focus for five minutes, please."

"All right, all right. Don't get your panties in a bunch." He smirked when her foot started tapping. "In my defense, I wanted to tell my lawyers in one go, but your man-cake forced it out of me." His gaze lingered on hers. "It's nice that you and your ex-husband are going at it again."

His words had the effect he'd hoped for. Joci's face turned red, and she wrinkled her nose. God, he loved that mannerism.

"Of course Adrian told you. Why wouldn't he?" she huffed.

"If you were the one who got away from me, I wouldn't rest until I nullified my mistake," he pointed out. He could watch her for days. The delicate blush caused by his doggedness set a welcoming hue to her skin. It was gorgeous and increasingly addictive.

"The timing of all this wasn't deliberate," she insisted.

It was Cameron's turn to fold his arms over his bare chest. "Mm, yes, I'm sure," he goaded. "Where's the hunky dude anyways? He's usually trailing you like a bloodhound."

"He's downstairs in his office."

Probably telling J.J. to screw off. Good. Maybe he'll take a bit of his own advice. Cameron's finger slid down her arm. "But you're welcome."

Joci's brows knit together. "For what?"

Stepping close enough to smell the raspberry heaven that clung to her hair, Cameron captured her eyes with his. "For getting you all riled up. It's unfortunate that it took another man to start your engines so you could screw your ex."

Joci's took aim, but he caught her hand before it could connect. She struggled in his grip but he wouldn't release her. Not until he had his fill, but he never saw that happening in their lifetime.

"If my touch is what your body needs to be with someone else, I won't offer it up again," he breathed, his lips inches from her parted ones.

"That's not what happened." Her gaze searched his. "You stopped us, remember? You did. I didn't want to."

Cameron snaked his palm around her neck and tilted her face up. "I didn't see you argue," he returned.

Her gaze faltered and she put space between them. "And I didn't see you chase after me."

His cheek twitched, but her argument didn't put him off. How could it when her eyes told a different story as they scoured his form like a famished doe seeing greenery after a bitter winter? "You may want to tell your body that, because I don't buy it and neither do you."

Joci gripped the doorframe and swung her gaze away. "You kept secrets from me, Cameron. My guess is that you're hiding a few more. Adrian doesn't do that."

It took every molecule of resistance to not spill the beans about her partner. He gave the man his word, but hell if he didn't want to break it then and there.

She clenched her jaw, then added, "I don't have to explain why I slept with him, but being truthful was at the top of my list."

"Keep lying to yourself, Joci. Let's see where that gets you."

She closed her eyes and took a breath before opening them again. "Look, we're stuck living together for the foreseeable future because of you, so don't pin your woman issues on me."

She looked too irresistible in that moment, but Cameron harnessed his patience and let out a sigh. Her comments were true. Their predicament was his fault. If he hadn't been an idiot, J.J. never would've left him near a corpse.

Yet as he observed the adorable way Joci nibbled her nail, he had to thank the jerk for reuniting the lost friends. He stopped short of wrapping her in his embrace when she folded her arms over her breasts. She wasn't prepared to hear his feelings for her, despite how badly it hurt to keep them hidden away.

"You're right. I am to blame for this shit storm," he admitted, and she stopped surveying the marble. "But I think it will be fun to live under one sturdy roof. I'm sure Adrian will like all of the extra attention you give him." He couldn't help but add, "After spending time with me," to get a rise out of her.

Joci let out an annoyed huff and spun on her heels. Watching her leave was the highlight of his day as he leaned his forearm on the door. He could handle the feisty brunette every waking moment, but he wasn't positive about her protective ex. Stepping into the hall, he sighed as he watched the sway of her hips. He couldn't help but follow her.

The courageous lawyer tossed him a malicious glare before she slammed the apartment door behind her. From the looks of it, facing J.J. was more tempting than avoiding the chemistry with Joci. His workload multiplied at the knowledge that she would be much too close and yet fathoms away from his arms.

— — —

Unpacking the suitcase thrown together in a hurry, Joci did her damnedest to ignore the hilarity from the living room. She pulled out a drawer and stuffed her bras in it as Rayna's voice filtered through the open-concept apartment. It was her brainy idea to have her friend tag along to her place to grab clothes. Joci wasn't sure what all to pack, since their time was open-ended. The trial was approaching at a fast pace thanks to her client insisting on keeping as close to the original deadlines as possible, but she had plenty of court appearances to make before then. Two of the security guards from the firm were assigned to trail her and Adrian during their jaunts in between the office building and court. The idea of being secluded to the firm and courthouse wasn't her favorite, but she didn't have any other option. Being in the same apartment as Cameron made her feel safe somehow. She wasn't sure why, but knowing he was nearby settled her nerves.

"I could do without the flirting," she muttered. Rayna claimed to be focused on her career, but Joci wasn't convinced. "If I make it out of this alive, I'm setting her up with someone," she vowed when Cameron's chuckle resounded.

She told herself she was just aggravated by the situation, and Rayna and Cameron's eye batting played no part in her mood, but she was fooling herself. He was a complete ass, yet she was drawn to his wit. To her, Cameron's jokes and cold shoulder were a coping tactic. One she didn't appreciate.

"I'll bet the therapist loves him," she snorted. He carried unearthed demons. The woman had hinted as much to her off the record. Maybe it was her bachelor's degree in psychology, or just plain curiosity that was the underlying reason for her attraction to the tatted-up man she used to play Barbies with.

She hung up the last suit jacket and hid her brown luggage in the closet. Opting to slip into less businesslike attire, Joci pulled on a pair of pink Victoria's Secret sweats and a purple V-neck tee. Wrangling her hair into a messy bun, she emerged from the bedroom ten times more comfortable.

"You look snazzy," Rayna pointed out.

"I might as well be relaxed during my stay with the world's most frustrating client," she replied with a sassy grin.

"Yep, that's me. I have to be memorable." Cameron's eyes lingered over her clothes. "As are the words on your ass."

Joci twirled around and shot him daggers.

"Love really does cover it," he insinuated, cocking his head to the left. "In both aspects."

Rayna coughed and tried to steer the conversation away from a potential mud-slinging. "I ordered Lucky Bamboo. I hope it's all right."

Taking the open love seat, Joci propped her legs up on the empty side. "Yum, Chinese food. It's been too long since I've had it."

Adrian strolled into the room, suitcase in hand, and surveyed the occupants. "Did I miss much?" He dropped the bag and moved Joci's legs to sit down before setting them back on his knees.

"Not really. I got my clothes put away, and Rayna entertained Cameron," Joci advised. "Pretty boring." She slid her gaze to the auburn work of art and their client on the couch together. "Unless those two are about to start something."

At her implication, the smile dropped from Cameron's face and his brown eyes melted into pools the color of cold coffee. He didn't have to utter a retort; she read his thoughts and they sent shivers down her spine.

"Joci, did you review the Hasselman proof brief?"

Rayna inquired, drawing her out of the Cameron stupor. "I think it's due on Friday."

"I skimmed it," she reported, switching her attention to her friend. "You did a great job. I'll review it more in depth and note the changes."

Rayna nodded, then began to prattle on about work. The last thing Joci wanted to think about was the job that never ceased. Even now, it was sucking away her life bit by bit while she spent it with a client. The irony wasn't lost to her. Yet, she couldn't complain too much. She wanted to be near him. Though having Adrian and Rayna accompanying her weren't in her fantasy.

"Hey, Rayna, can we talk shop in the morning?" Adrian cut in. "My brain is on overload, and being so close to the office isn't helping me turn it off."

Joci could've kissed him for interrupting, but she refrained. Rayna offered apologies, then got up to answer the knock at the door. "I swear it's like you're in my brain," she whispered.

"I do my best." Patting her leg, Adrian stood. "I'll help you with the food."

Joci sighed as she watched his retreat. Adrian was being overly kind since the threat. He rarely let her out of his sight. He truly was a one-of-a-kind guy. Her eyes traveled to where Cameron sat. *Speaking of,* she thought, recognizing the coy grin on his lips.

"Aw, you two are so sweet. It's disgusting, really," Cameron pestered in an annoying songlike voice. "He's a dreamboat, isn't he?" he asked, moving to the edge of his seat.

"For your information, yes, he is," she hurled back. Cameron's obvious envy encouraged her. He cared about her in more than an attorney and client way, but something was holding him back.

Joci's gaze flitted over the tattoos. Cameron was attractive, she conceded, but he was also an arrogant son of a bitch.

Adrian and Rayna appeared with bags of her favorite Chinese food. Studying the tall redhead, she had to admit that he was arrogant too. Probably more so than Cameron, but somehow she had grown accustomed to it. Her mind screeched to a halt. What other personality traits would she tolerate in the name of love?

Back when she worked with the juvenile courts, Joci was picky—too picky—when it came to the mental and physical attributes of the men she dated.

Adrian placed her order of spicy beef lo mein and crab rangoon in front of her on the coffee table. He was the reason she released her long list of desirables in a man. Adrian swooped in and saved the day by adding her to the firm's roster, but he also tilted her world in a different direction. He stole her affections before she knew what was happening. They were in a relationship even before she had the chance to break up with her boyfriend at the time.

Recalling her time before the enrapturement of the Petosa heir, Joci wrinkled her nose. She was dating a cop back then. One who transferred to Cedar Rapids due to their relationship's dissolution.

Grabbing her lo mein, she watched in silence as Adrian and Rayna conversed like old pals.

She locked eyes with Cameron as he ate his fried rice in silence. *Damn you,* she thought when he gave her a tiny smile. Even after he acted like a dick, he somehow set off the butterflies in her stomach. It was uncommon for her and yet felt perfectly normal when Cameron was the reason. Some part of him was good; she could sense it. She'd felt it.

Joci broke their gaze and focused on her food. She took two bites before her mind wouldn't allow any more. Too many possibilities swirled in her brain, and she couldn't siphon out the good from the bad. Adrian's role in her life wasn't planned, but it could have been avoided.

When she looked at Cameron, she felt the opposite. Somewhere in her subconscious, he meant something more, and she was determined to see it through. Without a doubt, Joci believed being appointed to this case wasn't coincidence—it was fate.

CHAPTER THIRTEEN

A week later, Cameron heaved the transcript away from him and rubbed his temples. He and Adrian had been going over trial prep for three hours, and his brain was about to explode. Nothing looked favorable. From the depositions to the evidence, everything pointed a thin, bony finger at him. J.J. outdid himself this time around. Normally, their squabbles were resolved with money or even drugs, but this time, the Mikkelsens wanted retribution for the Del Rossi mob getting in their way. He wouldn't admit to the ghastly events that led to the bad blood, but he knew enough to realize they weren't backing down.

Adrian's voice droned on in the background, but Cameron wasn't listening. After a while, the man's voice became nails on a chalkboard to his ears. He closed his eyes and winced as his headache doubled. With prison looming over his neck, the anxiety caused more verbal lashings than he cared to take credit for. It took every ounce of will not to finish the job he was sent to do. He eyed Adrian's necktie. It'd be easy to use it to his advantage—which was precisely what Jerry wanted him to do, after all—but he couldn't. Without knowing how Joci truly felt about the dick, he was stuck. Things were much easier before J.J. decided to frame him.

Just this morning, he'd yelled at the deputy during his frisk, made tears come to Rayna's eyes, and his most concerning, ran Joci off when she offered to make him a bagel. It was too much. Being in this proximity to her sent his emotions into turmoil.

"I'm heading out to check on Joci. She should be back from her pretrial conference by now," Adrian advised.

Cameron watched him shuffle the police reports, then stand. He would give his left testicle for the chance to leave the hellhole they called luxury and check on Joci himself. Other than polite exchanges in the apartment, the woman had avoided him like the plague for the last week. Even at the final hearing before trial, she shuffled their seating arrangement so she didn't have to sit by him. It was almost as if she was afraid to be alone with him, which was odd because she was much safer with him than with Adrian in his opinion.

"Sure. Get a few breaths of fresh air for me," he joked.

Adrian slipped on his suit jacket. It was a light charcoal color today. Exquisite and expensive like all the rest. "The windows open here," he noted. "They're just not big enough slots to wiggle through."

"It's not the same," Cameron complained, threading his fingers into his mangled waves. He was due for a haircut soon, according to Rayna.

The slender redhead nodded in agreement and snagged his cell phone from the tower of law books. As he treaded, Cameron's burner cell phone buzzed on the kitchen table.

Instantly, the attorney returned, his eyes wild. "Answer it," he directed, then fumbled with his phone. "I opened my recording app, so we're good. The police may need this as evidence later."

With wary fingers, Cameron flipped over the Nokia and saw no caller ID. Gaining courage despite his tumbling stomach, he connected the call. "Hello?"

"I take it you and my informant are cozy now."

Mind whirring, Cameron clutched the phone and saw Adrian's brow crease. He paused the recording app and shoved the phone back into his pocket. "Yeah, yeah."

"Good. I thought the two of you would get along."

"Fuck off, J.J.. You know what Del Rossi wanted me to do. You've been hindering it since you heard I was in town."

"Yeah, you're right. I just thought it was hilarious when Jerry hired the very guy you were supposed to silence," J.J. cackled

"What's he talking about?" Adrian asked, clearly oblivious to the danger he'd been in for the last few months.

Cameron wasn't going to spell it out for the guy. He was smart. He would figure it out. "What's the plan here? You know Adrian is staying here, and so is Joci. You can't get to her without hurting your own guy in more than one way."

J.J.'s laugh crippled the smirk on Cameron's face. "Maybe so, but I'm only interested in making sure Del Rossi leaves Iowa for good. If that means I happen to call the security guard who's supposed to be watching Ms. Dorous, then so be it," he hinted.

He looked up to Adrian. The man's face was suspicious and pained. They both knew what was coming next. "What did you do?"

Pausing for effect, the other man took a breath. "Are you familiar with Joci's whereabouts? It would be a shame to lose half of your legal team just weeks from trial." His low chuckle sent cold shivers over Cameron's arms. "Ah, what a pretty black skirt she's wearing today. And that gray trench coat sets off the green in her hazel eyes, doesn't it? I always liked girls with unique eye colors."

Cameron's mouth went dry as the click on the other end confirmed the end of the chat. J.J. was off the rails now. The man didn't care if he burned Adrian along with Del Rossi. J.J. was out for blood because of Cameron, and Joci might pay the price. He jumped to his feet and yelled, "Well call her, dammit!"

Thumbs flying over the phone, Adrian frowned. "I already am." He set off toward the window and glanced to the street below. "She's not the love of *your* life, remember?"

Deciding it was best to leave that subject alone, Cameron joined him and tapped agonizing knuckles on the pane. Speckles of people could be seen from their spot, but identifying someone was much more difficult.

"Joci, come on. Pick up the fucking phone," Adrian urged. His eyes shadowed when her voice mail message kicked in. "This is your fault," he barked, pointing at Cameron. Redialing the phone, he strode toward the front door with his client by his side.

"She has to be fine," Cameron murmured, stopping shy of the threshold. He couldn't pass through the door if he wanted to. From his spot, he saw Adrian continue to hit the dial button. He would never forgive himself if he was the root of her demise.

"Wait, how did he know what she's wearing?" Adrian asked, holding the door open.

"He's here. That's the only explanation." Cameron's heart pounded at the possibility. If the Danish drug lord was in Des Moines, he was royally screwed. No way would J.J. allow him to scurry off into the sunset. The man was here for one purpose, and any person who got in his way would be cut down.

"Great. Not only did you murder some guy, but you also brought a gun-slinging maniac to my hometown. He said he'd never hurt anyone here." Adrian called for the security guards and advised them of the new information they received.

Pacing at the doorway, Cameron willed Joci to sense the danger she was in. The fervor for her clients would be the death of her. Any other attorney could've covered her hearings, but no, she was as stubborn as he.

As Adrian's voice grew louder and more intense, the elevator chimed its arrival. The door sprang open, and all eyes swiveled to the passenger. Cameron held his breath, knowing there could be a dead body on the floor alongside J.J., or it could be the woman their thoughts focused on.

From beside him, Adrian let out a relieved groan while

Cameron fell back against the door. Standing in the elevator with a Starbucks cup in hand was a very much alive and unharmed Joci Dorous.

She stepped onto the tiled floor and lifted her eyebrows. "It's sweet of all of you to be gathered for my triumphant return, but it wasn't necessary." She took a sip of the brew. "My girl was innocent, and the judge figured it out. Took him forever, but nothing new with Judge Stillwell. I mean, his name should've been proof enough of his slow verdicts."

Before anyone else could speak, Adrian rushed to Joci and hauled her into his arms. "Thank God you're okay. I was so worried," he managed, then drew back. "Why didn't you answer my calls?"

Confusion crossed her face. She dug her hand into her purse and reviewed the phone's screen. "Oh, why did you call"—she glanced up, her eyes curious—"twenty times. It was on silent because of the hearing. I forgot to turn the ringer back up."

She glanced to Cameron, then back to Adrian. "After I got done, Joe, the security guard, said he had an emergency at home, so I told him to leave. I figured it wouldn't hurt if I treated myself to a coffee just around the corner from the courthouse." She swung her purse back on her shoulder. "Well, actually, some guy paid for it, but whatever. By the time I was done, the firm had sent Joe's replacement. I'm fine."

Cameron's blood froze in his veins, and he swallowed the lump in his throat. "What did he look like?" he asked, his voice hoarse.

"Blond, blue eyes, and a little shorter than me." She squinted. "Why? What's wrong? Why do you two look so relieved to see me? Did something happen while I was gone?"

Adrian shot blue icicles at Cameron. "He was inches away from her, Cameron! Inches!"

Regret filled him, but he couldn't react. His brain was processing the day's sharp turns. "J.J. Jepsen is here, Joci. He's the person who bought your drink."

She turned to Adrian, whose hands remained around her waist. "What?" she shrieked.

"He called us while you were gone and all but painted a picture of you. I thought for sure he'd nabbed you," Adrian admitted, and his voice caught. "You don't know how glad I am to see you."

Joci digested the words and took a long drink of her coffee. "All righty then. I guess Rayna is about to get a crash course in attorney 101."

Adrian hugged her to him tight. "Good. I'm glad you agree. I was afraid I would have to resort to tying you up to prevent you from sneaking away to the courthouse."

Treating a near-death experience with a cavalier attitude, she offered him a smirk. "Cuffs would've worked just fine."

Cameron witnessed Adrian's forced smile but was too distracted by Joci's face to heed the emotions transferred between the two of them. She might act like what nearly happened was no big event, but her eyes spoke the truth.

In agony, he couldn't tear his gaze away when Adrian soundly kissed her full lips. He didn't want to see. It was his own personal form of torture.

Sliding his back down the door until he was seated on the floor, Cameron watched powerlessly as another man shared as much love as he felt for Joci before his eyes. The things keeping him from breaking into their tender moment were the threshold that held him hostage… and her content expression.

— — —

"Remind me again why our Wednesday meal includes prime rib," Joci wondered, unloading the food from the containers. "It's like Thanksgiving and Christmas combined in late March. Very weird."

Adrian grabbed plates from the sleek cabinets. "Because my dad felt bad he wasn't here for any of the holidays, and because we're stuck with him." He nodded toward Cameron.

"Well, maybe he shouldn't fly to Jamaica with his British lover," she said under her breath. Cameron released a tiny smirk from where he was pouring wine into the glasses. She had to admit, it was nice to have more than one person with her to share a meal, even if she was with coworkers and a criminal. The last two years hadn't been so cheery. She understood now that it was because she wasn't with the right person. She'd steered clear of Cameron since moving into the apartment. She couldn't trust herself if she got too close. For some reason, all she wanted to do was jump him and tell the idiot how she felt… but she couldn't. Such an act required finesse, and not on the cusp of a homicide trial.

"Yeah, I'm not discussing my dad's philandering ways,"

Adrian remarked from the dining area, which was set up like a table ripped from a page of *Better Homes and Garden* magazine.

Eyeing Cameron, she was surprised when he didn't jump into the discussion and poke at Adrian. It was uncommon for peace to be involved when those men were in the same room. Setting the prime rib beside the turkey platter, Joci realized her animated client had dialed down his antics since last week. The only plausible conclusion dealt with the scene J.J. had created. She was aware of the warring mobs and their relation to Cameron, but he hadn't told her everything and she couldn't entirely blame him for it.

"All right, let's get our food on," she called, straightening a napkin.

Rayna appeared from the living room, sporting a black-and-white checkered sweater and navy jeans. "That smells so good. It's been driving me insane since they dropped it off." She took a seat beside Cameron's usual spot.

Joci swallowed a giggle when Cameron reviewed the place settings, then grabbed a chair kitty-corner to the auburn sprite. Rayna may have harbored undisclosed feelings for the drummer clad in black jeans and a red hoodie, but he did not reciprocate. It was entertaining to watch the ways he gently put her flirtation to the side. It was one of his more admirable traits. Part of her was jealous of the attention he gave Rayna, but she couldn't admit her feelings for him until the case was resolved. Even if they managed an acquittal, she wasn't positive she could be forthright with a mobster. For the time being, she'd batten down the hatches over her heart.

Opting to sit beside her friend, Joci plopped down in the chair and smoothed her white cashmere sweater. Wearing white was foolhardy, but it felt too good on her skin to resist.

Once Adrian joined them, crescent rolls in hand, Rayna spoke up. "This is nice. It's been forever since I had a meal that didn't include a TV dinner or from a restaurant."

Adrian screwed his nose up. "That's disgusting, Rayna. If you want to learn how to make a few easy dishes, I can help you out."

"Thanks. I'm a horrible cook. I burn spaghetti." Rayna beamed at him and spooned sweet potatoes onto her plate. "What about you, Cameron? Do you get together with your family much?" She grabbed the green bean casserole. "I mean, other than this year."

Pausing her hands over the carved turkey, Joci looked up but wasn't able to meet Cameron's eyes. Her friend's questions were polite, yet insensitive given the current relationship with his case.

Cameron set down the bowl of stuffing. "My parents were always on the road with their death metal band, so they dropped me off at my aunt's house the majority of the time," he disclosed, not taking his gaze from the food.

"Oh shit. I'm sorry," Rayna recovered. "Was your aunt nice?"

Digging his fork into the prime rib, he nodded. "I guess. She was better than nothing." His brown eyes skimmed up to Joci. "But one Thanksgiving, the girl who lived across the street from my aunt invited me over." He smiled at Joci. "Remember it?"

"Yeah, it was fun. I believe you stole the turkey leg I wanted." Joci paused in pouring gravy over the turkey on her plate. Cameron shoveled mashed potatoes into his mouth, signifying the end of the exposé of his private life.

"My dad tried to take me turkey hunting one year," Adrian recalled, filling the silence. "It didn't go over so well."

"I can't imagine your dad hunting," Rayna commented with a chuckle.

"Believe me, neither could I." Adrian continued to tell the story Joci had heard dozens of times from both Petosa men, but she couldn't concentrate on it. Her mind was preoccupied by Cameron's tale. Her family opened their home to others around the holidays, and having Cameron there when they were kids was one of the times she didn't hate the charitable policy.

"Do you remember what we did after dinner back then?" Joci asked.

Glancing to the duo of attorneys gabbing about family holidays, Cameron leaned closer. "Yeah, we went sledding and you broke your leg. Sorry about that, by the way."

"Oh, stop. It wasn't your fault. My backyard had a nasty hill."

"But it was my idea to build an ice ramp at the bottom." Cameron rested his spoon in the stuffing and gave his full attention to her. "Which resulted in us flying in the air." He cracked a smile. "Then me falling on you and snapping your leg like a twig."

She chuckled at the memory. Though it was painful

back then, the story was funny now that she thought about it. "Talk about a memorable Thanksgiving," she joked, not caring that their food cooled the longer they ignored it.

"It definitely wasn't something I'll ever forget."

"You brought me a teddy bear after I returned from the hospital," she reminded.

"And you had a bright pink cast." He wiped his mouth with the back of his hand. "When I saw what I'd accidentally done, my aunt gave me some cash and I ran to the store up the road."

"Then you brought back a brown bear holding a tiny red rose." She sighed. "I still have it."

"What? No freaking way. Really?"

She nodded. "Swear on my juris doctor. I could never part with such a sweet apology."

"I'm sorry, Joce. For then and now. I can't imagine you like being cooped up because of me." A lonely smile flashed on his lips. He took a bite of his roll. "But once this is all sorted out, I'll make it up to you," he promised.

Joci grinned at the hope that they'd indeed have a future instead of a bleak trial outcome. Losing him once and for all would be a punch to the heart. "I'll hold you to it."

"Deal. Maybe I'll even throw in a little sledding again," Cameron hinted with a quick wink.

"Don't you dare. I just got these legs," she joked.

"And they're perfect."

Joci's cheeks burned at the quiet compliment and they both went back to their plates. The remainder of the dinner went as smooth as possible, with Rayna only spilling white wine on her twice. After a quick and easy clean up, Adrian offered to escort the tipsy lawyer downstairs, to stretch his legs and prevent her getting into the wrong Uber car.

Joci hugged her friend, then collapsed onto the couch once the apartment door closed. She'd overeaten, but that wasn't uncommon when she was stressed. Cameron's trial was scheduled to begin in two weeks. They'd recently attended the pretrial conference and were prepared for trial. She had more than enough time to cram before a man's entire future rested in her hands. It happened often in her line of work, but this case felt different, closer to home somehow. *Probably because you like him.*

The clink of weights caught her attention, so she pushed up from her comfortable spot in search of the culprit. Entering the fitness room, Joci watched in silence as Cameron benched the barbell with 150 pounds of weight attached. It shouldn't have been attractive, but seeing his tattooed muscles strain beautifully excited her.

"I think there's a rule about working out too soon after a big meal," she teased as she neared him.

Cameron did another set, then safely replaced the weights in the cradle. "Probably, but if I'm going to protect myself in prison, I better bulk up as much as possible." He sat up and wiped a bead of sweat from his brow. The piercings he once wore with pride had vanished sometime after the nose ring.

In her opinion, he looked better without them, but it wasn't her concern. His case, on the other hand, was. "Adrian and I will win, Cameron. You saw the reasonable doubt we uncovered during depositions. We'll hit a home run. I need you to believe that."

He scooted closer to the bar and pointed to the empty part of the bench. Once Joci straddled the black foam seat, he spoke. "I have every confidence in the world in you," he reassured.

"Then why are—" His fingers over her lips silenced her.

"I don't trust the system. Never have." Cameron's finger traced her thigh. "Plus, J.J. or one of his guys will be in the courtroom. No doubt about it. He played me, and now I'm dealing with the results of his scorn." His fingers dipped to her chin.

"Then you didn't kill Nichols," she affirmed.

Letting out a sigh, he shook his head. "I couldn't kill him any more than I can kiss you in this moment." His eyes flicked to her lips. "I have control, even though it really sucks when you look so beautiful."

Joci's cheeks flamed at his compliment. "We're going to beat this. I won't let you spend another holiday alone."

Cameron tucked her hair behind her shoulder. "I wish I could believe you. Even if we win, I have no family. None who I care to share a meal with. My Del Rossi mates don't count as people I like."

"You can spend any holiday you want with me," she promised, moving closer. "There will always be a seat for you."

He released an uncomfortable laugh. "Thanks, but I can't."

"Why not?"

Tracing his hands up her soft sweater, Cameron leaned in. His brown eyes dared her to defy the intimacy of his act. "I can't watch you be happy with Adrian, or any other guy."

Joci rolled her eyes. Now would be the time to tell him about the ideal way he overtook her better senses with his lips, but she couldn't. Not until she knew he'd be safe. "Oh, come on. It's not like we did anything but kiss."

The look he sent her caused her smile to fade. "Maybe not, but I can't come to dinner and imagine another man touching you. I'd be too jealous to eat a morsel." He cradled her jaw between his hands. "You've given me hope for my future, but if I have to see you happy with someone else, I would rather serve life in prison."

"You don't mean that," she protested, out of breath somehow. This was insane, but she loved the madness.

Cameron kissed her lips sparingly. "But I do."

His breath clashed with hers, and all Joci wanted was to feel his touch more, longer, deeper. She didn't know how to react to his words. Their banter had led to more feelings than she ever anticipated. Never had she allowed herself to feel lasting emotions for a client. *But he isn't just a client.*

"I know Adrian is your ex-husband, and I think there's a good reason for it."

The urge to rip off her glasses so there was nothing between them ate at her. "Why would you say that?"

Searching her eyes with his, Cameron slid his fingers along her neck. "Because he's not your type."

"Oh really? And what is my type?" she charged.

He yanked her to him, stealing her breath. His gaze

hovered over her lips, and Joci's heart thumped out of control. "You would be happiest with someone unexpected. A man who can leave you guessing, but also knows everything you crave before you do."

Joci's hands curled around his biceps, the tattooed flesh artfully molding her fingers to him. "What else?" she voiced above a whisper, clinging to his next words.

His hands drifted beneath her sweater. The brash act caused Joci to gasp. Cameron quietly chuckled. "You need a man who will send shock waves through your body with a mere trace of him."

Frozen in her place, she reveled in how his hands traveled up her body. The heat in his touch created embers, burning low yet scalding her.

"A man who is so enraptured by your soul that ten years down the road when your three kids and fluffy Australian shepherd drive you batty, he still doesn't falter when another woman flutters her eyes at him."

His palms cupped her breasts, taunting. "But most important, you deserve a man who never gives up on you, who pushes you toward your dreams. You always spoke about helping people, Joce, and you're doing an amazing job so far, but I think someone can help you… motivate you to do more."

Joci panted, her eyes glazed over in desire. Cameron was barely caressing her, but the anticipation of what he could do overwhelmed her. "And where precisely am I supposed to find a man like him?"

Confusion stamped across his face and he withdrew his

warmth with reluctance. "I can't direct you to him. You have to find the guy on your own."

His obvious desire for her coupled with his retreat baffled her. This was the second time he'd done such an idiotic thing. She took in his gleaming skin and wondered what mysteries lay beneath his jeans and T-shirt. He was in excellent shape, more so than when she met him in jail, but it wasn't why she was attracted to him. "You know, you may fool others, but I see through those smokescreens."

One of Cameron's brown waves flopped over his forehead. "Is that so? And what do you see?"

Joci danced her fingers along his chest and pressed them over his heart. "You're more than a badass drummer who dabbles with mobsters. You have a good heart, but you don't always use it."

A slow grin etched over his handsome face. She was positive no one had ever been on the receiving end of this look. He filled her with both awe and sadness.

"You sure have me down, don't you?" He tapped the end of her nose with his thumb. "I wish my boy-band persona was all, Joci, but it's not." He sighed. "You know part of it, but there's more, and definitely not related to my case. It would send you running for the door. Everyone keeps secrets, Joce. Wouldn't you agree, Adrian?" His gaze shifted to the door, and Joci turned to look. Adrian's pale brows were knit together as he took in the scene in the downsized gym. She couldn't imagine what he was thinking. Cursing to herself, she wondered how much of their conversation Adrian had heard, and what he'd seen pass between them.

"Uh, sure," Adrian said, his baby blues more guilty than downtrodden. "Since the office is closed tomorrow for a judicial conference, Rayna will be by later to go over the case." He turned halfway, then added, "I think I'm going to head to bed."

Regret filled Joci as she watched the hasty departure. "You knew he was there," she accused. Her nerves flared at the apparent deceit.

Snickering, Cameron moved to the treadmill. "Calm down. He walked in five seconds ago. He didn't see or hear anything damning." He tore off his shirt and stepped on the machine. "Not that there was anything to see."

"You're running in jeans?" she wondered aloud, not bothering to rip her eyes away from his bare torso. There was more history on his body than mere tattoos. Deep scars and cigarette burns littered the spots his tattoos couldn't hide.

Walking backward, Cameron held up his hands. "I would strip down to my boxers if you weren't here." He smirked. "Unless you want to watch. I'm good with it if you are."

Grunting at his apparent mood change, Joci stomped from the room. *He only acts like this when Adrian's around,* she recalled. It made sense, since they both vied for her attention. She had a history with Adrian, but she saw a future with Cameron. *If the mob doesn't kill him first.*

CHAPTER FOURTEEN

Gray clouds filled the morning sky on the first day of trial. Monday never tasted so bad in Cameron's mouth as he stared out of the panoramic window. The week before had been torture enough with the jury selection, but now he dreaded the upcoming verdict. His life was about to be exposed to thousands of Iowans. Jerry wasn't fond of the possibility of dragging the Del Rossi and Mikkelsen mobs into the press and told him as much when Cameron received the phone call late last night. J.J. remained suspiciously aloof during the last month, making him curious as to why. Someone from the Mikkelsen crew would no doubt be in the gallery. His gut churned at the thought of Joci in danger because of him. Sure, she was in minimal danger thanks to Adrian, but J.J. wouldn't play fair no matter who was involved.

All of a sudden, he craved a blue-collar life over one spent behind bars. The gripping fragrance of berries wafted through the air. Yet he also wanted her, and that was almost as improbable as a murder acquittal. Still, it was all he'd dreamed of last night, a future with the prettiest criminal lawyer to ever set foot in his life.

"Are you ready?" Rayna's comforting voice asked from behind him.

"That's a loaded question," he managed, drawing in a deep breath. News vans littered the streets in front of the door. They didn't bother hiding their interest, sitting in plain view for all to see. He wasn't sure why the interest other than it was the most recent murder trial for the community.

Rayna's heels echoed on the expensive flooring. "I know. I'm sorry." Her amber perfume surrounded him like a mist. "But we need to go. Joci and Adrian are already downstairs."

Twirling around, Cameron tossed her a weak smile. "We mustn't keep them waiting then, must we?"

Running her hand over his hair one last time, Rayna nodded her approval at the new do. It was the shortest style he had sported since junior high. No doubt the frigid Iowa air would sneak right through his skull and freeze his already chilled heart.

"I don't know the final verdict, but in my opinion, you are innocent," she reassured, moving his green tie to the left. The damn thing felt like it was choking him.

"Thanks, Rayna. For everything." Cameron studied the attorney. He would miss her smile, and the bangs that wouldn't stay out of her eyes.

Offering him a dazzling smile, Rayna clutched her purse. "You can thank me a million times after we have a celebratory drink when the jury returns."

Cameron swung on his suit jacket. "If that's the case, I'll

buy the first round." He followed her to the threshold and hesitated before he stepped into the hall.

"Still getting used to no ankle bracelet?" she teased, strutting to the elevator and pressing the button.

An officer clicked on a pair of handcuffs and Cameron winced. "Yes, but I'll be even happier when I don't have to be used to these." He tailed Rayna and was disappointed when no one else appeared in the hallway. It wasn't that he wanted Joci to guide him through the process, but he did anyhow.

By the time the group made it to the first floor, Cameron's palms were sweating in anticipation. Gut churning, he took the first step toward his doom.

Adrian met them shy of the exit. His suave black suit with a pop of color in his blue shirt and striped matching tie made Cameron resent him more.

"There's a bigger turnout than we expected," the lawyer announced. "It seems a video was leaked online last night that showed one of your previous court hearings."

"It couldn't have been so horrible," Rayna defended.

Cameron attempted to wipe the perspiration from his brow, but his cuffs got in the way. "If it's the one I'm thinking of, it's very bad." His mind flashed back to the day in question, and he wished Rayna had brought an extra shirt for him. He may need to go through several before the day's end.

"He attacked another inmate while they were waiting for their hearings," Adrian filled in. "And it wasn't pretty."

Both attorneys stared at their client. "It happened five

years ago. The guy was asking for it," he pointed out.

"I thought you said you weren't violent." Joci's lips pressed together and made them all that more kissable.

Shrugging, he glanced to the floor. "Yeah, about that. In general, I'm not violent, but when somebody messes with a person I care for, I can lose my cool."

"Super. Just what we need, more character instability," Adrian seethed.

In reality, the inmate that Cameron had beat up deserved more than what he received. The guy knew his mom and said she'd whored herself out after concerts. Despite barely receiving birthday presents from the woman, he wouldn't allow the douche to talk down about her. He sure as hell wouldn't waste a bloody knuckle on her these days.

Rayna rolled her eyes and went in the direction of the awaiting crowd.

"How much does it show?" he directed toward the other man.

The deputy snorted and nudged him forward. "It's a bloody mess," he interjected, finding his tongue.

Cameron's legs longed to put as many miles beneath his feet as possible. "Great, even the police have seen it. I'm screwed." He started to pace, then paused when the sound of a camera's shutter echoed in the entry.

"Come on," Adrian griped, yanking on his arm. The man lowered his voice. "Kudos to you, though. You can throw decent punches."

A faint smirk flashed across Cameron's face as they moved toward the outdoors. "Thanks. I think." He didn't want to like the guy who was lying to Joci, but the lawyer had his good moments too.

As they reached the doors, Adrian instructed, "Say nothing. Joci is already on major damage control because of the video. We're hoping the jury hasn't seen it yet. The sheriff's van is waiting to take you a whole five blocks." He chuckled and opened the door. "Oh, and try not to act too cocky. The jury will hate it, not to mention me. It's annoying."

"Ugh, so many rules," Cameron grumbled, and got a scornful glower in retort. "All right, all right, I'll behave."

Brushing by him, Adrian mumbled under his breath, "I can't believe she was ever attracted to you."

If Cameron wasn't worried for his own life, Adrian's resentful declaration would've warmed his heart. As he moved into the flashing lights in the brisk spring air, the one thing keeping him rational was the fact that Joci wasn't entirely out of his reach.

— — —

The courtroom was filled to the brim with media and nosy Iowans. Her typical trial barely filled two rows, so Joci's nerves rumbled within her. Placing her left hand over her stomach, she attempted to settle the queasy sensation that wouldn't relent. The pitted ache had filled her gut since the day after their family-style feast. After chalking it up to a combination of too much food and unease from preparing for her opening statements, she told herself not to worry.

A camera flashed from the audience, and she focused

on the jury pool. It had taken a total of thirteen hours to whittle it down to the chosen twelve. With preliminary examinations out of the way, the battle was on the cusp of beginning. Glancing to her left, Joci spotted Adrian and Cameron chatting as the crowd awaited the judge's return. It seemed nature called too often for the man to ignore.

The circus earlier in the morning unsettled her until she reached the courtroom on the first floor. She knew Cameron had a colorful past, but actually seeing the footage didn't sit well. Jimmy Nichols's family didn't show, not that she expected them to. He wasn't a nice guy if the three ex-wives with protective orders against him were any indicator. Without a doubt, one of the gang members was present for the trial, though. Surely they wouldn't let the trial of their boss's suspicious death go unattended. Although, the courthouse was crawling with police, so it was possible no one save the prosecution cared for the outcome.

From the corner of her eye, Joci saw Quinn enter the room and make his way to the opposing counsel table and spoke in a hushed voice. Dozens of eyes turned in his direction, as if compelled. It was like seeing Ian Somerhalder in person; no one could ignore the exuding good looks and stamina. She gave him a polite grin before he quickly exited the courtroom, then returned her gaze to the two men beside her. Both Adrian and Cameron fixed their attention to her, their eyes filled with condemnation. Scribbling on her notepad, Joci ignored their obvious disdain. *A girl can still enjoy eye candy.*

The bailiff called for the audience to rise as Judge Keller

entered from within his chambers. "Sit," he grumped.

Eyeing the men beside her, Joci took a breath. Keller was fairly new as a judge, but one of the better magistrates in Polk County. His impartial nature and unwavering vigilance to the law both frightened and encouraged her for their case.

"Mr. Bell, Ms. Lord, you may begin," the judge acknowledged.

The county attorney buttoned his jacket, then shoved back his chair while his partner stayed seated. "Ladies and gentlemen of the jury, this is a case of a harrowing Halloween death caused by the defendant. After this week is through, you will see the tangible evidence against Mr. Shearer, including the weapons used and the drugs discovered at the scene of the crime. Coupled with testimony, you will have no option but to find him guilty on all counts."

Joci snuck a glance to her client. His brown eyes were vulnerable as the prosecution continued his opening statement. Over the years, she had been privy to many innocent and guilty eyes, yet Cameron's were a combination of both.

Worry dotted her brow as she met Adrian's gaze. He was the one person she could count on when it boiled down to it. Under the table, he squeezed her thigh in reassuring fashion. His unfaltering confidence in her sent her stomach fluttering for new causes.

"Ms. Dorous, Mr. Petosa, you may proceed," Judge Keller announced once Mr. Bell sat.

"Thank you, Your Honor." She stood and carefully positioned herself in front of the jurors. Without question, the majority of them didn't want to be there, so her goal was to give them a reason for their service.

"Ladies and gentlemen of the jury, you are here today because of an injustice that fell upon my client. He had no control over the damning situation or evidence from day number one. The same scenario could happen to you. During this week, I will prove definitively that my client, Mr. Shearer, was not capable of murder on Halloween night or today. He is a victim in this tragedy. Being at the wrong place at an unfortunate time is all that he is guilty of. The evidence I will show you will prove as much."

She took a slow glance over the people. "Over the next five days, I want you to put yourself in Mr. Shearer's shoes and imagine a life that you can never escape, as the prosecution wants you to believe. My faith is in the system, but oftentimes that same system fails one of its own. Let's not let that happen again at the expense of a young man's life."

After nodding a smile to the jury, Joci returned to the table and let out the breath she had been holding. Adrian winked at her, but Cameron's face didn't budge from a concerned expression. She may not have won over her own client, but at least she had one man on her side to begin this debacle.

— — —

The morning drudged by dreadfully slow for Cameron. Seeing the case against him all over again made his head hurt. It was like reliving that hellish night until his ears bled.

None of it was true, but the exhibits spoke another tale.

Any time the county attorney pointed to him, Cameron wanted to shrink into a speck of dirt. The nasty glances he received from both the jury and the audience didn't help his nerves either. Most of the first day was for the State's side of the case. From witnesses to exhibits, he wanted a stiff drink before they stopped for lunch.

Sitting beside only Adrian reiterated his dismal mood. Either he was pissy, hurt, furious, or a combination of all three. It made sense to be as far away from Joci as possible. She deserved better, but not Adrian. Adrian wasn't on trial for murdering a not-so-kind drug dealer, but he was still a scoundrel for being a Mikkelsen informant. Cameron was being the bigger man in this scenario, even if he dreaded every glance his two lawyers passed among themselves. It was cute in a peculiar sort of way. They tried to act like they didn't care for each other, but it was as clear as the gun found at the murder scene.

The one positive Cameron found in the dreary day was that he had an ideal view of Joci when she cross-examined the State's witnesses. Her tactics were tasteful and precise. She may pretend to be the girl next door, but when she was on a roll, her venom wasn't something to screw with. It reinforced his respect for her.

The defense's goals were to plant seeds of doubt within the State's evidence, then harvest a jury that couldn't agree to a case with shadows of doubts. Thus far, Joci had done a tremendous job of undermining the coroner's explanation of the stab wound and gunshot committed after Nichols was dead. She brought the rebuttal home with a lack of gunshot residue and blood splatter before the judge broke for lunch. It was similar to the depositions, but with more flair for the jury to see.

After seeing the panel scurry to their room off the courtroom, Cameron felt confident in their security for the first time all day. It wasn't easy when every other word the State used was 'murder.'

"Now what?" he asked as his attorneys tidied the table.

Adrian stood and craned his neck to the clock. "We'll reconvene in about an hour. Judge Keller is a bit fond of his lunch hour," he advised.

Cameron eyed the deputy. "And I'm guessing I have to stay here."

Taking a sip of water from her bottle, Joci nodded. "Unfortunately, yes." She pushed up her black-rimmed glasses. Her entire outfit was black today. She looked poised in that color. "You're not free yet."

Cameron wondered if the dark hue of blue was for show, or if she truly liked the blue button-up shirt beneath her suit jacket. Either way, he adored the subtle way it brought out the green hue in her hazel eyes. "I guess."

Joci placed her hand on Cameron's arm. "But honestly, you're safer here than if you went back to the apartment." She eyed the room. "I didn't see J.J., so I think we're in the clear."

Cameron chuckled low. "You think he would stand out? If he wasn't here this morning, he'll make himself known later on." He scoured the room, uncomfortable at the unknown.

"He's here somewhere. I can feel it."

Adrian and Joci exchanged glances. In that moment, Cameron coveted their connection. He had never been graced with one like it. It was enviable by anyone's standards. He wasn't positive where Adrian stood relationship-wise with Joci, but he hoped it wasn't close.

The deputy clapped on the handcuffs and prodded him away. "Be safe," the inmate warned. "I can't lose my defense team."

A flash of resentment crossed Adrian's face. The man quickly covered it with a sly grin. "It would make for a mistrial," he bantered, resting a palm on Joci's waist. "But we'll keep an eye out, all right?"

"Yes," Joci reiterated as the guard led him away. "Keep yourself alive too. We don't have a case without you."

Cameron lost sight of the couple when the sheriff's man pulled him into a back passageway through the courthouse. For obvious reasons, they didn't want the public exposed to criminals.

When they reached a holding cell with a sack lunch already waiting, Cameron scrunched his nose. "Wow, I haven't had one of these since high school."

"It's the best we can do," the man offered, taking the cuffs off and locking the door. "I'll be back to collect you before your trial starts again."

Sinking into the straight-backed chair, Cameron snatched the brown paper bag and emptied the contents on his lap. "Yum, mystery meat sandwich." He sniffed the white bread concoction, then tossed it back. He couldn't stomach eating.

Not when J.J. would poke his nose into the courtroom and ruin the case. He was a bundle of nerves that couldn't be quelled.

Popping open the small bag of off-brand potato chips, he loosened the tie around his neck. Maintaining his strength was a necessity, even if the chips tasted like ash in his mouth. He silently mulled over his options. Bashing his head against the bars until he passed out was tempting, as was slicing open his femoral artery with the tie clip Adrian gave him earlier. But he wouldn't indulge in either suicide method. He was determined to see this ordeal through. "Plus, someone may stab me on my way to prison," he surmised.

Time ticked by at a sluggish pace as he listened to the other inmates' chatter. Their idle musings and sexual innuendos drifted to him, but he didn't bother joining in. It was no use since they would return to the county jail, whereas he would be taken to his posh penthouse, courtesy of his attorneys. His situation would not go over well if the more dangerous criminals caught wind.

"Planning a jailbreak?" a stony voice inquired. "Because I can see you going all *Prison Break* on their asses."

Fear seized Cameron's hand, and the chips plunked to the dirty floor. "J.J.," he uttered, his voice low.

"You do remember me." The lanky blond stepped into view. A smug grin on his face made Cameron want to reach through the cell and smack it right off. "Good. I was afraid I was losing my touch."

Cameron sprang to his feet and gripped the bars. "You

shouldn't have come. The jailers will be making rounds soon."

J.J. leaned against the wall, and Cameron was surprised the man dared to muddy his designer coat. "Please. You think I didn't take care of them?" He grinned like a snake. "It's incredible what a few thousand dollars will buy you with these good ol' Iowa boys."

Clenching his jaw, Cameron wasn't surprised that bribes were involved. J.J. had more blood money than he cared to admit, and it served him well no matter where the man ventured. He hated to recall, but the drug lord's cash even helped him out of a bind a time or two.

"I will make this easy for you, Shearer." The tall man stepped up to the cell. "Give me Del Rossi's claims to the Midwest, and I will personally see that your case disappears."

Cameron's eyebrows furrowed. "And how will you do that?"

J.J. swept his hair over the left side of his forehead. "They can't prosecute a case without the defendant."

An arctic breeze trickled over Cameron's face. "Then you plan to kill me."

"Tut, tut. I'm not a monster." J.J. cleared his throat. "But perhaps our organization can point the prosecution in a different direction with one call. We have a more believable fall man ready if you play this right."

"And what am I supposed to do for this deal of a lifetime?"

"Tell Bernard that it's in his best interests to let the

Mikkelsens take a slice of the Iowa pie."

"Easier said than done. Jerry is adamant about keeping Iowa and the rest of the Midwest."

J.J. glanced at his fingernails. "Figure something out, then."

"How do I know you won't hurt me or my friends here if I do?"

The slender man shrugged and kicked his thousand-dollar boots at a crumpled ball of paper on the floor. "I wouldn't break my word. We're friends, after all."

"I wouldn't go that far, Jepsen. Threatening people I care for isn't how I show my friendship." Not trusting the promise, Cameron sat back down. If Jerry agreed to the demands, which he knew wouldn't happen, he had nothing left to protect himself with. No leverage whatsoever.

"I tell you what," he began with a forced smile. "Get my case dismissed and I'll set up a meet between you and Jerry. The two of you can hash out a deal."

J.J. contemplated the offer for a full five seconds before he chuckled. "You just don't get it, do you? I'm giving you the opportunity to do what's right for poor Mr. Nichols who left behind an orphanage of gangsters and drugs. If you don't make the call right now to your boss"—he held out a mobile—"I will have no choice but to proceed with plan B."

Already, Cameron didn't like the lunatic's backup plan. J.J. was well known for having more than one too. It was a constant in the man's life, unlike his relationship with one woman. "And what is plan B?"

Meandering to the exit, the European smoothed his

charcoal-colored jacket. "Let's say it revolves around the pretty lawyer of yours and leave it at that. It's obvious you like her. Hell, I like her, and all I did was see her in person once. I can't imagine what she would feel like in my arms." He winked. "But you know, don't you?"

"Leave Joci out of this," Cameron warned, coming to his feet once more. He never should've taken this job. It wasn't worth the agony of dealing with him.

"I see I've struck a nerve. I wonder what she would say about all your lying, cheating, stealing, and oh yes, fighting. You love the excitement, don't you?" the Danish thief alluded, greed exuding from his eyes.

Realization struck Cameron. "You're the one who posted the video."

"Folks, he's not as dumb as he looks." J.J. clapped in mock amazement. "Now don't prove me wrong and grow a conscience. Give me what I want, or I will visit the beautiful woman you dream about."

"I swear to God, I'll kill you if you lay a finger on her!" Cameron threatened, his fists ready for action.

A cynical grin spread over J.J.'s pale features. "You can't stop me from behind a cell door," he reminded. "But when you're ready to settle up, I'll be waiting."

Stealthily, he opened the door to the outside world. "You have until Friday to give me Del Rossi's seal of approval. Until then, I suggest your legal team doesn't venture out alone. My men tend to get handsy." He tossed Cameron a deviant wink, then vanished.

Regret laced with worry. Jepsen would keep his word.

He had seen similar circumstances deteriorate at a faster rate in Ohio.

Pacing the small cell, Cameron racked his brain for another way. If he didn't get his enemy out of his life, Joci would always be in danger, and so would he. He couldn't live with her life on the line.

"She deserves better," he affirmed. An idea jumped through his mind at lightning speed. It was foolhardy and dangerous, but it may work to his advantage.

A tan-shirted guard appeared through the door and ambled down the hall. Now was the time to act. His plan hinged on a hope that they wouldn't turn him down.

"Deputy, I need to speak with Officer Levi Quinn," he requested when the man reached him, chomping on an apple.

The man shot him a befuddled glance. "You want to have a chitchat with your arresting officer, huh? Do you want a sharp knife too? Maybe a camera-free room?"

"No, you don't understand," Cameron implored, running a hand over the back of his neck. "I have information about an international drug dealer in Iowa with open warrants he would be interested in hearing about."

Narrowing his eyes, the deputy took another bite of the fruit. "Hmm, he may want to hear what you have to say, then."

Cameron let out an uneasy breath as the man hurried down the hall. In the next few minutes, he was either going to sign his death certificate or liberate the life of the one woman he dared to love.

— — —

Wiping her mouth, Joci pushed off her knees and flushed the toilet. The salad she'd eaten for dinner hadn't agreed with her frazzled nerves. Other than odd behavior from her client following the lunch break, the first day of trial had gone better than expected.

She pulled at her messy ponytail, then cleaned her glasses. After returning from the new French bistro downtown, the county attorney had pulled her and Adrian aside to discuss the upcoming witnesses.

The pressure the State's attorney was up against had already drained Mr. Bell, if the sweaty brow was any indicator. The remainder of the afternoon sailed by without hiccups.

At Adrian's request, he took over the questioning of the police officers. Joci smirked, recalling the intense technique her redheaded partner used on Quinn. It was clear he wanted to destroy the cop on a number of levels, and she was somewhat pleased when he got Quinn to admit Cameron had no apparent motive to murder the victim. That right there was orgasmic to an attorney. Cheating the system never felt better. The rush of being on top of the world happened every day in the courthouse, and she never would tire of it.

Splashing water on her face, Joci reviewed her reflection. "There's nothing quite like sweats," she pointed out, then frowned. Her face was a tad white, but she guessed it was due to a bad batch of lettuce, or maybe the undercooked boiled egg.

She expected day number two to involve more nitty-gritty details about the murder. Given her shocking unease about the bloody photos shown in court earlier in the day, Joci was concerned she wouldn't be able to handle more. It wasn't normal for her to grow nauseous, no matter the case.

"Joci, are you okay in there?" Adrian asked from the other side of the door.

Stretching her neck, she blew her nose and swung open the bathroom door. Apparently, she hadn't been as quiet as she'd hoped if he heard her through the two doors. Adrian stood in the doorway in a faded yellow Iowa State University T-shirt and a loose pair of red sweatpants. He looked scrumptious. "I'm fine. Just a stomachache. Nothing to be worried about."

Adrian searched her eyes intently and rubbed his hands down her arms. "Are you sure? If you're getting sick, I can run to the pharmacy down the street and get you medicine."

Joci patted his cheek. "You're sweet, but I'm not sick. Give me a bottle of antacids and I'll be good to go." She brushed by him, and when she gripped the door handle, he stopped her from leaving the bedroom.

"Nope. No bending over case law until you pass out." He laced her fingers with hers. "You need a good night's rest so you're ready for tomorrow." He pulled her to the bed and settled her into her spot. "If you want, I can sleep in your room tonight."

Joci rolled her eyes when he all but tucked her in. "I can do it myself, Adrian. You don't have to baby me."

"But I like to," he countered. Placing his hand on her shoulder, he added, "Plus, I wanted to tell you how proud I am of you without somebody making a joke of it."

Tucking her legs beneath her, Joci leaned against the headboard. "Oh really? Is it because I obliterated the witness who was allegedly at the park the night in question?"

Adrian sat on the edge of the bed but kept a safe distance. "Your performance did turn me on a little too much, to be honest."

"Oh whatever. You're such a flirt." She didn't want to give him the opportunity to come even closer. If she wasn't careful, he'd take advantage of her queasy stomach and spoon her until she fell asleep. They'd done it many a time when they were together. She didn't need the condemning glare from Cameron if Adrian stepped out of her room the next morning. Plus, Adrian was still trying to convince her they could be together again.

"True, but you don't seem to mind."

"All right, I give up. Why are you proud of me?" she queried, dragging the conversation from the dangerous subject.

Caressing her with his enchanting blue eyes, Adrian smiled. "Watching you capture the jury with your flawless wit and the damning law made me remember why I fell in love with you. You're the ultimate dream girl for me." He organized the blanket over her in a protective manner. "I will spend the rest of my days as your second chair if you'd let me just be there to watch your grace."

Blushing, Joci was well aware of what his words meant.

He wasn't one to share the spotlight with anyone. "Are you sure about that? I might take advantage of your offer," she teased.

"I'm serious, Joci. If we were together, I'd be different. A better version of myself. You always had that effect on me."

Picking at her nails, she worried her lips together. "We don't work, Adrian. I've told you once and I'll tell you again."

"Is it Quinn? Did he change your mind?" His brows knit together in frustration.

"No, Quinn had nothing to do with my decision."

Realization crossed over his face. "It's Cameron, isn't it?"

She wanted to disagree, but she couldn't. Try as she might, the smile she attempted to hold in won out and broke over her lips. "Seeing him again woke me up. For the first time since we split up, I can actually see a future with someone."

Adrian crossed his arms. "He's a mobster, drug dealer, and probably murderer too."

"And he makes me feel alive." She toyed with the edge of the blanket. "He's almost done with Del Rossi, and then he's free. There's good in everyone, especially Cam."

A cruel laugh emitted from Adrian. "You honestly think that?"

"I have to."

A peculiar expression crept over his features. His lip curled up momentarily, then dropped when he shook his head. "Okay, but when your attraction to him blows up in your face, I'll be around to put you together again."

Joci couldn't understand Adrian's steadfast loyalty to the possibility of their relationship. "You need to move on, Adrian. Simple as that."

"Not happening anytime soon."

Before she could argue, her stomach gurgled and she sprinted to the bathroom, slamming the door. After she emptied her stomach, she rested her head against the wall. "Ugh, this sucks."

"Joci? You don't sound good. Do you want a ginger ale or something?"

She groaned in misery. Holding her head, she attempted to pull herself together. "Maybe a drink would be good," she managed before another round hit her.

Adrian swept open the door and his face fell at the sight of her clutching the toilet bowl. "Aw, hon." He swiftly grabbed a washcloth and rinsed cold water over it. Hustling to her, he pressed it to her forehead.

"Thanks." The soft material helped but didn't influence her stomach.

Brushing back her hair, Adrian dabbed another cloth at her neck. "You don't feel warm," he noted.

Bracing her forehead with her palms, she shrugged. "I told you. It's a twenty-four-hour bug or something. Maybe the chicken in my salad was on the raw side."

Her legs shook as she rocked up to stand. "It could be the case. It's been stressful these last weeks."

Adrian gripped her hips to steady her swaying body. "Could there be any other reason? You never throw up."

Pressing her lips together, she saw he had a point.

Even when she was ill, she avoided puking at all costs. Sorority Joci never got queasy after partying too hard. Another thought flashed through her mind. "What's today's date?"

"Um, uh, March 20," he stammered after glancing at his watch. "Why?"

She quickly calculated, her heartrate skyrocketing. Rustling through the bathroom drawers, she tossed items out as she looked for her birth control tabs. "Happy late St. Patrick's Day to me."

"What's going on?" he asked, urgently this time. "You're freaking me out a little."

Her heart dropped to her stomach when she found the mint-like tablets. Terror struck her as she reviewed the circular container. "One's still in there," she confessed, dropping it.

Adrian's face went from a joking smile to utter disbelief. "You don't think—" His voice trailed off when he picked up the medicine for himself.

"Shit! Shit! Shit!" she repeated in a panicked voice, wringing her hands together. This was not in the five- or even ten-year plan. She didn't want to ever have kids again. Not after the way she lost the first one.

She eyed Adrian, but found his new expression unreadable. "I take them at night because of my busy schedule. I think I forgot the night I invited you over." She bit her bottom lip. "And we didn't stop to take any preventative measures."

Keeping her eyes fixed on him, Joci cursed herself into

a frenzy. She wasn't this irresponsible. She made it her mission to stay in control at all times. This was not her definition of control whatsoever.

Adrian chucked the pills over his shoulder, not caring where it landed. The container clattered against the shower door. "You're sure you and Quinn didn't have a little rendezvous?" he asked seriously.

Narrowing her eyes into slits, she propped her hands on her hips. "No, you dick," she hurled back. She was surprised that he didn't suggest Cameron too. Adrian held his hands up but kept his lips shut.

Huffing at his silence, Joci stomped out of the bathroom and grabbed a spare blanket from the bedroom closet. "I think I'll work on some trial prep on the couch," she informed him. "At least it doesn't goad me about my sexual escapades."

She made it a whole ten feet before Adrian snaked his arms around her and hauled her against his broad chest. "Let go, you oaf," she demanded, fighting a useless battle against his strong hold. She was in no mood for his antics. She needed to think, and she couldn't do it when he inebriated her mind. If she was pregnant, it changed everything for her. Cameron wouldn't want to be bogged down by some other guy's baby. Particularly when the man was the one who despised him. She felt her body ready to hyperventilate.

"No, Joci, I won't let you go," Adrian's voice rumbled. "I'm not letting you go again." He spun her around to face him.

Cupping her jaw, he studied her face. "And I sure as hell

am not allowing you to go back to work after the day we've had." He pulled her close. "You need to rest."

Wetting her lips, Joci countered, "Fine. You go prepare the closing statement for Friday."

A chuckle escaped his mouth and calmed the raging storm inside of her.

"Look, I know this is going to sound quite odd given the new circumstances, but I need to ask you something." He dropped to his knee and dug his hand into his pocket.

"What are you doing?" she squeaked, panicking.

Adrian grabbed her hand in his. "I was going to ask you this after the case was done and I had time to prove that I wasn't the same guy, but I can't wait."

Her breath caught in her throat. If he was anywhere near serious, she just might faint.

"I've loved you since I met you, Joci Dorous," he continued with heartfelt vigor. "I screwed up when I stopped fighting for you. For us."

Her hands shook at his careful choice of words. She hadn't expected to hear any such sweet things for the rest of her life. Happiness wasn't theirs to keep. Not a second time. She'd made her peace with it years ago. Up until recently, she didn't want any type of future with a man unless it involved 'wham bam thank you ma'am.' Her head thrummed in anticipation of his next words.

Kissing her palm, Adrian produced a small, black ring box. "But I want to rectify my mistake. We deserve another shot, a new beginning."

"So you want to set out and be partners in a new law firm,"

she managed, hoping to steer the conversation to somewhere other than marriage.

"If that's what it takes for you to be my wife, then yes," he played along, opening the box. His pleading blue eyes bolted her feet to the floor. "Marry me, Joci." He smirked. "Again."

Joci's heart warred with her brain as she glanced at the ring. It wasn't the same shape or even carat as the first one. This one was unique in all possible ways.

At long last, she parted her lips to speak. "How long have you had the ring?"

"Since the day I found out we had a murder case together," he replied, a tinge of embarrassment in his words.

She marveled at his gumption. "Pretty confident in yourself, aren't you?"

"I knew what I wanted. Our union in the case was too perfect to pass up." He ran his thumb along her wrist. "You weren't going to slip through my fingers a second time," he advised.

Seeing the truth in his eyes, Joci inhaled and reviewed the facts with care. Starting fresh with Adrian scared her to death. In one night, she'd discovered the possibility that she carried his baby once more and he wanted to marry her. Those were two things she'd sworn she would never subject her soul to another time. She struggled with the possibility that her feelings for Cameron were a passing whim and not concrete. They hardly knew each other.

"What if I'm not pregnant and it's a stomach bug?" she questioned. "Would you want to try for another baby?"

"If you're not pregnant, then you're not." He sighed and squeezed her with tenderness. "I know what you said two years ago. If you never want kids, that's okay with me. I'll have you. You're all I want."

She cursed under her breath at his perfect response. "All right, then what if we don't work out?"

Adrian tipped off his knee and hopped to his feet. "Do you love me?" He kept his hold on her, but otherwise remained at a distance.

Joci mulled over the answer. Loving Adrian meant that she couldn't turn off her emotions like she endeavored.

"Well, yes, but not like—"

A small smile covered his face. "I love you. I know you think you like Cameron, but if you were willing to consider a future with him, can't you consider one with me instead?" He held up the ring. "I swear we will make this work no matter what. I can't stand to be without you in my life. I want to wake up to your slobbery pillow."

Shoving his shoulder, she tossed, "That's yours, jerk."

He chuckled and caught her wayward punch. "I know. I'm just making sure you're paying attention."

Rolling her eyes, she disclosed, "Always the smartass." She searched his face, cursing silently. What if he was right? What if the tremors she experienced around Cameron were one-sided? He didn't make an obvious move for her. Hell, he'd avoided touching her. She sighed. But there was something in Cameron's dark eyes that told her different. He protected her though he wouldn't admit it. If she gave up the opportunity she had to be with Cameron, she'd never forgive herself.

"Adrian, I can't. Not because I don't care about you or because you had your shot, but because I can't." She offered a guilty grin. "I can't give away something that wasn't meant for you."

Adrian's hopeful face dipped to a dismal frown. "Ah, yeah, okay. I get it. You love Cameron."

Joci couldn't help but smile. She'd never even thought the words, but they were true.

"Promise me one thing, though?"

She focused on Adrian. "Sure."

"Wear the ring until the trial is over."

"Are you freaking serious? Why would I do that? Did you hear what I just said?"

He cleared his throat. "You're still in danger, Joci, and if you are carrying my child, I don't want the Del Rossi or Mikkelsen mob to know you mean anything to Cameron. It'd make you a big fat target."

His plea made sense to her sleep-deprived brain. Staying safe was crucial now and any day. Meeting his gaze, she didn't think wearing a gaudy ring would harm anything. "Fine, but you need to stop calling me fat."

Adrian chuckled, relief washing over his face. "I'd never dream of it, but thank you. Even if you aren't mine, I don't want anything to happen to you."

He planted a kiss on her forehead. "I'll let you get some sleep. We'll talk about the baby situation later."

Yawning, she settled back under the covers. "Sounds like a plan."

Adrian's soft steps stopped at the door when he flicked off the light. "Nobody will hurt either of you. I swear on my life."

"You're such a drama king." Joci rolled over. "I'm not officially pregnant yet, Adrian," she muffled against the pillow.

"Then I'll be sure to buy a test tomorrow," he teased, shutting the door.

Sliding farther under the covers, she popped open her eyes and stared into the darkness. Adrian was being overdramatic, but he had a point. It was the only reason she agreed to sporting the diamond ring. Carefully, she placed her hands on her flat stomach. *Is it possible?* She wasn't sure, but the way Adrian reacted, he was more than thrilled at the potential child.

Cameron's low voice echoed under the door and reached her. But will he be all right with it? She couldn't be sure about anything until she had all the evidence. One she could easily get her hands on, but the other involved a man who was as unpredictable as winter in Iowa.

CHAPTER FIFTEEN

Spooning the last bite of square corn cereal past his lips, Cameron stared at the brewing coffeemaker. It sputtered out a caffeine addict's delight, but no one was there to drink it yet. The machine was on an automatic timer, but this morning the sound he slept through any other day annoyed him. He slid the blue porcelain bowl out of the way and twirled on the barstool. The instant the coffee finished was when Joci would appear, but today she was late.

Nervousness plagued him almost as much as the plea bargain J.J. offered the other day. The milk in his stomach soured at the thought of his Joci being harmed if he didn't comply. He stayed compliant with everything his boss told him to do until Joci's life became a bargaining chip. After speaking to Jerry last night, he saw Adrian emerge from her room. It pained him to see the joyful smirk on the man's face. He'd wanted to wipe it off the instant Adrian looked at him. Whatever happened behind Joci's closed door, he wanted to know even if it'd make him sick. He didn't trust Adrian since he was a puppet of the Mikkelsen mob, but also because he was shady as hell when it came to Joci. The man vied for her more than even Quinn, which was saying something.

The bedroom door cracked open somewhat, so he swiveled to face the kitchen. A shock of red hair met his gaze. Watching a triumphant entrance from Adrian was not high on his list of things to see in his lifetime. It was bad enough he had to be around the man who followed Joci almost as closely as he did. He hadn't seen him return to Joci's room the night before, so he instantly wondered why Adrian was in there.

"Fine, but when this case is over, you are going," the man in question directed, his shoes tapping the floor as he entered the room. He grabbed the coffeepot and nodded to him. "Good morning."

Cameron bobbed his head in return but didn't offer a greeting. It wasn't a good morning until Adrian didn't have a hold over Joci. She couldn't see it, but her coworker was bad news. His aura was always off, and that made Cameron's inspection of him intensify. Surely Adrian knew the risk involved when it came to the Mikkelsens. Of course, in his own experience, he didn't have a choice when he joined the Del Rossi mob.

The son of a wealthy lawyer, Adrian wore a watch that cost more than Cameron's first car. Coupled with shiny brown loafers and a pinstriped blue suit, the attorney was too good to be real. He resembled one of those television lawyers who always got what they wanted. If the Mikkelsens aided Adrian at all in the court system, Cameron guessed the redhead was more in debt than he thought.

Adrian poured sugar into his coffee and leaned against the granite. A peculiar smile splashed across his lips. It was one that made Cameron want to wipe it off with a mallet.

"Everything okay with Joci?" Cameron broke down and asked. He could stare at perfection for only so long. His eyes were starting to hurt from the pale skin.

The man took a sip of morning energy. "She's good. Excellent, really. Just a bit behind."

"Sure," he answered, curious at the reason behind the man's happy mood. This version of Adrian wasn't his favorite. He preferred brooding Adrian, or perhaps jealous Adrian, but this chipper façade was disgusting.

Before Cameron could speak again, Joci bounded from the bedroom and strutted through the kitchen like a new summer breeze. How he wished she would stop wearing fragrances that made him crave sunshine and bikinis!

"Are you sure you should be drinking that?" Adrian pointed out when she clutched the handle of the coffeepot.

"Why wouldn't she?" Cameron asked, not concerned. Joci always had coffee near her, a hint of the aroma clinging to her clothes.

Gripping a clean mug, she filled it halfway with the dark liquid. "Yes, Adrian. I can have my goddamn coffee." She flashed him a haughty grin.

"But—" he started, and her glare silenced him.

"Try and take it from me," she warned, then inhaled the steam wafting from the cup. "That's the stuff."

It was in that moment Cameron saw the ring on her

finger. That finger. The one he wanted as his. If she was attached to Adrian in the domesticated way, he was as good as in the slammer for life because the instant he didn't have witnesses around, he would knock the fucker's lights out. Joci was *his*, not the egotistical ass's who stared at her over the rim of his coffee cup.

Choking on air, he stood and the barstool screeched. "All righty, well if your repulsive lover's quarrel is about done, we should go. The judge won't wait for us." He took a step away and chuckled. "Oh wait, yes he will."

Not caring to hear a response from either of them, he hurried to his bedroom. Shutting the door, he rummaged through the pile of pleadings on top of his dresser with haste until his fingers touched the burner cell phone J.J. had sent him. There was no way he would call that piece of shit. He already had a deal going on with Quinn, specially crafted for the blond mobster. Regrettably, it didn't mean Joci was out of the woods yet; the Mikkelsens could still come after her if J.J. informed them of Cameron's attachment. He'd asked Quinn to take Joci into protective custody, but actually getting her to agree was another struggle. She wasn't the type to sit back idly and let the men handle things. She'd want to get her hands dirty if he knew her, and he did. No matter how many times Adrian reminded Cameron that he didn't know the tall brunette, he disagreed at every turn. She hadn't changed all that much since Ohio. Yeah, she was older and a hell of a lot prettier, but her soul was the same. How the hell Adrian convinced her to marry him again he couldn't think about. At the moment, he needed to focus on his trial.

Closing his eyes, he tried to picture his buddy's phone number. Memorizing contact information was an abnormality, but Cameron had forced himself to learn Jerry's. He usually didn't call. Jerry called him from various burner phones.

He swallowed hard. Calling in not one but two favors to the Enforcer would come with strings attached. Which strings, he wasn't sure of yet, but he had a few guesses. Both included his life in the firing line.

"And just when I thought I was done with mob shit," he muttered, punching in the numbers.

"I need to speak with Bernard," he stated when a henchman answered the call. Though Jerry to Cameron, his comrade was a stickler for formalities. Cameron gave his name and the man grunted.

The silence on the other end chipped away at his brilliant idea. This was his one-time get out of jail free card. "And it's the best use of it too," he confirmed.

The longer he waited, the more his arteries felt ready to explode. He needed to make sure Joci was safe. He didn't trust Quinn, not completely, and he sure as hell didn't trust Adrian. There was only one man who could make his wishes a reality.

"Cameron, is that you?" a rumbly voice queried in his ear.

"Last I checked."

Jerry chuckled, the sound not quite comforting. "Shouldn't you be in a courtroom with two expensive attorneys?"

"I'm heading there soon." Cameron pulled his tie away from his neck.

"And Jepsen, is he sticking with the original deal?"

"Yeah, I don't see him backing off. The Mikkelsens want Iowa too much to let go."

Jerry snorted. "Typical. Now what else do you have for me?"

Cameron swallowed past the bile rising in his throat when he heard Joci's light laughter and Adrian's voice accompanying it. It wasn't that he was jealous, but he was. He couldn't have her, so if she was going to resort to Adrian, Cameron needed assurances that she didn't wind up as a continued pawn for the Mikkelsen crew. So long as Adrian was involved with the lot, she would be no matter what. "I have a favor I need to cash in. I wouldn't bother you, but it means the life or death of the woman I love."

He paused and let those words wash over him. He'd never admitted his feelings for Joci out loud.

"Let me guess, your attorney?" Jerry hollered in Italian at one of his men.

Cameron caught the phrase "shut the damn door" before he rambled on under his breath. "Yeah."

Jerry chuckled from the other end. "What? You're not going to go into detail? I'd enjoy a bit of entertainment. Plus, I didn't think you were over my sister yet."

Ignoring the insinuation regarding his ex, Cameron pushed forward. "Not happening and you know it."

"Fine, fine. Now what is it?"

"I made a deal, Jer. It'll get rid of J.J., but I'm afraid Joci is going to get caught in the middle of a bullet fight."

"I see nothing wrong with that. He's a pain in the ass. What kind of deal did you make?"

Pacing, he did his best to keep his voice low. He didn't need Adrian to hear and tip off J.J. "As you know, Jepsen's drugs have a distinct chemical makeup. I promised the cops Jepsen and the Mikkelsen mob connections. Since J.J. has several open warrants in the States, his arrest would give the cops enough time to secure a good case against him while they wait for him to dish out the Mikkelsen information."

"What about Ms. Dorous? No doubt she comes into all this somehow or you wouldn't be bothering me."

"Yes. Quinn said he'd keep her in protective custody, but they have a history and she doesn't like to obey anyone."

"Sounds like someone else I know," Jerry added.

"True. She won't let the cops keep her away. That much I can predict for certain. Not unless they manhandle her. I don't see Officer Quinn doing it either, so I need help."

Jerry cleared his throat. "You're asking me to bring her under the protection of the Del Rossis, correct?"

He gulped. "Yeah. That's what I need."

"And you're aware that once she's under the Del Rossis, you can't be romantically involved so long as she is protected, right?"

Setting his jaw, he breathed in his fate. "Yep, I know." Rules of the mob weren't always followed, but this was one of the gray areas. Being emotionally attached to a protected party put the entire mob at risk. Obviously, the significant others were different, but being protected meant the Del

Rossis would wage war for the person. It wasn't a code to trifle with. Cameron understood it now more than ever. The mob's protection ensured Joci's safety from Adrian as well as J.J. He didn't trust that Adrian wouldn't throw her into the mix should the need arise. Even if he couldn't have her, she'd be nearby and far from harm.

"Hmm, you're asking quite a bit, Cameroni."

"And I'm not done either." He didn't wait for the boss to respond. "If I'm successful, I want out of the mafia for good."

Silence simmered in the conversation until Jerry spoke up. "Your request is bold. I always liked that about you. All right, Shearer. We'll do it your way. If you can deliver Jepsen and the Mikkelsens to the authorities and get them permanently out of my territories, I'll release you and the woman."

Just when Cameron's lips tempted a smile, the Italian added, "But if not, you're still in, and I may have need of an attorney in Iowa who will help us from time to time."

The stakes were higher than he imagined Jerry would offer. *It's worth it, though. She's worth it.* Try as he might, Cameron wouldn't let Joci fall prey to Jepsen or the dashing redhead who allegedly claimed her as his fiancée. He'd get down to the bottom of that conundrum later. For now, he'd sacrifice his heart and freedom for her sake. It may be a suicide mission, but it was one worth trying.

— — —

Checking her phone during one of the afternoon breaks,

Joci squinted when she noticed Rayna had called her three times. She put the iPhone back into the front pocket of her purse. *If it's important, she'll text,* she decided.

"Where did Prince Charming run off to?" Cameron asked from her side.

Joci turned her head to the left and took in her client's demeanor. He'd been off since she'd witnessed his brown eyes fade to black at the sight of the engagement ring. She should explain that Adrian and she weren't together, but they were rarely alone. It wasn't a conversation she wanted others to hear, given the physical and emotional risk on her side.

"He had to run to the office real quick. Something about another case he needed to check on," she informed him. "He'll be back before we close for the day." She stacked her notepad on the prosecution's exhibit book. "Why?"

Leaning back in his chair, he ran his eyes over her. "Just making sure he didn't abandon you."

"Adrian would never do that," she snapped, digging her nails into her partner's chair between them.

"Mmhmm, of course not," he mused aloud.

Studying him, she admired Rayna's choice of the dark blue shirt under his suit jacket. The hue reminded her of the tattoos sporting the same color that were visible when he didn't wear such professional attire.

Ignoring her longing to see the brilliant designs once more, Joci cleared her throat and eyed the courtroom. The jury was in their safe room, and a handful of spectators remained in their seats. To her relief, the case was slowing down. They were about to wrap up day two of the trial, and only three news interns were in the audience, compared to the five who were there before. One by one, she heard the spectators leave the room during the recess. She took it as a good sign. The case of a drug dealer wasn't of big interest. Nevertheless, she suspected the State would rest by the end of the next day. Mr. Bell was out of witnesses and running low on sweat. He'd need a transfusion if they continued on another few days.

"You may want to stay in the apartment after we win," Cameron advised in a quiet voice.

Joci flipped her straight, brown hair over her shoulder. "Why? What do you know? Is J.J. here?"

"As it turns out, yeah, he is," her client admitted. "I saw him yesterday." He moved to Adrian's seat to close the minimal distance between them.

"Why didn't you tell us? I need to tell Adrian." She pulled out her cell phone and moved to call one of the loitering bailiffs so they would step out while she phoned Adrian, but he snagged her arm.

"No, don't," Cameron urged. "One of J.J.'s guys is in the crowd. We can't make a scene."

Glaring at him with wild eyes, she wrenched free of his grip and stared at his hands. The same hands that had tenderly touched her not long ago. She shivered in remembrance. Casually, she snuck a peek over her shoulder. Sure enough, only one person sat in the back of the room, though he was intently studying his phone.

Two deputies headed their way, chatting casually.

"Ms. Dorous, we need to take him to one of the holding rooms until court resumes." The older of the two men hauled Cameron to his feet.

Joci stood as well. "I'm not done speaking with him." The man with jingling keys nodded for her to follow. Once they were safely stowed in one of the rooms just off the courtroom, she let out a breath when the click on the lock echoed in the small space. It wasn't a horrible spot, but was definitely in need of a thorough cleaning.

Glancing to her client, she cleared her throat. "Are you going to tell me why I shouldn't make a scene now?"

Cameron shot an obvious expression her way. "Are you serious?" She shrugged, not knowing what else to do. "Okay, if you want me to say it, then I will."

Steadying her breath, she braced her body for the next slew of words.

He leaned over until his cuffed hands closed over hers. "I need you safe, Joci, which means you have to keep your head down no matter what happens."

"What's going to happen?" she asked as her gaze flicked to his cuffs then to his lips before settling on his face.

Rubbing his thumb on the back of her hand, he met her hazel eyes. "Nothing, I hope, but I have a notion my nemesis will strike soon."

He took a deep breath. "And Quinn and I have a little surprise for him when he does."

Joci followed his direction. "You're selling J.J. out?" she guessed.

He smirked in that damn adorable way that forced her

lips to reciprocate. "Something along those lines. More of an exchange of favors."

"Wait, favors with who?" she questioned, now tightly gripping him. If he was going to put himself in danger's way, she needed to stop him. His eyes glued to her hands, but she didn't relent. J.J. and this case be damned, she couldn't live without knowing Cameron was protected.

Tracing his finger over her ring, he sighed. "I see you will soon be his forever again, huh?" Cameron chuckled. "It's funny. I didn't think you were a woman who passed out second chances like candy on Halloween." His eyes clashed with hers. "You sure didn't for me."

"We were never together," she reminded him in a hushed tone, letting the remainder of his observation stay open. She needed to correct him. As soon as possible if the glint in his eyes was any indicator.

He linked his hands intimately with hers. "Ah, right. How could I forget?"

Joci should move away from him. If anyone walked in to see their brazen intermingling, the Bar Association would have her job. "You're a client right now, Cameron, not my friend. You know whatever connection that passed between us was purely physical."

He leaned in close until his nose electrified hers. "I don't believe that, and neither do you."

Holding herself back from giving in to her desire to catch his bottom lip with her teeth, Joci focused on her breathing. That would've been easier if his mocha eyes didn't penetrate her resolve to look away.

"You're much more than a pretty face." He leisurely reviewed her body. "Or pretty every inch of you." Joci rolled her eyes, but he didn't cease. "You're the woman who's trying to save my life, yet there's more to you. The kindness you exude, though sometimes brash, intoxicates me almost as much as that damn perfume you wear." With bold fingers, he traced her lips. "You make me want to be someone other than a mob man."

The last bit startled her out of his magical haze. That fact moved her heart an inch. Clearly she meant more to him than an attorney or long-lost friend. "Why?" she whispered.

Cameron's eyes grazed over her. "Because you remind me of who I was. No one else has ever done that. I can't lose the feelings you shoot through my veins. It's better than any high I could imagine."

"Oh," she replied, still grappling with his statement.

"There's just something about you, Joce," he admitted. "I came to Iowa to hunt J.J. down. I never expected to like being at your mercy," he explained, his voice thick with emotion.

Joci sat back in shock. *Now would be a great time to say something, Joci.*

"Are you going to say something or just sit there and look pretty?" he asked with a low voice.

"Um, I don't know." She picked up her pen and started to write on the notepad.

Out of the corner of her eye, she saw him smirk at the gibberish. She couldn't focus if her life depended on it. Cameron's proximity only enhanced her sense of smell, and damn did he smell incredible.

"Do you remember our first kiss?"

Startled at the question, her pen paused and she looked up. "Yes."

Cameron drummed his fingers on the desk. "We were riding our bikes through the mud and you totally wiped out on the bike ramp."

Joci smiled at the imagery. She could see it as plain as day. "So did you if I recall correctly."

"Only because I was worried you broke another bone." He traced his index finger over her wrist. "You're a tad accident-prone."

"I never broke anything after I left Ohio, so you must've been my weakness," she teased. Her eyes bugged the instant the words flew out. *Shit!*

He let out a shaky breath. "Am I still your weakness?"

She didn't know how to respond. If she told him the truth, he'd be inclined to rub it in Adrian's face. "Anyways, you cleared the mud off my face, then kissed me. The end." She wrapped up the story with more haste than a tardy bell, then bent over the table and hoped he'd let the subject drop. She wasn't ready to admit her feelings. Not yet.

Carefully, Cameron grabbed her hand and held it between his own, compelling her attention back to him. "That's the gist, yeah, but I like my version better."

"What's your version?" she asked, breathless when she recognized the yearning in his eyes.

"Well, I skidded off my bike like a badass, not a pansy, and slid to your side. You were covered in mud from ponytail to sneakers, but I'd never seen anything so lovely." He moved as close as physically possible. "I knew right then that I had to kiss you. No other guy would be as lucky as when I pressed my lips against those muddy ones of yours." His gaze dipped to her mouth. "Though I am fond of the red tint to yours today."

Swallowing hard, Joci's body warmed at his words. There was no way in hell he was lying. Deciding now was as good a time as any, she confessed, "I think I'm pregnant."

"We were hot and heavy, but that doesn't make a kid, darlin'" came his response.

I know that," she snapped. "It's not yours. It's Adrian's."

Both his hands shot to his head and he let out a loud sigh. "Of course it is."

"What's that supposed to mean?"

"You're not sure you're pregnant? How're you not sure?"

Joci held up her hand as they talked over each other. "It means I haven't taken a test yet, okay?"

She watched Cameron's chest rise and fall while he digested. *Tell him, Joci, or you'll regret it.*

Before she had the chance to spill her guts, he asked, "It happened when I stopped us, didn't it?"

She slowly nodded. "It was the only time we slept together."

"Fuck," he groaned, rubbing his eyes harshly.

Joci shivered, imagining him using that word in a completely different context.

"So the engagement, is that because he knocked you up?"

He eyed the ring as if it were a snake.

"No. We're not engaged. It's a precaution," she explained, but was met with a squint, so she continued. "Adrian thinks it'll keep J.J. away from me if they know I'm taken."

"And a gigantic ring keeps you safe? I don't think so. He's playing you." Cameron sat up straight. "Because I can think of a bunch more ways to make it crystal clear you're mine, and none involve a piece of jewelry."

Joci opened her mouth to ask what he meant, but two deputies entered the room and stopped her. "We're right outside if you need us, Ms. Dorous."

She nodded. "Great, thanks, guys." Once they heard her response, they left again.

"We should focus on the case," Joci determined as she began to stand. Her knees didn't straighten before he yanked her back to the chair.

"Absolutely not. I'd rather discuss what you're going to do about the Adrian situation."

She tilted her head in annoyance. "What situation? I told you, he's trying to help me." It was his turn to tilt his head, so she slipped off the ring and slammed it on the table. "There, happy now? I'm single again."

He eyed the massive jewel, then returned his gaze to her. "I'd be happier if you skipped town and let Adrian finish the case."

"Not happening, Cam. I don't back down from anything."

He boldly tugged on a strand of hair resting on her collarbone. "I thought you'd say that. Don't worry, I'll make sure you're safe."

She rolled her eyes. "Adrian said he took care of it."

Cameron nudged his finger through her jacket's cuff. "Yeah, I don't trust him and neither should you. The Del Rossis will protect you from now on."

"What did you do?"

Pulling her close, he hovered over her ear. "What I had to." He moved back, his eyes skimming her lips.

Joci hated him for the delightful agony he put her through. It was all too much. He'd used his mob connections to protect her. It was insane, yet intensely seductive.

If she could clone the way he looked at her, she would be a millionaire in a day. It was what all girls dreamed of. An enchanting hold that made her insides jump with ecstasy as she swam in his chocolate eyes.

"Motherfu—" she began, but in all honesty wanted to finish the curse more in the physical sense. "Aw, screw it," she mumbled under her breath when he leaned over and planted a kiss on her lips.

She meant for it to last a second alone, but when she kissed him back, all noise fell away to quiet. Her stomach exploded with fireworks as he delicately caressed her lips with his own. Never had she traveled the world under a man's touch. Never until Cameron.

She pulled back reluctantly when her ears picked up the aggravating sound of incoming voices. The interruption was necessary, but she longed to throw sanity out the door and let him bang her more thoroughly than a gavel in the hands of a trigger-happy judge.

The scenarios her mind created involving Cameron were

too many to count, and she wanted to intimately explore each one. *Dear mother of mercy, I need to stop thinking like that.*

Joci's face heated when she comprehended what they'd just done. It was inexcusable, yet felt too natural to be wrong. Catching a glimpse of his swollen lips, her body urged her to return to his embrace and never leave it again.

"I should, um, get a few more bottles of water," she pointed out when the empty bottles caught her eye. She needed a distraction that didn't have a multitude of tattoos and a tongue as vigilant as the devil's.

He glanced to the table, then back to her. "Yeah, sure, good idea." Cameron stayed in his spot, observing her jerky movements.

After scratching his cheek, he grabbed a scrap of paper and scribbled on it. Handing it to her, he advised, "Here. These are Jerry's digits. If you get in a bind, he'll have your back."

With guarded precaution, she took the outstretched shred of paper. She didn't want to be in debt to any mob, but she was also fond of living.

"Thanks, I will," she replied, and his face slackened in relief.

Juggling the bottles, she made sure her phone was in her purse before promising, "I'll be back. It's a courthouse. They check for guns at the entrance."

Folding his hands in his lap, he retorted, "You don't need a weapon to kill someone."

She swiveled her head away, unable to meet the warning

in his eyes. He said the words as if he knew from experience. Despite the orgasmic sensations he sent through her body, Joci wondered if he was more dangerous than she'd thought.

Taking a step away, she froze when he added, "Or kidnap someone."

Not daring to look back, she pushed forward, her heels echoing through the room with each step. She may have bitten off more than she could chew by harboring emotions for the low-key mobster who stirred every desire in her existence.

— — —

Cameron wanted to rush after her, to bar the doors and take her on every surface possible until Joci gave in to the essence of them. Instead of using his handcuffs in a kinky manner, he sat there and watched her strut from the room. It was a beautiful sight to witness. The easy sway of her hips and the tight black pants ensured that standing up anytime soon would prove to be embarrassing.

"That's her, isn't it? The infamous Joci Dorous. She's stunning, Cameroni, but you already knew as much."

Slowly, Cameron pivoted. One person called him by the jokester name, and it was the same man who'd appeared as though from thin air. A steady smile covered Jerry Del Rossi's face. "Yeah, it's her, Jer."

The stocky mobster hadn't changed much since he last saw him, though the silver streaks in his hair were more prominent now. "She must be a vixen in the bedroom to wrangle you."

"It's not like that," Cameron defended. He wasn't even sure how the boss snuck passed security. He noted the second door in the back of the room, no doubt where the man entered from. "Joci and I used to live in the same neighborhood. She anchored me." His face clouded. "Until she left."

Jerry clapped a bejeweled hand on Cameron's back. "But you're reunited at last. I think there's a catchy tune in there somewhere." He chuckled when Cameron gave him no response. "How does your attractive lady feel about your wayward past, Cam? Is she overjoyed to have her heart in the grip of a killer?"

Cameron surveyed the tiny room in one quick movement. Other than five very Italian bodyguards, two in front of each door and one inside with them, the place was eerily quiet. Without a doubt, he was sure J.J.'s guy had disappeared from the courtroom not far away. Probably forever, if he knew his boss. How Jerry managed it, he'd never know.

"She's heard the tip of the iceberg, but after this is over, she'll return to her dick of an ex," he spat, the words tasting of charcoal.

The perfectly gelled eyebrows of the mob king rose. "Do we need to add a little bend and crack to our festivities?" He snapped his fingers and a man stepped forward. "Because all it takes is one word. I'd throw it in for free just to make you happy. The guy is a Mikkelsen puppet anyhow. No big loss."

Taking the righteous road never hurt so bad as Cameron

weighed the options. "No," he resolved. "She needs him alive." He swung his eyes to the door Joci had walked through moments ago. The air still held a hint of her fruity fragrance.

"That is an expression I never imagined I would see on you again," Jerry admitted, pulling Cameron back to the present.

"What do you mean?" He itched to break free from the cuffs, but Jerry wouldn't break him out. Cameron hadn't earned it yet. He still needed to get rid of J.J.

"The way you watched her leave a few minutes ago." Jerry leaned back, his chair creaking under his ample form.

Clearly he stopped going to the gym. "She's my friend. I care for her."

"Ha! It's more, don't lie to me." Jerry sat up straight. "You look at her with such passion even Bambina never received." He chuckled and laced his sausage-like fingers together. "What does Joci possess that my sister didn't?"

His temper flared at the mention of his long-lost lover. Bambi had been the epitome of a girl innocent in the ways of the mob—until she reeled Cameron into the realm, that is. Betrayal held all forms, but hers was the worst. "Bambi and I didn't work, Jerry. It's all I will say about her."

Jerry nodded in approval. "A wise boy I raised." He scoured their setting. "Iowa is quaint. I'm not surprised you like it here."

"Why would you say that?"

The mob leader shrugged. "Oh, maybe because you don't have eye candy like Joci in Ohio." He paused, then added, "I'd stay around too."

"The only thing about Joci you should be focused on is her safety."

Jerry grinned like a Cheshire cat. "Hmm, you like her a lot, don't you?"

Cameron's eye twitched, and all he wanted to do was bust someone's lip.

"Rest assured, your Joci will be kept out of harm's way."

He didn't want to ask how Jerry made it all possible. No doubt it involved bribes. No matter the way, he was thankful for the part the mobster played. One less life would be destroyed, and he could live with the results, whatever they may be. "Thanks, Jerry."

The man waved away the favor, which meant nothing and everything at the same time. Business was his main goal, and the deal he'd made with Cameron would prove to be fruitful no matter which way it played out. He'd either get rid of competition or secure Cameron and possibly Joci within the Del Rossi family. Win-win both ways.

A tall man with a buzz cut took a small step toward them. Cameron noticed him touch his finger to his left ear. After the man removed it, he spotted the earpiece.

"Well, it's time to make my services useful," Jerry joked as he stood. "My man trailing Jepsen turned up dead this morning, so I expect the Danish whelp will make a grand entrance within twenty-four hours."

Patting Cameron's shoulder in a brotherly fashion, Jerry leaned down and whispered into his ear, "I wouldn't be opposed to giving you more liberties within the ranks if you and Joci end up together. Then I'd truly have a good criminal attorney on my payroll without the need of our deal. You know she'd be happier with you."

Cameron held in his fury. It wasn't the time or place. His personal feelings for Joci were obvious, and the mobster would use those as much as he could to get his way. Jerry didn't want to lose him, so it wouldn't be a surprise if J.J. managed to slither away at the boss's command. Anyone could get rid of competition. Trusted allies were harder to come by. "She would never agree to joining Del Rossi."

Straightening his coat, the mob boss's crafty grin widened. "You'd be surprised what a girl will do for someone she cares about. Reminds me of someone else I know."

The entourage swarmed around Jerry, and like a mist, he vanished in seconds. Letting out a frustrated groan, Cameron planted his face in his hands. Even a deal with the devil wasn't as terrifying as a deal with the oldest Del Rossi brother.

CHAPTER SIXTEEN

Tucking her feet under her body, Joci lounged on the sofa while she reviewed the final words to the jury. She had written the lengthy closing minutes after locking lips with Cameron. For some reason, he inspired her, and the words flowed without obstacles. Pausing her pen, she stared into nothingness as her mind hurled back to the afternoon.

Kissing him had been a horrible idea, and yet she couldn't stop thinking about it. The scene played over and over in her mind the rest of the trial day, when she spoke to Quinn and Adrian, and even during dinner. The distraction overtook all relevant matters until she didn't notice when Adrian went back to the office instead of their guarded apartment. She was in a stupor, and the only way out was by Cameron.

"Why didn't you tell me you and Adrian got engaged?" Rayna's voice sliced through Joci's heavy veil.

Glancing to the energetic woman, her heart sank. "Oh yeah, the engagement." She eyed the massive ring that felt heavier than a boulder on her hand. "It's fake. Not the ring, but the engagement part. Adrian thought it may help somehow if J.J. knew we were in a relationship. I'm second-guessing it even now."

Rayna plopped down beside her and gawked at the ring. "Damn, girl." She pulled it off Joci and slid it on her own finger. "If I had a ring like this, I would marry the guy anyways." She returned the gem to her friend's hand, but Joci set it on the coffee table instead. "Is there anything else going on, or is it just the case?"

Coiling into herself, Joci didn't want to answer. Of course there was more going on, but she wasn't about to spill details about how she felt for Cameron. It was an atomic bomb waiting to ignite and cause mass destruction.

An alternative distraction piqued her interest. Turning toward Rayna, she disclosed, "I'm pregnant. Or at least I think I am. I haven't tested yet."

"What! Is it Quinn's?" was the first thing out of her friend's mouth.

"Quinn? No. Why does everyone ask that?" Joci mumbled.

Patting her friend's belly in a circular pattern, Rayna pointed out, "You and Quinn are… well, how do I put this?" She tapped her nose. "You seem like the obvious couple, whereas you and Adrian are more of a step backward."

"Great. Thanks for the confidence boost." Joci tossed her notes to the coffee table. "Adrian and I hooked up a while ago. It was reckless and a onetime thing, but you already knew that."

She stood and cocked her head. "We're pregnant. I'm

pregnant with Adrian's baby again." She skated her gaze to Rayna. "Does that sound as weird to you as it does to me?"

Rayna stretched out her legs on the couch. "Yes," she started matter-of-factly. "I mean, I understand, given your history, but do you think the two of you will get back together?"

"No, definitely not."

She yawned, then tugged on Joci's pant leg. "And what about Quinn?"

"Negative again."

Rayna smirked and wiggled her eyebrows. "Then that leaves one man. How about Cameron? What're your feelings for the handsome ex-con? Is he your true love?"

A distorted chuckle escaped Joci's throat. "I don't think true love exists, Ray. Hell, it could smack me in the face and I'd never know."

Silence settled between them, and the clock's ticking on the wall met their ears. After a minute, Rayna spoke up. "True love means he will do everything in his power to keep you safe. He supports you no matter how batshit crazy you can be." She smiled listlessly. "He wants you happy even if it means being happy with someone else. That is what true love is to me." She stood and hugged Joci. "Though I'm sure it varies by person."

Without another word, the younger woman tromped to the kitchen and fiddled with the coffeemaker. The racket she made was minimal compared to the noise erupting in Joci's brain. Matching a man to Rayna's explanation wasn't as hard, as she expected.

Sinking to the sofa once more, she was flabbergasted to realize Cameron fit just about every bullet point of the definition. The issue was he was all wrong for her.

— — —

Scanning the room, Joci was surprised the crowd had increased since yesterday. The media presence remained minimal, but more spectators had come to watch the trial wrap up. The video surveillance the P.I. found wasn't entered into evidence on either side since faces couldn't be determined. She wasn't certain if that was a good thing or not. In her mind, she guessed it was J.J. and his goons, but it could've been anyone. The witnesses stuck to as much of their deposition testimony as possible, but Mr. Bell managed to get the questioning back on track whenever she badgered a test result or testimony. No surprise exhibits or witnesses jumped out midtrial, not that she expected any. The State was doing their best, but in her opinion, they never should've proceeded to trial. Then again, she was more than biased when it came to Cameron. Keeping her attention on the jury, she watched them closely. The State was currently spewing their sob story and emotion-heavy closing, but she could see the jury wasn't swayed.

Taking their doubtful faces as a positive, she turned her head to the left. Adrian gave her a quick smile before he went back to writing notes. Cameron, on the other hand, didn't drop her gaze once he secured it. Their odd link worried her. It was more than sociable, yet teetered on a sensation that was brand new to her.

Adrian's head popped up again, breaking the sizzling connection. "You've got this," her second chair encouraged, squeezing her arm.

The prosecutor took his seat, and she hated to think of the poor fool who would have to sit there after the anxious man. No doubt the cleaning crew had their work cut out for them.

Standing, she ran her hands over her suit jacket to settle her nerves before she made her way to the jury box. "Members of the jury, you have been exposed to a substantial amount of evidence and testimony this week."

She took a breath. "Now, you must discuss your views for a verdict, but as you do that, I want you to remember a few key points. The State didn't have viable evidence for a conviction. Mr. Nichols died from asphyxia, an act any person could commit. Take the gun and knife out of your arsenal, because they aren't relevant. Those wounds were done after his death in hopes to throw the police off track. Many of you know Mr. Nichols was a drug dealer. This man had many enemies, and my client wasn't one of them. The dirt in the victim's nose didn't match the dirt under my client's fingernails. While Mr. Nichols's death is unfortunate, my client couldn't have committed the act. He was too loaded up on drugs to do anything but sleep it off. The prosecutor failed to fully establish my client as the perpetrator."

Joci snuck a peek at Mr. Bell and saw new perspiration trickle down his forehead. His partner didn't look any better. "Now, my client did admit to participating in recreational drugs that night, but it is not a motive for murder. The State could not support their complaint, since no solid motive was displayed for this case. Just because my client had drugs on his body didn't mean he had purchased them from Mr. Nichols before his untimely death."

She took a moment and surveyed the faces of the jurors. "If my client is guilty of anything, it is of his drug use. It was wrong of him, but he is not a threat to society and has since participated in drug rehabilitation. Mr. Shearer had no knowledge of his own location until the police advised him of such."

Walking toward Cameron, she extended her arm. "He was at Gray's Lake at the wrong time. That is all you can find him guilty of." She softened her gaze when his face relaxed. She shouldn't enjoy defending him so much, but it just felt right.

"Put yourselves in his shoes. You're in a new city. You play your heart out at a concert, and then you wake up to realize you've been charged with murder." She locked her eyes on Cameron. "I don't believe he killed anyone."

Swiveling to the jury, she added, "And neither should you."

Pausing for effect, Joci was pleased when several jury members turned reflective instead of judgmental. She returned to her seat, then glanced to the judge. The man nodded, then grabbed his gavel.

"The jury may now be excused to deliberate. Bailiff, you can take the defendant into custody when his counsel is finished with him. We are adjourned." He banged the tiny hammer and the twelve souls filed off to their room.

Once the judge removed to his chambers, she let out a sigh. It was over. She'd completed a murder trial and could still walk. Though her knees were a bit wobbly.

"You were incredible!" Adrian praised as he hugged her. "Epic by anyone's standards."

"Thanks." She offered a weary smile. "Now the hardest part: waiting." The courtroom cleared out quickly, a select few remaining behind. It wasn't uncommon once the judge and jury left. The court attendant would call back any spectators when a verdict was reached. Joci doubted many would stick around. It was nearly the lunch hour, and no doubt the jurors would take advantage of one last free meal. If deliberations went long, most would lose interest and head back to work.

"I bet it doesn't take too long," a new voice chimed in from behind them.

The tinge of an accent sent shudders down Joci's neck. She twirled, her gut dropping. Her eyes darted to Cameron, and she swallowed hard at the grim expression on his face. Without a doubt, the man before them was J.J. Jepsen. She didn't recognize him at the coffee shop but now she did. His blond hair and pale eyes made him look like he'd stepped out of a fairy tale.

"I must say, it was an excellent closing argument, Ms. Dorous. A sight to behold. I'll be sure to recommend you to all of my Iowa contacts," the preening criminal promised.

People filed out of the courtroom like cattle and the tall cretin stepped closer. His blue eyes dropped languidly to

Joci. "I see why you like her," he tossed to the man standing trial.

Cameron's jaw tightened, but he didn't utter a word. He had no way to protect himself, and that fact alone terrified Joci.

"I'm sorry, who are you?" Joci inquired with faux politeness as Adrian put his body in front of hers.

J.J. peeked over to Cameron. "Del Rossi went all out on your attorneys. This one is more than familiar, and that one is stunning. I think I'm in the wrong family."

"Why is he familiar?" Joci asked, leaning away from Adrian.

A knowing glance quickly passed between the three men. It made her heart drop to her stomach when Adrian's face blanched.

"Mr. Petosa and I are on speaking terms, to put it bluntly," J.J. advised. "I'm shocked Mr. Shearer didn't tell you about it. I'd thought he'd do anything for you. Apparently not."

"What?" She looked to Cameron, then Adrian and finally J.J., her eyes wild. "What does that mean?"

"Joce, I'm—" Cameron's words fell flat as Adrian opened his mouth.

"Joci, I, uh," started Adrian, but he didn't finish before J.J. interrupted.

"Your pal here owes the Mikkelsen mob a lot of money. We made a deal so he could keep his bones intact."

"What? No, you aren't serious," she stammered. It wasn't possible, but when she met Adrian's guilty blue eyes, she knew the truth. "It was gambling, wasn't it? You told me you stopped." She pressed a hand to her chest. "Oh my God, I can't believe I listened to you."

Glancing around the room, she noticed their group was secluded in a tight circle, giving the impression of intense conversation. It wouldn't be seen as uncommon for a case, but she was certain J.J. managed to manipulate the crowd somehow.

"And I did, but only after I lost at a poker tournament. I didn't know the Mikkelsen mob funded it or I never would've played the first hand." He reached for her arm, but she yanked it out of reach.

"Yes, you would've." She took a step toward Cameron, fully aware of the side she was choosing. Adrian's face fell at her act. He knew what it meant too. There'd be no second chance now. Not with his alliances muddied. Not with the lies he told her. Not with the danger he created.

"How'd the trial go? Sorry I missed it, but my men tell me it was interesting. It's too bad you couldn't use the security footage from Halloween night that Adrian tampered with," J.J. heckled. "He did a great job too. If it weren't for your P.I., I doubt the tape would've been cleaned at all."

"What did you do?" she seethed at Adrian. Instantly, Joci wanted to see the video before it was doctored. She was confident it would exonerate Cameron of all charges.

J.J. chuckled. "We make a great team, you and me. I think we'll continue our arrangement even after the verdict."

Joci's hands curled into fists as Adrian stayed mute. It all made sense. Why he stayed late at the office; who the 'boss' was; hell, he probably didn't go to the office whenever he snuck out of the apartment. He'd played her from the start, and she was the one who looked like a fool.

"You honestly thought I would go back to you after I found out you were sacrificing both Cameron and me for your gambling debts?" She couldn't stay silent. He more than deserved her wrath.

Adrian took a labored breath. "It wasn't my intention, Joci. J.J.'s boss wanted me to swing a few things their way in court. When Cameron's case was passed to us, the Mikkelsens promised to release my debt if I could secure a guilty verdict. You weren't supposed to fall in love with him."

Cameron's hand tightened around her wrist, and she was grateful he kept his mouth shut. She'd explain later. Right now, her ex needed a tongue lashing.

"How I feel for anyone doesn't give you a right to screw up someone's life, Adrian." She slipped off the ring of their fake engagement. "I was right about you not once, but twice." She stuffed the band into his hand and glared at him. "There's no way in hell I'm letting you near me again."

Shifting his weight, Adrian propped his hands on his hips. "Joce, I know you're pissed, but I didn't think it would get this far. My dad was supposed to give me the money to pay them back, okay? He hasn't, obviously."

"So you just went along with a mobster. Great idea." She crossed her arms over her chest.

"I didn't want to, I *had* to." He moved toward her, but she stepped backward. "If you'll let me explain, we can figure this out."

Chewing on her bottom lip, Joci studied Adrian's worried face. He wasn't a hardened mafia man or even a criminal. He just couldn't say no to another card deal. "I don't know if I even want to do that."

"You know, this is adorable. Lovers' quarrels are my favorite." Casually, J.J. looped his arm through Adrian's. "But I think instead of waiting it out with you and hearing you squabble, Mr. Petosa and I will chat outside the courthouse."

Joci caught her breath at the insinuation. Sure, she was mad as hell, but letting Adrian leave with J.J. wasn't safe.

"In the meantime, the two of you should discuss what color looks best on Adrian for his funeral." He pulled Adrian toward him. "I'm thinking pastel blue would be good."

"What? You said—" Adrian started.

"Shut up!" J.J. demanded in a hushed tone. "I can do whatever I want with you." He nodded to Joci and opened his jacket slightly. "And her too."

A glimmer of metal caught Joci's eye and she gasped. She didn't want to know how he managed to sneak a gun into the courthouse.

"Please don't," she begged, her gut roiling. Adrian didn't deserve being hurt despite his associations with the Mikkelsen mob. It appeared he was never supposed to survive the case, and by the expression on his face, he realized it the same time as her.

"I'd take you instead if I could." The man's eyes swung to Cameron. "But I need him focused, and what better way than to take the man in love with the woman he loves?" He chortled. "God, you Iowans are messed up."

Adrian's eyebrows shot up as he glared at Cameron, but he didn't speak. It was no use anyhow. He was well aware of how she felt about their client.

She couldn't meet Adrian's gaze even if she wanted to. She didn't need to see the terror in his blue eyes. Keeping herself together was all she could muster.

"We'll have a little exchange, Shearer," J.J. continued in a soft tone. "Bring the drugs that Nichols gave you."

Cameron's brow furrowed. "You know the cops have the drugs they found on me in evidence. I can't get to them."

"Well, I'll kill him if you don't figure it out. Easy enough, right?"

Joci looked up in time to see the blond's face light up with a smile. "Unless you would rather keep her for yourself." He clucked his tongue. "Though I doubt she'll love you if you kill her baby daddy on purpose." He nearly preened at exposing the secret.

"His man was here when I told Cameron," Joci put together. "You bastard."

J.J.'s grip on Adrian tightened. "Very good, Ms. Dorous. Your body isn't the only reason your client likes you."

Inching closer to the man, Cameron's voice turned as cold as death. "Hurt him and I will obliterate your existence."

"Oh, that's mighty chivalrous of you," the mobster mocked, guiding his hostage away.

"I'll be fine. Don't worry," Adrian promised. "And Joci, if something happens, I love you."

Tears spilling from her eyes, she nodded. She couldn't

say the words she didn't mean.

"Oh look, your jury is back," J.J. pointed out "Is it favorable when they return so quickly?"

Both Cameron and Joci turned toward the front of the room as the jurors filed in like robots. When she looked behind her, Adrian and his captor were nowhere in sight.

"What do we do?" she managed as the bailiff called the parties back to the courtroom. Her knees knocked together and her pulse raced as the room filled with people. She would have fallen had Cameron not held her up.

With his hands still shackled, the gentlemanly act was more awkward than comforting, but she couldn't fault him for trying. Joci's head thrummed in anticipation. After the last shuffle of feet, the judge captured everyone's attention.

"Foreman, have you reached a verdict?" the judge bellowed, somehow agitated by the short recess compared to usual strung-out jury deliberations.

"We have, Your Honor," the woman with springy curls replied. She turned toward the prosecution table and Joci gripped Cameron's arm, her nails digging in.

"We, the jury, find the defendant, Cameron Anthony Shearer...." She paused and eyed the defense table. "Not guilty on all charges."

A murmur rippled through the courtroom and cameras flashed.

Judge Keller's brisk nod secured the verdict. "Thank you, jurors, for your time. You are dismissed."

He turned his head and addressed Cameron. "Mr. Shearer, I hope this ordeal has taught you a thing or two."

"It has, Your Honor," Cameron echoed verbatim the words his lawyers had force-fed him.

"Good. I expect you to live along the laws of Iowa, should you stay here." He struck the gavel. "Deputy, please remove the handcuffs. You are free to leave." The judge pounded the wooden hammer one last time for good measure, then scurried back to his chambers.

No words could form on Joci's lips. *I won. I won a murder trial.* She let out a breath. *And in three days.* Her mind switched from victory to defeat when she recalled that the second attorney in this case was absent.

"Adrian. We have to find him," she urged in a hushed tone. "Where will J.J. take him?"

"I'm not sure. He'll call," Cameron advised as the officer took a step back, handcuffs in hand.

Rubbing his wrists, he lifted his eyes and a tiny smile spread over his face. "It's not the best time, but in case things light up, I wanted to thank you for helping me." He closed his hands over hers. "It meant a lot to have someone who not only believed in me, but also fought for me."

Despite her muscles feeling like jelly at the moment, Joci accepted the giant bear hug. For once, she was relieved to be in his arms without the possibility he would spend the better part of his life in prison.

Notwithstanding her comfort, the danger that lingered around him set off warning bells. Though he wasn't the reason Adrian was taken as a hostage, he'd known about the other man's involvement with the Mikkelsens. Trusting Cameron was a battle that continued to wage within her soul.

"Happy to be of assistance, even if your special mob friends stirred the pot a bit." She forced a smile.

Reporters swarmed around them as Cameron led them from the room, but she didn't appease one. As important as the case had once been, it was nothing compared to the issues at hand. Hunting down the bastard who not only took Adrian but also turned him evil and jeopardized her life trumped an acquittal anytime.

— — —

Cameron watched in curious silence as Joci made her way through the courthouse. People funneled around them at every step, but she handled them with expert skill. It was more than obvious Adrian was meant to wrangle the circus after the verdict. That fact alone made his heart break for her. It wasn't supposed to end with a manhunt for anyone.

He rubbed his neck as their next movement became clear. It was time to call Jerry, even if he wasn't keen on the idea. Joci needed Adrian alive despite the floundering loyalties, and Cameron needed Joci happy. Whatever cost it included, he was all in.

The need to shove the pestering bodies aside and whisk her somewhere tropical tempted him. But as he saw the polite smile plastered on Joci's face, he knew he couldn't do as he wanted.

The two ambled out the front doors and he spotted his devilish salvation. Jerry's bodyguards didn't surround him, but they were within lunging distance if gunshots were fired. He met the mobster's gaze beneath his bushy eyebrows and felt his insides cringe.

Taking Joci's hand, Cameron led her to his employer. When he glanced over at her, he was surprised her face held the remnants of a smile. She was still in attorney mode.

"I take it the jury found you innocent." Jerry smirked, then nodded to Joci. "I owe you my thanks, Ms. Dorous. Cameron is quite the addition to my business. I'm glad you managed to keep him out of the system."

Joci's stared at the man in a blue overcoat. "You can show me your gratitude by rescuing Adrian," she spat out.

Her candor amused Jerry, and he nudged Cameron's gut. "I like her." The man perused Joci's attire. "She'd be good for you."

Shifting, Cameron kept the subject on Adrian, lest he blatantly agree and send Joci into a tailspin. "J.J. hasn't made contact yet. I suspect he will before nightfall."

One of Jerry's men stepped forward with a cell phone, the one that had been in Cameron's locked and guarded apartment. After handing it to his boss, the man backed away and stood stoic.

"Ah, I see Mr. Jepsen reached out after all," informed the Italian, reviewing the phone. "Gray's Lake. 4 p.m." He flipped the screen toward them. "It seems like a special spot for you."

Snatching the phone, Joci read the text with hungry eyes, then glanced to Cameron. "We need to get moving." She clicked her heels on the concrete. "And I need to fill in Quinn on all of this."

As if he heard his name on the wind, the police officer

strode into the confines of their group. "Everything okay here?"

"Yes, just discussing how to get Adrian back," Joci informed.

"Wait, what happened to Adrian?" he asked with a lifted brow.

Joci swiftly filled in the officer with the details. Instead of words, the cop only let out a low whistle when she finished. "Cameron and his boss are going to help and they're taking me with them."

"Whoa there, Wonder Woman. You aren't going anywhere near danger," he instructed, his voice stern.

Cameron bit back a smile when she perched her fists on her hips in defiance. Pissed Joci was irresistible, even if she resembled the comic book hero by mistake.

"The hell if I'm not," she hurled in return.

"Joci, it's not a good idea. J.J. may switch tactics and use you as a hostage," Quinn argued.

"Or she could be the bait," Jerry suggested.

"Hell fucking no." Quinn skimmed the mystery man, then addressed Cameron. "I have a hunch of who he is, but I would rather not hear it for deniability reasons. I'm sure if I looked in the police database, there'd be an outstanding warrant or two." Jerry shrugged nonchalantly while Quinn eyed the surrounding men. "What's the real plan here? We're not using Joci as bait. I can have patrol cars at the lake within minutes to set a perimeter. If I know who we're up against, I can call in a favor with my SWAT buddies."

Jerry harrumphed. "Yes, because J.J. won't expect police

involvement." The short man pulled his coat closer to his neck as a chilled breeze whipped by them. "I can't believe I'm stooping to help the man who was helping my enemy. You should've just killed him, Cameron."

Shaking his head quickly, Cameron held his breath. He couldn't be sure if Joci heard him or not. Judging by the way she was speaking in low tones with Quinn, he went with not.

"My men are preparing as we speak," Jerry continued. "The Danish ass won't realize what hit him when they're through with him."

"I need him alive," Quinn reminded, suddenly back in the conversation. He took a step closer to Joci, as if to protect her from the criminal scum surrounding them. It was cute in an odd sort of way. A way that Cameron found admirable and enviable.

"And I need Adrian alive," Joci cut in before another man could speak. She stepped to where Jerry stood and captured his attention. "Do whatever is necessary to see he isn't harmed. I don't care the consequences."

Glancing to Cameron, then back to the spitfire attorney, Jerry's face brightened. It was a common expression when the mob man was given free rein. "I like your style. I assure you, it will be done," he pledged.

With her mind set, Joci let out a puff of air and turned on her stilettos. From her stance, Cameron could see she was shaken and terrified. He would be too, if it was her life on the line and the only people to trust were outlaws.

She headed in the direction of her office, and he sighed

when Quinn raced after her. It was better this way. Now was as good a time as any to put distance between them. Once Adrian was safe in her arms, Cameron would cease to matter. His case was over, and soon so would be their connection.

"You know this changes things, right? I'm helping you save a member of the Mikkelsen mob."

"He's not part of their family," Cameron argued. "Just a means to an end."

Jerry scratched his chin. "Either way, our original deal is dead."

Stuffing his hands into both pockets, he lifted his eyes to see Jerry studying him. "Then this better work," he mumbled against the wind.

Chuckling, Jerry slapped his back. "Which plan? The one where the redheaded attorney lives, or the one where you ride off with the girl?"

Keeping his face as complacent as possible, Cameron shrugged indifferently. "I don't know, Jer. I really don't know."

CHAPTER SEVENTEEN

Drumming her fingers on the back of the seat, Joci narrowed her eyes to slits when Officer Ollie Richards met her gaze through the rearview mirror.

"Don't look at me like I'm the big bad wolf," he instructed. "This wasn't my idea." She cocked her head and he held up his hands. "If you hadn't gone all crazy ex-wife on us, you could've watched this all go down from the safety of your apartment," he reminded her harshly.

Joci huffed and sank into the back seat of the patrol SUV. He wasn't wrong. She'd sent Quinn and Cameron into a tailspin when she insisted to be a part of the rescue mission. Her demands had been shot down by everyone present. Despite her outrageous floundering, Quinn managed to convince the mob boss and her ex-client of three hours to let her attend from a safe distance if only to keep an eye on her himself. That was only after failing.

She smirked. Quinn's chat with her hadn't gone well. Right after he left her office, she managed to escape the two cops he'd assigned, Ollie one of them, but was caught by Quinn in the lobby. Overall, she was satisfied to be near the action so she could be among the first to verify every person she cared about was safe. Sure, she was going to be the first person to slap Adrian, but she needed him to be okay.

She jiggled the door handle in frustration. "Are you serious? You babyproofed me in?" she whined.

Ollie turned in the driver seat. His eyes skipped over her in judgment. "Yep. It's a good thing too, apparently."

Static drifted over the radio and she sat up as fast as possible. The thing hadn't made a peep in the last hour, and she was getting perturbed.

Soon, Quinn's crisp voice broke through. "DMPD in place, along with an Italian hoagie."

She giggled at the pun but saw the young officer didn't. He was as preoccupied as she. "I won't tell if you let me sneak around a bit. I swear, I'll come back before the action starts," she attempted, batting her eyes.

Snorting, Ollie shook his head. "Uh-huh, right, because Joci always does as she says. I saw the opposite firsthand today, so you'll excuse me if I don't believe you." He clicked on the radio and soft guitar strums filled the vehicle. "Why did you switch sides?" he asked, not bothering to hide his scorn. "I swore you and Quinn would go the distance."

Settling sideways on the seat, Joci's hands went to her stomach. She couldn't blame an unborn child for her flip-flop since she'd broken it off with Quinn before conception, but the real culprit was on the loose and not what she wanted to admit to.

"I don't know," she settled on. "Quinn always knew we wouldn't end up in some little white-picket-fenced lot with rocking chairs on the front porch. He has a riddled past, and so do I." She rubbed her belly the more she thought. "It was a uniting of downhearted forces, and it worked for a while."

She turned to Adrian because Cameron admitted to murder. If he hadn't, she was confident she never would've slept with Adrian. It was juvenile for a number of reasons, but she wouldn't blame Adrian either. Though Cameron's lie came out later, Joci knew why he did it. Their attraction was genuine, but he tried to protect her even then from himself. *So much for that working out.*

Wind whizzed stray leaves over the hood of the vehicle, sending a chill through her body. Ollie kicked the heat up another notch, but didn't act affected by the winter winds.

"Hmm, I suppose I can accept it," he replied at last. He checked his phone again. His anxiousness wore on Joci. Her stomach had been in turmoil since the morning, and the meeting would occur anytime, only making it worse.

Turning her neck, she observed more squad cars arrive. The scheme Cameron, his mob boss, and Quinn had hatched was brilliant, but not bulletproof. As more officers filed into the unforgiving cold, Joci hoped each would return home safely.

Ollie's phone chimed a country ballad, and a grin stretched over his face. "I'm going to take this outside," he rushed to say.

Without a doubt, it was his gorgeous and very pregnant wife on the other end. Right then, Joci felt jealous of Ollie's new family. It was unsoiled by life's harsh realities. She followed the cop with her eyes as he walked around the car. His teeth showed wide with pride while his free hand hung in his warm coat pocket. She wanted that. A man ecstatic to be a dad, but even more so to have her as a partner. Adrian never looked off into the tree line with giddy eyes like Ollie in that moment. It was spectacular and shattering at the same time.

When she couldn't take the lovey-dovey expression on Ollie's face another second, Joci leaned through the opened divider across the back seat and clicked the doors unlocked. Ollie's attention being anywhere but on her gave a perfect opening, and she wouldn't miss it.

Bracing herself for the rebuke both Quinn and Cameron would serve on her, she slipped out of the SUV and snuck to the path. It was foolhardy and stupid, but she needed to see it all go down. She'd stick to the tree line and leave after the exchange. Nobody would know she was there until afterward when everyone was safe. "Watching the plan in action won't be so hard if I stay incognito," she assumed. "But I'm pretty sure they'll kill me if I'm seen." No doubt her presence would hinder any focus, which was why she was set on staying hidden. So long as she did that, she was golden.

Slinking along the trails, Joci listened to the quiet rustle of tree branches. Her patience paid off when the familiar and maddening voice of Cameron Shearer was the first to greet her in the woods. *Of course it's him. It's always him.*

— — —

It was rather adorable the way Joci tiptoed through the brush littered with spring snow. Had he not been accompanying the Del Rossi men on rounds of the area, Cameron wouldn't have spotted her. The charcoal trench coat caught his attention after some twigs broke beneath her boots. Stray leaves clung to the expensive material, and broken splinters of branches intertwined with her straightened hair. She couldn't look more appetizing unless she was in his embrace.

Creeping up behind her, Cameron resisted the urge to scare her. Knowing Joci, he would end up with a black eye. Still, feeling her heartrate skyrocket against his hands would be worth the trouble.

She shuffled between two pine trees, sneaking a peek at the clearing where J.J. was due anytime. The initial anger that had passed through him at first sight of her fled. He was looking forward to hearing how she'd escaped the vigilant Officer Richards a second time.

"I don't think hiding in a tree is what I had in mind when we agreed to keep you at a safe distance," he chided in a quiet voice.

Joci yipped in surprise and whirled around. "Dammit!" She met his gaze, guilt scrawled on her pink cheeks. "Are you going to take me back to Ollie?"

Cameron crossed his arms across his borrowed Carhartt coat. The bulky thing was warm. He had to give props to Quinn for preparing for the unusual Iowa weather. The limited clothes he possessed were either torn to shreds or dirty, save his favorite pair of jeans. It felt nice to be in his own clothes for a change. Well, the jeans were his, but the rest felt like it. The police department had retained his possessions for evidence, but since he was acquitted, they were returned after the trial.

Taking a step closer, he fished a leaf from her hair. "I haven't decided yet." She wrinkled her nose, and Cameron fought for control.

"Please, Cameron, I can't bear to be left out of this." She gripped his forearm and offered pleading eyes. "I need to know what happens. Adrian is an idiotic ass, but he's also the baby's dad."

"I know." He let out a breath and the cloud dissipated on the wind. "I take it you took a pregnancy test."

"Yeah. Rayna practically forced me into the bathroom. I swear she would've crammed in the stall too if I'd let her." Joci's lips curved momentarily. "I guess I'm going to be a mom. Weird."

"Well, I won't let either of you get hurt." He needed to believe it as much as her. He didn't give a shit who the dad of her baby was. It could be an alien and he'd still love Joci.

She nodded her acceptance. "I never heard all of the plan."

"For good reason, it seems."

Her eyes swiveled to the clearing where Quinn and Jerry were hunkered down. "What if it goes wrong?"

Sheltering her in his arms, he closed his eyes as her scent attacked him. It may be the last time he held her, so he wasn't about to let her go so fast. He couldn't stay in Iowa even after the fiasco was over. She'd no doubt forgive

Adrian, and it'd break his heart to watch her fall in love with the crook.

"It won't. Adrian will be safe soon." He met her worried eyes and their alluring green tidbits made him crack a smile. "And then you'll be happy."

Apprehension fluttered over her face. "Happy with Adrian?"

Cocking his left eyebrow, he allowed a small glimmer of hope. "Isn't that what you want? Who you want?" He needed to hear the reason behind her confusion.

Joci bit her bottom lip, tempting Cameron to do the same to the malleable flesh. "The only reason Adrian and I slept together is because of you," she confessed.

"I don't know if I want to take credit for that then," he forced out, biting the inside of his cheek.

"I slept with Adrian because I was pissed at you for shoving me out the door." Her soft words settled through the crisp air.

Relief mixed with remorse flourished through Cameron's veins. He had thought as much, but hearing it solidified his emotions. "Say the words," he prompted, tucking her hair behind her ear.

"It's wrong on so many levels." She struggled, unable to maintain his eyes. "I should be happy with the potential of Adrian and me. He is the safest choice for me. Well, okay, despite his Mikkelsen association." Her eyes fixed on his hair. "Then why does every particle of me crave you?"

Not put off by her rambling, Cameron adjusted the black beanie covering the hair his fingers itched to explore.

"You tell me, Joci."

Her lips quivered over the words. "How can I know what I feel for you is real and not mere fiction?"

The way she danced around the revelation caused a grim smile to cross his face. He wasn't about to guide her to the truth. She deserved Adrian and a life where everything made sense. He couldn't offer such a paradise.

"If you swear to not karate chop the men I send over, I'll let you stay and watch," he promised, hoping the change of subject would urge her to say something. He wouldn't do it. Not when he had more to lose.

He fought inner turmoil and dropped his hold on her before he studied the open space between the forests. When he moved to escape, her hand caught his arm.

"Your solution is to leave me alone with mobsters?" She frowned and tilted her head in concern.

Cameron chuckled. "Joci, you've been with a mobster this whole time." He smirked. "I haven't hurt you once, have I?" Her frown deepened, and he added, "Don't worry, if they even offer you a sideways glare, it will be their last."

She cracked a smile and he had to get out of there. Setting his feet in motion, Cameron whistled to the group of Del Rossi men in the forest nearby.

"Just like that, huh?" she called to his back. "No trying to convince me to be with you or anything?"

Grinding his teeth, he nodded and whirled around. Damn, but the woman wouldn't let anything go. It was part of why he cared for her.

"Yes, Joci, because you deserve a safe, rich man who

will love you," he ground out, the words tasting like muck.

Hopping over a fallen branch, she grabbed his hand. "I don't love him," she stated, her eyes probing his with more power than he thought possible.

"You'll learn," he dismissed automatically, jerking his hand away.

"You're an ass."

Cameron forced out a dark snicker. "I may be an ass, but you're alive because of me, so don't hate me too much when I'm gone."

Joci flicked her hand to the approaching bodyguards. To his shock, the men backed away without hassle. "I don't hate you."

He shrugged and let out an aggravated sigh. "Fine. Loathe, detest, abhor, use whatever fancy word you want to. It doesn't change anything." The wind picked up and ruffled his hair. "Once this is over, I'm gone. I have to return to my beloved Ohio and do as I'm told, so do me a favor and hate me." He hoped the words sounded as sarcastic to her as they did to him.

"Why?" she sputtered. She inched closer to him for a wind break. Her act made him want to both wring her neck and kiss it until she was permanently molded to him. "Why can't you stay?"

Cameron shook his head. Her constant battling confused him. She was too transparent in certain aspects, yet a complete shield of black in others. "Because I owe Del Rossi. I used the mob to protect you." He couldn't let her know the entirety of the deal he'd made with Jerry. In no way did he want to sway her. "Plus, I can't stay in Iowa because there's nothing here for me."

"Yes, there is." Joci clutched his hand between hers, daring him to break free. "Stay for me."

The thought tempted him, but he couldn't succumb to his darkest desire. Being with him would endanger her life. He was part of a mafia. Even though Jerry promised to let him leave eventually, it wouldn't happen. Not entirely. He couldn't put her at risk because of his involvement.

Capturing her face in his palms, Cameron let her innocence wash over him. She hadn't said the phrase he longed to hear, and he wouldn't say it himself. Instead, he would shove her right back to her ex-husband.

"Even if I wanted to do exactly that, I can't, Joci. I won't be responsible for your demise." He pecked her cheek, unable to help it.

"Then you're doing it again," she affirmed. "You're pushing me away just like at the apartment." Before he could confirm her suspicion, Joci covered his lips with hers.

The stunning contrast of her warmth and the flurries that fell on his nose pushed his resolve aside. Yanking her to him, Cameron engulfed her lips until all he sensed was her. The addicting taste of her tongue swirled his mind to anywhere but there. He clasped her to him, holding her neck to steady her movements. He needed her as badly as a beat to a new song.

If danger didn't lurk within the snowy trees, he would've had no problem with ravishing her among the woodland animals. Kissing Joci unraveled years of pent-up frustration.

"Oh, uh, I can come back," a teasing Italian accent broke into their embrace. "Or I can watch for a bit."

In slow motion, Cameron detached his lips from her and stared at her closed eyelids. She needed to leave them like that, or he might tell Jerry to go screw himself.

"No," he growled, shooting daggers to his employer. Jerry was a sick pervert when he wanted to be, so keeping Joci at a safe distance was Cameron's main concern. He turned and kept the swollen-lipped siren safe in his shadow.

"Ah, well, maybe next time." Jerry pointed to the clearing. "A car was spotted at the east entrance. It's time."

Settling his nerves, Cameron waved to the bodyguards. "She doesn't leave," he enforced with a stern voice. They nodded their understanding, so he set off with Jerry.

He couldn't force his head to turn back to look at Joci. He didn't want to visualize her with snowflakes on the lips that yearned for him, and forlorn hazel eyes. He was off to haggle his loot for a better life for her. *A damn good trade.*

— — —

Joci watched Cameron as the distance grew between them. It was for her own sake, but she wasn't convinced his personal security didn't play into his second dismissal of her. It was why she had to kiss him. She needed to feel his true emotions. Tracing her mouth with her frigid fingertips, she admitted that she wasn't prepared for the onslaught of havoc he wreaked on her.

Even from a hundred feet away, she could hear the idle chatter between him and Quinn. They looked homey together, as if the circumstances from the case had sprouted a peculiar kinship with the two.

Cameron's profile caught her attention, and she rubbed her hands together for warmth. She'd noticed the eyebrow piercing was studded once more, and the nose ring was back in place, but she didn't mind. She liked him no matter what he wore. He pulled a winter hat over his brown waves, and she missed watching them toss in the wind.

"Evidently, I have more than one type."

The rumble of cars in the distance whipped her attention to the present situation. Daydreaming about Cameron would get her nowhere. He was adamant she live out her years with Adrian. It was the most rational route, even if her heart wasn't on board.

Keeping her eyes fixed on the freshly parked vehicles, Joci stifled a cry when she caught sight of Adrian.

"He's alive," she murmured in relief, then slapped a hand over her mouth when the mobster bodyguards glared at her. She could give away the entire plan if she wasn't careful.

"You made it," the cocky blond sneered as he approached Cameron, Jerry, and Quinn. "Oh goody, you brought along a cop. Is he here to arrest me?"

She was aware of the horde of men in the trees but doubted J.J. had come unprepared. It wouldn't be smart.

"I'm not an idiot, J.J. He's here to make sure that if you try anything, I have a reliable witness," Cameron bit back. He jutted his chin toward Adrian. "Give me the attorney, and I'll secure a deal between our mobs."

With wary eyes, the abductor surveyed the surrounding trees. "I need more than words."

Cameron's jaw tightened when Jerry handed the mobster a yellow envelope. "The agreement is in there. Now give him back."

Joci's pulse echoed in her ears at the sight of Adrian. His face was battered and his bottom lip was split open, but he looked stable. "Come on, come on," she whispered when the warring mobster froze in his place.

In one fluid motion, he pointed to the forest, and the men accompanying him cocked their guns. "What did you do, Shearer?" J.J. taunted. "Jerry never shows up to meets. I know it isn't this easy."

The Del Rossi boss shrugged. "Chicago was getting chilly. I thought I'd travel."

Swallowing hard, Joci was glad Jerry insisted Quinn wear normal drab instead of his uniform. A glaring police presence wouldn't have gone over well with this bunch.

Cameron nodded. "It is." He motioned for Adrian, but the other man held him tighter.

Panic rushed through Joci as the plan unraveled before her eyes. Quinn's subtle scratch on the head set the timber ablaze with uniformed SWAT officers. J.J.'s men didn't ask questions before they started pumping metal toward the officers.

"You son of a bitch!" J.J. screeched, pointing his gun at Adrian. "You brought in the Feds?"

Cameron stepped toward his enemy at a slow pace, his hands up. Worry laced Joci's gut. The men she cared for were dancing on death's trapdoor, and neither had a gun to protect themselves.

"Hey, man, I just want him. I'll call them all off if you give him to me," the exonerated convict reasoned.

Gripping the branch at her side, Joci cursed so prolifically the bodyguards looked to her with unsettled expressions. "Shit! Come on, Cameron, you can do this," she pleaded, tearing pine needles. Despite Adrian's debt with the Mikkelsen crew, she didn't want him dead. Hell, he needed to help her raise their baby. He couldn't do that if he was dead. She may not love him as she once did, but she desperately needed him alive.

Gunshots peppered the woods, but the men didn't leave her side. They did, however, haul her back into the trees when she took a step away from the haven.

"Let me go!" she screamed when J.J. jammed a gun to Adrian's head. She watched in horror as Cameron attempted to talk the man down. No words met her ears over the deafening whiz of gunfire.

When J.J. crammed Adrian back into one of the SUVs, she struggled at the bodyguard's grip. Her gut pitched when J.J.'s gun directed toward Cameron. Ice filled her veins at the subtle kickback in the mobster's arm. Her legs buckled as Cameron staggered, then collapsed to his knees.

No longer in control of her actions, Joci bit her protector's hand until she tasted blood. Shoving him aside, she raced down the slope. Snow melted into slush beneath her speedy feet, resulting in a slippery jaunt to her goal.

Yelling for Cameron, she ducked when a bullet was fired

in her direction. The force of the shot that nearly struck her stunned her heart for a moment before she forced her feet to keep moving. If she couldn't save Adrian, she was determined to get to the only man who dwelled in her heart. She saw pain etch over Cameron's features and she picked up her pace. *If he doesn't get himself killed first.*

Surveying the area, she spotted Quinn nearby behind a tree, taking shots toward J.J.'s men when he had the chance. *He's safe at least. One out of three.*

Sliding along the mushy terrain, she spotted Jerry hunkered down between his bodyguards near a giant oak, clipping one of J.J.'s men. Ignoring the satisfied smile on Jerry's face, she reached Cameron as the vehicle accelerated right at him.

"Joci, run!" he bellowed, clutching his side.

Not listening, she quickened her pace and pushed him out of the way before the car struck him.

Fumbling on the stiff ground, Joci groaned at the slicing pain. "Ugh, football is a dumb sport," she complained after the brutal tackle.

Cameron crawled over to her military style. "What the hell were you thinking?" he chastised, surveying her body for injuries. "He could've hit you!" His hands traced every inch of her, his brows furrowed in worry.

"I'm fine," she argued, though her ribs smarted with each breath she inhaled.

Before Cameron had the chance to rebuke her more, the squeal of tires forced his eyes to the edge of the clearing. "Shit! No!" he called, but the clashing of metal drowned out his voice.

Lolling her head toward the sound, Joci's blood curdled at the sight of the three SUVs making their escape. Suddenly, she couldn't remember which one J.J. and Adrian were in. Spying two of J.J.'s men left behind, she gasped when one of them took a shot directed toward the vehicles. "Adrian!" she wheezed, her voice foreign to her ears.

Cameron rushed back to her, disregarding the blood dripping down his coat. The loud pop that reminded her of a firework reached her ears as he threw his body over hers. Peeking over her shoulder, her eyes widened as a giant flame sparked beneath one of the SUVs.

The blast lifted him from Joci and tossed their bodies carelessly in its wake. Debris fluttered over her, filling the air with smoke so she couldn't breathe. The sound of squealing tires was foggy but prominent as she gasped for air. Fluttering her eyelids, Joci caught sight of Cameron ten feet away before her mind blanked to pure white.

CHAPTER EIGHTEEN

The intense need for water shook Cameron to the land of the living once more. Cracking his eyelids open, he winced at the bright stream of sunlight on his face. His eyeballs ached as he rolled them to the window. *Curtains would be good.*

Squinting, he studied the room. *I'm in a hospital*, he concluded from the empty white space and whir of monitors. His hopes crashed and burned when Joci wasn't perched in the chair beside the bed. The machine keeping track of his heart rate bleeped in anger as his worst fears crumbled onto him.

She's dead. Oh God, no! She can't be dead. His mind spun out of control and he jerked at the IV in his arm. Air. He needed air to counteract the abundance of loneliness flowing from his head to toes.

"Hey, hey, hey! Calm down there, Cam," Rayna's gentle voice comforted.

Whipping his head around, he groaned when his neck kinked. "Ow," he rasped, his voice hoarse.

Rayna's manicured hands pressed him back against the pillow. She pushed the call button and sat on the bed. "Here, drink some water. You don't sound so hot."

Cameron eagerly accepted the straw and allowed the cool liquid to refresh his throat. "Thanks," he managed, though chapped skin wailed at his act.

"What happened?" he asked after licking his lips. He tried to piece everything together, but flashes of ambulances and the memory of gunshots muddled each other.

"You got shot and then one of the cars blew to smithereens, so says Quinn," Rayna advised. "I wish I could've seen it." She slapped her hand over her mouth. "Shit, I'm sorry. That's rude of me. I've just never seen anything explode before." She swiped her bangs to the side of her forehead.

Sighing, Cameron shrugged, wishing he hadn't. "It's fine. I'll bet it was a sight."

"And you were a kickass hero," a second voice insisted. Quinn stepped into the room, wearing his police uniform. "Glad you're up, Sleeping Beauty. You were out for a while."

Cameron tried to adjust the pillow behind him, but the uncomfortable act was pointless. He slumped back and held his side. "What the hell?" Peeling the covers aside, he frowned at the bloody bandage. "Fabulous."

"Oh, you're bleeding again! I'll get the nurse." Rayna shot the help button a glare. "Damn thing should work better." She left the room in a huff, and Cameron didn't envy the ear on the other end of the woman's complaint.

His gaze dipped to the plaster cast on his left arm. He

didn't feel any pain, but guessed the IVs were giving him ample medications. "And a broken arm too?"

Quinn poked the cast. "Oh yeah. You broke your ulna, shattered your radius, but just a hairline fracture on the humerus," he informed, reviewing the chart at the end of Cameron's bed.

"Wonderful. Just what I need, more brokenness."

Succeeding in taking another sip of water on his own, Cameron met the officer's bold green eyes. "How is she?" he asked, the cup shaking in his hands.

A broad smile crossed Quinn's face. "Joci's good. She has a few scrapes and a fractured rib, but she and the baby will heal up fine."

Relief flooded Cameron, and tears misted his vision. "Good." He cleared his throat to hide the emotion but saw he hadn't fooled Quinn.

"Your affection for her is deep, isn't it?" the cop put together.

"Yeah," he admitted. "It is."

Moving to the window, Quinn placed his hands behind his back. "I never thought I would say this about a woman I was once in love with, but I'm going to anyways." He pierced Cameron with his gaze. "She needs you."

Placing the empty cup on the bedside table, Cameron shook his head with as much vigor as he could muster. "Um, no. I'm the last person she needs. You or Adrian will do much better than me."

Quinn's brows knit together. "I saw the way you dove on top of Joci to protect her from the explosion. Most guys wouldn't be stupid and risk themselves for a random woman."

"She's not anyone random," he defended. "She's safe, and now I can leave her to Adrian." He stopped at the sorrowful look on Quinn's face.

"He's dead," the other man whispered. "Adrian is dead. One of my SWAT buddies swore Adrian was in the car that exploded, but we couldn't find his body. It's to be expected with such a high-velocity blast. The shell of the SUV was found, but the K-9 unit found minimal organic material. The techs are hoping to get some DNA off the samples, but don't hold your breath." He ran his hand over his chest. "We all got memorabilia from the event."

Clenching his eyes shut, Cameron held in his fury. "No! No! No! He wasn't supposed to die." The warm stickiness of blood seeped onto the thin hospital bedsheet at his frustrated flailing. "She's going to hate me with a passion now."

Tossing the sheet back, he swung his legs over to the side of the bed. "I need to get out of here. Sign whatever discharge papers." He got to his feet, and then all of his energy drained from him.

Before he could fall, Quinn caught him and settled him on the bed once more. "If you keep that up, your stitches will never heal," he teased, hitting the defective call button several more times.

The agonizing pain riddled Cameron's body. "She can't hate me if I'm dead," he joked back, sweat tracing his brow.

Quinn planted himself in the seat beside the bed. "That's bullshit, and you know it. Joci needs you more than ever.

She has a fatherless child to raise—"

"Joce can be a mom on her own. She's strong," Cameron cut in.

Scratching the back of his neck, Quinn nodded in agreement. "Okay, yes, she can, but there's also her freakishly strong feelings for you to think about." His tone grew serious. "She never had those for me, Cameron. Or Adrian, I'd assume. Her emotions for you are real. While your mob boss and I were fending off J.J.'s goons, she freaking threw herself in harm's way to save you from being turned into a pancake under a car. I don't think she would've done that for me."

"Like I said, she's a strong woman." He shook his head. "She'll find someone better." Chuckling, Cameron nodded to him. "Keep your phone on."

"You may wish such a fate, but it's not true." Quinn slugged his shoulder in jest. "After what I saw you do at Gray's, I think you have endless possibilities for your future." He pointed to his badge. "If you decide to stay, you should check out a life on the other side of the law. Maybe a confidential informant or something. I'd bet my superiors would be okay with you hanging around if you helped us out."

A nurse and doctor strode through the door, and Quinn offered him a tiny salute. "Think about it." He smiled to the attractive nurse. "See ya on the flip side," he called, heading out of the room.

Cameron was too preoccupied to watch him leave. The whole criminal consultant suggestion didn't sound so bad.

Joci has a thing for cops, he recalled, then laughed. *But I wouldn't be a cop.* His act caused the nurse to give him an odd glance.

He kept still as the doctor pressed a stethoscope to his chest. It was ridiculous to entertain Quinn's suggestion. His life was based on mob connections and drugs. Switching sides was a death sentence. Jerry himself would pull the trigger. Given the fact that there were no bodies recovered, it was plausible J.J. escaped. He wouldn't be free of the Del Rossi chain without proof of a body. Plus, as Jerry said himself, the original deal was dead. He was just as screwed as when he came to Iowa. More so, since his heart was on the verge of tearing in half.

The nurse poked him with a needle, startling him to reality. "I still need the arm," he grumbled when she didn't find a vein.

As the doctor droned on about the extracted bullet and his assorted broken bones, Cameron wondered if there was a sliver of hope when it came to Joci. He was the ultimate motive behind Adrian's ill-fated death. He didn't expect her to see beyond that, yet a promising future glimmered in the distance.

"Joci," he stated. "I need to visit Joci Dorous."

The aged doctor mumbled something about his recently set bones, so Cameron added, "Yeah, I'm doing this with or without your help."

He smirked when the nurse rolled her eyes and muttered in Italian to the physician. Her accent came as a good reminder. His body may be out of harm's way, but that didn't mean he was entirely out of the woods. If Jerry had dished out money for expert surgical staff, Cameron owed him for that too. No doubt the man bribed a few doctors to give them extra time in the hospital too. As kind as the mob boss was, he doubted love was a swaying explanation.

"If she even wants me," he reminded himself under his breath. Joci was full of twists and turns. If their brief time together had taught him anything, he couldn't bet his heart when she'd already stolen it.

— — —

Releasing the breath she had been holding, Joci stared at the end of the plain hospital bed. Waking up to bad news wasn't how she wanted this to go. "Adrian was supposed to be here," she repeated quietly, her eyes not straying from the wall. If she did, she would be forced to accept that Adrian was dead.

"I know. I'm sorry, Joci. I hoped we could've found him among the car parts, but it was impossible." He pulled his hand out of his pocket. "But they did find this." He plopped a ring in her palm.

"It's his class ring from Harvard," she gasped. It couldn't have been a coincidence. "He never took the thing off." She fingered the etched law building on the side and the Latin word *veritas*. Surely 'truth' meant more in this context than what Harvard originally hoped.

"If any of the tests come back with Adrian's DNA, I'll let you know." Quinn placed a comforting hand on her arm. "I wanted you to hear this from someone who cares about you.

I honestly wish my report was better."

"Me too." She cradled the blankets over her stomach. "Thanks for telling me, Quinn," she remarked, meeting his gaze. His face bore a hint of the explosion, with scrapes and one line of stitches above his right eyebrow. Even battered, he remained a vigilant friend.

She predicted his withdrawal from her side, but was surprised when instead, he sat on the bed beside her and wrapped his arms around her shoulders.

Tears pricked her eyes, but Joci held them at bay. Crying over Adrian was all she'd done after their divorce. Now she couldn't bear to let one drop free. It was obtuse yet made perfect sense in her mind. She loved Adrian, but not in the way to shatter her heart. That experience already happened once, and she never gave the glued pieces back to him before his death. Copious buckets of sadness were filled over the man. At one point or another, she would mourn him, but not today. Not while the families of police officers wailed for those slain at a mobster's hand. Not since part of the deaths were caused by Adrian's ignorance and association with the damn Mikkelsen mob.

Snuggling deeper into Quinn's sturdy embrace, Joci closed her eyes and just listened to the steady rhythm of his heart. It was a sound that comforted her in more ways than his hands ever could. The baby growing inside her would never know Adrian, which made her distraught. For her own soul, the loss of him reiterated the fact that they were never meant to be together. For a time perhaps, but not for eternity.

"He's okay," Quinn advised after she was almost lulled to sleep by his heartbeat.

She knew of whom he spoke, and remained mute. Her feelings were clear when it came to Cameron. She'd harbored the unspoken truth for months. Noticeably, he'd shielded her and took the brunt of the blast. Her one broken rib was her own fault for playing defensive lineman to protect him. But despite all of what happened, he was the moving force behind J.J. and played into Adrian's death in the end.

"You shouldn't blame Cameron," Quinn chided, who'd somehow switched alliances on her. Somewhere between bullets and handcuffs, the two had formed a comradery.

"I don't. Not really. I just think some of this may be his fault," she shot back, prying her eyes to him.

Quinn brushed her hair from her forehead. "It's not. He didn't force Adrian into debt with the Mikkelsens. Adrian got himself in that mess. He didn't take Adrian and refuse to hand him over after the deal was made. Cameron didn't shove him into the SUV and gun it." His green eyes softened. "J.J. Jepsen killed Adrian, and he got what was coming to him. End of story. No shifting blame. Cameron is doing enough for the whole county."

Regret tinged her. "He is?"

"Oh yeah." Quinn smirked. "And he's also being a stubborn patient. Nothing new there. I thought he was a pain in the ass when I arrested him, but damn, he's being a dick to the hospital staff."

Joci couldn't help but grin. The stubborn jerk was the

man she'd known since they were kids. She'd always been drawn to him. "He's infuriating," she complained.

"Yes, he is, but he also demanded to see you as soon as he woke up," the officer updated. "The damn fool frustrated the doctors enough that they gave up."

Sitting up, she glanced around the room. "He did? When did he visit me?"

"Ah, well, I stopped him before he rolled down the hallway. It was quite funny to see, to be honest." Tucking the sheet securely on her, he pointed out, "He needed to heal. You both did. If and when you're ever ready to see him, I'll pass it on."

"I don't want to see him yet," she swiftly inserted.

He nodded. "Understood." Kissing the top of her head, he added, "I'd be totally cool with you never wanting to see his mug again, but it's selfish of me."

Wincing, Joci leaned her body against Quinn's. She needed to be held even if it hurt like hell. Sitting there, she reveled at how much he didn't feel like home anymore. For almost two years, he'd been her haven and more, but since the inception of the murder case, the sensation had fallen away little by little. It wasn't replaced by Adrian either. Nothing felt the same since meeting Cameron, and she knew why.

He was just down the hall.

— — —

"She doesn't want to see me," Cameron repeated. "Great." He fumbled with the magazine Quinn had brought.

"Give it time," the man who resembled a friend more than a cop at present encouraged.

Two days in the hospital didn't dampen the man's positive mood, but Cameron enjoyed every second of it.

"She'll come around. It's a lot to digest." Quinn propped his feet on the bed. "Want to talk about all the pros of being associated with the good side of the law?" he offered, a gleam in his eyes.

"I get why Joci likes you. You're relentless." Cameron rolled his eyes.

"Takes one to know one," Quinn quipped cheekily, holding up a fake badge.

"I'm thinking it over." Cameron flipped a page. "I don't know if a black CI stamp is my style. I'm more of a green or orange jumpsuit type."

Quinn crumpled a flimsy tissue and threw it at him. "Aw, sure it is. Plus, it's not like it would be on very long when you're around Joci." He laughed at his own joke until his face was dark red. The sound was contagious, and soon Cameron joined in.

Cameron ducked out of the way of another tissue aimed at his head. "I didn't need to know all about your time with Joci, but thanks for the disturbing visual. It makes lunch sound horrible."

When Quinn's chuckle tapered off, Cameron pointed out the obvious. "Cops and mobsters don't mix."

Finding a piece of paper this time, Quinn formed a perfect airplane. "You know, you're right, but a person can hope, can't he?"

Observing the plane in flight, Cameron worried his lips together. It was peculiar for him to be wanted anywhere without strings attached. "Why are you set on me staying here? I'd think you would run me out of town to be with Joci."

The tall man pondered the query. "If there's one thing I don't mess with, it's fate," he divulged. "I was meant to arrest your ass."

"Which you thoroughly enjoyed."

"True." Quinn pointed his index finger at him. "But you and Joci were meant to cross paths again. She took a shine to you the instant she saw you, and hell yeah, it was tough to watch." He scratched his head. "Not as bad as the Adrian thing, but still difficult."

"Then why not ride in like the cavalry and trap her with your freakishly masculine charisma?" Cameron wondered.

Folding another aircraft, Quinn admitted, "Because you are the right guy for her."

"How do you know?"

"She was assigned to you by fate, Cameron. Appointed, if you will. Any other attorney could've been given the file," the man remarked with a smile. "The universe tossed Joci to you. Don't be a prick and throw her back. You'll never catch another woman like her."

Chuckling at the candor, Cameron snatched the plane and let it soar. "You might be right, but I'll deny I ever said those words." He exchanged a smile with his friend, and the two men tossed paper through the air, not caring where they landed.

"Am I interrupting a Boy Scout meeting?" Jerry's amused voice asked.

Cameron swung his gaze to the door as Del Rossi entered. The guards were stationed outside the room, which eased his gut for the moment. "Just having a bit of fun," he answered for both of them.

"I should go check on Joci," Quinn stated, standing. He locked gazes with Jerry, then swiveled back to Cameron. "I'll be back later. Maybe with a warrant, if I find an open one."

Jerry waited until the door closed before he jerked his thumb toward it. "He's a nice fellow for a cop. Were the two of you being chummy?"

Shifting on the bed, Cameron nodded. "Something like that."

Jerry plunked into the nearest seat. "So, what should we discuss as your broken bones heal? The oddly warm temperatures outside? I swear Iowa has weather patterns like a teenager." He studied his employee. "Or perhaps your plan to repay me? You owed me J.J.'s body and the Mikkelsens' influence out of Iowa. While you've been recovering, I got a message from one of the higher-ups in the Danish group. They're not finished with Iowa, which means you're not finished with me."

Swallowing the rising bile in his throat, Cameron laced his fingers together to halt them from fidgeting. He knew it wouldn't be as simple as an exploding car. "I wanted to talk to you about my proposal, as it turns out."

A crooked smile played over the mobster's face. "Go on."

"It's an unconventional idea, but I'm fairly certain you'll like it," he started, forcing his lips to part in a grin. "There's an opportunity for me to be a criminal informant for the DMPD. If I do that, you'd always know the status on gangs here and the police involvements."

Jerry placed his hands on his belly. "I have a better idea. I have pull in one of the police stations, and I'd like to build on that. You would be the perfect person for the job, but I don't want you to be a CI. I have a specific occupation in mind. One I desperately need."

Cameron swallowed hard. He wasn't 100 percent sure of this, but he owed it to himself to listen. A fresh body on a slab in the morgue was the worst possible outcome, after all.

— — —

Every channel on the hospital television failed to hold Joci's attention for more than ten minutes. Her mind was full and somehow void simultaneously. The doctors had cleared her for discharge, yet she remained in the teeny room. When Quinn advised her that an anonymous benefactor paid for all of her medical bills and continued stay at the hospital, Joci knew Cameron's mob boss had a hand in it all. Even her nurse told her she could stay up to a week, which was unusual. And another reason she was certain the Del Rossis were pulling strings. She should go home, but she didn't want to see an empty apartment. Her reasoning wasn't completely truthful. She wasn't ready to leave.

In the back of her mind, she knew Cameron would come for her. She didn't want to leave before he visited, even if she'd made it quite clear he wasn't welcome.

She tossed the remote aside and crawled under the covers. It was a girlish idiosyncrasy she couldn't shake. Her heart wouldn't allow her to leave without laying eyes on him.

Yesterday, she'd scurried down the hall and hovered two doors from his room. She couldn't complete the journey. Partially due to the men in black outside his door, but mostly because she was afraid of what would happen. He was intertwined with a notorious mob. The ho-hum life she led wouldn't satisfy him. It was foolish to believe anything else.

She glanced at her phone when a new message chimed. Checking it, she opted against a reply to Rayna. Between her and Quinn, Joci's time in the hospital was anything but solitary.

"I wonder if Cameron had any visitors," she said aloud, worried for him. Iowa wasn't his home. No caring friends would've clung to his side as he rode out bullet wounds and fractured bones. She was the only friend he had here. *Making me a horrible one.*

"I should've gone to him." She cursed at her cowardice, but seeing him in a hospital bed would make her care more. She couldn't afford another failure, since he wasn't going to stick around long enough for a snowman to be designed.

Her door creaked open and she whipped her head up. Quinn stood at the room's entry but he didn't move. "I think I'm heading home for a while before my next shift," he informed her. "Call me if you want a ride." He shot her a smile. "I'm more than happy to help."

"Thanks, Quinn, but I'll be fine," she countered. She loved the police officer, but not in the way he preferred.

He nodded and grabbed the handle. "Whatever you say."

As he swung the door shut, Joci stumbled over her next words. "Leave it open. Please."

A knowing grin dazzled her. "You bet. I'll touch base later."

As he left, Joci caught a glimpse of another body outside. Her mouth dried at the dark hue of the jeans with jagged holes. It seemed the hospital didn't stock up on new apparel after a blast took bites out of denim.

"Can I come in?" Cameron timidly asked as he filled the doorway. With street clothes and a cast on one arm, his silhouette stunned her.

Clicking the TV off, she slowly nodded. "Sure." She hoped she didn't sound as anxious as she felt.

He shut the door behind him with careful movements, then leaned against it. His left arm sported a white plaster cast with bright pink doodles. The urge to tease him overwhelmed her better judgment. "I see someone had fun at your expense," she pointed out.

"Oh, that. Yeah." He shook his head. "Quinn's a dick. He did it while I was napping the other day."

She smirked. "I rather like it." He shrugged, still not speaking. The silence between them was too much for her to handle. Trusting herself with him was a fatal flaw.

Her eyes fluttered over his clothes with dried bloodstains. Whose, she wasn't sure. Other than his broken arm, Cameron's short-sleeved shirt displayed one bandage over his right forearm. Joci couldn't halt the craving to touch him, if just to ensure his safety was genuine. He looked worse off than anyone involved, and it pained her to see his brown eyes filled with remorse.

"It's not your fault," she began, her confidence boldened. "J.J. killed Adrian, not you."

Slowly, he walked in her direction. "Is that how you honestly feel or how you're coping?" He rubbed the back of his neck. "I know Adrian meant a lot to you."

Hot all of a sudden, she tore off the blanket. "He did mean a great deal, but this is not me coping. I mean, I am coping, but not in the way you think."

Cameron paused, wary. "Okay."

"I lost Adrian a long time ago," she filled in. "Just like he lost me." Joci studied her bare finger where a ring once sat. "We never quite pieced the relationship back together. He wanted to, but I wasn't willing to put my entire soul into it."

"But you would have," Cameron interrupted. "If he lived, you would've made it work."

Rejecting the notion, she crossed her legs. "No. I wouldn't have."

"Why?" Cameron ran nervous fingers through his messy brown hair. He looked too sweet to pass up.

Heart pounding, she answered, "Because I already fell for someone else." She opened her lips to finish, but he stopped her.

"I need to confess something to you."

Though taken aback, she urged him forward. "Sure, go ahead."

He took a breath. "When you moved away from Ohio, you broke my heart."

"Oh." Her eyes dropped to the hospital sheet. It smelled too clean in the room, and she wanted to escape it the longer she remained there. *Or light a scented candle.*

Cameron inched forward. "After you left, I climbed the tree in your front yard." He looked off in reminiscence. "You know, the one you called a heaven tree because the blooms were so good you may as well be in the afterlife."

Joci snapped her hazy eyes to him. "Yeah, I remember it." Studying him, she noticed his face wasn't too beaten from the incident, though it held remnants of pain. He remained stoic of any hint of what he felt. It reminded her of the aftermath of the beating he'd received in the jail.

"Anyway, while I was up there, I promised myself to visit you." He paused and glanced to her. "And I did. Sort of."

"You came to Iowa?"

"Yeah. My parents' band had a gig in Ames a few years later, but I could never find you. It killed me since I knew you had to be somewhere among the cornfields."

She smirked. "I'm sorry. I wish I'd known. We should've kept in contact, like pen pals or something."

"It's okay. I think it's better this way. I got the chance to get to know you all over again." He smiled at the tale and his nose ring compelled her attention. She thought the damn thing would've been lost by now.

"Do you remember when we pretended we were archeologists? We dug up a bike ramp in your yard."

Cameron shook his head. "And your dad was so pissed when he saw our dirty masterpiece."

Chills scattered along Joci's arms. She knew the scene well. In her fuzzy memory, the images appeared before her eyes. Two kids cramped side by side with spades in their hands. The smell of Ohio soil drifted to her subconscious. "Yeah, I got a nice wallop on the butt for it."

"We dug up a moth. Do you remember it?" She nodded in remembrance. "It was the most beautiful thing we found out there." He pointed to a tattoo on his arm, one that captured her attention at first glance. "Come to find out, it was nothing special, but I kept our day alive when I put it in ink."

Joci's breathing increased as he finished. *Our time meant that much to him?* She couldn't fathom it unless he felt more for her. "I thought it looked familiar."

He adjusted the sling on his arm. "Yeah, and then your brother just had to get into trouble with the law." He sank onto the bed. "I don't know if I should thank him or hunt him down and make him pay for the time I lost."

Her lungs burned as she comprehended his words.

"It's funny, because the day we discovered the moth, we swore to marry and travel the world as renowned scientists." His brown eyes locked with hers. "That didn't quite happen, did it, Joce?"

Recollections flooded into her mind as fast as a bullet train. Every time they romped around in the mud or played tag in the driveway made her smile. "No, it didn't."

His fingers sought hers out. "But I'm not giving up on

the dream." He chuckled. "I can't even if I want to."

"Why not?" she asked, tears pooling in her eyes.

Instead of answering, he wiped a stray tear from her cheek with the back of his hand. "Those few years you lived across the street were the best ones of my life. I never wanted them to end." He kissed her fingers, one by one. "And when you were yanked from me, I had no one."

"I'm sorry. I—" she started, but he hushed her with his words.

"It's not your burden to bear. I chose my path." Dropping his hold, he moved closer to her. "But if I hadn't been a dumbass and done all the idiotic things, I never would've wound up with you as my attorney in Iowa."

The method of life unspooling forced her lips to rub together. "But what about...." Her sentence dropped flat. She didn't want to ask any questions about the mob. She knew too much already.

"When I discovered that my feelings for you didn't go away after all those years, I didn't tell you because I was afraid they would take you away again," he admitted. "I can't handle it a second time."

Either way the case ended, they had too much at stake. It was among the reasons she wouldn't allow herself to open up and be honest with him. If she lost him to prison or the underworld, her heart wouldn't be the same.

"There's always someone you can't shake. Someone you wonder what could've been. You're that person for me, Joce, and I don't ever want to let you go." He let out a shaky breath, his proclamation complete.

"I know what I want to say, but I'm afraid to say it." She blinked furiously, willing herself to spit out the words she longed to utter since kissing him.

Cameron sighed in frustration. "Joci Dorous at a loss for words. That doesn't happen often." He slunk toward the edge of the bed. His cast scraped obnoxiously on the sheet, and he ripped the clinging material off.

His movements, though strained, were also loveable. Joci pictured him from their youth and smirked. In reality, he hadn't changed much. Sure, he'd grown to staggering height and build, yet he remained the kid she'd had a crush on. His wandering ways got her into trouble then as they did twenty-odd years later. Regardless of the mishap, her affection for him didn't waver.

"Cam, I have a confession too," she noted, resting her hand on his arm.

Her childhood best friend, now all tatted and grown up and sexier than she'd ever imagined possible, turned his head in her direction. He offered her a slanted smile. "Oh yeah? What is it?"

Calming her racing heart, she tipped his chin to completely face him. The vulnerability in his eyes both startled and catapulted her courage. "I loved you when we were kids."

Her fingers traced his assorted ink. A listless smile came over her when she found more tattoos that reminded her of their adventures. His body was a map, one that led straight to a future with her.

"I always wondered what happened to the mop-headed

heathen from across the street." Joci returned her gaze to him. "You never strayed from my mind."

Agilely, she lifted her shirt and displayed her ribs. A singular tattoo of a pink flowering tree with two sparrows perched on a branch came into view despite the bulky bandage. "And you've always been close to my heart."

He traced the tattoo tenderly, then turned to the bandaged rib. His fingers scorched her skin, but not nearly as much as when his eyes met hers.

"I thought I lost you," he disclosed in a quiet voice. "Then when I woke up, my fear overtook me." His voice thickened with emotion. "I needed to see you were alive before I left."

Joci replaced her shirt. "Why didn't you?"

He took a breath. "I couldn't very well barge in on you."

"Like that would stop you."

Smoothing her hair, he conceded, "Yeah, you're right. Any other time it wouldn't, but I wasn't sure how you felt." His voice tapered off. "About me."

No longer able to dance around the subject, Joci grabbed his face and pulled it to her. "I love you, Cameron Anthony Shearer. I did when I was nine years old, and I do now." Her eyes softened. "As long as you love me, my mind will never change."

The crease in his brow eased at her final revelation. "You're sure? Because I'm really not—"

Her lips over his hushed any chance of a rebuttal, and Joci was never so glad for it. Without a care to either of their injuries, Cameron hauled her into his embrace and kissed her with every molecule she inspired.

Tangling her fingers through his curls, Joci gasped at the sheer intensity of their union. It was a kiss nearly thirty years in the making, and she wasn't about to miss a second.

Slipping her tongue between his lips, she tingled with desire as it clashed with his. The compelling hint of chocolate lined his mouth, and all she wanted was to indulge in him until she was immobile.

Without warning, Cameron pulled back. Only then did Joci realize she was straddling him as they teetered on the edge of the hospital bed. His face was marred in pain and she instantly remembered both their wounds. Their ardent embrace would have to wait until later.

"Oh, sorry. I guess we didn't really think that through," she said, embarrassed. When she attempted to move, his arms held her in place.

"No, don't. I like having you close," he whispered, inches from her lips. "For obvious medical reasons, I can't take you in all the ways I've imagined since I saw you in jail, though."

Goose bumps spread over Joci like wildfire. His low tone increased the longing she felt for him. "You're right." She struggled in her spot, but he remained stern despite his injuries. "I thought you said—"

"I did." He trailed his fingers up her back. "But that doesn't mean I'm against you sitting on me in a seductive yet torturous manner."

Joci rolled her eyes and scanned his face. "What am I going to do with you?"

A devilish grin crossed his handsome features. "I can think of way too many options, but for now, I need to know if you want me to stay."

Confusion ripped through her mind. She'd told him she loved him, yet he didn't see his place in her life. The thought instantly saddened her.

"Of course I do." She paused as she recalled his line of work. A mob player and criminal attorney would mesh quite well. "But—"

"It's the mob thing, isn't it?" he filled in. She shrugged and looked to the door. "I made a decision yesterday, Joce. One that would secure me in your life, but if you aren't certain, I need to hear it now." His eyes narrowed at her apprehensive nod. "I can't buy my way out of Del Rossi's debt right now, but it's my goal."

"How are you planning on doing that?" she inquired, suspicious of the answer.

"I'm going to become a cop."

Joci's eyes widened until she thought they would pop out. "A cop? As in police officer?"

He gave her a small shake of the head. "Yep. Jerry is going to get me in somehow. Our deal is that I'll feed Jerry minimal intel about the rival gangs here until I repay him. Shouldn't be more than five years." He bopped his index finger on her nose. "It's like probation for my past." She cocked her head, and he amended, "Okay, it's more like a second chance with the girl of my dreams with a horrible probation officer hounding me."

Racking her brain, Joci went over the possible outcomes.

"I don't like you owing him," she noted. "But I realize part of your debt is because of me, so I can't be too harsh."

Cameron's finger circled her face. "The Del Rossi mob protected you. If I'm a part of them, they will continue to do that." His gaze lowered to her stomach and carefully placed a palm to it. "For all of us."

Her trepidation with the situation loosened when he added, "And I'll be right beside you to make sure of it. This baby—our baby, if you let me—will grow up climbing trees and playing on a dead-end street just like we did." She nodded in agreement with tears threatening her eyes at his underlying promise to their future. Cameron placed a featherlight kiss to the end of her nose. "Good. And we'll watch the little guy—"

"Or girl."

"—or girl ride bikes with the neighborhood kids, and then the three of us can pretend we're archaeologists like we used to." His lips covered hers briefly, the adoration in his brown eyes warming her all the way to her toes. "And I swear I'll never give you a reason to move away from me. Ever."

She covered his hand on her belly. "That sounds perfect to me, and you'll be safe too, right?" The question caused a toothy grin to cover his lips. "Because if not, it's a deal breaker," she clarified. The little she knew about any mafia; a person didn't leave unless they were dead. If Cameron believed he could buy his way out, she'd trust he knew what he was doing. She didn't know Jerry well enough to determine whether it was possible or not. But even if he never left the Del Rossi mob, she could live with it. He was all she desired, mobster and all.

Tilting her chin up, Cameron lowered his lips to hers briefly. "Oh yes, I'll be safe too." He kissed her again, lingering on the taste of her. "I'll be safe because you love me." Their lips passionately collided once more. "And because I love you, Joci Dorous." He nipped her bottom lip. "And I have the tattoos to prove it."

Laughing, Joci swatted at his shoulder, then captured his mouth with hers. No other kiss echoed throughout her body like Cameron's. It was as if her soul had been awaiting him and sprang to life when they discovered each other at last. Being caught in his arms was home to her. All others paled, and comparison wasn't necessary. He was it.

Breaking free, she found her breath and rested her hands on his chest. "Fate may have brought you here, but I intend on keeping you in my life." She wiggled her eyebrows. "In any way necessary."

"Counselor, I believe I have the exact pair of handcuffs you desire," Cameron teased with a wink. "And once I'm a cop, good luck getting them off me."

Wrapping her arms around his neck, Joci insinuated, "I like the way you bargain, Officer. We have a bright future ahead of us."

"We better get started, then. I have a lot of time to make up for." Cameron's lips touched hers delicately, the static in the kiss electrifying them both. Joci was never so certain about a case in her life until Cameron's. With him, she was positive they would continue to defy the odds.

ACKNOWLEDGMENTS

First, I'd like to thank my wonderful publisher, Hot Tree Publishing, for their incredible dedication to their authors. A multitude of thanks to the editors, beta readers, cover designers and every person who made this book come to life.

Finally, I owe many thanks to my writing partners who encourage me on a daily basis. Amazing things happen when women support each other.

ABOUT THE AUTHOR

Skye McNeil began writing at the age of seventeen and has been lost in a love affair ever since. During the day, she moonlights as a paralegal at a law firm favoring criminal law.

Skye enjoys writing romantic comedies and cozy mysteries novels that leave readers wanting more and falling in love over and over. She writes contemporary and historical novels ranging from sweet and sassy to steamy and sultry. Her constant writing companions are two cats and two dogs. When she's not writing, Skye enjoys spending time with family, photography, volleyball, traveling, and curling up with a cup of coffee and reading.

Skye love to connect with her readers.

FACEBOOK: WWW.FACEBOOK.COM/SkyesTheLimitWriting

WEBSITE: WWW.SKYEMCNEIL.COM

TWITTER: HTTPS://TWITTER.COM/SKYE_MCNEIL7

INSTAGRAM: WWW.INSTAGRAM.COM/MCNEILSKYE

ABOUT THE PUBLISHER

Hot Tree Publishing opened its doors in 2015 with an aspiration to bring quality fiction to the world of readers. With the initial focus on romance and a wide spread of romance sub-genres, they envision opening up to alternative genres in the near future.

Firmly seated in the industry as a leading editing provider to independent authors and small publishing houses, Hot Tree Publishing is the sister company to Hot Tree Editing, founded in 2012. Having established in-house editing and promotions, plus having a well-respected market presence, Hot Tree Publishing endeavors to be a leader in bringing quality stories to the world of readers.

Interested in discovering more amazing reads brought to you by Hot Tree Publishing or perhaps you're interested in submitting a manuscript and joining the HTPubs family? Either way, head over to the website for information:

WWW.HOTTREEPUBLISHING.COM

www.ingramcontent.com/pod-product-compliance
Lightning Source LLC
Chambersburg PA
CBHW032204180726
48284CB00001B/184